Praise for Daniel Lyons's *Dog Days*

"This first novel comes as close to a good
'summer read' as I have found."
—*Boston Globe*

"The novel at first seems as if it may click over onto a track
already covered by *Microserfs* or any number of Hollywood
scripts involving the Internet . . . But when it leaves this
insular world for the outside world's realities of bad
neighbors, bad relationships, and bad decisions, *Dog Days*
heads in a different direction from the rest of the pack."
—*New York Times Book Review*

"Sure to charm a wide range of readers . . . chock-full of
genuinely amusing one-liners . . . Reads like a good situation
comedy—intricately woven yet never overbearing."
—*Booklist*

"Hilarious and refreshing . . . delightful, witty, smart,
and self-assured."
—*Fast Company* magazine

DANIEL LYONS is a journalist who has written for various newspapers and magazines, including the *Boston Herald*. He was
short-listed for *Granta*'s "Best of Young American Novelists"
competition, and won the *Playboy* college fiction award for a
short story that became the basis for *Dog Days*. He lives in
Charlestown, Massachusetts.

ALSO BY DANIEL LYONS

The Last Good Man

Dog Days

Daniel Lyons

A PLUME BOOK

PLUME
Published by the Penguin Group
Penguin Putnam Inc., 375 Hudson Street, New York, New York 10014, U.S.A.
Penguin Books Ltd, 27 Wrights Lane, London W8 5TZ, England
Penguin Books Australia Ltd, Ringwood, Victoria, Australia
Penguin Books Canada Ltd, 10 Alcorn Avenue, Toronto, Ontario,
    Canada M4V 3B2
Penguin Books (N.Z.) Ltd, 182–190 Wairau Road, Auckland 10, New Zealand

Penguin Books Ltd, Registered Offices: Harmondsworth, Middlesex, England

Published by Plume, a member of Penguin Putnam Inc. This is an authorized reprint
of a hardcover edition published by Simon & Schuster. For information address Simon
& Schuster, Rockefeller Center, 1230 Avenue of the Americas, New York, NY 10020.

First Plume Printing, June, 1999
10 9 8 7 6 5 4 3 2 1

Ⓟ REGISTERED TRADEMARK—MARCA REGISTRADA

The Library of Congress has catalogued the hardcover edition as follows:
Lyons, Daniel.
    Dog days / Daniel Lyons
        p.   cm.
ISBN 0-684-84000-6
        0-452-28096-6 (pbk.)
    I. Title.
    PS3562.Y4483D6   1998   98-10949
    813'.54—dc21   CIP

Printed in the United States of America

PUBLISHER'S NOTE
This is a work of fiction. Names, characters, places, and incidents either are the products of the author's imagination or are used fictitiously, and any resemblance to actual
persons, living or dead, events, or locales is entirely coincidental.

BOOKS ARE AVAILABLE AT QUANTITY DISCOUNTS WHEN USED TO PROMOTE PRODUCTS OR SER-
VICES. FOR INFORMATION PLEASE WRITE TO PREMIUM MARKETING DIVISION, PENGUIN PUTNAM
INC., 375 HUDSON STREET, NEW YORK, NEW YORK 10014.

For Meri

DOG DAYS

A T SOME POINT things started going way too well for me. I was twenty-four years old, living in Boston, doing advanced research at the world's fifth-largest software company, and dating a woman who had rowed at Harvard and done postgraduate work at Oxford.

How had this happened? I didn't dare ask. I do not believe in God, but I do believe there is an order to things, an energy that holds the world together; and maybe somehow I had tapped into that. On warm autumn afternoons I would ride my bike along the Charles, past the rowers and joggers, past the cars caught in traffic, past the brownstones and boathouses and rusty bridges, past the stinking Haymarket fish stands and the shouting Italian fruit vendors and the shy Asian women who sold flowers in the street—and suddenly, for no reason, I would burst out laughing. This was my life. I had to keep telling myself that.

I was raised an Irish Catholic, and the most central of our many self-defeating superstitions is the belief that when good things happen, bad things are just around the corner. So with each new stroke of good luck I grew a little more afraid. At night I woke shivering from a dream in which I was winched off the ground, higher and higher—five hundred feet, a thousand—and then dropped.

I kept thinking about those stories in Greek mythology where the gods play tricks on people. One day, I figured, I would step outside and see a meteor racing toward me, or a bolt of lightning, or a speeding car. Either that or Alan Funt and the crew from *Candid Camera* would step out of the bushes and explain the joke, and I would blush and try not to look too foolish. But somehow, sooner or later, the spell would break, and my good luck would explode and scatter like a clay pigeon, blown right out of the sky.

The key was faith. You had to have no faith at all. You had to keep telling yourself that this was all going to end tomorrow. You could not allow yourself to enjoy your good fortune, not even for a moment. This exercise required tremendous concentration of the juggling-while-riding-a-unicycle-on-a-tightrope variety. For a long time I managed to do it. But then I slipped.

This happened at Wonderland Park, a dog track north of the city. It was a Tuesday night in late October: a sharp wind with a taste of winter, thin clouds scudding across the sky. The track was Jeanie's idea. Her father used to take her there when she was a kid. She led me up to the back row of the grandstand. I can imagine the way others might have seen us: a young couple huddled together, their breath rising in little plumes, the woman red-haired and gorgeous, the man scrawny and bespectacled and out of his league, peering out from beneath a Detroit Tigers cap, blowing into his hands.

We were eating Wonderdogs, drinking hot chocolate. On the track, under the glare of the klieg lights, the greyhounds were restless, high-strung, tugging at their leads. I had placed a ten-dollar bet on a jet-black one-year-old named Coco. She was running in the first race of her life, at nine-to-one odds. When the gates burst open, Coco leaped into the lead and ran with such force that the other dogs looked as if they had been drugged. She ran the way you might run in a dream, with no effort at all. She flew. She won by thirteen lengths.

Everyone rose. A strange electricity hummed in the air. Then came the announcement: a track record. The monitors ran a replay. We all stood there, dumbfounded. The man beside us said that in forty years of going to the track he had never seen anything like this. "It's like the freaking *Twilight Zone*," he said. His breath stank. "A thing like this makes you want to go have kids, just so you can tell them about it." We laughed and said, sure, whatever you say, and ran off to collect. But I knew what he meant. Greatness is a rare thing, and you're lucky if once or twice in your life you get to bear witness to it. Those of us who saw Coco run could count ourselves among the lucky.

"How did you know?" Jeanie asked me. "You didn't place a bet all night, and then you put ten dollars on that dog. Why did you do that?"

We were out in the parking lot, trying to find her Saab. I could feel the ninety dollars in my front pocket—nine crisp ten-dollar bills, folded in half, rubbing against my leg. The air was cold; it felt almost like snow, except that the sky was clear, and it was too early in the year.

"I liked the sound of her name," I said. "Coco. It sounded lucky."

She stopped. She put her fingers to my forehead, the way my mother did when I was a kid and she was checking my temperature. "You've got it," she said.

"What? The flu? The mark of the beast?"

"The *chi*." She brushed my hair away from my face. "Buddhist monks get it. They get in this zone where they're on a different plane. They can use their minds to control their body temperature. Some of them can fly."

I stood on my toes and flapped my arms. Nothing happened.

"Stop," she said. She pushed me against the fender of a Jeep, and pressed herself against me. "Reilly," she said, her voice going husky, "I don't know if I can wait till we get home."

On the way back into the city we put on the Cure, a band we both admitted with some embarrassment to having liked during our painful, angst-filled, adolescent loser phases. We spoke of those phases as if they had taken place years before, but in fact my depressed loser phase had extended all the way through college and had ended only recently, when I moved to Boston and met Jeanie; I didn't tell her that, though. We were driving over the Tobin Bridge and the song was "Lovesong," and when Jeanie sang, "I will always love you," I managed to believe that she meant it for me. Which proves, I suppose, that in fact my pathetic loser phase hadn't ended at all, because what kind of person finds meaning in the lyrics of a Cure song?

But there I was, drumming my hand on the armrest, grinning like an idiot. For the first time ever, I believed: My good luck was not luck, it was skill; I was not getting more than I deserved, I was getting my fair share. From the bridge I gazed down at the Navy Yard, where the lights spilled like dye into the inky harbor. Beyond that the Bunker Hill monument loomed over the rooftops of Charlestown. Suddenly my future was unfolding before me like some glorious movie landscape: I would become a millionaire, and marry Jeanie, and nothing bad would ever happen to me.

Of course this was ridiculous. About six months later things fell apart, the center could not hold, and Jeanie and I broke up. Strictly speaking, I broke up with her. But I only did it because she confessed that she had slept with Mort Stone, a vice president at our company, a man with degrees from Yale and Harvard and a summer house on Nantucket. I marched out of Jeanie's apartment on Beacon Hill, ignoring her apologies, telling myself that at least I had kept my dignity. But as I crossed the threshold a thread of fear tightened inside me: It occurred to me that Jeanie had tricked me, that in fact she had wanted to break up with me and had only pretended to be contrite. Yes, she had asked me not to leave; but there was something perfunctory about her pleas, as if she were reading them from three-by-five cards, or reciting them from memory.

For a moment I stood on the sidewalk gazing at the door I had just slammed, a shiny black Beacon Hill door with a brass knocker and a semicircular window above it that looked like a setting sun, and I felt like a kid who has run away from home and then panics when no one comes looking for him. I waited for the door to open, for Jeanie to come running out after me. She didn't. I started to knock, but then thought better of it. Instead, I peered in the window. She was on the phone, holding her hand to her face and gazing dully at the ceiling; she looked like someone who has just returned from having a pet put to sleep. I figured she was talking to Mort. "Love takes such a toll on us," I imagined her saying in a weary voice. This was one of her favorite expressions; she used it all the time.

It was May, a cool evening, the late sun going pink in the pale sky. Everyone on Beacon Hill was doing their spring cleaning. I walked down Hancock Street past boxes of junk: old records, worn-out shoes, sweaters so ugly even the Salvation Army wouldn't take them. And I couldn't help feeling that this was how Jeanie saw me, like some bit of clutter that had been taking up space in her life and now, at long last, she was rid of. My run of good luck was over. I had been shot down out of the sky, and now there was only the slow twisting descent, the engines coughing and sputtering smoke, the final fiery crash. On Cambridge Street a bus approached, and I had all I could do not to throw myself under the wheels.

N O WHITE MAN has a right to complain, Evan said. Evan Weiss was my *Nation*-reading roommate and my partner at work. He did not share my sense of tragedy. "Woe is you," he said. "You're a twenty-four-year-old white male, gainfully employed, reasonably decent-looking, living in a city overcrowded with desperately lonely college girls. Please."

Of course he was right. There were lots of people who would have killed to be me. That, at least, was what I kept telling myself. And who knew? Maybe a few hundred episodes with desperately lonely college girls would erase Jeanie Sullivan from my memory. But I didn't think so.

Jeanie was stunning: tall, pale, freckled like a leopard. Her eyes were green, her lips were full. Her breasts were the kind that other women paid plastic surgeons to build for them. People stared at her. She spoke French and German, ran a 10-K in forty-five minutes, drove a red turbo Saab, and was planning to make vice president before she turned thirty. At work she peppered her presentations with references to Proust and Nietzsche, and nobody knew the way she grew up: a tenement in Dorchester, brothers who molested her, a father who drank and did the same. She had lost her Boston accent and replaced it with something vaguely mid-Atlantic, and if someone asked where she grew up, she would say, "Oh, we kind of grew up all over the place." Most people believed she was some kind of diplomat's brat. She did nothing to dispel the notion.

And me? Put it this way—if I were a comic book character, my name would be Average Man. Five ten, one sixty, brown hair, brown eyes, glasses. I grew up in Detroit and I was never the best at anything, not even as a kid. In school I was happy to do nothing and get B's. To me it seemed like a better return on investment. In woodshop, when other kids were making jewelry boxes and dining-room tables, I contented myself with crooked candleholders and lopsided picture frames. When the science fair rolled around, I dragged out my trusty papier-mâché volcano, the same one I'd used every year since third grade, and filled it once again with baking soda and vinegar. Still, my test scores were good, and with a bit of luck and a certain amount of charm I managed to wheedle my way into the University of Michigan, where I did a computer science degree and actually held my own.

After graduation I talked my way into a job at Ionic Development Corporation, a legendary place in Cambridge on the Charles River, a huge brick building with a lobby the size of a cathedral; every time I walked in, I felt as if I should genuflect. On the company e-mail list my name appeared next to Stoney Reinach, whose books on artificial intelligence I had studied in college. Reinach was a god: He taught in the Media Lab at MIT and consulted at Ionic, and there was his name, right next to mine. And there, in meetings, right across from me, was Bill Whitman, our founder and president, a man who once had been bigger than Bill Gates, a man whose picture I had seen a thousand times, everywhere from *Forbes* and *Fortune* to *Rolling Stone* and *Spy*.

There also in meetings was Jeanie Sullivan, making eyes at me. Every time I looked at Jeanie I was struck again by how beautiful she was, as if I was seeing her for the first time. And I would feel two things: first, a little charge of desire; then a tinge of fear. The combination, I have to admit, was not entirely unpleasant. It was, I suppose, the way a dog might feel toward a cruel owner: he's scared, yet he can't help being loyal. After all, life at home may not be great, but the alternative is a lot worse.

ALL SUMMER I SUFFERED. I couldn't sleep, couldn't eat. In the evenings I gazed down at the tourists in the streets of the North End, where Evan and I lived, and wished that I too could be boisterous and stupid, wearing a fannypack and having the time of my life. At work, I played Quake with the dressed-in-black Goth trolls in the telecom department and pretended not to know that the software project that Evan and I were working on was going down in flames. One day I went out and got a stupid-looking Caesar haircut and a pair of wraparound sunglasses. I told myself I was a hipster, a loner, a dangerous type. I tried a goatee, and then a soul patch. During a trip to San Francisco I got my ear pierced, but then the hole got infected and I had to let it heal shut.

At night I went to Xeno, on Lansdowne Street, and I danced for hours, like a maniac, never stopping, as if by staying in constant motion I could churn Jeanie out of my system. By July, it was working: I went a whole day without thinking about her. Still, there were relapses. One night I went to see *The Umbrellas of Cherbourg* in a theater in Brookline, and left feeling as if I'd been cracked across the skull with a lead pipe. At home I put on an extended mix of

"Lovesong," and wept about what a ridiculous figure I'd become.

One night I got into a fight. This happened in Caffe Vesuvio, a wiseguy hangout on Hanover Street. Evan liked to go there on weekends, late at night. He would put Bobby Darin on the jukebox and smoke cigarettes and admire the Italian girls who came in dressed like models from MTV videos, in high heels and tight dresses.

It was Friday night, two in the morning. We'd been out dancing with Maria Bava, our landlord's niece. Maria had graduated from Northeastern and was waiting to hear from the Peace Corps. She had been on a waiting list for six months. Apparently there were all sorts of people lining up for the privilege of working for no pay in some skanky corner of the Third World. Evan and I found this shocking. Maria said we were capitalist tools. We said we'd drink to that. For now, Maria was working in her uncle's grocery store, on the first floor of our building. She had long black hair and a body like Venus. Sometimes I would stand outside the store and watch her work. I could imagine her in a pair of safari shorts, teaching English to a bunch of African kids. Evan said they would be the luckiest kids in the Third World; he would gladly eat nothing but porridge if he could spend his days staring at her.

The fight started over our bill. We had ordered three cappuccinos, and the waiter charged us seven dollars. This wasn't a big deal. Waiters in the North End always padded the bill. But Evan was showing off for Maria. He asked the waiter how three identical items could add up to seven dollars. The waiter asked Evan if he had a problem. Evan said, no, he didn't have a problem, but he wondered if the waiter had a problem when someone ordered just one cappuccino, for two dollars and thirty-three and one-third cents, and the waiter had to make change for that third of a cent. "What do you do then?" Evan said.

"You know," the waiter said, "I think you *do* have a problem."

He slapped Evan's face. He smiled when he did this, as if he were being playful. But it was a serious slap. Evan tried not to seem scared. But probably he was flashing back to his childhood in the South

Bronx, where every day he got robbed of his lunch money by kids from the projects. He forced a laugh and said, in a schoolmarm voice, "Well, mister, that kind of thing isn't going to get you a lot of tips, I can tell you that much." His eyes were dashing madly back and forth behind his glasses, like two big fish in a fishbowl.

At the front of the café, the owner, Davio Giaccalone, had turned in his chair and was staring at us. Giaccalone was a dime-store mafioso. He wore shiny track suits and lots of gold chains. In addition to Caffe Vesuvio, he owned a Laundromat on Prince Street and various other businesses whose nature involved unmarked doorways and empty storefronts and thick-necked men who carried baseball bats. Supposedly he had once cut off the thumbs of a driver who had stolen from him.

Giaccalone said something to his nephew, Tony, who got up and headed toward our table. Tony was a miniature bodybuilder with feathered hair and a Gold's Gym tank top. He was also an aspiring stand-up comedian. He did open-mike nights. Maria said he was awful. She and Tony had grown up together. When they were eighteen, Tony had asked her to marry him. She told him that she hoped he wouldn't take offense but that she wasn't planning to spend the rest of her life in the North End. Now she was twenty-five and every time she saw Tony those words came back to haunt her.

"Maria," he said, "what the hell are you doing with these two faggots? What's going on here? Are you with these guys?"

"We're just leaving," Maria said.

"Right," I said. I put a twenty-dollar bill on the table. "We're leaving."

He looked at me, then at Evan. "You know," he said, "it's bad enough that little weirdos like you move into our neighborhood. But what the hell do you gotta come in here and start causing trouble for?"

Maria said we weren't causing trouble, and we were all just going to leave, and there was no need to make a scene—but Tony cut her off. "Maria," he said, "I think you ought to go wait outside."

The people around us started edging away. Maria told Tony to calm down. He grabbed my shirt. He was shorter than I was, but wider. Up close I could smell his cologne. I pushed him away. He grabbed me again. I shoved him into a table, which toppled over, sending a tray of plates and glasses crashing to the floor. A woman shrieked. Tony snarled and got back on his feet. I was reaching for a sugar dispenser when Evan grabbed my arm.

Later I would explain to Evan the rule about breaking up fights, which is that you don't grab your buddy, you grab the other guy. Before I could pull my arm free, Tony nailed me. My head snapped sideways, my lip exploded. Blood ran down over my shirt. The waiter grabbed Evan, and Tony grabbed me. They dragged us out to the sidewalk and threw us against the hood of a car.

It wasn't much of a fight, really. I hadn't thrown a single punch. The greasers hanging around on the sidewalk were snickering. I felt dizzy and embarrassed. I thought I might have suffered a concussion. I got one when I was a kid, playing street hockey, and I seemed to remember it feeling like this.

"What day is it?" Maria said. She snapped her fingers in front of my face. "Do you know who you are?"

I got to my feet. "Unfortunately, yes," I said, and started for home.

NATURALLY WE WANTED REVENGE. Evan's fantasies were violent: dismemberment, disembowelment. In high school he'd been a big Dungeons & Dragons freak. He definitely had a dark side. He had a scrubby beard and thick curly hair that grew wild, like shrubbery. He wore mountaineering sunglasses with little leather flaps on the sides. He looked like a revolutionary, someone whose picture you might see in the post office, wanted for crimes involving explosives.

As a high school student, Evan had won a national chess tournament and had been rated one of the top one hundred players in the world in his age group. At MIT, he had tested out of the entire undergraduate math curriculum. He went straight into graduate study as a freshman, and did concurrent bachelor's and master's degrees, finishing in four years. He was recruited by everyone—IBM, DARPA, Lucent, Xerox PARC.

So he was brilliant. He was also a geek. He belonged to *Star Trek* newsgroups, and kept a Spock costume, complete with wig and ears, in his closet. I knew this because one day, when he was out, I went through his things. Bless me, Father, for I have sinned, but you can't be too careful with roommates, especially ones who have committed entire episodes of *Star Trek: The Next Generation* to memory.

Evan belonged to a Japanese *anime* club on the Web, and spent thousands of dollars on phone sex. He squandered even more on records and stereo equipment. He owned a Luxman tube amplifier that cost four thousand dollars and looked like a small refrigerator. He owned three McCormack pre-amplifiers—one for the California Audio Labs tuner, one for the Sennheiser headphones, and one for the Lynn turntable. He'd spent a thousand dollars on special cables to connect all of these things to his five-thousand-dollar Vandersteen speakers.

He read Freud and Nietzsche and other things that I didn't understand and which I suspected he didn't, either. But he could toss the bullshit. One time, at a party in Somerville, I saw him drive an earnest, hairy-legged Cambridge girl to tears by insisting that he no longer believed in anything. The next morning I found her sitting on the couch wearing Evan's NeXT Inc. T-shirt and drinking a cup of instant coffee.

"We should bury that waiter up to his neck and then run over his head with a lawn mower," he said. "Or tie him to a tree and shoot arrows into his legs. Or skin him alive. The Aztecs did that. They flayed people, then wore their skin."

It was late Saturday night, and we were driving home from Salisbury Beach. Evan was sprawled out in back. Maria was up front, riding shotgun, looking out for cops and keeping an eye on the radar detector. We were maintaining a cruising speed of about one hundred miles an hour.

Every so often we spent a Saturday night slumming through the beach towns on the North Shore. Evan liked to pretend we were the hosts of a cable show: *White Trash Weekend with Evan and Reilly.* Tonight we'd had dinner at the Hilltop Steak House in Saugus before driving to Salisbury Beach, where we had visited a country-western bar, a karaoke disco, a strip joint, a heavy-metal club full of bikers, and finally a place called the Beachcomber Lounge that had red leather booths, a ratty pool table, and five glum drunks sitting at the bar listening to Patsy Cline on the jukebox.

"We should kidnap Tony," Evan said. "We should tie him up and take out his teeth with a pair of pliers."

"Go to sleep," Maria said.

We got back to the North End at three in the morning and discovered that there were no parking spaces in the entire neighborhood except for the one on Hanover Street that was reserved for Giaccalone's Mercedes. I did something that I would not have done if I had been sober: I moved his barrels. "To hell with Giaccalone," I said. "I live here too, right?"

"I love it when you get all drunk and Catholic and indignant," Evan said. "You're like James Joyce—portrait of the asshole as a young man."

He stumbled away toward our building. I walked Maria home. "You really should move your car," she said.

I pretended not to hear her. At her door there was an awkward moment, a bit of fumbling for keys. I'm no whiz kid with women, but I know when a girl is waiting to be kissed. And I couldn't believe it. I'm always astonished when a woman likes me. It's not that I'm an ogre. But I definitely could use some work. My eyes are too far apart, my nose is too big, and there's a gap between my front teeth. My hair looks like something that was stolen off a mannequin. Luckily, I'm not fat, although I probably will be when I get older. For now I'm just pale and undermuscled. I haven't exercised since college, and even then all I did was play Frisbee. I can't bear to look at myself naked, at least not with my glasses on. With my glasses off, everything gets blurry enough that I can almost believe I look normal. I'm definitely not someone who makes love with the lights on.

So maybe I was only imagining that Maria wanted to kiss me. Either way it didn't matter because I wasn't going to let it happen. There was a rather serious impediment to my forming a relationship with Maria, which was that ever since the breakup with Jeanie I had been more or less impotent. I had discovered this one night with a woman who invited me home from a bar in Faneuil Hall. I tried to concentrate, but this only made things worse. The woman said something mean, then laughed while I put on my clothes and ran out the door. Since then the idea of sex terrified me. On my own, I was fine. But with a partner, nothing. I accepted the curse, and resigned myself to a life of baby oil and Kleenex. Evan called me Onan the Barbarian.

Maria took my hand. "Are you okay?"

"Sure." I smiled, and stepped away from her, into the street. "I'll talk to you tomorrow," I said.

"Okay." She seemed puzzled.

I waved—a dorky gesture, more of a flip than a wave—and said, "Well, good night."

She squinted, as if there were something written on my forehead and she was trying to read it. Then she said, "Okay, good night," and opened the door.

For a long time after she went inside I stood across the street, staring up at her windows, wondering if I had only been imagining things. I watched her lights come on, and then go off. I thought about how she would look naked. Part of me wanted to rush up there and take her in my arms. But then I imagined the rest of the scene: We tear off our clothes, fall into bed, and then—ta da!—there's Mr. Shrimpie, refusing to play ball. Who was I kidding?

I walked home. The streets reeked. Even now, in the middle of the night, the air was as hot and humid as the inside of a greenhouse. We were having a heat wave. The forecasters said we were close to breaking a record. The sidewalks were heaped with rubbish from the restaurants, the pavement sticky with the runoff from the trash bags. Rats rustled in the bags and scurried along the cobblestones, swarming through the puddles of light and vanishing into the gutters. At home I fell into bed and dozed off thinking about ways to kill myself.

Next morning I awoke with a plan: I would buy the Sunday *Times* and a bag of bagels and show up at Maria's apartment. In the time it took me to shower, I managed to envision an entire life with her: a house in the suburbs, a bunch of dark-skinned children, a little bedroom with floral wallpaper and a crucifix hanging over the door. Maria went to mass every Sunday. She wasn't the type who would cheat on you, or leave you. I saw in her the possibility of a sane life. In the bakery, waiting in line for the bagels, I imagined her meeting me at the door in a T-shirt, the two of us drinking coffee and then falling into bed as the afternoon stretched into evening.

This reverie was interrupted, however, when I walked around the corner and found my car slumped onto the pavement, with all of its tires slashed.

GIACCALONE SAID he didn't know anything about any tires on any faggot's car. He was sitting at his usual table, eating a cannoli. Sunlight slanted through the window and spilled across the floor. A fan spun thrummed lazily overhead. Outside, the temperature was rising. At night the air fell to about eighty degrees and then in the morning the temperature started climbing again. Even now, at nine in the morning, I was sweating.

The café was quiet. The only customers were three old men who sat in back playing dominoes. The little tiles clicked on the table. They looked up at me and murmured to each other in Italian.

I stood in front of Giaccalone. He picked up a section of the newspaper and fanned himself with it.

"You're telling me," I said, "that nobody here saw anyone near my car."

"Nobody here saw nothing," he said. "And you'd better get that shitbox out of my space, bucko."

My car was not a shitbox. It was a 1975 BMW 2002 Turbo, which I'd bought from its original owner, a professor in Ann Arbor who called the car Sigrid and only drove it on weekends in summer. Only 1,672 turbocharged 2002s were ever built. Officially they were only sold in Europe, but a few were gray-marketed into North America. My car still had its original white paint, no dings or dents, with a spoiler on back, racing stripes on the sides, and the words "2002 TURBO" written in reverse script on the front air dam. It was way too nice a car to keep in Boston, and I could have made a killing if I sold it; but I couldn't bear to sell it.

The 2002 Turbo produced 170 horsepower, weighed 2,200 pounds, and boasted a top speed of 130 miles per hour. Sometimes, in the middle of the night, I drove out of the city and played boy racer on Route 128, running at full throttle against Bimmers and Porsches. Fair enough, it was stupid. But everyone has their obsession. Evan had his records and his stereo equipment; I had Bilstein shocks and Bridgestone tires and Kugelfischer mechanical fuel injectors. In Detroit, where I grew up, this was considered normal.

Jeanie said the whole boy racer thing was a form of projected homosexual desire. "You've got a bunch of guys out there, cruising around, going one-on-one against each other. You get all revved up, *zoom-zoom,* and then you get on his tail—you get *on his ass,* as you put it—and then there's a little spurt and it's over. And you don't think there's something homoerotic about that?"

"No," I said, "I don't."

"Oh, Reilly, you're so . . . midwestern."

Jeanie had never been to the Midwest, except for stopovers at O'Hare to change planes. But like everyone else from the East Coast she claimed to know all about the Midwest—more, in fact, than people in the Midwest did.

"If you weren't so homophobic you'd see it," she said. "All you guys need are some leather motorcycle hats and you could be the cast from *Cruising.*"

Looking back, I think this might have been the point when things started to go bad between us.

*   *   *

The desk cop gave me a report to fill out. There wasn't much they could do, he said.

"You're kidding," I said.

He looked up. His name, I noticed, was Incorpora. He had a long, sallow face, a high forehead. It was Sunday morning. He needed a shave. In the back of the office they had hung a wet towel over the front of a box fan. The towel slapped and spun in the wind. But it didn't seem to be helping any. Incorpora's face glistened with sweat. He kept dabbing himself with a paper towel.

"It's obvious who did this," I said. "All you have to do is find someone who'll testify. I mean, go look around a little, ask a few questions. Maybe pressure an informer or something."

"An informer? What do you think this is, *Starsky and Hutch*? You want me go see if Huggy Bear's heard about any tire slashers out on the loose?"

Behind him, a fat cop put down the meatball sub he was eating and began laughing so hard that pieces of bread fell out of his mouth. "What'd you do?" the fat cop said. "You move somebody's barrels?"

"That is precisely what he did," Incorpora told him. "Not only that, but in the North End. On Hanover Street."

"Jeez." The fat cop whistled. "Whose barrels?"

I told him.

"Kid," he said, "you ought to get your head examined."

They were still laughing when I left.

That afternoon a crew from a Firestone shop put my car up on blocks and changed the tires. Among the hecklers who gathered to enjoy the spectacle was Gus Garibaldi, Maria's uncle. He stood outside his grocery store hurling insults at me and laughing at his own jokes. Gus was our landlord. He charged us fifty percent more than everyone else in the building. The phrase "Old World charm," which his advertisement in the *Globe* had promised, turned out to be meant literally: We had roaches, no air conditioning, crumbling exposed brick walls, and a toilet that ran incessantly. When we threatened to break our lease, Gus said we should consider how awful it would be to come home and find our belongings, well, *interfered with*.

"Looks like somebody got a Sicilian parking ticket!" he bellowed. "You watch out, or next time you might lose a couple fingers, huh?"

He wiggled his fingers in the air. The simians on the sidewalk grinned and leered and cackled and pointed: it was like being the featured attraction at the circus of the retards. The one who laughed hardest was Lucia Ronsavelli, our neighbor from across the hall. Lucia was Gus's mistress. She believed that nobody knew this. But of course, everybody knew. Gossip spread in the North End like mildew in a wet basement. It was impossible to keep secrets, Maria said.

Lucia was about fifty years old, and had a white stripe bleached into the front of her hair. We called her "the Bride of Frankenstein." She hated us. Then again, everyone in the North End hated us. The old men sitting on their folding chairs muttered, "Faggots," when we walked past them on the sidewalk. Kids threw firecrackers at us from rooftops. The fruit vendors wouldn't speak to us; they just grunted and took our money and gave us the worst pieces from their carts.

Maria said we had to see things their way: The yuppies were moving in, and taking over; the rents kept going up; and the Italians were getting pushed out of their own neighborhood. The yuppies treated people from the neighborhood as if they were servants. You couldn't blame the Italians for being resentful, she said.

"You're lucky you're still alive!" Lucia shouted. She brayed like a donkey. Everyone laughed, but this time at least part of the laughter was directed at her. She was wearing oversized sunglasses and a stretchy green minidress that clung to her lumpy hips and made her look like an overstuffed sausage.

Maria pushed through the crowd. "I hate to say I told you so," she said.

"Good," I said. "So don't." My head was killing me. It felt as if it were going to split open.

"You're one of those people who has to learn things for themselves, right? You won't take anyone else's word for it."

"Whatever you say." It was ninety-eight degrees with a heat index that made it feel like four thousand. I smelled like a homeless person. All I wanted to do was lie in front of a fan and smoke dope and wait for it to be Monday. "You know," I said, "only in the North End could a greasy, shit-filled crispelli like Davio Giaccalone tyrannize an entire neighborhood and have everyone love him for it."

"I thought you grew up in Detroit," she said. "I thought you knew all about stuff like this."

In Detroit, I told her, a pimp like Giaccalone would get his ass kicked. There were a lot of mob guys in the downriver towns. At school we always knew which dads were wiseguys because they were the ones who went out of their way to make themselves invisible. They didn't go to church, or come to cookouts. They didn't wear gold chains and flashy suits; and they most certainly did not drive flashy cars. They wore hunting jackets and work pants, and drove old beat-up American cars. When you ran into them, they were polite, but that was it. The wiseguys in Detroit would take one look at Giaccalone and burst out laughing.

"Maria!" Gus shouted. "Come on, get over here. I'm not paying you to hang around outside with these stunads."

"Stunads?" Evan said. "Now we're stunads? What the hell is a stunad?"

Maria laughed. "You don't want to know. Look, I'll see you guys later."

She ran back into the store. I grabbed Evan. "So what do you think?" I said.

"About what?"

"There." I nodded toward Tony, who stood in the doorway of the café, winking and blowing me kisses—his extremely subtle way of clearing up any confusion I might have had about who had slashed my tires.

"What should I do?" I said.

"You," Evan said, "should move your car."

"WE COULD SMASH his windshield," Evan said.

"Too obvious. He'd know it was us."

"We could wake him up with prank phone calls."

"Right. That's a good idea."

It was Sunday night. We were sitting with Maria on the roof deck. Our apartment was on the fourth floor, and we had a ladder in the living room that led through a skylight to the roof. We had a view of the harbor on one side and the city on the other; this almost made the place worth what we were paying for it. The apartment itself was pretty bare. We had Evan's stereo stuff, which took up one wall, and then we had a couch, a 27-inch Sony TV, a Sony PlayStation, a stack of video game cartridges, and that was about it, other than a few aluminum lawn chairs we'd stolen from Quincy Market.

We were stretched out on the chairs now, trying not to move. If you held very still you could almost not feel the heat. But if you stood up, or moved even slightly, you began to sweat. The air was so sultry that you felt as if you were drinking it. Earlier that day I had seen people jogging; I could not imagine how they managed to breathe.

Evan had put on a special-pressing Miles Davis record. The music was slow and lazy; the fat notes plopped up out of the skylight like bubbles of warm air being pressed through a chimney. At home, Evan listened only to vinyl. He insisted that it sounded better. Personally I couldn't hear the difference, and it seemed to me that CDs made more sense if only because you didn't have to keep climbing down the ladder and turning the record over. Evan said that if that's all you cared about music you might as well slit your wrists now and get it over with. Fair enough, he was a purist. I felt the same way about people who drove cars with automatic transmissions.

Evan handed me a joint. I took a long hit, and watched the rooftops go fuzzy. A thick slow bass line spilled up out of the roof. I wondered if humidity affected the way music sounded. The vibrations moved through the air, after all.

"We could steal his car," Evan said. "Or something else maybe. What else does Fat Boy have that's worth money?"

"He's got a dog," Maria said.

"Let me guess," Evan said. "A pit bull, right? Either that or a Rottweiler. Or maybe a Doberman."

"Actually, it's a greyhound. Apparently she's some kind of champion. Supposedly she's worth a hundred thousand dollars. Her name's Coco."

I hadn't been paying attention, my thoughts were wandering. "Hold on," I said. "Did you say Coco?"

"He just got her. Her trainer owed Davio twenty-five thousand dollars. Davio told the guy he could have his thumbs, or he could have his dog, but he couldn't have both."

A cold sweat began forming on my back, between my shoulder blades. "I saw that dog run in the first race of her life," I said. "I won ninety dollars on that dog."

Evan sighed. He'd heard, too many times, the story about me and Jeanie and our night at Wonderland. "I'll pay you another ninety," he said, "if you stop right now and don't finish that story. I'll pay you nine hundred if you promise never to tell that story again, for as long as you live."

"What story?" Maria said.

"Jesus." Evan clapped his hands. "Here we go."

"What's the story?"

I sat there, staring into the distance. The record ended. I closed my eyes. It was past midnight, and we were mightily baked. The neighborhood lay silent, except for a thin humming sound which gradually I recognized as the sound of fans—hundreds of them, whirring.

"Look," Evan said, "we'll put sugar in his gas tank, all right? What does that do, anyway?"

I gazed at the Custom House tower, and beyond it the rooftops of Beacon Hill. I thought about Jeanie. Where was she now? Probably in her apartment, lying in bed with Mort Stone.

"Reilly."

"Huh."

"What does that do?"

"What?"

"The sugar. When you put it in the gas tank."

"It fucks up the engine."

"Yeah, but how?"

I shrugged.

"I thought you were from Detroit," he said. "I thought you were Mister Motor City."

"Look," I said, "if I asked you how the *Starship Enterprise* manages to keep running for all those years without ever having to stop for fuel, could you tell me?"

"Of course."

Maria giggled.

"Sadly," I told her, "he's not lying."

"It's cold fusion. There's a reactor—"

"Buddy," I said, "please."

Maria said she had to go home. We climbed back into the apartment. Evan said probably we should just forget about Giaccalone. We had enough things to worry about, he said. Like work, for example.

"Let's not talk about work," I said, and felt my stomach tighten as it did whenever I thought of the place.

JEANIE ARRIVED wearing a white sleeveless dress and sporting a sunburn. Mort walked in a minute later, also sunburned. Apparently they had spent the weekend on Nantucket, sailing. Jeanie sat down without looking at me and began writing something on a legal pad. She and Mort did not sit together, but if you watched them carefully, you could catch them trading glances. It made me sick.

It was Monday morning, eleven o'clock. Evan and I were giving a progress report. We did this once a month. In attendance were the president of the company, Bill Whitman, whom everyone called Whit, and a dozen sales and marketing drones who sat tapping their gold Mont Blanc pens on their blood-colored leather portfolios, which they no longer bothered to open. In the old days people took notes when we talked to them; now they fought to stay awake.

Evan and I worked in advanced research and development, affectionately known as ARAD, and we were developing a Web-based groupware application called Nectar. We were six months late, way over our heads. The code was crawling with bugs. When we fixed one, we created two. Evan had designed the program, and he insisted that he could make it work. But it seemed to me that Nectar would never run on anything other than an overhead projector.

In recent months our presentations had grown tense. Today was the worst ever. Hostility crackled in the air like heat lightning. I was shivering. The air conditioning was cranked. Whit said cold air kept people alert. What he didn't say but no doubt knew was that cold air also made women get nipple hard-ons; which also kept everyone alert. We were on the fifth floor, on the side of the building that faced the river. Outside, sailboats danced on the choppy water, zigzagging back and forth. How I wished I were in one of them.

Evan and I had a regular routine: he was the magician, and I was the lovely assistant. My job was to stand there glowering at the sub-humans, like Charlton Heston in *Planet of the Apes* appearing before the ape tribunal, while Evan stood at the whiteboard scribbling acronyms and drawing arrows and talking about transport protocols. Evan was a masterful bullshitter. Today, he responded to a rather pointed question about our e-mail interface by launching into a tutorial on the seven-layer OSI model. He was halfway through when Whit cleared his throat and said, "Hey, Evan? Evan? Hold on, okay? Put down the marker."

The room grew silent. The drones stopped tapping their pens and sat up straight. They looked like sharks smelling blood. I had the feeling we'd been ambushed. Whatever was about to happen, they'd all known about it before the meeting began. First thing that morning I'd checked the e-mail server but had found nothing out of the ordinary. Still, it was possible they'd passed information in interoffice mail. Or maybe they'd met in hallways. People were always conspiring at Ionic. You couldn't go for coffee without having some kind of conspiracy. The place ran on paranoia. The whole industry did. Paranoia did for us what greed had done for Wall Street in the eighties: It drove us. It gave us fuel.

Evan and I stood at the front of the room like a pair of captured outlaws. I glanced at Jeanie. She looked away. Mort, however, was looking right at me, and smiling. He had a bland, handsome face, the kind you see on TV announcers and airline pilots: steely eyes, strong jaw, good teeth. He wore suits from Joseph Abboud, and got his hair cut on Newbury Street. He was vice president of marketing. I hated him more than I hated myself.

"Here's the thing." Whit sighed, and put his hands to his face. "We've got to put a stake in the ground, you understand? We've got to make some decisions. So here's what we're going to do. We'll go another month, and then after Labor Day we'll take a look at what we've got, and then we'll decide either to productize, or, I don't know, I guess we'll cut our losses." He gave us a sad smile. He did not seem angry. "Does that sound okay?"

I shrugged. This wasn't exactly a surprise. For months we had been intercepting e-mail messages in which Mort and others recommended that the company scrap Nectar and fire us. But I guess we'd never thought Whit would really do this. I focused my attention on a woman named Ginny whose nipples were threatening to tear holes in her blouse; then she glared at me and I looked away.

Evan began blinking his eyes. He was trying not to cry. Poor Evan. In his entire life he'd never failed at anything. The worst part was that I had dragged him into this disaster. His modules worked fine. Mine looked like they were designed by retards.

Evan said Whit should consider the enormity of the task that we had tried to tackle. Nectar contained almost two hundred thousand lines of code. "It's like writing a novel," Evan said, "with the extra condition that if there's even a single typo, the whole book is unreadable."

He had used this line before. The drones were rolling their eyes. Whit said he understood how hard we'd worked on this. "Nobody's saying that you didn't work hard," he said.

"But look," Evan said, "if you were Dostoyevsky's publisher, and he was writing *Crime and Punishment,* and he was running a little bit late, would you go to him and say, 'Hey, Fyodor, another month, babe, and then we'll have to cut this thing short. We'll do *Crime* now and *Punishment* later.' Would you do that?"

Before Whit could answer, Mort said, "In a word, yes." The

drones burst out laughing. Evan looked out the window. If it weren't sealed shut, he might have opened it and jumped out. Whit sighed, and looked down at his hands. Whit hated conflict. He never should have been running a company.

Bob Lull, our supervisor, said, "Look, a month is fine." He was standing in the corner, keeping his distance from us, as if we had some contagious disease and he didn't dare get too close. In fact we did have a disease: it was called Dead Man's Disease. We were marked for slaughter. Lull was thirty-something, middle management, hoping to make vice president. He had a master's degree in psychology, and he operated under the assumption that he understood more about other people than they did about themselves. He wore Peruvian sweaters, and drove a Volvo station wagon; but beneath the fuzzy Cambridge exterior he was an ambitious back-stabber, as slippery as a watermelon seed, just like the rest of them. He had cut his teeth at Data General and then at Digital Equipment, and he had seen the kind of office treachery we could not even begin to imagine. Evan called Lull the "Great Satan." One day, he said, we were going to turn on the television and see the police digging corpses out of Lull's basement.

"I don't see why we're even waiting a month," Mort said. "Why let it drag on?"

Whit said it wouldn't hurt to wait. He didn't like rushing into things. He told us he was sorry. We had nothing to be ashamed of, he said. We'd had a good idea, and we'd worked hard. "We can't let these projects go on forever," he said. "We've got the pressure of the market to contend with. We've got the assholes on Wall Street breathing down our neck."

Whit hated the investors. Sometimes it seemed to me that he hated the whole company, too. Certainly Ionic wasn't anything like the company he had started in his garage fifteen years before. In the early days they'd had a beer blast every Friday afternoon, and everyone came to work wearing shorts and sandals and Hawaiian shirts. Now Ionic had investors, and a board of directors, and marketing fiefdoms run by people like Mort Stone. The only reminders of the happy hippie days were the photos that Whit kept on the walls of his office. "I wish you guys could have been around in the old days," he said one day when Evan and I were at his house for dinner. "Now . . . well, you know." He sighed. "Now it's a *company*. It's a job."

Evan said Whit was a sad case, a guy who'd got lucky and made a fortune and now didn't know what to do with himself. He had drifted into computers after dropping out of graduate school. Somehow he had bluffed his way into a job working nights writing COBOL on mainframes at the NASA Jet Propulsion Laboratory. In his spare time he tinkered with an Apple II, writing little programs using Bill Gates's version of BASIC. When IBM developed the PC, in 1981, Whit took a program he'd written for the Apple II, ported it to the IBM, and hit the jackpot. To Evan, this was revolting. To me, it was an inspiration: Whit was living proof that even people without talent could succeed in life.

"Is there any other business?" Whit said. He was wearing a Hawaiian shirt, the pocket stuffed with three-by-five cards. He carried them with him at all times and was constantly making notes to himself.

Mort said, "I just want to say again that I think it's cruel to let these projects linger."

Whit pretended to think about that for a moment. Then he said, "Okay, back to the salt mines."

AFTER THE MEETING I hid in a conference room and waited to ambush Jeanie. When people walked by, I pretended to be writing on the whiteboard. I knew this was pathetic. But I had to see her. I had to talk to her. I had to tell her about all of the ways I was suffering, all of the places I could no longer go: Fenway Park, the Swan Boats, the Thai restaurant on Newbury Street, the maparium at the Christian Science Center. I wanted to tell her how every morning and every afternoon I rode my bike over the Longfellow Bridge and tried not to think about the night in February when we had managed to fumble open enough clothing to have sex against the railing behind one of the towers, with a fat moon hanging in the sky and the cold air stinging our skin and Jeanie making jokes about my sturdy little long fellow. I wanted to tell her that if she knew how much this was hurting me, she wouldn't do it.

Instead, I leaped out and cornered her and then couldn't think of anything to say. She stood there, gazing down at me. In heels she was five eleven, sometimes six feet. I motioned toward the conference room. She followed.

"What happened to your mouth?" she said.

I'd forgotten: my lip was swollen, and had turned blue. I told her about the fight in the café. I told her what they'd done to my car.

"That must have been tough for you," she said. "I mean, for a man, and his car—men have so much of their self-worth tied up in objects, you know? And the whole deflating thing. The tires. I mean, symbolically, you know, it's pure Freud, right?"

"Actually," I said, "that's not what I wanted to talk about."

"Isn't today . . . ?"

"What?"

She looked away. She seemed puzzled. "I'm sorry. I must be mixed up." Sometimes it seemed to me that Jeanie was suffering as much as I was. A few times since the breakup I had come home and found blank messages on my phone machine—somebody had called and then not left a message. One time I used star-sixty-nine to dial the number of the last person who'd called me, and sure enough, I got Jeanie's machine. She was confused, I figured. She'd had a fling with Mort, and confessed this to me, and like a fool I refused to forgive her, and now she was stuck with Mort. But you can't end a relationship the way we had done it. It's too sudden. It leaves too many loose ends. One day we were officially in love, and the next day we were broken up, and we'd never talked about why this had happened, or what it meant. You can't do that. Love is like an oil tanker: You have to start slowing down a long time before you stop.

"So what did you want to talk about?" Jeanie said. She glanced at her watch. As a child, Jeanie had mastered the art of appearing to have no feelings; she'd had to do this in order to survive her father. But I could see in her eyes that she was as nervous as I was. Her eyes were dark green, flecked with gold; they made me think of sunlight spraying through trees. They were the only place where sometimes, if you looked really carefully, you could still see Jeanie the way she had been when she was a kid, before she had gone to Harvard and changed her voice and figured out how to claw her way to the top.

Other people resented Jeanie for her ambition, but to me her struggling only seemed sad, because it was so obviously fueled by fear. All day, every day, she lived with the fear of being found out, of being exposed as a fraud, of losing everything. In her worst nightmare she ended up back in Dorchester, being chased by her father. She was determined never to go back there, never to be poor, never to have to depend on anyone for anything. What people at work didn't understand was that Jeanie was not so much trying to get ahead as she was trying to get away. She dragged her past behind her like a swimmer towing a buoy, and the effort of this had made her tough. But sometimes in her eyes you could see the original Jeanie, the skinny kid with the big ugly glasses and the big ugly secret that all these years later still made her wake up in the middle of the night, reaching for breath.

"I want to talk about us," I said. "You and me."

She sighed, theatrically. "Reilly," she said, "I care about you. You know that. But you have to get on with your life, don't you think?"

"No," I said. "I don't." My face was getting hot. I knew that I was making an ass of myself, that ten years from now I would not be able to look back on this time without wincing. But sooner or later everybody goes through a period of lunacy over a love affair; and this was my turn. "You've changed," I told her. "I don't even recognize you anymore. I mean, your *hair*."

She had got a new cut: short, blunt, severe. Evan said that when you reached a certain level in marketing, they brought you in and did the lobotomy and the "Lady Republican" hairstyle at the same time.

"Look who's talking," she said. "You've got this concentration-camp haircut. What's next? Are you going to go buy some wide jeans and wear them down off your ass like some hip-hop kid? Are you going to start riding to work on a skateboard? Look, Reilly, change is good, if it's change in the right direction. And if it's genuine. I'm growing up. Maybe someday you will, too."

When I first met Jeanie, she would come to work wearing black 501s and Italian boots. Now she wore suits, and she looked like the people we used to make fun of—the people who kissed ass and worried about promotions.

"I don't understand what went wrong," I said. "One day we were fine, and the next day—wham."

She asked me if I'd considered medication. Prozac, Zoloft. They leveled you out, she said, and then you could go into therapy. "There are things you need to work on," she said.

"You know," I said, "I'd do it, if I felt that I was doing it for a purpose. I mean, if we were going to couples counseling or something."

She looked at her watch. "Shit, I'm going to be late."

"Jeanie."

I grabbed her arm. She looked at me. Her eyes were blank, as if I were a stranger, some madman standing next to her on the T and telling her about the microchip that the space aliens had implanted in his penis.

"Jeanie," I said, "for Christ's sake, you're wearing nail polish. You sold out." Tears were forming in my eyes.

She pulled her arm free. "Reilly," she said, "I'd love to sit here and play Sandinista with you, but I've got a meeting."

NABEEL AND UPENDRA said not to worry, that nobody had ever been fired from Ionic, and there were people who had done far worse things than screw up a piece of software. "One guy stole a NeXT workstation," Nabeel said, "and even he didn't get fired. Curious case. I never understood why anyone would want a NeXT workstation in the first place. You couldn't pay me to use one." He lifted a slice of pizza from the platter. "Here, dig in. Where's Evan?"

"Working. He says he's got thirty days. That's seven hundred and twenty hours. He's not going to sleep."

"He's crazy," Upendra said.

"This is true."

The restaurant was noisy, the tables filled with software types from Kendall Square: lots of beards, not many neckties. We were sitting in a booth in back.

"Do you have any idea," Nabeel said, "how many products they've funded and then killed off? This happens all the time. It doesn't even bother them."

Nabeel was from London. His mom and dad were both doctors,

but he affected a Cockney accent and played at being working class. He said *kiwwed* for *killed, bovver* for *bother.* He wore Doc Martens and black 501s, and when he heard me arrive in the morning he would put "Lovesong" on his stereo, just loud enough for me to hear it.

Nabeel had been at Ionic for five years and still had not produced anything. Nevertheless everyone in management considered him a genius. He arrived at nine and left at five and never spent less than ninety minutes on lunch, and he expected to continue doing this for the rest of his life. The trick to surviving in ARAD, he told us, was to develop ideas that were esoteric enough to be impressive but flawed in some way that made them impossible to use in a commercial application. When we first developed the Nectar prototype, he took us aside and suggested ways to hobble the software. Evan told him to fuck off; but now sometimes I wished we had taken his advice.

In addition to his amazing record of nonachievement and his string of spectacular car accidents—all of which, he claimed, were not his fault—Nabeel was famous at Ionic because of something he once had done to a girl in the sales department. Her name was Amy, and she was cute, and although she was not particularly bright, she was clever enough to trick Nabeel into buying her several expensive dinners before she remembered to mention that she had a boyfriend. "I'm sorry," she said. "You didn't think that you and I were, um, dating, did you?" Nabeel, ever gracious, said of course not. In fact, to prove that there were no hard feelings, a week later he took her out again, this time to a restaurant in New Hampshire, where he ordered lavishly, ran up a huge bill, and then walked out, leaving her stranded.

"I wouldn't say this to Evan," Nabeel said, "but just between us girls, I think he's being a bit naive about this whole thing. Nectar wasn't ever going to work, okay? And even if it did, they wouldn't sell it. You're too late. A year ago, maybe it would have been viable. But now? Forget it. I can't believe they've let you chase after it for as long as they have. If anybody's to blame, it's Whit, really. I've seen this happen a million times. The sales guys blow some wind up his arse and he gets all excited. But he doesn't stop to think about whether something will actually work. Now I love Uncle Whit, right? I do. But the fact is, he doesn't know a thing about software."

Upendra said Nabeel was right, we were better off having them kill Nectar now. "God forbid you should have them put the product into the market and then have it die. That kind of thing can destroy your career. At least now, on your résumé, you look okay."

Upendra knew what we were going through; he had once spent two years on a project only to have Whit kill it off at the last minute. Since then he had stopped caring. He put in his hours and lived for his vacations, which he spent on rock-climbing expeditions. Upendra was a California kid, with soft features and a surfer accent. He had a master's degree from Stanford and lately had been talking about going back to finish his doctorate. Like me, he had recently gone through a painful breakup—his girlfriend had taken a job in Silicon Valley and met a guy out there—but unlike me, he wasn't moping about it. Life went on, he said. These things happened. I envied him for this equanimity. I figured it had something to do with his being Indian. Once I asked him if he could teach me to meditate. He stared at me, then shook his head.

"Even if they let you go," Upendra said, "it's no big deal. And they'll have to give you something like a year's worth of severance pay. I mean, I'd love to get fired. But I'll tell you, it's not easy to get fired. They don't want to fire people. It makes them look bad. Plus, you could go work for a competitor. For them it's actually worth it to keep you around, even if you do nothing. I mean, look at us. We've been here for five years."

"The worst they'll do is move you," Nabeel said. "They'll put you down with the zombies."

The zombies were the people who worked in customer support and low-level R&D. They worked side by side in a vast room the size of a football field, all of it the color of oatmeal. Our offices overlooked their cubicles. When I watched them, I felt heartsick, the way I did when I saw puppies in cages at a pet store. All day long the zombies sat in their little pens, writing bug patches and device drivers, and the worst thing was, they were happy. They loved their jobs. They were the biggest losers I'd ever known. They decorated their cubicles with plants and photographs and Dilbert cartoons; they wore off-brand relaxed-fit jeans and got eight-dollar haircuts. Evan said we should take a photograph of them and mail it to college career-counseling offices with the warning, *Don't let this happen to you.*

"They're not so bad," Nabeel said. I looked at him. "Okay, they *are* that bad. But you'd get used to it."

"I would die a thousand deaths before I got used to them," I said.

"Speaking of which," Upendra said, "Janet Scuto was looking for you."

Janet Scuto was the zombie team leader in charge of spellcheckers. She also was in charge of the kitchen on our floor. Every so often she would send around a questionnaire asking what new items we'd like to have stocked in the vending machines. I requested Ecstasy. Evan asked for handguns.

"Apparently," Nabeel said, "the coffee machine was left on all night. A pot was ruined. Your names came up."

"It wasn't us," I said.

"Tell that to the judge."

Janet's rule regarding the coffee machine was that whoever took the last cup had to start a fresh pot. Evan and I insisted that it was bad enough to get the last cup from a day-old pot without the added insult of having to make a fresh pot for someone else. Why not let the next person make their own coffee? Janet wrote a memo to Bob Lull in which she threatened to revoke our kitchen privileges unless we complied. She complained also about Evan making coffee, using four bags instead of one—producing a drink he called "crystal meth in a cup" that had sent one of the zombies home early complaining of chest pains. Basically, Janet Scuto didn't have enough to do, and so had to find ways to make the people around her miserable. No doubt she dreamed of being moved into management where she could torment entire groups of people at the same time.

After the memo incident, we decided to fight back. We sent Janet a dozen roses, with a card signed: "Your secret admirer." Janet was short and fat and hopelessly single. She kept pictures of her cats tacked to the walls of her cubicle, as if they were her children. The appearance of roses on the shelf above her desk was guaranteed to create a commotion. Sure enough, that afternoon a gaggle of female zombies gathered around her desk, while Janet Scuto blushed and beamed and said, "I don't know, I really don't, I have no idea."

Since then we had built on the strategy by waiting for Janet to leave her cubicle and then dialing her extension. At the far end of the room she would stop, turn, listen—and then she would fly back as if she were attached to her desk by a rubber band, her stubby legs churning, her breasts flopping, her face contorting into a spastic grimace. Gasping, short of breath, she would grab the phone and try not to shout: "Hello?" And we would hang up. *Click.* For a few seconds Janet would stand there, looking ready either to cry or start smashing things.

Lull had warned us to leave Janet alone. Evan told Lull to mind his own business. Lull just stood there, speechless. On the one hand you had to admire Evan for being so fearless. On the other hand, there were times when I thought Evan was simply being a dick. Evan said he just couldn't take orders from people who were not as smart as he was. I tried not to think of Evan's attitude as being either good or bad; he just wasn't meant to be somebody else's employee, that's all.

"Janet came in this morning," Nabeel said, "and I swear she looked like her head was going to explode."

"It's true," Upendra said. "She looked like the Tasmanian Devil."

The waiter started clearing our plates. I stood up to leave.

"What's the hurry?" Nabeel said. "I mean, look, you're a dead man, right? You might as well enjoy it."

"I guess you're right." I sat back down. We ordered cappuccinos. Nabeel poured an enormous pile of sugar into the foam on his. The sugar caramelized. It looked like lacquer. He followed it with about a pound of powdered chocolate, then stirred the whole thing up.

"Reilly," he said, "take my advice, okay? Just forget that Nectar ever happened. Put it behind you. Move on."

NECTAR WAS EVAN'S IDEA. He stumbled on it almost by accident. We were supposed to be looking for ways to build e-mail filters. But Evan, the boy genius, started tinkering with Web protocols, and instead of coming up with a filter, he came up with an application that let people share documents over the Web. It was pretty straightforward. There was a central database from which you could retrieve documents using a Web browser. Then he incorporated e-mail. Again, simple enough. But then he realized that the technology could be used to let people shop on the Web. You stored product information in the database, made it accessible from a Web browser, and used messaging protocols and encryption software to handle the transactions. Suddenly we had a product with mass-market appeal. Lull showed a prototype to Whit. Whit showed the prototype to the drones in marketing. The drones drooled. Whit gave Evan a budget and a deadline.

At that point I figured Evan would go off on his own. It was his idea, after all. But Evan had a theory that great products come not from lone inventors but from pairs of people. Usually the pairs were lopsided: there was the visionary genius and the pragmatist. Think of

Gates and Allen, he said. Or Jobs and Wozniak. It was binary. You needed both bits, the one and the zero. It was obvious which pair of the binary coupling I represented. Still, I stood to make a fortune. That helped me swallow my pride.

Evan negotiated a new contract in which we would receive royalties tied to sales of Nectar. The idea was to give us the incentives that we would have had if we were running a start-up, but with the safety net of a big company. I never knew the details. But figures in the one to five million range were mentioned. Somehow, word got around— Boston is a pretty small city. That summer the *Globe* did a story about us, and *Boston* magazine put us in their annual "Boston's Most Eligible Bachelors" feature. On weekends I visited Porsche dealerships and wondered whether I wanted a coupe, a targa, or a cabriolet.

Now when I thought about those days I felt like an old man looking back on his youth, seeing everything bathed in a golden light. Jeanie and I had started going out, Evan was my new best friend, and Nectar looked like a sure thing. But somehow in the course of fifteen months everything had managed to go terribly wrong. The problems had less to do with Nectar than with the Web itself. The Web is great for publishing static information, but not so good at handling interactive transactions. In effect we were trying to make it do something that it wasn't designed to do. Nabeel said we might as well staple jet engines to a turkey and expect it to fly like a stealth bomber.

We split up the work: Evan did the guts (database, messaging, file I/O) while I did the cosmetics (output drivers, user interface). We missed our first deadline. Lull told us not to panic. There were always delays, he said. This was back in the early days, when we still liked him and he still liked us. He offered to put more programmers on the project. We said no, we were okay. We could work harder.

We put in eighty hours a week, then one hundred, then one hundred and ten. At that point we were basically doing nothing but working and sleeping. We ate meals in the office, and showered in the company gym. Sometimes, late at night, we would go dancing at Xeno, then go back to Ionic, shower, and write code until dawn.

Somehow in the midst of all this I managed to have a relationship with Jeanie. Mostly this consisted of me showing up at her apartment at about midnight and collapsing on her bed. Sometimes we ate lunch together, usually in her office; and sometimes one thing led to another. When I got back to the lab, Evan would demand to smell my fingers; and sometimes, if I happened to be in a good mood, I would let him.

Most of the time we worked in a kind of trance, speaking in little half sentences, sometimes not speaking at all. In the middle of the night we would roam the empty hallways, wired on caffeine and lack of sleep, feeling like the astronauts in *2001: A Space Odyssey,* marveling at the hum of the fluorescent lights and the smell of disinfectant and the carpeting that stole away the sound of our footsteps. We broke into offices, and played hide-and-seek with the security guards. In the morning, when the zombies came in, we would giggle at them and close our blinds.

Our code was a world unto itself, a labyrinth of caves and tunnels. Sometimes in the morning we would go out to get coffee and bagels and the real world would seem only vaguely familiar, like a place you might have visited when you were a kid, but you weren't sure. At home we nailed blankets over the windows and slept for eighteen hours straight. Then we got up, ate a bowl of Cap'n Crunch, and went back to work.

The second deadline approached, and we missed again, and again, Lull told us not to worry. Worrying was wasted energy; it stole from the work. But at the same time we could sense him pulling away—he had sniffed out trouble, and was already working out a version of the story that would absolve him of responsibility. Every Friday we met with Lull for a code review. These meetings became increasingly unpleasant. Lull offered less and less help. Really there wasn't much he could do.

People over thirty can learn visual programming languages, but only the way tourists learn a foreign language. So we were more or less on our own. And the code was out of control. Meanwhile, the drones in marketing kept requesting new features, and we tried to accommodate them, but usually this meant we had to undo the modules we'd finished. The madness grew worse. We were explorers lost in the jungle, constantly changing direction. We were wrestling Jell-O. We were dogs on ice. One night, on Nabeel's recommendation, we rented *Aguirre, Wrath of God*. Halfway through, when Klaus Kinski's doomed conquistadors started dying off, we stopped the tape. Evan didn't talk to Nabeel for a week.

Whit told us to take a break. He flew us to Puerto Escondido in his private jet. He gave us each a corporate credit card and a bottle of sunblock. "Get drunk, get laid, get whatever," he said. "Do anything you want except talk about Nectar. Don't even think about Nectar." He called this the "tabula rasa" strategy. The idea was for us to come back with fresh minds.

We followed his orders: we slept late, drank tequila, smoked enormous joints, went snorkeling. We met two Mexican girls who allowed us to believe that we had picked them up, and then turned out to be hookers. Evan paid. I passed. My decision turned out to be the correct one. The hookers left Evan with a dose of crabs. After an unsuccessful course of qwell treatment, he was forced to shave his pubic hair.

We returned to Boston feeling vaguely sick, and less eager than ever to look at the code. It was February, the weather miserable. Snow fell constantly, like a plague. The streets became piles of slush, an arctic landscape. The T barely ran. Every day hundreds of people were left stranded in the big switching stations where the Red Line and the Green Line and the Orange Line converged. The people stood waiting for the trains, bundled up and shivering, like refugees. We decided not to bother going home. We had cots brought in, and camped in our office. At night we were the only ones in our wing except for Shaky Jake, an old alcoholic janitor from Roxbury who kept bottles of Old Crow whiskey and a stash of incredibly rude porno magazines (*Bound to Please* and *Big Butt* were two titles I remember) in his trash cart. We would invite him in and give him slices of pizza and he would tell us stories about Malcolm X, whom he claimed to have known when he was a kid.

During the day we wandered into the East Wing like anthropologists going among the pygmies. The East Wing was the Dead Zone, home of marketing. Everyone wore suits and had very white teeth. Evan and I pretended to each other that we were visitors in a zoo, staring at the strange creatures in their furnished cages. At the same time the creatures were staring back at us, equally incredulous. We were wearing shorts and T-shirts and sandals—and outside it was snowing. We hadn't left the building in days. The reaction from the Dead Zone creatures was always the same: their eyes went quickly to the ID badges clipped to our T-shirts, and then for a moment there was a look of relief—okay, they're employees—followed by a look of astonishment. How, they seemed to wonder, did these dopes come to be working here? And who let them out of the mailroom? Sometimes we waved to them; other times we just stared for a few minutes and then moved on.

Always our journey ended with a visit to the sales department, where we would hunt for new secretaries and rate them in comparison to the ones we already knew as part of our ongoing Sexual Attractiveness Survey. The rating system was fairly standard: looks, personality, and something we called the "W Factor," which referred to Willingness and was based on the degree of hostility with which our entreaties were met. Extreme hostility produced a negative W Factor, which could reduce a contestant's total score substantially. Signs of high willingness, on the other hand, could offset physical drawbacks and raise a contestant's score. A physically unattractive woman could in theory move into first place, if she seemed willing enough. Currently our front-runner was a woman named Gayle Hammond who was both attractive and friendly. In last place was Janet Scuto, who scored low on physical attributes and then was dragged lower by her personality and lower still by her W Factor.

In April, the snow began to melt and I began to suffer panic attacks. These occurred on the bike path outside our office. I would stand there, paralyzed, gazing up at the Ionic building, a huge brick monolith with a glass maw carved into the base. I imagined myself

being swept into the mouth of a monster and devoured in its ma-
chinelike gullet. Sometimes the fear was so great that I would turn
and cycle home and call Lull with an excuse about the flu. Evan too
came up with reasons to stay away: a conference in Palo Alto, a sick
aunt. But no matter what, Nectar was always waiting for us, like a
nightmare from which we couldn't wake up.

11

IT'S MY FAULT," I said. "We would have made it, but I couldn't pull my weight. I blew it. I'm sorry."

It was four o'clock. I had just returned from lunch. After the cappuccinos, Nabeel had started ordering rounds of Sambuca.

Evan was wearing his rubber Spock ears. He wore them when he felt anxious. He said they helped him think. He gazed at me as if I were a stranger.

"I'm going to take Nectar to Microsoft," he said. .

"Sure you are. Don't even pretend."

Evan hated Microsoft. They had recruited him out of MIT. He flew to Redmond expecting a perfunctory interview and a sweet offer. Instead, they took him to a bare white room where two guys from Cal Tech grilled him for three hours with math problems. Apparently he didn't do so well. He left feeling like a survivor of an alien abduction, still smarting from the rectal probe. He vowed he would become homeless before he would work for Bill Gates.

"I'm gonna do what I gotta do," he said, and resumed typing. Probably he had been sitting at his desk since I left. He could sit in one place for hours without moving. He was like a plant.

"I'm ruined." I fell into my chair. "It's Jeanie. She ruined me."

"You're not ruined," he said. "You're drunk."

I belched, and looked out the window. We had a corner office with a view of the river. We'd been moved there when Nectar got approved. Whit even had the office redone for us: fresh paint, new furniture. Now the carpet was ruined, the air stank, and everywhere there were piles of equipment and debris: Jolt cola cans, pizza boxes, monitors, cables, hard drives, floppy disks in piles like playing cards, coffee cups from Starbucks, Post-it notes, stacks of printouts, photocopies, compiler manuals, newsletters, a photograph of Steve Jobs as Satan, a drawing of Bill Gates hanging from a cross, and a montage called "Assholes of All Time," which included pictures of Jobs, Gates, and other so-called visionaries: John Sculley, Jaron Lanier, Marc Andreessen, Mitch Kapor. We hated them for being phonies and hucksters, for letting the bozos at *Forbes* and *BusinessWeek* believe that they really did have some clairvoyant ability to see into the future; but also, to be honest, we were jealous of them.

Along with our "Assholes" montage we had a shrine to Dan Bricklin—a cluster of photographs clipped from magazines, all of them showing poor old Bricklin smiling out from behind his beard and glasses. Bricklin invented the spreadsheet, and he could have made billions except that Mitch Kapor stole his idea and built a company called Lotus Development, whose product, 1-2-3, put Bricklin out of business. Bricklin ended up doing ads for Dexter shoes and lobbying for free speech on the Net. Sad stuff.

"I couldn't even do those device drivers," I said. Being relegated to device drivers was like being demoted from mechanic to oil-change boy. A chimp could do device drivers. Janet Scuto could do them. But not me. My code was full of dead ends and patches and work-arounds. I spent a week floundering with the drivers before Evan finally took them away from me and wrote them in an hour. But this was precisely why Nectar was late. Evan was trying to do my share of the work in addition to his own. It just wasn't possible.

"I'm slowing you down," I said. "We're like those two hikers on

K2, and I'm the guy with the broken leg. You're going to have to leave me here. You're going to have to let me die."

"Shut up," he said.

"I haven't written a decent line of code in months. I've lost it. Whatever crappy little bit of talent I ever had, I've lost it."

Every day was the same. I arrived, sat down, stared at the screen, and . . . nothing. After a while I would look out the window and think about Jeanie and try not to imagine the way she was spending her lunch breaks these days, and then my mind would start buzzing and there would be nothing but white noise. So I would go outside and walk along the river. And then the sky would be dark and I would realize that another day had gone by without me doing any work.

"I'm going to be homeless," I said. "I'll be living on the Common, eating McDonald's leftovers out of the trash, collecting cans for the deposits. I'll have to move back to Michigan and get a job at Kinko's."

Outside, the lab was quiet. The zombies were having a meeting. They were always having meetings. Soon, perhaps, I would be in there with them, enduring their awful jokes. I felt woozy.

"Okay, enough's enough." I sat up and clapped my hands together. "What are we working on?"

He gave me a sour stare. For a moment he really did look like Mr. Spock.

"*We?*" he said.

"Right. What do you want me to do?"

He shook his head. "Go home."

In Kendall Square there was a bank with a date-and-temperature sign and as I rode past I looked up and saw something familiar and then I stopped and stood there and wondered how on earth it was possible to forget your own birthday. But there it was. I looked again. It was one hundred and one degrees; and August 10. How could this happen? Maybe if you were eighty years old, you could forget your own birthday. But I was twenty-four. Twenty-five, now. I was twenty-five years old, living in Boston, pathetically in love with a woman who had dumped me. I was about to lose my job, and now celebrating my birthday by myself in a ratty apartment in the North End. I was truly pathetic. And the fact that I knew this and did nothing to change it made me even more pathetic. I considered Jeanie's suggestion about medication. Maybe she was right. A month in a hospital might not hurt, either.

At the top of the Longfellow Bridge a couple were leaning against the railing, kissing, near the spot where Jeanie and I had stood on that winter night under the cold moon. I cut out into the traffic, between the cars, and pedaled as hard as I could.

THE PHONE WAS RINGING as I walked in the door. The air was dead, stale. There was a sour smell. Probably we had lost power again, and the milk had gone bad when the refrigerator was down. For days, Boston Edison had been asking people to go easy on the air conditioners. The power grid kept tapping out. The phone rang again. It occurred to me that this might be Jeanie calling. Maybe she had remembered my birthday and had got me a present. She'd say it was nothing much, she didn't want me to take it the wrong way, but she wanted me to know that she still cared about me. Or maybe things weren't going so well with Mort. So we would have dinner, and drink some wine, and I would walk her home, and at her door she would lean toward me, and then away, and then toward me again and we would kiss . . . and then fifty years from now we would look back on this night and laugh and tell our grandchildren about it.

I picked up the phone, my hands trembling.

"Happy birthday!" my mother shrieked. She was calling from a cellular phone. The signal was spotty, breaking up: she sounded like an astronaut calling Houston control from the space shuttle. "Did you get my card?"

"Got it," I said, and picked up the Federal Express envelope that had been propped up outside the door. The airbill on the envelope had been filled out by Mom's secretary, Madeline. So had the card, which had a picture of a cake in the shape of a vodka bottle and the words "Absolut Birthday" underneath. I knew what had happened: the scheduling software on Mom's Newton had prompted her about my birthday, and she had called Madeline and told her to FedEx me a card.

Mom was a lawyer. She'd put herself through law school at Wayne State, and then had put me through college at Michigan. Back when Nectar was going well, I had entertained a fantasy in which I made a million dollars and then wrote Mom a check for fifty thousand to pay her back for my tuition. Now I was lucky when I could pay my Visa bill.

"So, Glen," she said, "what are you doing to celebrate?"

Ah yes: the issue of *Glen*. Glen is my name. Glen Timothy Reilly. Hardly anybody knows this. How I got this name, I have no idea. We have no ancestors or relatives named Glen. What were my parents thinking? Glen isn't a name, it's a curse. I have not called myself Glen since the eighth grade, when, in a fit of painful adolescent self-consciousness, I made the leap and became G. Timothy or just Tim. But I was small, and was called Tiny Tim. So then what? There was no going back to Glen. For a time, in high school, I used initials. I became G. T. Reilly, which fit well with the car fetish, but unfortunately sounded a bit like the name of a cartoon character. It also gave rise to variations such as "goat turd." For a while I was known at school as "Goat Boy," a name I liked, and "Turd Boy," which I didn't. In college, I started going by Reilly.

"Are you having a party?" Mom said.

"Of course," I lied. "But it's supposed to be a surprise. I'm not supposed to know about it."

The line crackled, then went out. Then she came back. "Are you there?"

"I'm here." I looked up at the ceiling. The plaster was coming loose in a spot where we'd had a water leak. I went to the refrigerator, trying to track down the smell. It was like opening the door to a crypt. The inside was sweating. I emptied the milk down the drain and rinsed the carton while Mom rambled on.

"I'm in Chicago," she said. "A malpractice case. This doctor. This guy, honey, I swear, we gave this guy a Drano enema. He walked out of there with blood in his pants."

"Mom, please."

Mom's family was pure bog Irish, from downriver Detroit. Sometimes it showed.

"What, suddenly you're a prude? Okay, we cleaned him out, is that better? God, I think I'm coming down with something. I've been getting a sore throat all day. There's something going around here."

Mom was a full-blown hypochondriac. She was always coming down with something. Over the years she'd had whooping cough, tuberculosis, emphysema, and several forms of cancer.

"You wouldn't believe the traffic here. I'm out on Lake Shore. I've never seen it like this."

The signal broke up. She kept talking. The effect was like hearing someone spin a radio dial—vowel sounds, bits and pieces of words. She asked me if I'd heard from my father. I told her I hadn't.

"That's just like him, isn't it?"

"I guess so."

Dad lived in northern Michigan, near Traverse City. He had moved there after the divorce, and now was a quasi-survivalist. He wore olive-drab T-shirts and camouflage pants, owned a short-wave radio set, and referred to his house as "the compound," even though really it was just a log cabin in the woods with a fence around the yard. Sometimes when I drove up from Ann Arbor, I felt like Captain Willard going up the river after Colonel Kurtz. Dad lived with an overweight girl named Brittany who had graduated from high school the year after I did. He wrote articles for magazines like *Sports Afield* and *Outdoor Life*. Trout fishing, deer hunting. Apparently you could make a living doing that.

When I was a kid, Dad worked at Dow Chemical, in Midland. He had a Ph.D. in chemistry from Purdue. When I was little he taught me about the periodic table. He hung the chart in my room, and explained the different-colored squares. He told me to think of them as building blocks. Everything in the world could be broken down to these elements, he said. To me, the world seemed to be a vast and mysterious place; but to my father there was no mystery. The world was carbon and hydrogen and a few dozen other things. That sense of certainty—the sense of a world in which every question has an answer and every problem can be solved—is what drew me, I suppose, to writing code.

For my seventh birthday Dad bought me a Commodore 64 computer and a BASIC manual, and from day one I was hooked. Other kids played with model trains; I created video games. At night I would work in Dad's office in the basement; we shared his desk. I would write code, while he sat beside me trying to prove Fermat's Last Theorem. It was all very Norman Rockwell, at least until the layoffs started.

I was nine years old when it happened. The company was losing money, cutting back. Dad hadn't done anything wrong. But I guess he tended to be a little more outspoken than other people. So his number came up. Mom said we could move, he could get another job. But the layoff had taken the heart out of him. His confidence was gone. There was a long winter in which he spent all of his time at his desk in the basement, wearing the same ratty L.L. Bean sweater, shivering beside the space heater, a haunted look in his eyes.

After the breakup, Mom and I moved to Detroit to live with her parents. We moved on Easter weekend. Ever since then, Easter has made me feel creepy: the colored eggs, the man in the bunny suit.

My grandparents had an old-people house: water-stained wallpaper, frayed furniture, a half dozen cats. There was a smell of dried urine, and also of something that Mom said was creosote, although I have no idea what creosote is or whether there was ever any of it in their house. As a kid I used to think that the smell was the smell of my grandmother's skin, which was dry and white and always flaking off. The air, I imagined, was filled with tiny particles of her dead skin.

At twelve, I wore a surgeon's mask in the house and refused to take it off. My grandfather took to wearing one too, in solidarity. He took me to Red Wings games, and taught me how to box. We went fishing on Belle Isle, and he pointed out the black people, whom he hated. When he died, I was the one who found his body.

When Mom's law practice got going, we moved out and rented a little house in Sterling Heights. Since then she had started making serious money and had bought a house in Birmingham. She drank too much, and didn't date. She said she was too busy to find a man. The truth, I think, was that the divorce had hurt her more than she admitted, and she wasn't going to risk going through that again.

"Is Jeanie there?" she said. "Let me say hi to her."

"She just ran out." I cleared my throat. "She's getting champagne."

"She's a great gal."

"She sure is."

"And you're lucky to have her, mister. You'd better remember that, you hear me? Shit! Jesus Christ! Hey! Hello? Anybody home?" Brakes screeched. Car horns blew. Mom dropped the phone. Then she was back. "Sorry about that. You can't believe the way people drive here. Look, I'd better go before I kill someone. Give Jeanie a hug for me."

OUTSIDE A BAKERY I stood watching a man in a T-shirt arranging pastries on sheets of wax paper: marzipans, cannolis, cream-filled shells shaped like lobster tails. He frowned when he saw me. I walked away. Night was falling. The brick buildings leaned against one another as if they were holding each other up. A few stories up, old women sat perched in their windows like little gray birds, across the street to each other, complaining about the heat.

On Hanover Street, cars were double-parked and triple-parked in front of the bakeries and cafés, leaving a space just wide enough for one car to get through. Traffic was backed up. People were blowing their horns. The greasers on the sidewalk shouted at them to shut up. The air stank from the heat and the trash and the smoke venting out of the restaurant kitchens. The tourists ambled through the crowded sidewalks, getting shoved and jostled and insulted, loving every minute of it. Across from Giaccalone's café I stopped and glared at the wiseguys hanging out on the sidewalk. They had Coco on a leash and were taunting her with cannolis, making her jump. I wanted to do something. I wanted to be Charles Bronson. I wanted to go over there and turn the place upside down.

Instead, I ducked into World's Worst Chinese and took a booth by myself in back. World's Worst Chinese was run by Palestinians and decorated with pictures of Jerusalem. The busboys scooped leftover fried rice back into the steamers. We'd seen them do this. Once Evan had found a human tooth in his wonton soup. There was no air conditioning. The men's room was like something out of the Middle Ages. Most of the patrons were elderly Italian men with respiratory ailments who coughed constantly and struggled to bring up phlegm, which they spat into napkins. It was a perfect place to spend your birthday.

I forced down an egg roll and an order of General Tso's Chicken, then wandered back out onto Hanover Street, past a flower shop and a dentist's office and a butcher shop, where skinned rabbits hung by their feet and a cow's head stared up from the display case. I walked under the Central Artery, past the flower sellers and the buskers and the bums, past the fish markets and the boarded-up vegetable stands, through Government Center and up Beacon Hill, where I found myself, as if by accident, standing outside Jeanie's building.

Her lights were off. Her car was not on the street. I set up an observation post. Ten o'clock came, and then eleven. Not until midnight did it dawn on me that Jeanie was not coming home.

At a pub on Charles Street I ordered a Sam Adams and a shot of tequila. I took a stool at the bar. At the far end of the room clumsy, flannel-shirted frat kids with cheery Irish faces, and names, no doubt, like Mike and Eileen, were leaping around in what passed for dancing in a place like this. Here were the people I had despised in college, the ones who majored in business and discussed without irony the challenges facing the Greek system, and they hadn't changed a bit. They were still flushed and drunk and soaked with sweat, still wearing Banana Republic shorts and Black Dog T-shirts, still having the time of their lives.

A girl with red hair sat down beside me at the bar. She was wearing cutoff jeans and a Bowdoin sweatshirt. Her name was Sally. I told her that a friend of mine had gone to Bowdoin, and made up a name.

She said she thought she knew him. I bought us beers and shots. Sally tossed down her tequila and dragged me to the dance floor. She danced as badly as the others. I don't mean to be a snob, but these people danced like deaf mutes. Sally's big move involved thrusting out her arms and shivering as if she were gripping a high-voltage wire.

Oddly enough, however, here among the faux-preppy proles I was feeling something that I'd felt with Jeanie: I felt as if I could become a normal person, one of those hip twenty-something guys you see in ads for snowboards and Volkswagens. I had always secretly wondered what it would be like to be one of them. In high school I had belonged to the computer club, and learned about parties the week after they happened. At college I found friends, but they were all fellow computer science majors. The thing about CS types is that we spend a huge amount of time interacting with machines. Consequently we tend to get along well with each other, but not so well with civilians.

"I like your ass," Sally shouted. I stared at her. I must have seemed confused. She pointed. "Your *glasses.*"

"Oh," I said. "Thanks."

But I think she liked my ass too, because we hadn't walked more than a block from the bar when she pulled me into an alcove and made a fleeting but deliberate move for my zipper. To my astonishment, Mr. Happy responded. "'Srighthere," Sally kept saying, and pointing to the next corner. Now that we were outside, I saw that she was drunker than she had seemed in the bar, and not as pretty. We stopped outside a brownstone on Joy Street. She fumbled for her keys, found them, dropped them, hunted around in the shadows for them, found them, and then started trying to figure out which one fit her lock. By then, God forgive me, I had opened her shorts.

At Michigan we were given seminars in which counselors told us that if sex involved force, coercion, or alcohol, then it qualified as rape. I'd left the sessions in horror. I'd had sex with three women, but if it weren't for alcohol I would never have slept with any of them. I considered calling my victims to apologize, then figured it was best not to open old wounds.

Now here I was, once again using alcohol to open doors, only this time I was not freezing to death on the Diag in Ann Arbor but sweating to death in Boston and admiring the glow of the streetlight on the pale orbs of Sally's ass. "Wait," she said, pulling up her shorts. "I found it."

We climbed to the second floor. I sat down on the stairs while Sally hunted for the next key. Moonlight slanted through a window. She sat down beside me. We started kissing again.

"You know what?" I whispered. "Today's my birthday. Or yesterday. Before midnight."

"Well," she said, kissing my cheek, "I've got a really good present for you."

The door opened with a click. Inside, there was a little kitchen and a living room decorated with Monet prints—water lilies, a bridge, a cathedral. I recognized the pictures. Every girl at Michigan had them in her room. There was a law about this, apparently.

Sally led me down a hallway to her room. She shut the door behind us, and switched on a lamp. She had a little twin bed with a pink-and-white comforter, stuffed animals arranged on the pillows. There was a desk, a bureau, lots of photographs: Sally on a ski slope, Sally at her graduation, Sally in Europe, sitting in a café.

When I turned around, she was taking off her clothes. She fell onto the bed. I glanced down at her thatch of pubic hair. She wasn't really a redhead at all. "Come on," she said, "it's your birthday." She tried to sit up, then got dizzy and fell back down. "Whoa," she said. "Oh my." I knew where we were headed. I got her to the bathroom and held her hair back away from the toilet.

I got her a glass of water, helped her brush her teeth, and led her back to her room. "I'm sorry," she said. "We can still, you know . . . I'm sorry." I pulled the comforter over her. She fell asleep. I ran my fingers through her fake red hair. I thought about Jeanie. I wanted to cry. On the way out, I saw one of Sally's roommates. She was standing in the kitchen, backlit by the glow from the refrigerator. I smiled. She shook her head.

It was four in the morning. The sky was gray. I imagined the sun struggling to lift itself through the humidity and wishing it could take the day off. In the North End, at the end of Hanover Street, I saw a black dog rummaging through a pile of trash bags. I whistled. The dog looked up at me. It was Coco.

I crouched down, made a little kissing sound. She trotted over, her nails clicking on the pavement. She had a face like Sophia Loren, eyes like saucers of milk. I held out my hand. She licked it. She looked up at me with an expression that seemed to contain both sorrow and sympathy. It was as if she understood how I was feeling.

And why not? She had been taken away from her owner and brought to live here with a bunch of thugs who treated her like a mutt. Probably she was as homesick as I was. I rubbed her head. I thought about taking her home with me. Then suddenly something spooked her, and she ran off around the corner.

14

EVAN SUGGESTED THERAPY. He said this in a nice way. "It doesn't mean you're crazy," he said. We were sitting at an outside table in Faneuil Hall, drinking margaritas with double shots. It was Friday night, and now, according to the weather station, we had officially set a record. The story had been in the papers that morning—the longest and hottest heat wave on record, and it showed no sign of breaking. If anything, it was getting worse. The air pressed down on us like the hand of God. It wasn't even weather anymore; it was a biblical plague.

For Evan, this all came as a surprise. He had been indoors at Ionic, working around the clock in air-conditioned comfort, since Monday. Now the heat and exhaustion and alcohol had combined to make him look like a zombie. His hair had gone crazy from the humidity; his eyes were bloodshot, and there were dark circles under them. He looked as if he'd just returned from an electroshock treatment.

"I went to therapy after my father died," Evan said. "You just talk, that's all. You talk things out. And it helps. You could at least try it. Go once, see how it feels."

In fact I had been thinking about seeing a psychologist earlier in the week, after I spent an evening watching the man who lived in the apartment across the street and fearing that I might end up like him. We called him "Lonely Man." He was about forty years old, and lived with a cat, which he fed from his plate. The thing is, he was not some fat loser sitting around dreaming of leading Boy Scout camping trips. He was clean-cut, decent-looking.

Yet there he was. Standing at his stove with his pan of soup he seemed not so much sad as confused, as if he couldn't understand how his life had come to this. One time I spotted him coming out of *The Umbrellas of Cherbourg*, hurrying away into the night, his face tight with grief. And I wondered, who was his Jeanie? What were his wounds?

Nabeel and Upendra returned to our table carrying slips of paper with phone numbers from two blondes they'd met at the bar. Nabeel had told them he was an oncologist at Brigham and Women's with a specialization in childhood leukemia.

"Ten bucks says the numbers are fake," Evan said. Sure enough, one was disconnected and the other was for a restaurant. "Women like that have a list of guys they're looking for," Evan said. "Number one, professional athletes. Number two, airline pilots. *Little Pakis who lie about being doctors* aren't even in the top ten."

Nabeel drained his margarita and said if he didn't get drunk in the next thirty minutes he was going to start thinking about how long it had been since he got laid, and then he was going to have to go shoot himself.

"I'll drink to that," I said.

"You'll drink to anything," Evan said.

"I'll drink to that, too," I said.

That afternoon we had put up a prototype of Nectar that actually ran for about an hour before something got snagged and crashed the server. Evan swore he was close to getting the thing to work. He made a proposal: the four of us could move to San Francisco, get venture capital, finish Nectar, and become millionaires.

"Sure, just like that." Nabeel snapped his fingers.

"I'm serious," Evan said.

"I know you are," Nabeel said. "That's the sad part."

Nabeel insisted there were better ways to get rich. These included "Drugs Not Hugs" T-shirts and bumper stickers, which would sell well on college campuses, and a line of plastic floating babies that people could toss into their neighbors' pools in the middle of the night. "We could expand," he said. "We could do toddlers, children, pets." He'd talked about this before. Once he'd sent a proposal to toy companies. The one person who wrote back suggested he seek psychiatric help.

"I know you don't believe this," Evan said, "but Nectar is going to work. If I can't do it at Ionic, I'll do it somewhere else."

Nabeel flagged down a waitress and asked her to bring us a straitjacket.

"A what?" She took out her order pad.

"Never mind. Forget it."

Daylight was draining from the sky, and I was feeling numb and buoyant, almost there but not quite. One more margarita would do the trick: a gentle push away from the dock, and I'd be floating. Suddenly, as if on some signal, all the lights strung around the plaza snapped on, and a little ripple of applause swept across the square. A woman at a table nearby said something about *The Remains of the Day,* a movie I'd seen with Jeanie. I got up in search of the men's room.

When I returned, our table was empty. Nabeel and Evan were talking to a group of women at a table in back. They were using the Rain Man ploy. They did this all the time. They would bring over a phone book and tell the women to read out any ten names and numbers. They would bet a round of drinks that Evan could recite the entire list without making a mistake.

I watched as Nabeel tied a napkin around Evan's head and then gave the women the phone book. Upendra waved to me. I shook my head. Watching other people have fun only made me feel worse. I felt like that comic strip character who has the rain cloud over his head, following him wherever he goes. I figured I'd go to the North End and see if Maria was around. At least then I'd only ruin the evening for one person, rather than a whole group. .

I stepped out into the street and slid between the cars. When I was halfway across, I heard a burst of laughter and applause. I turned and saw Evan tearing off his blindfold, taking a bow.

MARIA WAS IN THE STORE, closing up. Outside, the streets were jammed with tourists who were apparently unfazed by the weather. It was the Fisherman's Feast. Maria said I had promised to take her.

"I did?"

"Well," she said, "you should have."

She went home and took a shower and came back wearing a short yellow summer dress and a pair of sandals that showed off a set of freshly painted toenails, bright red. Her hair, still damp from the shower, hung in long shiny curls halfway down her back. The last thing I wanted to do on a hot night was to go shove my way through thousands of sweaty people; but on this night I would have followed Maria across the desert.

She took my hand and led me into the fray, where vendors shouted, music blared, and a cloud of greasy smoke hung in the air above the sausage carts. Kids on rooftops were tossing packs of firecrackers out over the crowd: they exploded in the air above our heads. At one street corner an orchestra played, and the old men who usually sat grumbling on their folding chairs were jitterbugging in the street with the old ladies who usually sat up in their windows gossiping.

We pushed through the crowd, holding hands, yelling, "Hey, Jim-MAY!" and, "Yo, Chuck-EE!" On Hanover Street a Knights of Columbus marching band—twenty fat men in ill-fitting uniforms and plumed hats, playing out of tune—plowed through the mass of bodies, followed by a float carrying a statue of the Blessed Virgin that bobbed along, tilting from side to side like a ship on a rough sea. The Virgin was decorated with money. Strips of bills hung like streamers from all sides of her body.

The procession stopped outside Caffe Vesuvio. Giaccalone came out and attached a huge strip of fifty-dollar bills to the Virgin. A cheer went up. Giaccalone waved like a politician. He was wearing a silver track suit. He looked like a spaceman in a fifties sci-fi movie. A priest stepped up and kissed him on both cheeks.

"Look at this," I said. "They worship the guy. It's unbelievable."

"Davio does a lot of good for people. He gives money to the church. He lets old people live in his buildings without paying rent."

"He slashed my tires."

"You parked in his space."

I stared at her.

"Come on," she said. "Let's go for a walk."

We got Italian ices from a street vendor and went to the garden of St. Michael's Church. The garden was on Hanover Street, behind high brick walls covered with ivy. It was lush and crowded: flowers, shrubs, sprawling plants whose leaves cast wide shadows, a grape arbor overgrown with vines. The air was sultry and wet; the smell of lilies hung like perfume. We sat on a bench looking up at a stained-glass window that depicted a saint crushing a snake. I felt bad for the snake: it lay there, limp, its eyes bulging, its tongue hanging out of the side of its mouth. It looked the way I felt. Even now, this late at night, the temperature was well into the nineties. Maria's lips were red from the raspberry ice. I could imagine the taste of fruit on her mouth. Down the street an orchestra was playing "Macarena."

I thought about the day I met Maria. It was a weekday afternoon.

She was alone behind the counter in the grocery store. I was in line behind two yuppie women, one of whom was complaining to her friend about the North End. Maria was bagging the woman's groceries. "The people here," the woman said, "I swear, they're worse than the Italians in Italy, and that's saying something. They're gruff, they're rude, they're surly. They speak some language that I don't know what it is. They think they're speaking Italian, but trust me, that's not what they're speaking. I don't think it's Sicilian, either. It's some weird hybrid, some mix of English and Italian. Miss, don't put the soap in with the vegetables, okay? Please? Right, a separate bag. No, a plastic bag. Right. You see what I mean? You've got to watch them every minute."

I caught Maria's eye. *I'm not like them,* I wanted to tell her. She scowled at me, and looked away. God only knew how much crap like this she put up with every day. The women left without saying thank you or good-bye. As the door fell shut, I noticed a little bug-eyed kid, maybe eight years old, standing at the counter. He had been lurking there, and now he made his move: he pinched two Milky Way bars and slipped them into his pants. Maria saw him. She shouted. The kid made a break for the door. I caught him by his shirt and pulled him back to the counter. "Come on," I said. "Hand them over."

He pulled the candy bars out of his pants. I put the candy bars on the counter with my groceries. "Add them to my bill," I said. The kid took a step for the door. "Freeze," I said, and he did. He stood there, trembling, his eyes as wide as dinner plates. Maria rang up my order and gave me my change. I gave the kid the candy bars. He glanced at Maria, then bolted.

Maria stood there staring at me and tapping her fingernails on the register. I smiled. She didn't smile back. I stood there waiting for the shouting to begin. In the North End, people were always shouting at me and Evan. If we walked in the street, they told us to walk on the sidewalk. If we walked on the sidewalk, they told us to walk in the street.

But Maria didn't shout. She asked me, in a quiet voice, if I always went around doing good deeds, and if so, shouldn't I be wearing a pair of tights and a cape? I told her it was no big deal to let the kid go. How much did a candy bar cost—fifty cents? If that's what it took to keep a kid out of trouble, I was happy to pay it. Especially if the kid learned a lesson.

"I see," she said. "And what lesson is that? Go ahead and steal, and if you get caught, the Yuppie Avenger will pay for your candy?"

First of all, I told her, I was not a yuppie. Second of all, that kid would never steal again. "Believe me, I know," I said. "I've got first-hand experience." I told her my story: I was nine years old, and we had just moved to Detroit. The person who paid for the candy bars was an old black woman with gray hair and red-rimmed eyes, the first black person I'd ever spoken to.

"And what? You learned that it was wrong to steal?"

"No, I learned that I wasn't as sly as I thought I was." I told her what the old woman had said to me: *Child, you 'bout as smooth as a figger skater wid a clubfoot.*

At last, Maria laughed. She had a gorgeous smile. "Fair enough." She held out her hand. "My name's Maria." A strand of hair fell down across her face. She pulled it back behind her ear. "You live upstairs, right? You're the one with the car."

I nodded.

"Tell me something," she said. "What *is* that thing?"

How do two people go from shaking hands in a store to kissing in a church garden six months later? How does friendship deepen into love? And was it love that I felt for Maria, or something else? These were the questions I asked myself as we sat kissing in the garden at St. Michael's. She said she was crazy about me. I wished I could say that I was crazy about her, too; but unfortunately I only felt crazy in a kind of generic, non-person-specific way. Maria was great—smart, pretty, funny. And yet something made me hold back.

Maybe it is hard to believe that I could prefer Jeanie to Maria; but there it was. With Jeanie, I had felt a kind of electric current, as if I'd grabbed a power line and the juice was surging up through my arms and into my body; while Maria, despite her many wonderful qualities, was strictly low-voltage. Certainly she was attractive, and sweet; but maybe she was too sweet. It seemed to me that going out with her would be like drinking Sanka instead of double espresso, or taking methadone instead of heroin.

Jeanie was all edges and angles, snares and traps, pits filled with sharpened sticks. Maria was curves and cushions. In television terms, Jeanie was Ginger while Maria was Mary Ann. And in bed? Forget it. Jeanie was ferocious. Think of Linda Blair in *The Exorcist* and you've got the picture. Women who grew up in crazy families were always like that, according to Nabeel, who attended support group meetings (abuse survivors, children of alcoholics) hoping to find them.

As for Maria in bed, I could only speculate. But the key word, probably, was *modesty*. Whips and chains? No way. Ditto for stockings and garters. We were talking flannel nightgowns and white cotton panties territory; maybe, if things got really crazy, we'd do it somewhere other than the bedroom.

But Maria and I did not talk about these things. What we did talk about, in between kisses, was how messed up I was over my job and my future and everything else. I didn't say the word *Jeanie,* but I didn't have to; Maria had seen me through the worst days of the breakup, and she knew as well as anyone how Jeanie hovered like an evil spirit over every part of my life.

As evidence of my deranged condition, I told Maria how I'd forgotten my birthday. She said this was no big deal. But I could tell she was taken aback. Normal people simply do not forget their own birthdays, no matter how busy they are. I described the nightmare I'd been having: I was working at Kinko's, wearing one of those stupid aprons, and I couldn't keep up with the machine, and I got fired, and everyone was laughing at me.

Maria said failure could be an agent of change. She said that she didn't mean to criticize but that sometimes Evan and I were a little full of ourselves. So maybe getting the wind knocked out of us would do us some good. Besides, she said, what would life be like if you succeeded at everything you did? I said I didn't know, but I wouldn't mind finding out.

We kissed again. The raspberry on her lips reminded me of Kim Donowski, my high school girlfriend, who wore fruit-flavored lip balm and left me for a goalie on the hockey team. After refusing for two years to let me touch her below the waist, Kim slept with the hockey player on their first date, and at first I hated them—until I learned that Kim was pregnant and that the goalie was leaving school to get a job on the line at General Motors, and then I counted my blessings and wished them both the best of luck.

In the distance the orchestra was playing "Amore," and people were singing along. Then the band broke into a polka, which made no sense here in the North End, but then again so much of the North End made no sense; and listening to the music I thought about my father, and the days of his disintegration, when he would sit at the kitchen table singing, "I don't want her, you can have her, she's too fat for me," while my mother, perpetually overweight, served dinner and forced a laugh.

I thought about how life ruins people. Fate, in the form of a lay-off, had ruined my father. Then my father had ruined my mother. Now Jeanie had ruined me.

"A year ago," I said, "I was cruising along, doing fine. Now I'm roadkill. I mean, let's face it, I'm not going to make it to the list of Boston's most eligible bachelors this year, am I? Unless maybe they have a 'Most Eligible Homeless Men' category. What am I going to do? Join the military? Become a priest? I'll be working in some bank, writing COBOL for the rest of my life."

"Maudlin self-pity is such a turn-on," Maria said. "Seriously. It's very attractive."

She said I should come with her to the Peace Corps. I said I didn't think so. "The pictures I've seen show people doing things with shovels," I said. "I have this rule about using shovels."

"Which is?"

"I don't." In college I spent summers working construction, and I vowed that when I graduated, I would never do manual labor again. No mowing lawns, no shoveling snow—nothing.

I told Maria that with all due respect I couldn't see why anyone wanted to join the Peace Corps. "I mean, in the sixties, when the job market was tight and there was this flood of baby boomers with nothing to do, okay, then it made sense. But today I don't know why you would want to turn down a good job and go off and build irrigation systems for people, or give vaccinations, or whatever it is they do."

What I didn't say was that to me the Peace Corps seemed like something that you might think was cool when you were about seventeen years old; but by the time you were twenty-five you should know better.

Maria said that as long as we were being brutally honest, she had to admit that she didn't know how people could spend their lives doing something as boring as writing software, and on top of that, could go around acting as if it were some kind of really cool job. "You work seven days a week, under all of this pressure, and for what? So that people can shop on the Web? Half the world is starving to death and you want to devote your life to saving people from having to get into their car and drive to the mall? That's criminal. And I think it messes people up. I mean, here you are, ready to jump off a roof because you didn't walk into your first job and become a millionaire. Do you realize how unbalanced that is?

"You guys talk about putting a computer on every desktop. But guess what? Most of the world doesn't have a desktop. Most of the world would be very happy if they could count on a bowl of food once a day. You talk about Windows and the World Wide Web as if these were important things. I think you need to get some perspective. You're not doing cancer research, okay? You're making office equipment. These software companies take guys like you and they brainwash you. They dangle a bag of money in front of your face, and what do you do? Do you ask yourself whether the world really needs software that lets people shop on the Web? Do you ask yourself whether this is something that is really worth spending your life doing? No. You sit down and start typing. The smartest people in our society are being used to create appliances. I think that's tremendously sad."

I pointed out that while it might be crazy to have no goals other than making money, it was just as crazy to think that money didn't matter. "There's nothing noble about being poor," I said. "Trust me, I've got firsthand experience."

She said I didn't have to tell her about being poor. She had grown up in New Jersey, and apparently her parents were pretty well off. But when Maria was twelve years old, her mother died in a car accident and the family sent her to live with her uncle Gus and his wife, Angela, in their little apartment in the North End.

Maria talked about New Jersey as if it were some lost paradise. And maybe it was. I had seen photographs of the house where she grew up: a big brick place with a wide lawn. There were photographs of her mother, but none of her father. "That," she said, when I asked, "is a subject that I would rather not discuss."

At least half of the women I knew hated their fathers. There was no telling what Maria's dad had done to her. She was always cheerful, and yet there was something sad about her too, as if something—her mother's death, perhaps—had left a kind of aura around her. It seemed to me that the more I got to know Maria, the less certain I was about who she was.

Sometimes when I came downstairs in the morning, I would see her sitting behind the counter, reading the *Herald,* and in that slant of early sunlight she would seem weary, and older, and I could see how she would look in middle age; and a wave of sorrow would move over me, the same kind of sorrow I felt when I walked past the orthopedic store on Prince Street and saw, in the window, the tiny leg braces made for children. Anyone watching Maria would know that she didn't belong in that grocery store. Worse still, you could tell that Maria knew this, too.

The store was hot, and dirty. The narrow aisles were crowded with little Italian widows dressed in black and shoving packages of cold cuts in Maria's face and complaining that they'd *axed* for their prosciutto sliced thin and did you call this thin and where was Gus, I want *him* to slice it this time. Then Gus would come over and say that maybe Maria thought she was too good for this place, and Maria would say, no, she was sorry, and she wouldn't let it happen again.

We walked home, holding hands. The feast was winding down. The air felt cooler, but probably that was an illusion. I told Maria about growing up in Detroit. I was feeling homesick. Detroit is a great place, despite what people say. I told her about the muscle cars on Woodward Avenue, the black radio stations playing Motown records and John Lee Hooker, the soul food restaurants on the East Side, near the river.

Maria told me about *Jane Eyre*. It was her favorite book. She had read it over and over, so many times she practically had it memorized. I could imagine the twelve-year-old version of Maria, trapped in some awful apartment and reading about Jane, the orphaned girl who finally finds happiness. What Maria wanted now was the same as what she'd wanted then: simply to get away.

We got to her building. She asked me if I wanted to come in. I mumbled an excuse about being tired. "It's not that I don't want to," I said. "It's just . . . it's complicated."

"It's not complicated." She smiled. "It's Jeanie, right?" She pinched my cheek, as if I were a kid. "Right?"

I shrugged. I knew I was being stupid. Even now, months after the breakup, I couldn't let go of Jeanie. In some dark corner of my imagination a bunch of evil little gnomes were cruelly keeping alive a fantasy about her still loving me. I could hear them back there, stirring the cauldron, fanning the flames, whispering to me. As soon as I fell in love with Maria, Jeanie would be on the phone, wanting to get back together. And then what would I do? Would I tell Jeanie to go away? Would I really be able to do that? Somewhere in the distance a pack of firecrackers went off: *pop-pop-pop.*

Maria kissed me on the cheek and went inside. Once again I found myself standing across the street, looking at her windows. I thought again about what she'd said about the work I did. I'd never known anyone who would say things like that. I felt like a priest who'd just been told, by an angel, that in fact there is no God, that everything he believes is wrong. My thoughts spun and tangled in my head; they zoomed around like bees in a jar.

Maria's lights went off. I trudged home. On Prince Street, a boy and girl were kissing—high school kids at the end of a date. I wished I could be that age again, and could love the way teenagers love, without hesitation, without fear. I wondered if I would ever be able to love anyone the way I had loved Jeanie. Maybe your heart had only so much capacity; and maybe I'd used mine up.

I turned away. Tears stung my eyes. What was wrong with me, when something as lovely and innocent as a kiss could make me want to cry? How on earth was it possible to turn down a woman like Maria Bava? What kind of monster had I become? Up above, a weak moon struggled to make itself seen through the haze. Somewhere a dog barked. I hurried around the corner, feeling more alone than ever.

A S I WAS GETTING UNDRESSED, I looked across the street and saw Lonely Man holding a woman in his arms. They kissed, and then laughed. Music drifted from his open window. Fighting back tears, I closed the shade. I put a bowl of ice in front of the fan and aimed the breeze at my bed so that the wash ran across my face and chest. It was not as good as an air conditioner, but it was close. The ice cubes would last for half an hour. The trick was to get yourself to sleep before then. I was drifting off when the couple upstairs came home and I was treated to the sound of their moaning and groaning, the headboard pounding against the wall.

I opened my eyes. The clock radio glowed. The woman upstairs was shrieking like a cat caught under the wheel of a truck. Once again there were tears in my eyes. The whole world was in love, it seemed, and I was doomed to a spectator's role. I felt like the kid in the Jimmy Fund poster, sitting in his wheelchair at the ballpark, holding a glove, saying, "I can dream, can't I?"

I lay there listening to them. The man was wheezing like a steam engine. I imagined them bursting through the floor and crashing down on top of me. What a way to die. After a chorus of "Oh God oh

God oh God oh God" they finally fell silent. But my torture was far from over, because seven hours later I woke to the sound of a hissing shower and a giggling female voice—Evan, the boy wonder, had scored.

He had warned me that this would happen. This was earlier in the summer, when a flight attendant on a red-eye from San Francisco gave him her phone number. "It's happening," he said. "I can feel it. Your energy is crossing over into me."

I told him this was ridiculous. We were sitting in first class, drinking Heinekens. We had spent two days at the San Mateo office meeting with engineers from HotSpot, a Web company that Ionic had acquired. The goal was for us to get ideas about how we might use Java in Nectar. The problem was that when we began developing Nectar there was no such thing as Java; so adopting Java was going to mean undoing a lot of what we had done. The HotSpot developers were younger than we were, and they were typical West Coast guys: facial piercings, surfer accents, no clue that there had ever been computer programming prior to the development of HTML.

We knew they weren't going to help us. Why should they? Sure enough, we showed them our code, and they yawned and said they'd follow up with some ideas in a week or two. Still, it had been nice to get out of Boston, especially since we managed to rent a Mustang Cobra, which we drove down the coast to Santa Cruz and then up through Route 17 back to the Valley, where Evan showed me his shrines: Sand Hill Road, the Xerox Palo Alto Research Center, the building at Stanford where Sun and Cisco had been born. Evan came alive in the Valley. It was as if there were current actually flowing in the streets, and he was tapping into it. I, on the other hand, always felt tired, as if we were walking on a grid that drained your energy when you plugged yourself into it.

Very late, near midnight, we drove back up into the hills and looked down at the Valley and all of the flat buildings arranged in rows like chips on a circuit board. Everything was glowing, as if nobody ever stopped working. It was an amazing place. You could imagine the millions of hours being spent here each week, the hundreds of thousands of little human turbines spinning at top speed. The air hummed with energy and desperation; beneath everything else, beneath the singing of birds and the distant whoosh of cars on Route 101, you could hear the low thrum of lives being spun away. Here was history being made, Evan said. Right now, right this moment, somebody was working on something that was going to change the world. And we were a part of it. Every time we came to California, he said this.

And now on the plane he had shifted into his theory about my sexual powers crossing over into him. There was no sense resenting him, he said. "It's not my fault you're on Queer Street. I'm not the one doing this to you. I'm just feeding off your karma. Besides, you could break the spell at any time. All you have to do is hook up with someone else. As soon as you do, Jeanie will want you back. Until then, however, you're trapped in the vortex. And my powers will continue to grow."

"That's . . ."

"Frightening. I know."

"Insane is what I was going to say. Also, for the record, Jeanie did not break up with me. *I* broke up with *her.*

"Sure you did. Buddy, you've said it yourself—it was a ruse. She didn't have to tell you about Mort. If she really wanted to stay with you, she would have kept her mouth shut. But no. She fucked Mort, and she told you. That, my friend, is evil. She wants out of the relationship, but she gets *you* to do the dirty work. You have to admit, she's good. I almost respect her for it."

"Maybe I should have forgiven her," I said. "I should have told her I didn't mind. I should have said, 'Okay, I forgive you.'"

"Sure, that's a good plan. And hey, while you're at it, why not join a cult and cut off your nuts? Look, I don't want to be a jerk, but here's the truth: Jeanie used you. She saw you as this hot developer, you were going to make a fortune on Nectar, and she wanted a piece. As soon as things got rocky, she bailed. And where is she now? Mort's a vice president. Face it, she's a climber. And you did the right thing breaking up with her. You did the only thing. Because if there's one thing that will destroy your soul, it's living with a woman who cheats on you. Take her back? Forget it. She'll run you around like a monkey on a leash."

"I thought you were saying that's what I should do."

"No, I said that's what you *could* do. It *could* be done. But not so that you can stay with her. I would not in a million years advise you or anyone else I care about to make a life with Jeanie Sullivan. You know my policy. Zero tolerance. One slip and they're out. So all I'm saying is that yes, in theory, it would be possible to make Jeanie want you back. And if you want to do it, fine. Make her come crawling back, sleep with her a few times, and then—wham!—shove her face into the mud. Why not? She deserves the punishment, and I could use the entertainment."

"You seem to have some anger toward women."

"Any guy who suffered the kind of adolescence that I did deserves to be angry at women," he said. "Besides, I don't make the rules, I just play the game. And it's so easy. Just hook up with someone. It doesn't matter who she is. Ugly, fat, mean, whatever. Hook up, and the spell is broken. Your karma is restored. Jeanie comes back. The fun begins."

"But what about the new girl?"

"Jesus. Hello?" He snapped his fingers in front of my face. "You dump the new girl."

"What if I like her?"

"What's to like? She's fat, she's ugly, she's mean to you. What can you see in her?"

"You're saying I should hook up with a grimbo."

"Not too grim. If she's too grim, it won't work. Otherwise you could just go to a nursing home and pick up some elderly woman. 'Hey, I'm dating Millie, it's great, we're in love, we're planning a family.' No. She has to be believable. But within the range of women to whom you could possibly be attracted, she should be as grim as possible. That way you don't feel so bad when you dump her. And it's easier on her, too. If she's really grim, she won't be surprised when you dump her. She had you for a month, and it's the best month of her life. She's happy, she's got her memories. She can marry the boy in the trailer next door. Look, this happens all the time. How do you think grimbos get dates? They get used to lure back ex-girlfriends. They know this."

"You're saying there's this whole category of women who get used as bait, and who accept this?"

"Look, the grimbo you go out with isn't going to blame you for going back to your old girlfriend. All she asks is that when you do dump her, you do it kindly. Have a little respect. If she's going to blame anyone, she's going to blame herself for hooking up with someone who was so far out of her league."

"Oh, like me and Jeanie."

"Well, that's how you saw it. Frankly, I never saw the appeal of Jeanie. I mean, she's cute. Fair enough. But she doesn't exactly stop traffic. I know she *thinks* she does. And look, back in the projects in Dorchester she probably did. But in New York, girls like Jeanie are a dime a dozen. You remember that meeting when she went on about Nietzsche? She didn't even get it right. Believe me, I know my Nietzsche. She was talking out her butt, man. Reilly, Jeanie is *nothing,* okay? She works in *marketing.* But if you want her back, fine. We'll go up to Salisbury Beach. The place is crawling with grimbos. It's grimbo season right now. We'll put on pith helmets and safari coats, we'll get nets and tridents, and we'll have us a grimbo expedition."

"What do you use for bait with grimbos?"

"I don't know. A Camaro? Aramis cologne? Acid-washed jeans? Look, here's the thing. When you do hook up with a grimbo, you can't be halfhearted about it. You have to *believe.* You can treat her badly. That's okay. She'll probably like you better for it. Grimbos respond to mistreatment. Reminds them of their dads, I guess. But no matter what, you have to really believe that you're going out with her, okay? Otherwise your karma won't be restored. And that's why she can't be too grim."

"But if she's not truly grim, I might actually like her. Then what do I do?"

"Look, here's a rule for you. In general, try not to like the women you date, okay? That, if I may say so, is the mistake you made with Jeanie."

"You mean that I liked her."

"Liked her? You *loved* her! That was an accident waiting to happen, my friend. It was like watching one of those car-crash-dummy films, in slow motion."

"You're saying that I should only go out with women that I don't like."

"I'm saying they should have a flaw. Something that bugs you. Nothing repulsive. We're not talking about missing limbs, or harelips. But something that will keep you from falling in love with them."

"That's crazy."

"Really? Which one of us has spent the past six weeks sitting in his own filth, unable to get a hard-on, and which one of us is here holding the phone number of an airline stewardess?"

"Flight attendant, bucko. Not stewardess. Flight attendant."

"You see? That's why you get stomped on."

"All I want," I said, "is to find someone who'll be faithful to me. I don't think I can deal with getting my heart ripped out and fed to me again. I want someone who'll make a commitment."

Evan stared at me, astonished. "This is worse than I thought," he said.

EVAN'S NEW COMPANION was Agnes Rizzo, a woman from the quality assurance lab at Ionic. Apparently they had crossed paths in a restaurant in Chinatown. They went dancing, found an after-hours club in Allston, did some Ecstasy. Now they stood before me, wearing towels and a pair of shit-eating grins. I was on the couch, watching cartoons.

"I didn't know you were here," Evan said.

"I live here, Spock."

"You vanished on us—"

"There's coffee," I said.

I wanted to be happy for them, I really did. Agnes was nice enough. She wore cat-lady glasses and Salvation Army clothes and for a while she had published a zine called *My Head* that she distributed at work. She spoke with a lisp and had bleached blond hair and a tattoo of Marcia Brady on her shoulder. The tattoo was not very good. I wouldn't have known that it was Marcia Brady if she hadn't told us. She and Evan had been flirting for months. At least once a week Agnes would show up at our office and stand in our doorway, smiling her goofy smile and making *Star Trek* jokes. Evan loved zany psycho alterna-chicks, or "Z-PACs," as he called them. The more tattoos, the better. The fact that Agnes was also a *Star Trek* fan drove him around the bend. Now she stood in the doorway of our bathroom, in a cloud of steam, wearing my Netscape beach towel. Her legs were pink from the shower.

"Hey, Reilly," she said.

"Hey," I said, and turned back to the cartoons. It was stupid to be jealous. I knew that. I told myself to calm down. But then when I got into the shower I could not help thinking about how the two of them had just been standing in this very spot, all lusty and soapy and fruitfully multiplying, and for a tiny moment I allowed myself to hate them.

Brunch was the plan. Lovers must have brunch, and the bigger the better. There was a Portuguese place in Somerville that had the best breakfast in town, Agnes said. They served farina and cinnamon bread and linguica. I could picture the scene. They would order pancakes and ham and linguica and potatoes; they would pass each other the ketchup and pour syrup on each other's plates and chow down greedily and say do you mind if I have a sip of your juice and then they would giggle and give each other tastes of whatever they were having.

I called Maria and invited her. She met us downstairs. She gave me a hug, which surprised me. I'd half-expected a knee to the groin. "Come on, I'm starving," she said. We walked holding hands, and for a moment I managed to pretend that we were a happy couple, the kind you see in an Eddie Bauer catalogue, healthy and well-scrubbed, spending Sunday morning the way all healthy well-scrubbed nondysfunctional Eddie Bauer couples do, with a big fat copy of the Sunday *Times* and brunch with your best friends.

The fantasy was somewhat spoiled by the fact that we all, except Maria, looked like AWOL soldiers from the army of the dweebs. Evan wore Birkenstocks, plaid shorts, a Bay Networks T-shirt that he'd stolen at COMDEX, and a pair of little rectangular prescription sunglasses. Agnes wore Evan's "Friends don't let friends listen to the Grateful Dead" T-shirt and a pair of his cutoffs, which she managed to cinch around her waist with an olive-drab Boy Scout belt. They were holding hands, and giggling, and calling each other "Jumanji." The significance of the nickname eluded me, and for that I was grateful.

They ran ahead of us, like two happy nerds on the day of the class trip to the science museum. Then we came around the corner and found them frozen in their tracks. Sigrid was smeared with eggs and shaving cream. Her new tires were slashed. The word FAGGIT had been scrawled on the windshield with soap. In the glare of the sun the letters were melting, bleeding across the glass. But you could still make out the word.

"Jesus," I said. "Holy Jesus and baby Jesus."

Maria put her hand on my arm. "Stay calm," she said. "Just stay calm."

"I'm calm," I said, and felt a blood vessel about to explode in my forehead.

Evan said this had to be Tony's work. Maria said we didn't know that. It could have been teenagers, playing a prank. I said that of course she was right, that we couldn't be one hundred percent sure, but that the spelling of the word *faggit* did tend to direct suspicion at Tony, since the average teenage vandal probably had enough command of the language to render that word correctly.

A woman leaned out a third-floor window and started shouting at us. "What's wrong with you people?" she said. "Leaving that heap out there—it's a disgrace! What are you, crazy? You think that's funny? Come on, get that piece of junk off my street."

I looked up at her, and tried to speak. But I couldn't. What came out, finally, was a kind of whimper. Evan ran home to get a bucket of water and some sponges. Maria and Agnes led me to a bench and told me to take some deep breaths and try to think about something pleasant. I closed my eyes and imagined my hands around Tony's throat, his face going red. I smiled.

"There," Maria said, "that's better."

THIS TIME I didn't confront Giaccalone, or go to the police. I called the Firestone store, dished out another eight hundred dollars, endured another round of abuse from Gus and the rest of the retards, and started dreaming again about revenge. Maria said I should put the Bimmer in a garage and forget about Giaccalone. "Whatever you do to him," she said, "he'll just get back at you worse." She was right. And probably I would have taken her advice—I would have cooled off, let things slide—if fate had not intervened later that night.

It was Saturday, the second night of the feast. Once again the neighborhood had become a madhouse. Evan and I were up on the roof deck, doing bong hits and listening to a Thelonius Monk record, which I had to admit sounded great, but not so great that I'd have spent a hundred dollars for the record and fifteen thousand for the stereo.

Maria and Agnes had gone to the movies together. Something about teenage lesbians in Australia. I had been tempted; but Evan refused to see foreign movies. He liked big stupid Hollywood pictures, the more escapist the better. "Why do I want to pay to go to the movies and get depressed?" he said. "I can get that for free, right here."

That afternoon the four of us had gone to the Gardner Museum, and Maria and Agnes had become fast friends. Evan said this was a uniquely female capability. "Men compete," he said, "but women bond. Half an hour after they meet each other they start talking about their periods and their boyfriends. They don't have boundaries the way we do. It's as if all the women in the world are really just one person who's been split into billions of pieces. Then they meet and trade notes. 'How's it been for you?' 'What do you take for cramps?' That kind of thing."

"Fascinating," I said.

In the distance, heat lightning flashed. The sky was a gray soup. It seemed as if it wanted to rain, but couldn't work up the energy.

"Buddy," Evan said, "have you ever been tied up in bed?"

I looked at him. I told him I was wasted, but not *that* wasted.

He scowled. It was about Agnes, he said. The night before, she had tied him to his bed. Not only that, but she was shaved. He asked me if I thought that meant she was promiscuous. I said I didn't know, but I could assure him that there were worse things than what he'd encountered with Agnes. Case in point: a girl I had dated at Michigan, an exchange student from England, whose pubic hair sprouted like wild plants from the edges of her underpants and grew like creeping ivy down the inside of her thighs. In pantyhose, she looked like Willie Nelson robbing a bank. Evan said all European women were like that, which was why you had to avoid them. We moved on to a more general discussion of female body hair—armpits, mustaches—but that's when fate interrupted us.

There was a disturbance in the alley, trash cans toppling over. We went to the edge of the deck, looked down—and saw Coco rooting through the garbage.

I suppose it took a few seconds for the data to be processed. All day we had been talking about revenge, and now . . .

"It's fate," I said. "It's God sending us a message."

"And what exactly is the message?" Evan said.

But he knew. Seconds later we were out on the back steps,

whistling to Coco. She looked at us, then went back to eating. I called her name. This time she stopped eating and looked at me, with her ears up straight. "Come on," I said, and patted my legs. She trotted over, wagging her tail. She was enormous. I bent down and rubbed behind her ears. She gave me a big dog grin. When I stood up, she rose up on her back legs and put her front paws on my chest. She was almost as tall as I was.

Evan looked around. He was getting nervous. "You know," he said, "maybe this isn't such a good idea."

"You're right, it's a terrible idea," I said, then opened the door and led Coco up the stairs.

She darted around our apartment, sniffing everything: the futon couch, the armchair, the running shoes. She stuck her nose into empty potato chip bags and pizza boxes. She scouted Evan's bedroom, then mine. I put out a bowl of water and some leftover potstickers from World's Worst Chinese. She wolfed down the pot-stickers and then came and sat with me on the couch. I ran my hands over her back, and up behind her ears. "The great Coco," I said. She sighed, and pressed her head against my chest.

Evan fired up the bong. Coco sniffed the air. She seemed to like the smoke. She rolled onto her back, with her head on my lap, and let me rub her belly. Her skin was soft and supple. It slid back and forth over her ribs. She sighed and closed her eyes. When I took my hand away, she reached out with her paw and pulled the hand back.

Maria and Agnes called. They were in a bar in Brookline. There was a band in the background. They wanted us to come meet them. Evan went. I stayed home with Coco.

Later, when I went to bed, she followed me to my room and curled up beside me on the bed. A minute later she was asleep, and snoring, her hot breath on my face.

I lay there, wide awake, my mind racing. All my life I had played it safe: I did my homework, stayed out of trouble, graduated on time, got a job. Now, for the first time ever, I had done something truly reckless. I had acted without regard for consequences. This seemed significant.

I thought about Jeanie. Where was she right now, in the last hours of a Saturday night? Maybe she was lying in bed and thinking about me, just as I was here thinking about her. I remembered the first time we spent the night together, and how I had admired the view from her bedroom: in the distance you could see the Citgo sign in Kenmore Square. In the morning we walked down to Charles Street and ate breakfast in a café. Then we went to the Public Garden and rode on the Swan Boats. Even then, on that first day, I knew that I was in love, but I didn't dare tell her. I didn't want to scare her off.

Six weeks later we went to the maparium at the Christian Science Center and Jeanie told me that she was in love: the tour was over, and we'd stayed behind, standing at opposite ends of the bridge, whispering into the corners of the globe, letting the words run like smoke up along the curve of the glass. That's when I heard it: *I love you.* I was leaning out over the Seychelles, thinking about Brenda Starr's scientist boyfriend, who worked with rare black orchids found only in the Seychelles . . . and Jeanie's words rolled down over Polynesia and up across Antarctica, arriving in my ear like a whisper on a trade wind. I turned around. Jeanie was smiling. My heart leaped. My whole life seemed to open up in front of me. You can't help it. You fall in love, and you build up this whole future: a house, a dog, a bunch of kids riding in the minivan. It becomes real to you. You accept it as fact. And then *whoosh,* it's gone. You look into the future and there's . . . nothing. A blank screen.

Worse still, I had only myself to blame. Because at least part of the reason that Jeanie slept with Mort was to get back at me for going on a lunch date with a girl named Meghan, a secretary in the legal department. What can I say? A cute girl asked me to lunch. I was in the zone, invincible. That year at the company Christmas party, a girl had come up to me at the bar and kissed me full on the mouth. And now secretaries were asking me out. Would I have slept with Meghan? I might have. Except that on on our first lunch date we were seen by Susan Kohl, one of Jeanie's friends. Unfortunately, we did not see Susan, and so when I got back to the office and Jeanie asked me what

I had done for lunch, I told her I went for sushi with Nabeel. She slapped me and walked away. That weekend I went to Detroit and Jeanie slept with Mort.

Jeanie didn't take an eye for an eye. She took both of your eyes, and your head, and any other appendages she could get her claws into. Not only did she sleep with Mort; she also told me all about it, in detail. "I didn't even enjoy it," she told me, feigning remorse. "He's too . . ." She blushed. "Well, he's kind of big. It really hurt." In her eyes there was a gleam, a predatory delight, which made me shiver.

Coco stirred, and shifted her legs. She curled up and started snoring again. I thought of Captain, the dog I'd had as a boy, a cheerful little dachshund who had helped me through some rough times. I imagined myself back in that funny-smelling house in Detroit, snuggling up with him, wearing my Detroit Lions pajamas. Good things were on the way, I told myself.

NEXT MORNING, SAME AS EVER, the white cups gleamed in their racks behind the counter at Caffe Vesuvio, the pastries lay in rows in the cases, and the air had that wonderful, bitter taste of espresso. But anyone could see that something terrible had happened to Giaccalone. He sagged in his chair, and stared out the window like a zombie. His hair had not been combed: it stuck out in all directions. He was chain-smoking. He ignored his sweet roll and coffee. He picked up the paper, then put it down. He sat wringing his hands and looking out the window at the street, which was baking in the sun.

"Look at Mr. Shit-for-Brains now," I said.

We were sitting at a table in back, pretending to read the paper. Evan had spent the night with Agnes at her place in Allston, and had just arrived home. His wrists were bruised. I didn't ask.

Tony ran in and whispered in his uncle's ear. Giaccalone said something. Tony shook his head. Giaccalone cuffed him and said, "Then try again," and Tony ran out.

Evan held the *Globe* up in front of us. "Christ," he said, "this is better than sex."

"I can't remember what sex feels like."

"Like your hand, only warmer. You think he suspects us?"

"This guy couldn't suspect his way out of a broom closet."

We brought a cannoli home for Coco. She met us at the door, wagging her tail. She had finished the bacon and eggs that I'd put out for her in the morning. Now there was a fresh loaf of dog crap on the newspaper under the kitchen table.

"Jesus," Evan said, waving his hands in the air. "What'd you feed her? Napalm? My eyes are watering."

It wasn't Coco's fault, I told him. Evan said he was not trying to assess blame, he was simply stating a fact. I rolled up the newspaper and carried it to the trash. "It's leaking," Evan said, and pointed to the trail of turd juice, the color of spat tobacco, on the kitchen floor. I mopped the floor and put out fresh sheets. We had air freshener in the bathroom, and this helped a little. Coco seemed not to notice the commotion. She stood off to the side, snapping up the pieces of cannoli that I had put into a bowl for her.

"Wait a minute," Evan said. "My *Star Trek* cereal bowl? A dog is eating out of my *Star Trek* china?"

"Relax," I said. "A dog's mouth is way cleaner than a human's. Everybody knows that."

"I don't know that." He picked up the bowl and put it in the sink. "Don't use this again," he said. "I'm serious."

Coco would sit when we told her to sit, and she would come when we called, with a smile on her face, her little claws clicking on the tiled floor in the kitchen. But she would not roll over, or beg, or give us her paw. She was too dignified for tricks like that. Evan found this disappointing. He said he'd always wanted to have a dog that would roll over.

"Go buy a mutt," I told him. "Mutts will do anything for a doggie treat."

He was stuffing CDs into his backpack, getting ready for another marathon session. His goal was to work straight through until Friday, or until he dropped, whichever came first. "I still say she should be able to roll over," he said.

Coco came back with the balled-up tube socks I'd thrown for her. She dropped them at my feet. I rubbed behind her ears and down along her neck. She was a marvelous animal: lean forelegs, broad shoulders, strong haunches, a long, sly smile. When she walked, her muscles rippled beneath her skin, and even when she was sitting still she seemed powerful: she gave the impression that there was a great amount of force contained in her body.

"The way her head is shaped," Evan said, "it looks like her neck just tapers off to a point. She looks kind of like a freak, don't you think?"

I reminded him that the dog he was looking at, the dog who stood there wagging her tail and holding a pair of my tube socks between her teeth, was a member of a noble breed, and that even among the members of that noble breed she was considered royalty. Imagine Montezuma, king of the Aztecs, held in captivity by the Spaniards, I told him.

"Actually," he said, "his name was Moctezuma. It's a common mistake."

That was beside the point, I told him. The fact was that Coco might very well be the fastest dog on the planet. Given a chance, I said, Coco might prove to be the fastest dog in history, the most elite athlete of her kind, ever. Think of Michael Jordan, I said. Or Wayne Gretzky.

"That's great," Evan said. "But she can't stay here, okay? You understand that, right? You're going to let her go, right?"

"Sure."

He gave me a look.

"Buddy, trust me," I said. "I've got the whole thing worked out. I know exactly what I'm doing."

He shook his head, put on his headphones, and rolled his bike out the door.

*   *   *

By Sunday evening, less than twenty-four hours into Operation Coco, the stress was taking its toll on Giaccalone. His face was gray. He looked like a corpse. He sat at his table in Caffe Vesuvio, talking to a priest, while the wiseguys stood around in a circle, talking into their cell phones, looking concerned.

Maria and I stood in the shadows across the street, watching.

"The poor guy," Maria said. "Look at him."

"Yeah," I said, and thought about the sixteen hundred dollars I'd spent on tires. "The poor guy."

Neighborhood kids had been taunting Giaccalone all day, Maria said. They called the café and claimed they had the dog. When he walked down the sidewalk, they barked at him from the rooftops. That morning the priests at St. Michael's had let Giaccalone address the congregations at the three morning masses. He had asked everyone to look for his dog and also to stop calling him with prank calls because it tied up the lines. He said they had to keep the lines free in case . . . in case . . . and then he broke down, sobbing.

"He's on the verge of a nervous breakdown," Maria said. "It's driving him crazy, not knowing what happened to her. For all he knows, the dog is dead."

For a moment I considered telling Maria the truth. I could take her to the apartment and show her.

Instead, I said, "Come on, let's eat."

We went to a place on Hanover Street, and had veal parmesan sandwiches. Maria kept asking what was wrong with me, why I was acting funny. I told her I was fine. This time, when I walked her home, she didn't ask me to come upstairs.

At the corner, I stopped at a pay phone and called Giaccalone at the café. When he came to the phone I growled a little, then whimpered, then barked. He hung up, swearing in Italian. Anyone who saw me walking down Salem Street—a man by himself, laughing out loud—surely would have thought I had just escaped from an asylum.

Coco was waiting for me when I got home. I put some hamburger in a bowl and broke an egg on top of it. This was the meal we used to give Captain as a special treat. Supposedly, eggs keep a dog's coat shiny. Not that Coco needed it. Her coat was inky-black, as shiny as shoe polish. She ate with a delicacy that was unusual for a dog, reaching her long face down toward the bowl and carefully snapping up pieces of meat with her long, muscled tongue. She chewed slowly, and didn't spill food everywhere, the way Captain used to. Her ears, I noticed, were slightly darker than the rest of her face, and her eyes too were ringed by darker fur, which tapered back to a point like the eye makeup on pictures of women in ancient Egypt. At certain angles there was something definitely wolflike about Coco's appearance; and at other angles she seemed almost human.

She finished eating, had a drink of water, and then looked up at me as if to say, *Now what?* She had big eyes, with honey-brown irises. From her nose back along her upper lip ran a row of whiskers, with one big whisker at the very back, at the corner of her mouth. She sat beside me, and yawned. "Ready for bed?" I said. She followed me inside and jumped onto the bed. We lay in the dark. Her face was close to mine, and one of her paws rested on my arm. I listened to the sounds from outside the window: voices, footsteps, cars on the expressway. For a moment I felt as if I were standing on an island in the middle of a raging river, watching everything rushing past.

NEXT MORNING AT SEVEN O'CLOCK I found Evan at his desk, wearing his Spock ears, staring at his screen, typing like a madman. Beside him, sitting at my desk, was Whit, who explained that he'd been unable to sleep and so had gone out for a drive at one in the morning and ended up at the Ionic building. In the lobby, he saw Evan's name in the overnight register. He went upstairs. They talked. That was five hours ago. Now the sun had come up and the two of them looked like vampires who had failed to make it back to their coffins in time: pale skin, sunken eyes. Whit was wearing a T-shirt, cotton shorts, and sandals. His hair was greasy and matted to his head, his eyes were wild from Evan's quad-strength pots of coffee, and he was grinning like a priest in a hot tub full of altar boys.

"Come on, sit down, get a chair," he said. He was wired. His right eye was twitching. "I'm redoing some of your interface."

My heart sank. I could only imagine the damage he had done. I looked at Evan, as if to say, *How could you do this?*

"Here, I'll show you," Whit said. "We can split up the code. Use that workstation over there. Go get some coffee. The stuff's amazing. It'd kill an elephant. Seriously, we're kicking some ass here. We

opened a can of whoop-ass on this thang. Whew." He looked at Evan.
"We bad, right? We bad."

Evan gave Whit a high five. "Right on, my man. We bad." He
glanced at me, and shrugged.

Outside, in the lab, a few ambitious zombies had started to strag-
gle in to work. Whit got up and closed the blinds. He didn't want to
be seen working with us. Lowering his voice, his hands shaking from
the caffeine, he confessed, in a halting staccato, that he had not
wanted to give us the ultimatum, but had been forced to do it against
his will. There was something sad and creepy about this. A boss can
either be loved or feared; and Whit wanted to be loved. But he wasn't
really the boss. He was more of a puppet. I felt bad for him. From the
way he described his job, it sounded as if he were being held hostage
by the board of directors and the various vice presidents.

"I just want you to know—I've already told Evan this—but I want
you to know that I'm on your side, okay?" he said. "But at the same
time I also figured, well, sometimes the threat of extinction can wake
people up and get them to finish a project. So maybe now you'll get
this thing out the door. I know you're pissed at me. But when it's over
and done and everyone's making money, you'll thank me, okay? Because I believe in this project. I really do. I wouldn't be coming in
here in the middle of the night, I wouldn't be sitting here now, if I
didn't."

I had to admit, it was pretty amazing for a company chairman to
come down into the trenches and write code. The only problem was
that Whit didn't really know much about writing code. He certainly
didn't know how to do the kind of work we were doing. There's a big
difference between hacking out a little BASIC program and creating a
million-line program in C++. One is a birdhouse that you build in
your basement and hang in the backyard; the other is the Trump
Tower. Far be it from us, however, to tell Whit that he didn't know
what he was doing. There was a time, in the early eighties, when he
had been the most famous programmer in the business.

Whit's first product, the one with which he founded Ionic, was a communication program called TalkTalk which even now, after almost twenty years, was still renowned for its elegance: the first version shipped on a single 5.25-inch floppy disk, with room to spare. In those days personal computers had 64 kilobytes of memory, so programs had to be tight. TalkTalk was tiny, but brilliant. We'd read the original code. It was like reading haiku. According to legend, Whit and his partner had written the entire TalkTalk program in a single weekend, and posted sales of twenty-five million in their first year. They couldn't hire people fast enough to take orders and fill boxes. It was the kind of problem we imagined ourselves having, in our wildest dreams.

"Here," Whit said, "you see how I restructured this?" He pointed to a screen that contained what used to be my code. It was like a photograph that's been digitally altered to look like a Picasso painting: eyes on the side of the head, the mouth upside down. In five hours he had managed to re-entangle the messes that I'd spent the previous three months untangling.

"You see where this is going?" he said.

I nodded. I felt sick.

"Looks great," I said, and told myself that as soon as he was gone, I would go back to yesterday's build and start from there.

"So you work on these modules, and I'll do these," Whit said. "Here, I'll close this on my screen, so you can get at it. Let me log the revision. Here."

We were using a code-management tool called Viking. Somehow Whit knew how to use it. I had no idea how this could be, unless he spent his free time learning every development tool that was used at Ionic. Or maybe he had learned Viking in order to stumble down here and try to look like a genius. He sat beside me, slouched in his chair like a Formula One driver in his cockpit, half-reclining, with his head tilted forward. He stared at the screen with eyes that seemed able to burn holes in the glass. He pounded the keyboard with his stubby fingers. His keystrokes came in little bursts, like flurries of Morse Code: *click-click-click.* He was sweating profusely. Probably it was the coffee. Evan's quad-strength lit up your nerve endings like

Fourth of July sparklers. I could imagine the chairman of our company keeling over from a heart attack, and the two of us trying to explain what happened.

At nine o'clock, the phone rang. We let it ring. A moment later Nabeel barged in saying he knew we were in here and what the fuck were we doing, having another circle jerk, and why wasn't he invited? Then he saw Whit sitting there, bathed in sweat, slumped in his chair, and for a moment Nabeel was too baffled to speak but then he said, "Oh, um, I didn't know . . . well, ahem, Evan, I just wanted to know if I could borrow that, um, Visual C++ manual." He grabbed a book from Evan's shelf and ran off.

"In all my life," Whit said, after Nabeel had shut the door, "I've never known anyone who was better at avoiding work than Nabeel. And I've known some real pros. You have to admire him. He's good."

We looked at him, not sure how to respond.

He laughed. "Don't worry," he said, "I'm not a fink."

Strange days indeed, when the chairman tells you not to worry about him ratting you out to your boss. Things became even stranger when Whit asked us if the stories he'd heard about us tormenting Janet Scuto with flowers and phone calls were true. Again we found ourselves at a loss for words. How did he know these things? There were people who said that all of Ionic was rigged with hidden cameras, that we were all under constant surveillance. Maybe they were right.

Whit asked if we could keep a secret. We shrugged. The secret, he said, was that he hated Janet Scuto as much as we did. He called her "the Rhino," and he wanted to fire her, but he didn't dare, for fear of getting hit with a lawsuit.

"Is that true?" Evan said.

Whit swore that it was.

"Okay," Evan said, "come here." He pried the blinds apart. Whit peered through the crack. "You see Janet Scuto? In a minute she's going to go to the kitchen. When she makes her move, you tell me."

Whit said he felt like Marlon Perkins in *Mutual of Omaha's Wild*

Kingdom. He was trying not to laugh. Suddenly he stiffened. "The Rhino is up," he said. "The Rhino is moving."

"Okay, stay cool, and wait till she gets to the end of the lab," Evan said. He picked up the phone. "Make sure she's all the way across."

Whit held his hand up in the air, like a TV producer giving a cue. "In five, four, three, two . . . *one,*" he said, then pointed to Evan, who dialed Janet's extension.

"Oh mother of God," Whit said. I could imagine what he was seeing: Janet sprinting across the lab, bowling people over. Whit fell into a chair, holding his hands over his mouth, tears running down his face. "You know," he said, "maybe you won't believe this, but I envy you guys. You get to do battle with psychos. I have to take *orders* from them."

He told us a story about a psycho he'd worked with at NASA Jet-Pro. Every day, after lunch, the guy would take a crap in the men's room and leave the toilet unflushed. The theory was that the guy was expressing his resentment toward his coworkers. When they confronted him, he denied everything. This went on for months. Finally one day Whit slipped a massive dose of Ex-Lax into the psycho's sandwich. The guy spent the afternoon on the toilet, doubled over with cramps, then left and never came back.

"I've forgotten how much fun it is just to sit at a desk and write code," he said. "To work, like an ordinary person. To fool around. To slack off, or to work through the night. All of this. That's why we get into this, right? I mean, sure, there's the money. But this is where it begins, right here, you and the machine. I mean, there's a certain kind of humor, a way of looking at things, that programmers have and the rest of the world doesn't. And I mean, if you don't love that kind of life, you might as well forget about it."

Evan and I grunted. There was kind of an unspoken rule that you didn't talk about this. But Whit was right; there is nothing more absorbing than creating software. In school I liked every subject, and loved some, but nothing came close the way I felt about writing code. Probably it is not hard to understand why a kid whose family has disintegrated finds solace in a computer. For me it was love at first sight.

More than love, really. Obsession. I would get going on a program and not be able to stop. When I did have to put the work aside—for dinner, for school, for sleep—my mind would race with ideas, and I couldn't wait to get back. And then to see it run! You are Frankenstein, standing by the table as the lightning rips into the wires and the monster—flawed, clumsy, but *alive*—sits up and growls.

People talk about doctors playing God, but it seems to me that doctors are basically just fancy automobile mechanics: something breaks, they fix it. We, on the other hand, create. We type instructions and bring a machine, or a whole network of machines, to life. The world around us may be breaking up into a million pieces, the people we love may leave us; but upstairs, in our room, on our computer, we can put everything back together.

At noon Whit went home. The coffee had given him a migraine. Evan said it was a good thing too, because he had made plans for lunch: he was meeting a friend from MIT who now worked at McKinsey and who was bringing a friend who worked at Kindell, Parker, Sloan, a big venture capital firm. Evan was going to take a shower and put on clean clothes and meet them at the Sail Loft. He asked me if I wanted to come.

"You were just sitting here with Whit," I said, "talking about being a team, slapping high fives—and now you're going to go stab him in the back?"

Evan pointed out that Whit had done a good deal of backstabbing himself over the course of his career. It was common knowledge, for example, that Whit had more or less stolen the idea for TalkTalk from NASA JetPro; Whit's original TalkTalk was simply a personal computer version of a program that JetPro used on mainframes. Then there was the story of Jimmy Burke, the programmer who helped Whit write the original TalkTalk. When sales took off, Whit refused to give Burke a share of the royalties. Burke sued, and Whit settled, but for next to nothing.

"This whole industry is based on treachery," Evan said. "Do unto others before they do unto you, right? Or what was it that Whit said that time? 'The limits of your success are determined by the degree to which you can impose your will on others,' right?"

This was, in fact, something Whit had told us, one night when we were at his house for dinner and he had drunk a little too much wine and was in an advice-giving mood.

"You've got a guy," Evan said, "who made himself rich by stealing an idea and screwing his partner, and you want me not to protect myself from getting screwed by him, too? Please. Whit's a nice guy, and he came here and put in ten hours of work, but I've been working on this fucking thing for two years, okay? This is *my* idea. *Mine.*"

I stared at him. Until now it had always been *ours*. He was standing up, snapping his fingers. He was so wired that he didn't even realize what he'd said.

"What?" he said.

"Nothing."

He picked up his gym bag. "So are you coming or not?"

I didn't know whether to feel hurt, or embarrassed, or just sad. I guess what I felt was all three.

"Not," I said.

"Okay. *Adios,* amoeba."

I rode my bike home and checked on Coco. She was still on the couch in the same place she'd been when I left that morning. Lunch was hamburgers: mine was cooked, hers was raw. We watched a little TV, and I gave her fresh water. "I'll try to get home early," I told her. "And then tonight we'll let you go, okay? Until then, you be good." She smiled, and licked my hand; and although she had been mine for less than two days, I felt sure that I would miss her when she was gone.

HAD EVERY INTENTION of keeping my word and returning Coco that evening. I would have done that—I would have waited until the middle of the night, and led her down the back steps, and set her free—except that at six o'clock, when Evan and I returned to the North End, we discovered that Giaccalone was offering a five thousand–dollar reward. The flyers were bright yellow, and they were everywhere: on telephone poles, in the Laundromat, in the windows of the markets. There was a badly reproduced photograph of Coco, and lots of misspelled information about how to collect the reward. As we stood there reading the flyer, a pack of nuns fanned out past us, shaking boxes of doggie treats and making kissing noises.

"Folks," I said, folding up a flyer and stuffing it into the pocket of my shorts, "it's a whole new ballgame."

Evan told me not to be an idiot. We got back on our bikes and rode into the neighborhood. The place was a madhouse. Kids were running around calling Coco's name, elbowing each other out of the way and racing past the old ladies who stood on the corners shouting themselves hoarse. These, no doubt, were the tenants that Giaccalone allowed to live in his buildings without paying rent.

"He's mobilized the neighborhood," I said. "They're like his private army."

"The army of the halfwits," Evan said. "Speaking of which, look at this."

Tony and Gus were standing outside our building. Side by side they created a study in contrasts. They were about the same height, but Tony was chiseled and overblown, his arms and chest swollen with muscles; while Gus had an enormous gut and tiny arms and two fat man-breasts that strained the fabric of his white tank shirt.

"Muscle Man meets Mammary Man," Evan said. "Talk about a meeting of the minds. They could combine their IQs and almost break one hundred."

Evan's theory was that the North End represented an example of reverse evolution: Anyone born with normal intelligence moved away, leaving the subnormals behind to breed with each other. Hence the man who sat at the counter of the Cozy Corner diner with a trail of spooge hanging out of his mouth, or the old morons who sat in folding chairs arguing with the shopkeepers about where to put the trash bags. Hence the priest who walked around talking to himself, and who claimed once to have spoken to the Blessed Mother in the garden of St. Michael's. Hence the hundreds of people who stood in the garden holding candles and waiting for the Virgin Mary to appear again. Hence Gus and Tony, who stood smirking at us like a pair of apes when we rode up to our building.

"Hey," Tony said, "it's my friends with the nice car. How're those new tires working out for you?" He had been at the gym. He was wearing red Spandex shorts and a green tank top. He was soaked with sweat, drinking Gatorade.

"They're great," I said. "How's the missing dog?"

"Why, you got her? You two taking turns with her?"

"You sound jealous."

He stood there, rolling up onto the balls of his feet, probably trying to decide whether it would be worth the damage to his hands to pound the crap out of me. I glanced down at his sneakers. They were extraordinarily small.

"You know what I think?" he said.

"I didn't know that you did think."

"That," he said, "is funny. Seriously. That's good." By virtue of his two miserable performances at an open-mike night, Tony now considered himself the local authority on humor. "Now let me tell you something. Here's what I think." He took a sip of his Gatorade; he was working on timing, learning how to hold off on the punch line. "What I think," he said, "is that you two wouldn't know what to do with that dog, because it's a female."

Gus burst out laughing, so hard that his breasts shook.

"Tony," I said, "you keep bringing up this gay thing, which makes me wonder if maybe you've got some issues with that."

He chuckled. "Yeah," he said, "I got some *issues* with that. I got an issue right here, just for you." He grabbed his crotch.

"Hey," I said, "look at the size of that thing. What have you got in there, a lucky rabbit's foot?"

"I'll put a rabbit's foot up your ass."

"You see? That's what I'm talking about. This obsession with fucking me in the ass. What's up with that?"

"Let me get this straight. You're saying *I'm* gay?"

"You do spend a lot of time at the gym."

"And?"

"Well, you've got this big roomful of guys, all grunting and heaving and groaning, all covered in sweat, all checking each other out in the mirrors . . ."

"You're saying those guys are gay? Let me tell you something, any one of those guys would kick your ass. You don't see them out riding around on bikes, dressed up like Beavis and Butt-head."

"We have to ride bikes," Evan said. "It's part of our parole agreement. We're not allowed to ride the subway."

"We'd use my car," I said, "but every time I leave it in the street some retard goes and misspells words all over it with soap."

Tony scowled. After the *faggit* episode, his buddies had started taunting him. Maria, bless her heart, had spread the story.

"So tell me this," Tony said. "How come you never wear shoes?"

"We always wear shoes."

"Yeah? What're those?"

He pointed at our feet. I was wearing Birkenstocks. Evan was wearing Tevas.

"Those," Tony said, "are sandals."

"And sandals," I said, "are a subgenre in the category of shoes, which is itself a subgenre in the category of footwear."

"Is that supposed to be funny?" Tony said. "Because I'll tell you, that's not funny." He looked at Gus. "Is that funny?"

"No," Gus said. "That's not funny at all."

"It's not funny having a toilet that runs, either," Evan said. "When are you going to come fix it?"

Gus gave us a "fuck you" gesture—he flicked his fingers under his chin—then went back down into the store, muttering to himself. Tony wandered in behind him.

Maria came outside. She had her hair pulled up, and was drinking a bottle of Pellegrino water. Three kids blasted by on bikes, screaming Coco's name. They nearly knocked over the fruit display. "Can you believe this?" she said. "Davio gave a thousand dollars to the church. They're saying two masses a day for Coco. And the kids in school are all praying to St. Anthony."

Evan asked what that meant. I explained to him that St. Anthony was the saint you prayed to when you lost something; supposedly he could help you find it. Evan said that was ridiculous. It was also ridiculous, he said, for everybody to be making such a big deal about finding Coco when the dog would undoubtedly show up on her own. "Dogs always do this," he said. "They run away. They have adventures. And then they come back. Doesn't anybody know that? I bet she'll be back by midnight tonight." He shot me a look. "Don't you agree?"

I said I didn't know, it was hard to say. Maria said she would take Evan's bet, no problem. She said Coco wasn't going to just show up. By now, in fact, she was probably a million miles away.

"A million miles," Evan said. "Where would that be? China? The moon?" He'd been in a sour mood all afternoon. Apparently the guys he met for lunch had not been too enthusiastic about Nectar.

Maria said Coco could be anywhere, but one thing was certain: These people running around in the streets were wasting their time, because no way was Coco still in the North End. I looked up at our windows; they were shut, with the curtains drawn. It was amazing, but Coco had sat up there all day, thirty feet above the commotion, listening to all those people calling her name, and she'd never made a sound. She was probably sitting there now, with her nose between the curtains, watching us.

"The dog was stolen," Maria said. "It's obvious. Davio knows that. He knows who did it, too."

The prime suspect, she said, was Coco's original owner. His name was Karl Wilson, and he had a kennel in New Hampshire. A week ago he had traveled to Boston with twenty-five thousand dollars and tried to buy Coco back from Giaccalone. Giaccalone said he would sell the dog, but not for twenty-five thousand. He wanted fifty. Wilson begged Giaccalone to have a heart. The dog had two good seasons left, maybe three. She could make history. Wilson offered to give Giaccalone a share of Coco's winnings, and to let Giaccalone keep Coco as a pet after she retired. And still Giaccalone had refused.

I told her I didn't understand—if Davio knew that Wilson had stolen the dog, why did he post the reward? Maria said the reward was a smoke screen. Giaccalone wanted Wilson to believe that he had got away with it; he was trying to fake him out.

I pointed out that if Giaccalone had been reasonable and agreed to Wilson's offer to buy back the dog, none of this would have happened in the first place. Maria said Davio was only being a business-man. The dog was worth a hundred thousand dollars, and all Giaccalone wanted was fifty. What was wrong with that?

"What's wrong with that," I said, "is that first of all, it's extortion, which is a crime. But more important, that dog was born to race. That's what she does. To keep a dog like that from racing, just because you're having an argument over money, it's not fair to the dog. These two idiots are having a squabble, and the dog gets caught in the middle of it. That's all I'm saying."

Maria said there were other issues involved. Believe it or not, she said, Giaccalone had become attached to Coco. And he didn't trust Wilson's promise that he would get the dog back after she retired from racing. He was thinking that maybe he would race her himself. He could hire a trainer, rent a kennel.

Maria said Giaccalone was lonely. His wife had died the year before, of cancer. They hardly knew she had it and then all of a sudden she was dead. Giaccalone had been devastated. He was fifty-something years old, and all alone in the world.

You had to understand, Maria said. Giaccalone didn't have a lot of friends. He had people who owed him favors, people who owed him money. But no friends. Everybody was nice to him, everybody said hello. But people were afraid of him. They kept their distance. Coco had been a comfort to him. He took her everywhere. He put her in his car and they drove out to the beach together and went for walks.

"And now that she's lost," Maria said, "it's like Davio is reliving his wife's death. The worst part is he just doesn't know for sure what happened to her. I know this doesn't fit your comic book view of the world, but you have to understand that Davio is a human being. He has feelings. And now he's a wreck. This is driving him crazy. He can't eat, he can't sleep."

For a moment I imagined how awful this must be for Giaccalone. Before I could really savor this thought, however, Tony emerged from the grocery store and started giving Maria a hard time for hanging around with us. "It's one thing to rent to these guys," he said, "or to sell them groceries. That's one thing. But what do you want to be friends with them for? People are going to think you're a fag hag or something. You know? And then they'll think—I don't know—they might think you're the kind of person who likes to hang out with that certain kind of person. You know what I'm saying? The kind of gal who wears comfortable shoes?"

Evan said Tony shouldn't wear such tight shorts, because people could see his prehensile tail through the back of them.

"My what?"

"Forget it."

"What, is that a gay thing or something? Did I miss something?"

"Don't worry about it," Maria said.

"Okay, but you see?" Tony said, in an instructor's voice. "That joke wasn't funny. You see how it just fell off? Part of it is that word. What was it?"

"Prehensile," Maria said.

"Right, whatever. Big word, doesn't work. Not a funny word. And your delivery was wrong." He looked at me and Evan. "Do you see what I mean, ladies? What do you think?"

"What I think," Evan said, pursing his lips, "is that you're just the hunkiest little piece of fried calamari I've ever set my eyes on." He sniffed the air. "And sister, what *is* that cologne you're wearing?"

Tony started to say something—then he just walked away.

"Well," Evan said, "time for my bubble bath." He opened the door. "Sweetie," he called, "are you going to come join me?"

"In a minute," I said.

A woman walking out of the grocery store stopped and looked at us. Then she blessed herself and hurried away. Evan went inside, cackling. Maria said we shouldn't freak people out like that. I said, how did she think it made us feel to walk around knowing that everybody thought we were gay? Everywhere we went, we got the gay treatment. Women pointed at us and giggled. Men made kissing noises. The woman who ran the drugstore on Prince Street winked and asked us which one of us did the cooking. I consoled myself with the fact that at least she had guessed it was Evan.

"I realize we're not the most macho guys in the world," I said, "but it's not as if we're running around in hot pants and high heels, trying to pick up sailors."

"Thank you," Maria said, "for that mental image."

She said she couldn't explain why people believed the things they did. Rumors got started, and people believed them. But who started the rumor? That's what I wanted to know. Maria said she didn't know. Lucia, maybe. Or Gus.

"Great," I said. "Good old Gus."

She asked me if I wanted to see a movie later. I told her I couldn't, and made up a lie about having to go back to work. "We've got five hundred hours left," I said. "We've got to make the most of them."

She looked at me. She didn't believe a word of it. "Reilly," she said, "are you avoiding me?"

"Of course not."

"So what is it? Are you afraid?"

"Afraid?" I tried to look puzzled. "What's there to be afraid of?"

Just then, Gus stuck his head out of the door and started yelling at Maria to get back to work. For the first time ever, I was glad to see him.

EVAN'S FAMILY WAS ORTHODOX, and although Evan claimed to be an atheist, I suppose you couldn't grow up in a family like that without having some of it rub off on you. "We're talking about grand theft," he said. "It's a felony."

It was early evening. I had just returned from a pet store in Somerville, with a bag of Science Diet dry dog food, a food-and-water bowl set, a beef-scented chew toy, a leather muzzle, and a variety of odor-killing products. I'd loaded them all in a big duffel bag and carried them through the North End, right past Giaccalone's café, past Gus, who sat on a chair outside the grocery, and up the front stairs of our building.

"We're not going to get arrested," I said.

"No," Evan said, "we're going to get killed."

I reminded him that I had stuck by him when he got caught planting a virus on the sales department's e-mail server, and had taken half the blame, even though it had been entirely his idea. I reminded him that I had loaned him a hundred dollars six months before, and had never been repaid.

"You owe me," I said. "And Giaccalone owes me for those tires.

So don't pull this Old Testament bullshit on me. All of this King Solomon and the Ten Commandments stuff."

"King Solomon had nothing to do with the Ten Commandments."

"Whatever," I said. "You know what I mean."

He insisted that we didn't have room for a dog. We had a tiny living room, a galley kitchen, a bathroom with a shower stall and a miniature sink. Our bedrooms were eight-by-ten, just big enough to hold a bed and a dresser. I told him what Maria had once told me: At the turn of the century an apartment of this size would have been shared by two entire families of Italian immigrants—ten or fifteen people, all crammed in here. Compared to that, what were two guys and a dog?

"Besides," I said, "it'll only be a few days."

"A few days? Are you serious? Do you have any idea how hot it is?"

"No," I said, "I have no idea how hot it is. You see, Evan, what you're looking at is a hologram—a projected image that looks like a real person. Right now I'm actually standing at the North Pole, and the temperature here is a cool, comfortable thirty-five degrees. I've heard something about this heat wave you're having, and I do sympathize."

He looked out the window. Outside, a bunch of kids were calling Coco's name. "Do you hear that?" he said. I told him not to worry. But telling Evan not to worry was like telling ice not to melt. Evan grew up in the Bronx. He was born to worry.

"It's not fair to the dog," he said. "Even a little dog would be crowded in here. And Coco is not a little dog."

In fact, Coco stood thirty-two inches at the shoulder, which made her six inches taller than the average female greyhound and four inches taller than the average male. But greyhounds are perfectly happy living in close quarters, because they've spent their whole lives in cages. This was one of the greyhound facts I'd learned that afternoon while scanning the Web for sites devoted to greyhounds and dog racing. The greyhound, it turned out, was one of the seminal breeds from which all other dogs are descended. The ancient Egyptians kept greyhounds. The Spanish conquistadors brought them to the New World and used them for hunting. A greyhound could see a rabbit standing a half mile away, and could catch it in thirty seconds.

A fast greyhound could run at forty miles an hour. Coco had been clocked at forty-seven, according to her biography, which I'd found on a dog-racing site. Coco held track records up and down the East Coast. There were lots of photographs of her, as well as descriptions of her parents and siblings. In the world of dog racing, she was Secretariat.

"Who?" Evan said.

"It's not important," I said. "The point is, she's not going to have a problem staying in an apartment. It's more room than she's used to."

Evan said it was bad enough to steal a dog; but to steal a dog from the mob? It was suicide. I told him Giaccalone wasn't a mobster, he was just some fat guy who ran a café and played at being a wiseguy.

"Tell that to the guy whose thumbs got cut off," Evan said. "I'm serious. They'll cut off our thumbs. And then what'll we do? How do you type without thumbs? Have you thought about that?"

"You tap the space bar with your stump," I said.

Coco was sitting nearby, watching us, smiling. "Look at that face," I told Evan. "Look at her. She loves it here. How can you resist that?"

"Easy," Evan said. "No problem at all."

I tried a different approach. I told him that whatever money we got, we'd split it fifty-fifty. I figured this would sway him. He was desperately broke. He had maxed out two Visa cards, and American Express had been calling him at work, demanding payment. He had no concept of how to manage money. He just saw things and bought them. Records, stereo gear—he couldn't resist.

"We'll get five thousand bucks," I said. "You can take your twenty-five hundred and pay off your American Express bill. And then you can start overspending again."

He still wasn't convinced. He stood there hemming and hawing. Finally I couldn't stand it. There are times when you just have to grab people by the nape of the neck and drag them to their destiny. "Buddy," I said, "whether you like it or not, I'm going to do this, okay? So you might as well help me." He closed his eyes. I handed him the bag of dog food. "Here," I said. "Put this under the sink."

I was setting out a bowl of fresh water when Lucia knocked on our door. Coco leaped up and started scrambling around the room, figuring she was going to go outside. Whenever we went near the door she would spring up and start wagging her tail. I looked out the peephole. Lucia was wearing huge glasses that magnified her eyes. Her face was distorted by the lens. She looked like a creature from outer space.

"It's the Bride," I said.

"What the hell does she want?"

"What, I'm a mind reader? Come on, get the dog out of here."

Evan dragged Coco into his bedroom. Lucia knocked again. She kept us under constant surveillance, and was always coming across the hall to complain about something. One time she brought Gus, who said that Lucia had informed him that there had been black people visiting in our apartment, and that he hoped this wouldn't happen again. At first I didn't know what they were talking about; but then I remembered that Nabeel and Upendra had come over to watch a movie a few nights before. I started to protest that our friends weren't black; but then that seemed wrong, and I just sat there, staring down at the floor, aghast.

This happened all the time in the North End. There was no such thing as privacy, or personal space. For me, this had been the most difficult aspect of adjusting to the North End. People in the Midwest have a highly developed sense of privacy. The boundaries are broad and brightly lit. In the neighborhood where I grew up, you could park a purple Winnebago in your driveway and the neighbors would never mention it, for fear of seeming nosy. In the North End, however, nothing was sacred. People leaned out their windows and yelled down to their friends in the street about their gas pains and upset stomachs and the diarrhea they'd had all week.

"Who is it?" I said.

"You know who it is," Lucia said. "You were just at the door. I saw your feet."

I opened the door. She was wearing a white tank top and a pair of leopard-print stretch pants that displayed her potbelly to some advantage.

"Lucia," I said, "are you expecting?"

"Yes," she said, "I'm expecting to see you two idiots get thrown out of the building."

I told her that we'd be more than happy to leave if Gus would tear up our lease.

"He'll tear you up a new asshole maybe."

"I love it when you talk dirty."

"Laugh, clown, laugh. But I'm telling you, keep that music down. What the hell was this noise you were just playing? It sounds like pots and pans clanging together. It's giving me a goddamn migraine."

Evan had been listening to Art Institute of Chicago when I got home. To be fair to Lucia, AIC did sound like pots and pans clanging together—and I think that was because they were in fact clanging pots and pans together.

"It's jazz," I said.

"Yeah? Jazz this."

She pushed past me into the apartment. "One more time," she said, "and I'm going to tell Gus. I'm not kidding."

I said that Lucia seemed to have formed a special relationship with Gus. "He's up in your apartment all the time," I said.

Her face tightened. "I've got a mouse," she said.

"A *mouse*? Is that what you call it? I've never heard a mouse yell like that before."

Her face started shaking. I steered her toward the door. That's when she spied the newspaper on the kitchen floor.

"What's this?" she said. "You have a pet?"

"Right," I said, "we've got a pet mouse. It must be related to the one you've got. Maybe they're cousins."

"Where is it?" She spun around. "There's no pets here. Not even cats. That's the rules. Mr. Tomasino, down the hall, he got a kitten once, but I told Gus. If I can't have a kitten, then neither can he. And neither can you. Gus makes the rules, not me. Do you hear me?"

"Loud and clear. Thanks ever so much for visiting." I shut the door in her face.

Evan came out of his room. Coco ran straight to me, wagging her tail. I crouched down and gave her a hug. She licked my face.

"Hey," Evan said.

I looked up. He did not seem happy.

"Come here," he said.

I followed him. He pointed to a dog turd and a puddle of piss.

"She was scared, that's all," I said.

Coco ran off, whimpering. The thing about dogs is that they always know when they're in trouble.

"I'm losing patience," Evan said.

I got paper towels, a sponge, and Lysol. Even after the crap was cleaned up, Evan said he couldn't sleep in there. The smell was too strong, he said. He was pacing back and forth.

"It's not that bad," I said.

He went out. A few minutes later he came back with a dozen pine-tree air fresheners and hung them from the ceiling in his room. The air fresheners, however, smelled worse than the dog shit. I told him he could sleep in my room. He went in there, but came out a half hour later.

"It's no use," he said. "I can't sleep."

I was stretched out on the couch, reading *AutoWeek*. Coco was lying beside me. Everywhere I went, she came with me. Evan said this was because I had dog breath, and reminded her of her kennel-mates.

"I'm going back to the office," Evan said.

It was ten o'clock. He'd been awake now for thirty-eight hours.

I asked him if he wanted me to go with him. He shook his head. "No offense," he said. He packed up some CDs and a change of clothes. At the door, he stopped. He looked at me. "Look," he said, "how much longer are you going to keep this dog?"

Twenty-four hours, I told him. Forty-eight at the most. He groaned. I went to the window and watched him ride his bike down Salem Street. Coco stood beside me. She was holding her chew toy—she wanted to play fetch. I tossed it, and she brought it back. We played like that for a while, until she got bored. I stayed up for another hour or so, watching TV. Coco sat beside me on the couch, pressing her head against me so that I would keep rubbing her ears. When I went to bed, she followed me there and curled up beside me.

I lay on my back, watching the light from the street play on the ceiling. Down below, there were voices in the street, the last people leaving the restaurants, saying their good-byes. I rubbed Coco's head. I thought to myself that after she was gone, maybe I would go and get myself a dog. I liked having a dog around. Coco sighed, and flapped her tail against the covers. Soon she was asleep, softly snoring.

I dreamed about Maria: we were at the beach, somewhere tropical, maybe Mexico, and Coco was with us, and we were all in the water, scuba diving, and the guy who ran the dive shop had rigged up a scuba system for dogs too, so Coco could swim underwater with us. There were huge schools of tiny yellow fish, shimmering and rippling like pieces of cloth unfurling, and Coco was chasing the fish. It was a weird dream, but a good one, and the next morning I woke up smiling.

AGNES WORE a Salvation Army dress and a pair of high-top sneakers and was sitting beside Evan, staring at him like a groupie. He was typing, staring at the screen, as if he didn't even know she was there. It was nine o'clock. Evan had been up all night, again on the quad-strength coffee. He was developing facial tics. Every so often a muscle at the right side of his mouth would go into a spasm.

Agnes asked me if I had heard about this dog thing. She showed me the *Herald:* COCO COMMOTION IN NORTH END was the headline, over a photograph of Coco. The article described the madness that Giaccalone's reward had created. It said also that the police had become involved.

Boston Police spokesman Sgt. Michael Doyle said police have few leads at this time.

"It may be that the dog simply ran off," Doyle said. "But we are also considering other possibilities."

Doyle would not confirm whether the dog's previous owner, Karl Michael Wilson, of Derry, N.H., is a suspect.

Wilson, 45, has not been seen at his home on Willow Road in

Derry for several days, police said. Efforts by the *Herald* to reach Wilson by phone have been unsuccessful. At his business number a woman answered but refused to comment. Later that line was disconnected.

Meanwhile, the *Herald* has learned that a man matching Wilson's description was seen yesterday at Montreal International Airport, boarding a United Airlines flight to Frankfurt, Germany. Records show a dog carrier was also boarded on that flight. Wilson's sister, Judith Lindquist, is a United Airlines employee. Lindquist could not be reached for comment.

I was reading the story out loud. I stopped and looked at Evan. He was staring down at the floor, shaking his head. The muscles in his face were jerking around like Mexican jumping beans. Enormous sweat stains had formed under his arms. I knew what he was thinking: Wilson hadn't fled to Germany, he'd been grabbed by Giaccalone. Oddly enough, when I thought about Karl Wilson, I pictured Carl Wilson, the Beach Boy. I could see the poor guy being dragged from his bed in his underpants, struggling as they carried him to the trunk of a car, swearing that he didn't have the dog.

"What's wrong?" Agnes said.

Evan groaned and turned back to his screen.

"For all we know," Evan said, "they've already killed him. He's probably lying in a ditch someplace."

It was noon. I had spent the morning undoing the code that Whit had written, while Evan met with Whit and Mort Stone and lied about how well the project was going. Now we were in a Guatemalan restaurant in Central Square and I was trying to get him to calm down.

"Maybe Wilson really went to Germany," I said. "Think about it. That's what any sensible person would do. You'd get the hell out of the country as fast as you could. So maybe he heard that the dog was missing, or maybe Giaccalone called him up and started accused him of stealing the dog, and so he split."

"Maybe this, maybe that." He stared down at his plate.

"I know how we can find out," I said.

There was a pay phone out back, in the hallway near the kitchen. I held the phone between us, so Evan could listen. As I was dialing, the waiter who had served us our lunch, a little guy with a dark Indian face, came out of the bathroom zipping his fly and wiping his hands on his pants. He smiled. He had a gold tooth. I made a mental note not to finish my tamales.

Someone answered the phone at Giaccalone's café. I told him I had Karl Wilson on the line and that we wanted to talk to Davio right away. Giaccalone came onto the line. "Karl, where the fuck are you?" he said. "What the fuck are you pulling on me here?"

I hung up. I looked at Evan. "Satisfied?"

He walked away. I followed him to the table. Evan said the fact that Giaccalone seemed surprised to hear from Wilson did not prove a thing. "Think about it," he said. "If Giaccalone is holding Wilson, and somebody calls pretending to be Wilson, what's Giaccalone going to do? He's going to play along. He figures it's the cops, trying to trick him. So he plays along."

He was rocking back and forth in his chair, his eyes darting around, as if at any moment he expected a hit man to walk in and start spraying the place with machine-gun fire.

"Reilly," he said, "here's the thing. We've got a lot of pressure on us right now. Too much pressure. This is not a good time for a dog-napping."

"So what do you want me to do?"

"I want you to make this problem go away," he said. "Just make this be over."

My idea was to arrange a hostage swap. We would choose a super-market outside the city, a place with good access to a highway. There was a Star Market in Weston, near the Massachusetts Turnpike. Giaccalone would put the money in a shopping cart at the far end of a supermarket parking lot, near the entrance. We would arrive in a rented van, wearing gloves and ski masks. We would scoop the money out of the shopping cart, drop off the dog, and be gone.

"Clean, simple, elegant," I said.

We were in our office, with the door closed. I was getting ready to make the call.

"Childish, low-tech, thoroughly unworkable," Evan said. "What if they follow us?"

"They'll be trying to catch the dog."

"What if the cops trace the phone call?"

"We're not dealing with rocket scientists here."

I dialed the hotline number. Tony answered. He was using a cordless phone, which was whistling and crackling as if he were calling from the space shuttle. "Jesus," he said. "Hold on. Lemme change channels on this fucking thing. There. Nope. Shit. No, I don't know. Here, let go—"

The line went dead. I redialed. This time, the signal was clear. I was using a voice changer which I'd bought on the way back to work. They have them in every electronics store. Basically it's just a frequency modulator. At the high end it could make you sound like a chipmunk, while at the low end you sound like Darth Vader.

I chose the Darth Vader setting. "Get out a pen and paper," I told Tony. "I have instructions for you."

"Jesus," he said. "Look, stop calling here, okay? You're tying up the line." To someone in the background he said, "No, it's those fucking kids again."

Then he hung up.

I put down the phone.

"Hey," Evan said. "Great plan. Seriously. You're a genius. How much did you spend on that voice changer? Good investment, I'd say."

I asked him if he had a better plan. He said he did. We could take the dog down to the café, tell Giaccalone that we found her, and collect the reward. I stared at him. I couldn't believe how stupid he could be sometimes.

"What?" he said. "What's wrong with that?"

"What's wrong with that? Gosh golly, Evan, why don't we go jump in front of trucks on Route 93? Why don't we go wander around in Dorchester late at night? They won't pay us—they'll kill us."

"We'll tell them we found her. They'll love us."

"They won't love us," I said. "They'll beat the crap out of us. And even if they don't beat the crap out of us, they sure as hell won't pay us."

"So who cares? I don't care about the money. I just want to get rid of the dog. I mean, I'm sure she's a great dog, a nice dog, all of that, but I mean, she took a shit in my room, okay? I can't even sleep there. I can't even sleep in my own room. And now, to make it worse, the cops are looking for her. For us. Let's just wait till the middle of the night, and set her free. Let her run home."

"Impossible," I said. "No can do."

He got up. For a second I thought he was going to leap at me. But then Lull appeared in our doorway and put his hands up on the doorframe as if he might try to swing from it. He had the look people get when they come to say good-bye. I wondered if maybe he had got an offer from another company. Middle management guys were always getting wooed away. "Bit ripe in here, isn't it?" he said, making a sour face. "You know there's a men's room down the hall that you can use. You don't have to go in here."

We stared at him.

"Right. Okay." He cleared his throat. "Well, look, first thing *mañana*, there's going to be a video conference, and your presence is requested. Or maybe you know that already, if you've read my e-mail. I never know. Have you broken into the server yet today? Or is that scheduled for later?" He laughed. We didn't. That made him laugh even harder. I wondered if he drank during the day. "You *can* hear what I'm saying, right? Or you can at least read lips, right? You understand that I am speaking to you right now? I am addressing you?"

We nodded.

"Good. And do you think you'll remember what I'm telling you when the Ecstasy wears off later? Or should I write it down? Here, give me a pen."

He took a sheet of paper and wrote in Magic Marker: NINE A.M., DUANE. The conference rooms in our wing were named after members of the Allman Brothers Band: Gregg, Duane, Dickey, Butch, Jaimoe, Berry. In the East Wing the rooms were named David, Stephen, Graham, and Neil.

Lull taped the paper to Evan's monitor.

"Why don't you tell us what's going on?" Evan said. "Who are we meeting with?"

"Wait and see," Lull said. "Wait and see."

He slipped away across the lab, snickering.

"Bob Lull," Evan said, in a TV-commercial voice. "Husband. Father. Lithium user."

24

THEY DREW ME in with a ruse about a surprise party. Maria told me it was Agnes's birthday. We ate dinner in a restaurant on Salem Street: candles on the tables, opera on the stereo, a Coco poster in the window. The waiters wore white shirts with black bow ties. They spoke with accents. We had antipasto, then pasta, then entrees. Along the way we drank three bottles of wine.

Evan was guzzling. He said tonight he was going to sleep even if it meant drinking himself into a coma. His eyes were red, his hair sticking out. It was Tuesday night, and he'd been awake since Sunday morning. He kept proposing toasts to Agnes and Maria and telling them that they looked like something out of a vision.

Which was true. Maria wore a white linen dress, pearl earrings, a pearl necklace. Agnes wore a short blue dress, high-heeled shoes, and black stockings which Evan informed me (when Maria and Agnes were in the ladies room) were held up by a black garter belt. In a dress, and without her glasses, Agnes seemed like a different person. It was like one of those movie transformations where the librarian lets down her hair and becomes a vixen.

Agnes asked Maria about this dognapping thing. Maria said

trucks from all the TV stations had been in the neighborhood that afternoon, causing a commotion. "I saw it on the news tonight," Agnes said, "and all I could think was, what's up with this lunatic who kidnapped the dog? What's his name? Wilson? And he just vanished? I can't believe they can't find him."

"Actually," Maria said, "he called Davio today. Davio didn't tell the reporters. He's trying to keep it quiet. But Wilson called him, and they talked for a few seconds, and then Wilson hung up."

Evan stared down at his plate. His facial tic had suddenly returned: the muscles in the right side of his face were going into spasms.

"The cops played back the tape," Maria said. "They could hear people in the background speaking Spanish. They figure he's in South America."

I looked at Evan. He wouldn't look at me. His right eye was blinking wildly: he looked as if he were sending Morse Code signals with it.

"That guy must be scared to death," Agnes said. "I mean, wherever he is, he's out there, he's got his dog back, but now what's he going to do? It's like people who steal paintings from museums. What can they do with them? And it's probably not too easy to hide a dog, right? It's kind of romantic, though. He must really love his dog. I kind of feel bad for him."

Maria said if Agnes felt bad for the guy now, just wait until Giaccalone and his friends caught up with him, because then there would really be something to feel bad about. "Nobody gets away with something like this," she said. "I mean, stealing from the—you know." She lowered her voice. "Stealing from people like Davio? You've got to be crazy. Davio says he doesn't care what it costs, he's going to find the guy. He says he's going to cut off Wilson's hands and nail them up on the wall of his café."

"Would you pass me the wine?" Evan said. He put his hand over his eye to stop it from blinking. As soon as he let go, it started blinking again. I handed him the bottle. He poured a glass and drank it off in two gulps.

The waiter arrived with our dinners. Agnes had ordered salt cod.

She said she'd never seen it on a menu in Boston, but she'd had it all the time when she was on her trip to Italy. Maria said she dreamed of going to Italy.

"You'd love it," Agnes said. "I went two years ago, with the woman who was my girlfriend at the time. She was Italian. I mean, not really Italian. Her parents were Italian. Or her grandparents. Whatever. She could speak a little bit."

Evan cleared his throat and asked Agnes about the word *girl-friend*: When she said that, did she mean a *girl* who was her *friend,* or did she mean a *girlfriend?*

Agnes and Maria burst out laughing.

"What?" Evan said. "I don't get it. Did you get it?"

"No," I said. "I did not get it."

Maria said she wanted to go to Sicily and find the village where her family came from. Agnes said Sicily had been her favorite place. "The people are beautiful. The women! They've got this amazing thick black hair—like yours."

She reached out and touched Maria's hair. Maria blushed.

"Here," Agnes said, "try some of this." She cut a piece of her salt cod and put it on Maria's plate.

"Then you try some of this," Maria said, and gave Agnes a piece of her osso buco.

Evan and I were trading looks. I wasn't sure, but it seemed to me that Evan's date was hitting on my date, and my date seemed not to mind. I am not a prude—at least, I don't like to think so—but I have to admit that this was freaking me out. Agnes refilled Maria's wine-glass, and asked Maria if she liked the salt cod. Maria said she wished she'd ordered it.

"Really?" Agnes said. "Because I wish I'd ordered yours."

They traded plates. I looked at Evan. He was eating steak. I was eating salmon.

"Forget it," he said.

Evan asked Maria if she'd heard anything from the Peace Corps. She told him she was still waiting. There was a huge list, she said.

Evan said he still found it amazing that people were duking it out over the chance to go work for free. Maria said, yes, it was incredible, but there actually were people who wanted to do something meaningful with their lives. Evan said money and meaning were not mutually exclusive. For example, we were going to make lots of money *and* we were going to change the world.

Maria said that with all due respect, she thought a piece of software that let you shop on the Web was very nice but it wasn't the kind of thing for which you won the Nobel Prize. If you really wanted to talk about changing the world, you could look at people like Jonas Salk, or Watson and Crick. Someone like Bill Gates was not even in the same league.

Agnes said she agreed. She said it was cool what Maria was doing. "People get all hyped up about money," Agnes said, "but there are more important things than money."

"Really? Name five," Evan said.

That did it. Agnes launched into a tirade in which she denounced capitalism and said her father had been laid off from his job after twenty years and Nike paid Asian workers fifty cents a week and American corporations shipped toxic waste over the border to Mexico and poisoned people. What any of this had to do with what we had been talking about, I had no idea. I half-expected her to stand up and start singing the "Internationale."

Finally she fell back against her chair, out of breath. Evan put on a TV announcer's voice and said, "Thank you, Mr. Marx, and now back to our regularly scheduled pogrom."

The waiters started clearing our table. I got up in search of the men's room. When I returned, the conversation had turned to *Star Trek*. Apparently there was a movie marathon coming up, twelve hours of Kirk and Spock and the rest of the crew pretending to fall sideways as the *Enterprise* received enemy fire. Evan and Agnes were planning to go, and they wanted us to go with them. Agnes said we could all dress up as characters. Maria could be Lieutenant Uhuru, and I could be Scotty, or Bones. She told Maria about Klingons and

Romulans, about Kirk and Picard, and about the difference between Trekkers and Trekkies. "Trekkies," she said, "are people who like the show, while Trekkers are basically insane losers who have no life. The kind of people who invent a Klingon dictionary, and actually can speak the language."

"For example," Evan said, "I'm a Trekkie, and Agnes is a Trekker."

"That's bullshit!" Agnes said. She was not as drunk as Evan, but she was close. "You've got a Spock outfit! You wear Spock ears at work!"

"You've got a Yeoman Rand costume!" Evan said.

They had been getting louder all night. But this exchange was loud enough that the people at the next table, two middle-aged couples, turned in their seats and glared at us.

"Yeoman Rand," Evan said, in his Spock voice, "we're receiving hostile signals from life forms in an adjacent galaxy."

"Set phasers to stun," Agnes said.

They turned and began firing, making laser-gun noises. One of the men, a thin guy with blond hair and glasses, tried to flag down a waiter. We were saved when the lights went down and a waiter came out carrying a cake covered in candles and singing "Happy Birthday." Everybody in the restaurant joined in, except for the people at the table next to us, who sat there looking unhappy.

I leaned over to Agnes. "Was it a surprise?" I said. "Did you know this was coming?"

The waiter, however, set the cake down in front of me. There were twenty-five candles, and the words HAPPY BIRTHDAY, MONKEY BOY written across the top. People were clapping.

"I'm sorry," Maria said. "I told them. I hope you're not mad. Are you one of those people who doesn't like surprise parties?"

I started to tell her that I didn't know, since nobody had ever thrown me a surprise party before—but before I could say anything, Evan shouted, "Hey, Mister Fucking Loser, you think you can have a birthday and not tell us? Huh?" He grabbed me by the throat and pretended to throttle me.

"Buddy," I said, and made a gesture for him to calm down. The people at the next table were shaking their heads. The man with the blond hair said something about moving to a different table. Evan either didn't hear him or didn't care. He stood up and addressed the room. I'd never seen him this drunk. He put his hand on my shoulder and said, "This joker turned twenty-five and he didn't tell us!" His accent had grown stronger. He might have been back on the streets of the Bronx. "We're his best friends, and he didn't tell us! I want to make a toast, to the biggest lying sack of shit I've ever known!"

The two couples at the table next to us got up and headed for the door. Somebody said, "Oooooh," and Evan said, "Hey, people spend fifty bucks for dinner and they expect the whole world to turn into a Merchant-Ivory movie, right?" Everyone burst out laughing. The guy who was holding the door for the others followed them out and slammed the door behind him, which only made everyone laugh even harder. The maître d' ran out into the street.

"And this," Evan announced, pointing to Maria, "is his beautiful girlfriend, who arranged this whole surprise, and who loves him very much, for reasons I can't understand." I looked at Maria. She looked away. "Okay, she's never actually said that she loves him. But it's true. And look at her! Then look at him! This woman actually is attracted to this man. And if he doesn't marry her, I'm going to take him out and have him shot! A toast to Maria! Hey! *Mazeltov!*"

Another cheer went up. Our waiter came over and urged Evan to sit down so that he could cut the cake. Outside, the people who had been sitting next to us were arguing with the maître d', waving their arms and pointing at Evan.

"I love you, man," Evan said, and gave me a hug. "Now blow out the candles! Come on! Make a fucking wish, buddy!"

I took a deep breath, and blew them out. Another cheer went up from the room. The cake was chocolate with chocolate frosting, my favorite. We gave out pieces to everybody in the restaurant.

Evan asked me what I'd wished for. I told him I had wished that he would pass out soon.

"Come on!" he shouted, "tell the fucking truth!"

I looked at Maria. She was smiling. I suppose she knew what I had wished for. And maybe my wish was coming true, because deep down inside me I felt something letting go, like ice on a river melting in the springtime, cracking and breaking free. My grandfather used to say that he had fallen in love with my grandmother because of her kindness. To me, this was baffling; I was fifteen years old, and kindness was not on the list of things I was looking for in a girlfriend. But now, all these years later, I understood.

"Should I say what I wished for?" I asked Maria.

She shook her head. "You might jinx it."

Outside, the men were shoving bills at the maître d'. He came back inside, rolling his eyes. He was a small man with a little mustache that looked as if it had been drawn onto his lip with a pencil. He looked like a circus ringmaster; and felt like one too, no doubt. "These people! I offered them free desserts, compliments of the house. They don't understand somebody wants to have some fun. No harm, right? A little fun. But please, if I can ask you, please keep it down now, okay?"

Evan and Agnes got up and thanked him for being so obliging. Agnes kissed him. He smiled. Who could resist? They asked him if he would take them to the kitchen so that they could thank the rest of the staff. A moment later we could hear Evan telling the chef what a fucking great fucking chef he was.

Maria leaned over. She kissed my cheek. "So, do you think you're going to get what you wished for?" she said.

"I don't know." I turned in my chair. "Is there a Porsche parked outside?"

"Bastard."

"Darling."

"Don't call me that."

"Sweetheart." I took her hand, and pressed it to my lips. Her fingers were slender and delicate, her nails painted red. "You know what I wished for," I said.

"Do I?" Her voice was petulant, her mouth twisted into a pout. "Maybe you'd better tell me."

"I thought you said that would jinx it."

"That's a chance you'll have to take."

I leaned close, and whispered in her ear. "Hmmm," she said, and laughed. "That's a good wish." I kissed her neck, and breathed in her perfume. She lifted her head and gave me more of her neck. I told her about the rest of my wish. She gave a throaty laugh, and turned and kissed me.

Her lips were soft. Her mouth tasted of chocolate, and other flavors—salt, fish, wine, garlic—and as we kissed, I imagined all of the other tastes of her body: the ripe smell of her feet, the dank flavor in the spaces between her toes, the salt in the small of her back, the musk of her armpits and behind her knees. I kissed her neck, tasting the tiny beads of moisture that had formed there. She sighed. I drew my finger down along the inside of her arm into the crook of her elbow. She pushed her chair back from the table. She smoothed her dress, and tried to appear calm. "Come on," she said. "Let's go home."

N EXT MORNING we showed up in the Duane room at the appointed time and took our seats in front of the video conference cameras. Lull was already there. He wasn't looking as gleeful as he had been the day before. I didn't know if this was a good sign or a bad sign.

"I'm ready for my closeup, Mr. DeMille," Evan said. He had spent the night with Agnes and was madly in love with himself. He leaned toward the camera, pursing his lips. The technician ignored him. Probably he had only heard that joke about the closeup a few million times. The technician was enormously fat, and was wearing oversized clothing that was meant to make him seem smaller: his T-shirt could have housed a revival meeting, and the pockets on his denim shorts were the size of legal pads. He looked like a kindergartner who had been subjected to some bizarre growth-hormone experiment.

"So how'd it go?" Evan said, leaning back beside me.

The last time I had seen him was outside the restaurant, getting into a cab with Agnes.

"Fine," I said.

"And? What happened? Come on, girlfriend, give it up. Talk to Oprah, honey. Has the Eagle landed?"

"Roger that, Houston."

"Holy mother of God." He slapped me on the back. "I'm proud of you, son. You've given up your domicile on Queer Street and rejoined the company of men. Welcome back."

"Thanks. It's great to be here."

"So what was she like?"

I looked at him.

"Okay, strike that," he said. "Look, we should celebrate. We'll do something tonight, okay?"

I said we might want to hold off on celebrations until we saw what happened on the video conference. From the way Lull was acting, I had the sense that we might not be sending out for champagne. Lull was sitting a few feet away, trying to pretend that he wasn't listening to our conversation. He looked like a mourner at a funeral— bored, sad, his face as gray as the carpet and chairs.

"Okay, let's try this again," the technician said, wheezing from the exertion of connecting and disconnecting cables.

The screen came up. We caught a glimpse of Whit. Then we lost the signal. The technician fiddled with the cameras. He disconnected the cables and reconnected them. He shut the screen off and turned it back on. Whit's face flickered and went out. He was trying to say something; the audio signal was garbled.

"What's going on?" Evan said. "We're meeting with Whit? Where's he calling from?"

Lull didn't answer. Suddenly the signal held, and there was Whit. "I've got a migraine," he said. "We'll have to keep this short." His face was distorted on the screen; it looked wider, moon-shaped. He was wearing a white shirt, the pockets stuffed with pens. He was in the Ionic offices in San Mateo, where it was now six o'clock in the morning.

There were the usual jokes about the Great and Powerful Oz, the requisite nervous laughter. Then Whit said he was going to tell us straight out: He was pulling the plug on Nectar. "We had to move up the decision," he said. "I'm sorry. Microsoft has something that they're going to announce next month and ship by fall COMDEX. They're six months ahead of you guys, maybe more. Maybe a year. It's that Elvis project."

"I thought they killed that," Evan said.

"They did," Whit said. "And now Gates has unkilled it. Elvis is alive. The King lives."

Earlier in the year the Cringely column in *Infoworld* had run a rumor about Microsoft working on a Web-based shopping assistant that was code-named "Elvis." A few weeks later, *PC Week* shot down the rumor in its Spencer F. Katt column, saying that Gates had decided that the project wasn't viable. Whit hired someone to do some snooping. The conclusion he reached was that *PC Week* was right: the Elvis project had been shelved.

"Are you sure about this?" Evan said, his voice rising. He was clutching the edge of his seat, his knuckles turning white.

"A hundred percent," Whit said.

"You've seen the code?"

"With my own eyes. Don't ask how."

We never knew how Whit got his information. There were all sorts of espionage stories: bugs in the rooms at the Airport Marriott in San Francisco, spies who hung out in bars in Kendall Square. Supposedly there were people who made hundreds of thousands of dollars doing nothing but buying and selling rumors. For this reason we were forbidden to talk about Nectar in public places, and we were not allowed to bring diskettes into or out of the building. Every software company had the same policy. But still, word got around.

"So how is it?" Evan said. "How's the code?"

"Not as good as Nectar would have been, if that makes you feel better. It's not as ambitious. But it's clean. And anyway, that's not the issue at this point. It's not a matter of whose code is better. It's just numbers. We ran the numbers, the cost of productizing, testing, packaging, advertising, plus the cost of all the development we've put into it already, and we measured that against what we can expect to get back, what kind of market share we could get and what that would be worth, and we can't make the numbers work. It sucks, I know. But it's not personal, okay? It's business. It's numbers."

"Numbers," Evan said. He stared into the screen, clenching and unclenching his fists.

"I'm going to give you guys some time off," Whit said. "When something like this happens, it's like a death. You have to go through all the stages. Anger, denial, grief. So do that. Take some time to heal. And then we'll get you going on something else, okay? All right? Buck up. We're expecting big things from you guys, okay? I'll see you soon. We'll talk when I get back."

The screen went blank. Lull sighed. He was trying not to seem too happy. But I knew he must be loving this.

Evan stood up. "Well," he said, "I've been waiting a long time to say this." He took off his ID badge and handed it to Lull. "Bob," he said, "the day you've been waiting for has finally arrived. I quit."

Lull put the card on the table. He said he was going to pretend he hadn't heard that.

"Well," Evan said, "tell me if you hear this." He leaned toward Lull and whispered, "Fuck you, ass-munch."

He marched out of the room. I started after him. But Lull stopped me. "Close the door," he said. "Sit down. Hear me out for a second."

He talked about being an adult and accepting responsibility and learning how to fail and how even though things might look bad right now I could still have a good career at Ionic and maybe I ought to think about distancing myself from certain people and mwah mwah mwah mwah . . . he sounded like one of the adults in a *Peanuts* cartoon. I watched his mouth moving, heard sounds coming from him, and I nodded and answered, like a hypnotized patient, and all I could think was that this bad news could not have happened on a better day because I was still blissed out by the events of the night before, still living in a kind of haze, and nothing was going to ruin my mood.

Maria and I had gone to her apartment and everything that was supposed to happen did happen. All of my parts were back in working order. The curse had been broken. In theory, we had gone upstairs to have coffee. I was standing in the living room, looking at the photographs of her family, and when I turned around she was taking off her clothes.

She led me to her bedroom. The air was hot. The windows were open. In one window, a fan whirred. Outside, there were sounds in the street: people laughing, joking with each other, a car horn tooting. Maria laughed as we got undressed; we were like kids getting ready to go skinny-dipping, and dove into bed the way you might dive into a pond, slipping quickly under its surface. We lay together in her bed, talking, kissing, listening to the voices coming up from the street, and there was none of the awkwardness that I had thought there would be. I've always wanted to be one of those James Bond guys who knows what to do; but instead I've always been a dork. I never know how to proceed. Do we undress each other, or do we undress ourselves? When we finally do manage to get naked, will she like my body? Will she think I'm clumsy? Will I be able to get it up? And if I do, will I last long enough? If I don't, will she laugh at me behind my back? One of my friends in college learned to his dismay that his ex-girlfriend referred to him as "Flu Shot Pete"—as in, "A flu shot lasts longer than Pete does." God only knew what my nickname might be. Needle-dick? Shrimpy? Peanut?

But with Maria, somehow, it was different. Maybe it was the wine. But things just happened, and although I don't think I was anywhere close to James Bond, I wasn't a dork, either. The condom was in the drawer beside the bed, suspiciously handy, but at that point who complains?

Afterward our clothes were strewn everywhere around the room, like debris after a plane crash. Maria got out of bed. I lay on top of the sheets, listening to her in the kitchen, pouring glasses of water for us. The fan blades thrummed the air, a low drone that made me sleepy. She came back with the water, and put my glass on the table near the window. Already we had fallen into a pattern; this was going to be my side of the bed. This table would be where I put my watch and my water glass and whatever book I was reading.

I slid down into the bed. She slid down beside me. We kissed. The room was dark, the bed was soft, and I was exhausted; I felt myself sinking. She rolled over onto her side, and pulled my arm around her waist.

She slept quietly, her body rising and falling under the sheet, her hair fanned out across her pillow. For a little while I managed to sleep, too. But then I woke up, and for most of the night I lay awake, staring at the ceiling. At six, I got up out of bed and hunted for my clothes. I left a note on the table on Maria's side of the bed, next to her water glass. Then at the door I stopped. I couldn't slip out on her like that. I went back and put my hand on her arm and said, "Maria."

She woke slowly, her eyes still half-shut.

"I have to go," I said.

"What time is it?"

"Six."

She groaned. "Call me later."

Outside, pale sunlight lay in bands across the buildings. The air was cool. The smell of fresh bread drifted from the bakeries. Birds sang on the telephone wires. At home, Coco was waiting for me. She was freaked out from having been left alone all night. She scurried around in circles, leaping and whimpering, following me wherever I went—even into the bathroom, where she stood beside the tub while I took a shower, and then into my bedroom, where she watched me get dressed. You have to feel bad for greyhounds. For years they're kept like prisoners, and all that isolation makes them needy.

Coco carried her rubber mailman into the bedroom and dropped it at my feet. We played fetch for a while, and then we sat on the couch and watched TV. On Channel Five they were showing a tape made the afternoon before: Skip, the weatherman, was outside in Government Center wearing a chef's outfit and frying eggs on the sidewalk. On my way to work I stopped at a florist on Hanover Street and ordered a dozen roses to be delivered to Maria at the store.

A LITTLE GROUP had gathered in our office: Nabeel and Upendra; Agnes and her friend Sylvia, a Goth girl from the QA caverns; and Jake, a guy from testing who had been friends with Evan since college. People come out of the woodwork to witness bad news firsthand; I suppose it's the same as motorists slowing down to see a car crash. Also present was Meghan, the legal department secretary, who had shown up for no reason, just looking to say hi, but had chosen the absolute worst day ever to do this. She had been hustled into the room partly against her will and now stood there looking as if she wanted to leave but didn't dare say so.

Evan and I were sitting in chairs, and the others were all standing around us, like mourners at a wake.

"Dude," Jake said to Evan, "at least you'll get some vacation time, right?"

Evan didn't laugh. He just sat there looking as if smoke might start coming out of his ears. I wished I could be like him, all pissed off and indignant. I wished I could feel angry, or sad, or upset, or something. But I felt nothing. It was the same way when my grandfather died and all of his old VFW buddies showed up and they were blubbering and crying and I couldn't understand why. My grandmother was crying too, although more quietly. She kept turning her face away, as if she wanted to keep her tears to herself. I could not squeak out a single tear, even though I was the one who had come home from school and found him collapsed in the driveway, his face blue-gray, the color of the wool suit he would wear in the casket. It was February, and he had been shoveling snow, which he knew he wasn't supposed to do. At the calling hours I stood looking down at his rouged face and thinking that really there must be something wrong with me for not being more upset.

"You'll get extra options," Nabeel said. "Next pay period, you'll get a second envelope. Wait and see. A thousand shares, maybe two thousand."

Evan said what the fuck did he care about options because options didn't mean anything until you were vested and he certainly wasn't going to stay here long enough to become vested.

"Don't talk like that," Upendra said. "Take the vacation, use the bonus money, whatever. Think things over. And then if you want to quit, fine. But don't go off half-cocked."

"He's right, dude," Jake said.

Evan sat there, rocking back and forth in his chair, muttering about what an asshole Whit was, and how Whit had lied to us, and how management sucked, and they were all a bunch of phonies. Everyone kind of muttered along.

There's nothing that middle-class white kids like better than being able to play the role of rueful workers rising up against their greedy capitalist overlords. Agnes and Sylvia once had helped organize an effort to unionize the employees at Ionic. They wore buttons, handed out leaflets. The issue was put to a vote and shot down immediately. Unions are fine for the little moles and proles, people in dinosaur industries, garment workers and auto riveters, people who wear shirts with their names sewn onto them. But software developers like to think they're different.

"They all suck," Jake said.

"Totally," Agnes said.

"Definitely," Sylvia said.

Meghan turned to me, looking for help. She'd only come over to say hello, and now look what she'd got herself into. She was wearing a skirt and blouse and shiny black high-heeled shoes. She looked like the lone adult in a group of skateboard punks. Agnes and Sylvia made a point of ignoring her. Somewhere in their manifesto there must have been an item declaring that women who wore makeup were considered the enemy—unless the makeup consisted of black lipstick and vampire eye shadow.

"Management, dude," Jake said. "You know? What does that word even *mean*? I mean, what are they managing, right? It's all just about money."

Everyone muttered and mumbled and grumbled. I tried to play along, but I couldn't really muster up any anger at Whit, or Mort, or Lull, or any of them. What was there to be angry about?

Outside, the zombies were gathered in little clusters in their veal pens, talking in low voices and nodding in our direction. No doubt they all enjoyed seeing us get wiped out. And why not? We'd been jerks to them from day one. Every so often a zombie would walk by our window and glance in and then look away.

One of them, a little red-haired guy named Larry Gay, actually stopped and stared at us through our window. He stood there, slope-shouldered, sipping his coffee, his eyes moving back and forth between Evan and me. Larry Gay had been in ARAD years ago and then had been demoted. He was divorced, and lived in the Back Bay. He mumbled when he spoke, and never looked you in the eye. Now, however, he had become emboldened: he stared right at us. His face was blank. Evan gave him the finger. Larry Gay sipped his coffee and kept staring. Then he walked away. Evan got up and closed the blinds. He launched into a harangue about Lull ("He's a dick, he'll do anything to save his ass, he sold us down the river"), which was interrupted when Janet Scuto knocked on the door.

"I know this, um, isn't the best time," she said, trying not to smile, "but now that you're not, um, *under deadline,* I wanted to talk to you about a certain coffeepot that was ruined recently."

Evan picked up a mug and held it in his hand, as if weighing it. Then he turned and fired the mug at Janet Scuto's head. He missed, but not by much. The mug smashed into the wall and burst into little pieces.

"That's it!" Janet said, and ran off.

Meghan moved toward the door, keeping an eye on Evan, who now had turned to face the window and was rocking in his chair like an autistic child. No doubt Meghan realized that being in a room where mugs were being thrown at people's heads was not likely to be viewed positively when the next six-month review rolled around. She said good-bye (actually, I believe she said *"Ciao"*) and then ran off before security could arrive.

Security did arrive—two fat guards who carried what appeared to be real guns. They were followed by Lull and by Janet Scuto, who kept shouting, "Son of a bitch! Son of a bitch!" The guards asked everyone what had happened and at first we all played dumb, but then the guards started finding shards of mug in the carpeting and Evan admitted that yes, he'd thrown a mug, but he'd thrown it well over Janet Scuto's head and only to scare her.

Janet Scuto insisted that the guards call the police so that she could file charges. One of the security guards reached for his radio. But Lull managed to smooth things over. He convinced the security guards that a compromise was in order: Evan would leave the building, Janet could take the rest of the day off, and the police would not need to be called. So Evan left, under escort from the guards. Agnes went with him, and Sylvia went with Agnes. Nabeel and Upendra drifted away too, mumbling something about meeting for drinks later on.

I closed my door and called Maria. I was wondering how much of a disappointment I had been in bed. Women try to be kind—they say, "Wow, that was really . . . *nice.*" Maria hadn't said anything like that. Not exactly, anyway. But I could tell that the earth hadn't moved. Women will tell you it doesn't matter, that they don't need to have an orgasm every time. But how can it not matter? You know they're always waiting for that one guy, the *über*-lover, the one who knows precisely what to do.

Evan's theory was that you shouldn't worry about competing against that imaginary guy because that imaginary guy did not exist, and the reason he did not exist was because there was no way on earth to give a woman guaranteed orgasms, no matter who you were. The female orgasm was too unpredictable. There was no fixed set of techniques; hence, no way to practice. Clockwise? Counterclockwise? Hard, soft? Gentle, rough? Talk dirty, talk sweet? Don't talk at all? And you couldn't even focus on one woman and get it just right with her, because every woman was different every time. "Imagine if every time you played Quake, all the keys did something different," Evan said. "You couldn't be blamed if you didn't make it to the next level."

Evan said the female orgasm was part of a feminist conspiracy whose goal was to destroy patriarchy. Sometime in the late sixties or early seventies women had figured out a kind of jujitsu strategy, which involved using our own male psychology against us. "They give us a task," Evan said, "knowing that we'll take the challenge, because we have to, because men are task-oriented. It's wired into our circuitry. We can't resist. But at the same time we can't succeed. It's like feeding us an infinite loop and letting us cycle and cycle. *Voilà*. We're hoisted on our own petard. And they take over."

I tried not to blame myself for what had or had not happened with Maria. And I knew that asking her might only make things worse. But I couldn't help myself.

"I've been thinking," I said. "About last night."

"Great." She groaned. "Here we go."

"What?"

"You're freaking out, right? The commitment thing, right? Jesus. I knew it. Hold on. I want to go to another phone."

In the background I heard customers talking, and then Gus chortling. Maria picked up the phone in the office and called to Gus and told him to hang up.

"Just once in my life," she said, "I'd like to sleep with a guy and have him not immediately run away. Hold on." I heard papers rustling, a chair scraping on the floor, a door shutting. "Okay, I'm sitting down. So let's get it over with."

"Get what over with?"

"Whatever it is you're going to tell me."

"I just called to say hi. Did you get the flowers?"

"You sent me flowers?"

"I ordered them this morning. At Bonetto's. They're right around the corner from you."

"They're slow. It's okay. You sent me flowers?"

Someday I'd like to be suave, even for a day. I'd like to know how to dance, and how to say something charming. I'd like to sweep a woman off her feet, instead of stepping on her toes. I'd like to order flowers and have them arrive without me giving away the surprise.

"I wasn't calling about the flowers," I said. "It's just . . . I don't know. I was worried. About last night. Because I thought that maybe, you know, because you didn't . . ."

"Didn't what?"

"You know."

"Oh, *that,*" she said. "I would have. I mean, it's not that I don't like to do it or anything."

"That's not what I'm talking about," I said. "What I mean is, you didn't . . . well, I wasn't sure if you, like, *enjoyed yourself,* you know?"

"Oh my God. Is that the new euphemism?"

"You didn't, right?"

She paused. I could hear her breathing. "I can't believe we're having this conversation," she said.

"Why? Did you?" A glimmer of hope shone before me.

"No," she said. "I didn't."

"Oh."

"Reilly, don't be weird, okay? Don't be Mr. Sensitive New-Age Guy, Mr. I-Won't-Quit-Until-You-Have-One, because women hate that, okay? It's passive-aggressive. And it's not even about the woman; it's about the guy trying to earn his little merit badge. That's why women start faking it. And I refuse to do that, okay? So look. It was fine. I enjoyed it. It was really nice."

There it was: the N-word. I groaned. "*Nice?* Maria, I'm shriveling up here. My manhood is curling up like a fiddlehead fern."

She told me to relax, that it was always weird the first time.

"You have to get used to someone," Maria said. "The first time, even the first few times, you just have to get through those, so you can get to the other side."

"So you see this phase we're in now as a kind of endurance exercise."

"I'm not saying I didn't enjoy it."

"I hope so. You made enough noise."

"Shut up."

"And it's really weird, because, well, you'd never suspect it, I mean, just from knowing you, you'd never suspect that you were such a demon. But look, it's okay, right? Loud is good."

"Just shut up, okay?"

"That's what I wanted to tell *you*," I said. "'Shut *up*, lady! *Keep it down!*' I thought I was going to have to put a pillow over your face before somebody called the cops: 'Hey, get here right away—there's a woman being strangled to death! Somebody's killing a cat!'"

"Now you've made me self-conscious. Maybe we'd better not do it again."

"I wouldn't go that far."

"I didn't think so. But look, I want you to tell me the truth. Do you think we're moving too fast? Is it freaking you out? You didn't sleep very well."

"I never sleep well."

"Maybe you feel like I'm pushing you into something."

"Or maybe you're projecting."

"Or maybe you," she said, "are projecting your projection onto me."

"You're the one who brought this up."

"And you're the one who called me."

"I had to call you. It's protocol. You sleep with someone, the next day you've got to make the Call."

"So this is a duty call," she said. "You didn't want to talk to me, you just had to, because of some rule in your *Boy Scout Guide to Dating.* How charming."

"*Chahming,*" I said.

"Don't start on that."

"*Staht?*"

"When you make everything into a joke it just makes me think that you're freaking out."

"I'm not freaking out," I said. "I'm feeling very Zen about this. Which is how we both should be. We should take a Buddhist approach."

"You mean shave our heads, the whole thing?"

"Right, that's it. Exactly."

"Do we have to sell flowers at the airport?"

"Those are Hare Krishnas."

"I thought they were Moonies."

"Moonies work the traffic coming out of the airport, at the Callahan Tunnel."

"So which are we going to be?"

"We're going to be Buddhists. It's a different thing altogether."

"Do we sell flowers?"

"No."

"Do we wear robes?"

"No."

"What do we do?"

"We live in the moment. We take things as they come."

"I see." She paused. "So basically what you're saying is that you're freaking out."

"I'm not freaking out."

"You don't sound optimistic."

"I just lost my job," I said.

"You've still got your job."

"You know what I mean."

"Well, if you do start freaking out, if you start getting cold feet, if you feel like you're not ready for this, just tell me, okay? Don't keep me in the dark. Keep me informed. We can talk about things, all right? We can communicate."

"I can communicate," I said. "If I want out, I'll tell you."

"Great. And then I'll have you killed. Okay, sweetie?"

"Nice."

"I'm just trying to be honest."

"Okay, *sweetie.*"

"See you tonight?"

"Do I have a choice?"

"Not really."

We hung up. I leaned back in my chair. I laughed out loud. Here the soundtrack swells, the string section soars: Love had returned. Life was good. Outside, a swath of sunshine sparkled on the river. The Hancock and Prudential towers loomed above the rooftops of the Back Bay, their windows glinting. Nectar was history. I was free. I felt as if I could fly. For the first time in months I had nothing to worry about. I could go home early. I could sleep late. I could slack off. I felt like Data, on *Star Trek,* learning what it's like to have emotions. *So this,* I thought, *is happiness. How . . . extraordinary.*

The moment quickly passed, however, when I saw that an e-mail notice had popped up on my screen, FR: JEANIE_SULLIVAN. For a long time I sat there, staring at the monitor. There was a tingling inside me, as if a cord that ran through my body were being slowly tightened, like a piano wire. I couldn't believe this. I told myself to choose "Delete," or even "Read Later." Instead, I clicked "Read Now," and held my breath, not knowing what to expect.

A N HOUR LATER I was pulling a truly bastardly stunt: I was sitting across from Jeanie in a booth at Pop's Diner in Central Square and wondering how I would break the bad news to Maria. I really couldn't believe this was happening. Twelve hours after sleeping with Maria I was having lunch with Jeanie. I didn't know karma could work that fast.

Jeanie was wearing jeans and a T-shirt. Her hair was dirty, pulled behind her ears. She put down her menu and stared off into the distance. She looked as if she had just got up out of bed and still didn't know where she was. "This place is ghastly," she said.

Pop's was a retro diner, the kind of place that never seems authentic if only because of all of the effort that has been put toward making it seem authentic. The tables were edged with stainless steel, the floor was done in black-and-white linoleum tiles, and the walls were decorated with neon signs: BREAKFAST ALL DAY! EAT! FREE JAVA REFILLS! The music was all fifties—Buddy Holly, Bill Haley. The menu boasted items such as "Vanilla Shake Rattle 'n' Roll" and "Beantown Franks 'N Beans," which cost a decidedly nonretro fourteen dollars and ninety-five cents. The waitresses wore old-fashioned pale blue polyester uniforms with names like *Bonnie* and *Millie* sewn onto the front in yellow cursive letters. Our waitress was about twenty years old, a little Ivory Soap girl with big blue eyes and big pale breasts. The name on her dress was *Francine*.

Jeanie took out a pack of Marlboros. She shook out a cigarette, lit it, and blew a cloud of smoke up into the air above our heads. She looked at me. I was staring. I'd never seen her smoke.

"Don't start, okay?" she said. "Just don't."

"Rock Around the Clock" came on the jukebox. A bunch of businessmen, guys in their thirties wearing white shirts and ties, started drumming in unison on their table.

I told Jeanie about our meeting with Whit. She told me she'd heard about it. Of course she had. She'd probably known for days. "Evan threw a mug at Janet Scuto," I told her. "They made him leave the building."

She stubbed out her cigarette and said that Evan was an idiot. She had always hated Evan. He accused her of being an anti-Semite. She said she didn't hate Jews; just him. She asked me what I was going to do now. I made a bad joke about going to Disneyland. She didn't laugh. We sat there, gazing around. At one time we had been able to talk for hours; we would stay up all night, just talking. Now we couldn't get through lunch.

Francine brought our food. When she leaned across the table I saw her breasts, which were full and beautiful and milk-white, and ready, in my imagination, to spill out of her dress: I could imagine the rosy nipples that lay hidden beneath the fabric of her bra. How, one wonders, is it possible for a man who has spent the night making love to a beautiful woman, and who is now having lunch with yet another beautiful woman, to be startled and struck anew by the sight of a pair of breasts, as if he has never seen breasts before, as if he were a baby, roused and hungry, yearning for milk? I do not know. But there it is. I forced myself to look away, hoping Jeanie hadn't noticed. It used to drive her crazy if I looked at other women.

I had a steak bomb and a side of fries. Jeanie had a tuna sandwich and a glass of ice water. She stared at her plate, then pushed it away and lit another cigarette.

"So," she said. She tried to smile.

"So." My hands were shaking. I put them under the table. "I was surprised to hear from you."

More silence. She was not going to make this easy. She opened her purse, looked for something, then stopped looking.

"I need to talk," she said. "About us."

I read once about baseball players who can sometimes get into a zone where they can see a pitch coming toward them in slow motion. They can see the ball spinning. They can see every stitch. That's how I felt. I picked up my sandwich, but my throat was too tight and I knew I wouldn't be able to swallow. I put the sandwich down.

"I need to ask you a favor," Jeanie said. "As a friend."

I nodded. I had expected there would be conditions. No more roving eye, no more flirting with waitresses, no more lunch dates with secretaries.

"I want to call a truce," she said. "I need you to give me some space."

"I see," I said. "A truce."

"Right."

My face felt hot. "I didn't know we were at war," I said.

Suddenly she began to cry. Her shoulders were shaking. I took her hand. I asked her what was wrong. She said it was her father. He was sick. He had cancer. She started crying again. She was trying to catch her breath. The cancer was all through him, she said. His pancreas, his stomach. He'd gone to the doctor thinking he had the flu and found out he had six months, maybe less, to live.

Jeanie had gone to visit him over the weekend. Mort went with her. Until then she hadn't told Mort about her family. She hadn't told him anything. But on Friday she finally broke down. She asked him to go to the hospital with her. He agreed. That was Saturday. On Sunday morning, Mort called and said that he thought maybe they should take things a little more slowly with the relationship; this apparently was a Beacon Hill way of telling someone that you wanted to break up.

"What a bastard," I said.

She started crying again. "I'm sorry. You're the last person who wants to hear this, right? I'm sorry. But there's nobody else. I mean, there's nobody I can talk to. I don't see my shrink until Monday. I tried to get an appointment but he's booked. I don't know. I'm sorry. You don't want to hear this."

She got up and started to leave. I took her hand. I told her that no matter what, she'd always have me. "I'm crazy about you," I told her. "I'd take you back in a heartbeat."

"Oh, Reilly. That's not what I meant." She sat back down in the booth. Maybe she could see what I was thinking. Suddenly it seemed to dawn on her. "You thought—" she said. "Did you think—"

"No," I lied.

"You did, didn't you?"

"Okay," I said. "Yes. I guess so."

She took my hand. She told me she needed a friend. That was all. A friend. "Maybe that's asking too much," she said.

"No, it's fine." I smiled. I wished I meant it.

I could imagine Mort going over to the house in Dorchester, sitting in the den. I went there once, for Thanksgiving. I dreaded meeting Jeanie's dad. I knew all about him. I figured it would creep me out. And it did, in a way. Knowing what I knew. The old man was a wiry little guy, a little whippet, with a smoker's face and glassy eyes. He kept a portrait of Reagan on the wall of the living room and a stash of porno magazines in the basement. He worked at the post office. His table manners were atrocious. Eating dinner with him was like sitting in the front row at a Gallagher concert. You wanted to bring sheets of plastic. He drank Scotch and complained that the turkey was too dry. Jeanie's mother sat there not talking. She hated him as much as Jeanie did. Now that the old boy was sick, maybe she was happy. Who knew?

After dinner I had to go sit with him and the brothers in the living room. Jeanie's brothers were all like her father: dog-faced Irish guys in various stages of alcoholic decline. They swore in front of their kids and yelled to their wives to bring them more beer. We sat in big stuffed chairs and watched the Notre Dame game while the old man lectured me about college football. The more he drank, the louder he got. He told me stories from his mailman days—dogs he'd maced, kids he'd frightened.

"I know you're angry at me," Jeanie said. "But you have to let go. You can't stay angry. All anger does is destroy you. Look at my father. All his life he's been angry. Now it's eating away at him. You can't let that happen to you, Reilly."

I laughed. My head ached. I felt foolish and ashamed. I hated this diner: the smell of the fried food, the businessmen chortling and joking and ogling the waitresses, the waitresses flirting. All of life seemed ugly and grotesque, a mean and stupid entertainment. What were we? Why were we here? Look at this place, this fake place, with its shiny walls and neon signs and ridiculous music, and all of these people, these bags of atoms, moving and jabbering and tormenting each other, teasing each other and arousing each other, falling in and out of love—and to what end? What was the point? What was the point of love? Or work? Or computers? I felt myself growing smaller, like some stupid cartoon character, shrinking on a bench.

"I loved you so much," I said. I didn't care what she thought of me now. I was already a fool. It couldn't get any worse.

"I loved you, too," she said.

"So where does it go? Where does love go? How can you love someone and then not love them? How can we sit here with each other like this?"

"I don't know." She took my hand. "I don't think love goes away. Maybe it changes. But it doesn't go away."

She blinked. A tear fell from her eye. From the back of the room there came a crash and then a table of men burst into laughter. One of them whistled to a waitress and said, "Honey, get us some paper towels, would you?"

I stood up and took Jeanie's hand and led her toward the door. Outside it was a postcard day: bright sun, blue sky, no clouds, sailboats on the river. We held hands. I remembered how it had felt when we were first going out.

The night when she told me about what her father did to her, we were lying in bed at her apartment and I got so upset that I cried. He would come in at night, she told me. She had her own room. She would be lying there, awake, listening to him climbing up the stairs and hoping he would just go to bed. But then the door would open and the crack of light would move across the floor and up across the covers on her bed and she would smell the liquor on his breath, feel his hands at the bedspread, and she would pretend to be asleep for as long as she could. She had never told anyone about this, she said. But she trusted me. She said she felt as if we knew each other in some special way, as if we were two halves of the same person and we had been split apart a long time ago and now we had reconnected. I told her I knew what she meant because I felt that way, too.

And now I was feeling that way again, at least flickers of it, as we walked along the river toward Kendall Square. Buses heaved through the traffic, cabbies blew their horns, joggers ran along the path by the river, and nobody looked twice at two scruffy people standing at the end of the Longfellow Bridge, with their arms around each other and tears running down from behind their sunglasses. The world is full of heart-break and sorrow, they're everywhere, and nobody notices: We're worried about work, or bills, or errands; we're thinking about what we'll have for dinner. One evening in winter I was riding on the Green Line and there was an attractive woman—about thirty years old, well-dressed; a lawyer, maybe; she was carrying a briefcase. She was sitting by herself, in back, and sobbing. Not just little sniffles—big, heaving sobs. Everybody pretended not to see her. At the Government Center stop I got off and turned back and saw her sitting in the empty car, still sobbing, all by herself in the glare of the incandescent light.

Now, standing by the river with Jeanie, I thought of that woman and wondered again what her tragedy had been. And what had become of her? Where was she now? Was she happy? How hopeless the world can be: here we stood, Jeanie and I, with our lives falling to pieces, and there was nothing we could do for each other, and everybody was rushing past us, too busy to care.

"I'm sorry," I said. "For everything I ever did to you. I'm really sorry."

"I'm sorry, too," she said.

She put her hand on my face, like a blind person trying to read someone's features. I kissed her palm. I wondered whether it mattered that we were sorry. What good was it? There was nothing to do but stand there and cry. Which is what we did. Then we kissed, a real kiss, as if we had just met and we were kissing for the first time, as if none of the bad things had ever happened.

For a moment the old feelings were rushing through me and I wanted to remember forever the taste of her mouth, the softness of her lips. I wished I could have the memory of a machine, pure and perfect and complete, so that even when I was eighty years old I could open a file and replay this moment. But I knew I would forget. In a week, or a month, these sensations would fade—they would vanish, and disappear, like fog on the river, evaporating up and away. Even now the memories were fading: as quickly as things happened they began to erase themselves. In thirty years I wouldn't even remember Jeanie. She'd be—what? A footnote. A bunch of old letters saved on a diskette, a few photographs. Maybe that was a good thing.

We stepped apart. Jeanie smiled. She was the most beautiful woman I had ever known. It hurt me just to look at her. She brushed a lock of hair away from my face. Then she took my hand and we started walking. At the Ionic building we stopped, and hugged again, and I felt her body against mine, and it occurred to me that I would never touch her again, and I didn't want to let her go.

"If you need anything," I said. "If there's anything I can do."

"I know." She kissed me on the cheek. I stood outside, in the sunlight, and watched her walk into the lobby, her figure vanishing into the shade, growing smaller and dimmer, until at last she was gone.

I SPENT THE AFTERNOON trying to track down Evan. He'd gone to lunch with Agnes at a Mexican restaurant, and according to Agnes he had drunk four margaritas before stumbling down into a T station, saying he was going to go home and crash. When I called home, I got the machine. "He's probably passed out," Agnes said. I figured she was right. But when I got home, he wasn't there. Coco was sleeping on the couch. She barely noticed me. A vision flashed through my head: I could see Evan on the top of the Tobin Bridge, preparing to do a swan dive. I told myself not to think like that. I went downstairs and asked Maria if she'd seen him. She said he had come into the store and told her to tell me to meet him at the Frog Bar at seven o'clock. "He said it's important," she said.

She showed me the roses. She had put them in a vase out back, in the office. She was beaming. You can never underestimate the power of roses.

We went for iced cappuccinos at a café on Hanover Street, and Maria pointed out the two guys that Giaccalone had hired. They were standing at the corner, watching everybody who came into the neighborhood. It was six o'clock, and everyone was coming home from work. The sun was sliding below the rooftops; but still the heat was tremendous.

The "hired guys," as Maria called them, wore gray pants, blue blazers, and sunglasses. They must have been dying in those outfits. One was tall and thin, middle-aged, with gray hair and a pockmarked face: his cheeks looked like waffle irons. The other was younger, with a weightlifter's build and brushed-back hair.

"They look like security guards," I said. "They look like they should be working at a mall."

"Not quite," Maria said. She directed my attention to the bulges under their left arms. "They're from New York. Davio's paying a thousand dollars a day for them. He's raising the reward, too. It's going to be in the paper tomorrow. Ten thousand dollars. They're printing up new flyers tonight. He hired these guys to go door-to-door through the neighborhood. Davio figures maybe somebody knows something and they're not telling. It's like the Inquisition. They came to the store this afternoon. I mean, it's all very polite, but you can tell they mean business."

The older guy turned and looked at us. In the glare of the late sunlight, his face looked eaten away: he looked like the world's worst bee-sting victim. I picked up the *Herald* and pretended to be reading it. My hands were shaking.

"What's the matter?" Maria said.

I glanced over the top of the paper. The guy was still looking at us. I wondered if I should tell Maria about Coco. I had been thinking about telling her all day.

"We should go," I said. I stood up, and put some money on the table.

We walked past the goons. I could feel them staring at us. Maria said hello to them; they said hello back. They remembered her. At the corner we stood in a crowd of tourists, waiting for the light to change. Cars streamed out of the Callahan Tunnel, crawling all over each other, horns blowing. A bus lumbered forward, struggling to change lanes; it looked like a dinosaur caught in a tar pit. On the ramp to the Central Artery an ambulance sat trapped in the traffic, with its lights on and its siren wailing; nobody would move aside. On the sidewalk next to us a flower vendor was calling out: "Roses, tulips, cah-nations. Roses, tulips, cah-nations."

Mr. Bee-sting was still staring at us. I hoped that this was because he had a thing for Maria. I wondered if ever a woman had been able to get past that face of his and actually fall in love with him. I turned to the flower vendor and pretended to be interested in a bucket of tulips. Sweat formed on the back of my neck.

The light changed. We started across the street toward Faneuil Hall.

"Wait," I said. "Hold on."

I took her arm. We were standing in the middle of the crosswalk, with people shoving past us in both directions. "Get out of the way, for Christ's sake," somebody muttered.

Maybe I was making a big mistake. But seeing the goons had spooked me. I had to tell her. "There's something I have to show you," I said. "Back at the apartment."

Five minutes later Coco was standing up on her back legs, licking my face, and Maria was standing in the kitchen, looking pale and sick, as if she were seeing a ghost. "You know," she said, "sometimes I wonder if you really are dumb, or if it's just an act. But now I'm sure. Because clearly you're either retarded or you're mentally ill. You ought to be working on the grounds crew at Fenway Park with the rest of the mongoloids."

I told her there was nothing to worry about, that Giaccalone and his thugs would never suspect me and Evan. We were faggots, remember? Probably the thugs had already gone through our building and had passed by our apartment, like the angel of death passing over the Israelites in Egypt.

"The what?" she said.

"Forget it."

"I wish I could," she said. "I wish I could forget that I'd ever been here and seen this. Because you, my friend, are out of your mind."

I tried to defend myself. I told her how it had started as a prank and then got out of hand. I told her we were going to give the dog back as soon as we collected the reward. She asked me how we planned to do that. I said I wasn't sure. She looked as if she didn't know whether to laugh or cry or take a swing at me. She said we could take Coco downstairs right now. Nobody would see us. Lucia was out visiting her mother in East Boston. Gus was at home having dinner. The store was closed. "There's nobody around," she said. "Nobody will see us."

No way, I said. I wasn't going to let that dog go without the money.

"Reilly," she said, "if that dog is found here, it won't only be you that gets in trouble. It'll be Gus, too. And maybe even me. You get it? It's Gus's building. They'll blame him. You don't understand how these people think."

"Let's go out," I said. "Forget meeting Evan. We'll go get some dinner."

Coco was standing at my side, holding up her chew toy. I took it, tossed it, and off she ran. Maria stood there looking disgusted.

"We can go see a movie," I said.

She smiled. "Maybe some other time. Like when you get out of the hospital, maybe."

She opened the door.

"Maria," I said.

But she was already gone.

EVAN, NABEEL, AND UPENDRA were sitting at an outside table, and Evan was in the middle of a harangue which we had all heard before and which Nabeel referred to as Evan's "Why Boston Sucks" speech. The gist of it was that despite a few tall buildings and the presence of Starbucks, Boston was not a real city—not like New York or Los Angeles or San Francisco. Certainly not like London, Paris, Rome, Athens, Hong Kong. Boston was a provincial capital, a cultural backwater. There was no jazz scene. The sports teams sucked. The nightclubs closed at one-thirty. Black people walked into restaurants and were told that those empty tables were being held for people who had reservations.

"And this weather!" he said. "Can you stand it? I'm dying here. Look at my shirt. It's stuck to my fucking body!" He lifted his margarita. "Friends, I'm here to make you an offer. I'm moving to the West Coast, and I want you to come with me."

He was drunk but coherent. He had spent the afternoon in Sleepy Pete's, an arcade in Central Square, playing Mortal Kombat and beating junior high school kids out of their allowances. Now he was working on his fifth margarita and getting dangerous. Our waitress arrived: young, blond, vaguely preppy. They all looked like that. It was a requirement. I ordered a margarita. Evan said he'd take another one, too. The waitress said she had just brought him one. He said he would finish it by the time she got back. She looked perplexed. The bars in Faneuil Hall got busted all the time for serving people too many drinks. I told her we would be leaving in half an hour, and we would look after him. Nabeel and Upendra concurred.

"You see?" Evan said. "You see what I mean about Boston? She wasn't going to serve me! I'm not even fucking drunk! What's up with this town? All these little fake preppies, with their moccasins and their khaki pants. And all these faux-bos."

"Faux-bos?" Upendra said.

"Faux bohemians. Faux intellectuals." He waved his hand in the direction of the people around us. "These fucking NPR listeners, with their *Prairie Home Companion* T-shirts and their Labrador retrievers and their fucking Volvos."

He started singing the melody from *All Things Considered*. He was getting just loud enough to make me worried. The bar was full of fratboy types. Plus there was the regular quota of greaseball teenagers from East Boston and Revere. At the far end of the plaza, a mime was juggling bowling pins for a crowd in front of Quincy Market. Two beefy cops were leading a guy in handcuffs toward a paddy wagon.

"We should order some food," Nabeel said. He looked at me, then glanced at Evan, as if to make sure I understood. I nodded. We ordered nachos and quesadillas, and Evan said that now that everyone was present and accounted for, he could explain why he'd called us together. His plan was this: We would leave Ionic, move to San Francisco, and start a company of our own—Nectar Inc. "It's in our contract," he said. "If they fail to bring the product to market, the rights revert to us. You understand? They just made us millionaires."

Nabeel said he didn't want to rain on the parade, but had Evan considered that there might be a reason why Ionic had decided not to bring Nectar to market?

"Yes," Evan said, "because they're brain-dead. Because the company is run by marketing people who wouldn't know a line of C code if it jumped up and bit them on the ass."

Nabeel started to say something, then didn't. He sighed, smiled, and slumped back in his chair. Upendra looked as if he might burst out laughing; I prayed he wouldn't. Evan seemed not to notice. He said he had friends who could help us, guys he'd known at MIT. One was at Goldman Sachs; he could help us line up investors. Another was at McKinsey; he might agree to become president.

"We'll walk out of Ionic," Evan said, "and in twelve months we'll be millionaires. The day we go public I'm going to call Whit up on the video conference system and show him my ass and tell him he can kiss it." He looked at me. I didn't know what to say. Somewhere behind us two frat boys were singing the Bowdoin fight song. *"Rise, sons of Bowdoin, praise her name . . ."*

Nabeel said it was a nice revenge fantasy. Evan said it wasn't a fantasy, it was going to happen. Nabeel said Evan sounded like one of those guys who's in a local rock band and really, really believes he's going to be famous; and when you ask him what he'll do for a living if he doesn't become famous, he says, I don't know, because that's not going to happen, because I *am* going to be famous. "You know what I mean?" Nabeel said. "People think they can make something happen simply by refusing to believe that it might not happen. But that's not logic, that's madness. If you ask me, you should go ahead and get drunk and forget about it."

"I already am drunk," Evan said.

"So get drunker."

"Is it *drunker*?" Upendra said. "Is *drunker* a word? I thought it was *more drunk*."

"Drunker, more drunk—who cares?" Nabeel slid a napkin and a pen in front of Evan. "Here, write up your business plan. You can draw a little org chart, and put all of our names on it. Then go home and pass out, and we'll see you in the morning. And take a fucking shower, okay? You need one."

For a moment I thought Evan was going to hit him. But then he

said, in a calm voice, that he was going to make us all one last final official offer, right here and right now. "We'll take equal shares, the four
of us, and we'll work our asses off for six months, get the code into
shape, and we'll make enough money to live on for the rest of our
lives," he said.

Nabeel said he would have to take a pass. Evan said he was going
to write down on a napkin that on this exact date, in this exact spot,
Nabeel was offered a share in Evan's company and had turned it
down. He said Nabeel could keep this paper and show it to his grandchildren someday and tell them how he might have become rich. He
scribbled away on the napkin, and handed it to Nabeel. He began to
laugh; but it wasn't a happy laugh. It was an evil laugh, a threatening
laugh, the laugh of the movie villain who is about to put someone into
a vat of acid. Nabeel laughed back. For a long time they sat there
laughing at each other.

"You're going to be sorry," Evan said.

"I'm sure I will," Nabeel said.

"What about you?" Evan said. Meaning me.

I told him I was thinking about becoming a bike messenger.
When I first moved to Boston, I shared a house with a bunch of bike
messengers. They were happy people. They didn't worry about vested
options and 401(k) plans; they worried about car doors. "I've already
got the mountain bike," I said. "All I need are some hockey pads. It's a
good job. You're outside, you're getting exercise, you get a tan."

"You make four dollars an hour and cabbies hunt you for sport,"
Evan said.

"Plus," Upendra said, "you have to move to Allston and get your
face pierced and wear cutoff army pants with long underwear pants
underneath them. You have to go to the Middle East Café on week-
nights and listen to really shitty bands."

"Fair enough," I said.

Nabeel suggested a life of crime. The two of us could be partners. He said he'd always wanted to be a cat burglar, robbing jewelry
stores at night, that kind of thing. "A thief," he said, "but a cool thief.

Not a fucking bank robber, shooting people and shit. High-tech. We'll put on those really tight black clothes and slide through skylights and elude motion sensors."

"Are you sure you're heterosexual?" Evan said.

Nabeel said we already knew about computers. All we had to do was learn about security systems and police logistics. We would approach it like a profession. It was like doing arbitrage on Wall Street: You identify the opportunities, minimize the risk.

"Thank you, Charles Manson," Evan said. "Now back to business. No more fucking around." He drained his margarita. "I need to know if you'll come with me," he said. He wasn't kidding. I knew him well enough to know that. "I need an answer right now."

I tried to imagine the two of us living in California, running our own company. I thought about the time when we met with the guys from HotSpot, and I was the oldest person in the room, and it had frightened me to think that people like me were creating the future. Still, what did I have to lose? I was twenty-five years old. Even if we screwed up completely, I could still get a job.

"Okay," I told him. "I'm in."

THE NEXT DAY the *Herald* ran a photo of Giaccalone on the front page, with the headline: LOST DOG BRINGS $10K REWARD; *"She's Like My Child," Cafe Owner Says.* Giaccalone was holding a picture of Coco and looking distraught. Evan and I had both arrived at work carrying copies to show to each other. He had spent the night with Agnes, who had an air conditioner in her bedroom. I had spent the night with Coco, with a huge fan aimed at the bed; all the fan did, however, was move the hot air around. I hadn't been able to sleep. All I could do was lie there, sweating, and pray for the heat wave to end.

"Anyway," I said, "ten thousand bucks, right? I feel like goddamn Franco and Vanzetti."

"Excuse me?" he said. "Who?"

"With the Lindbergh baby," I said. "Franco and Vanzetti."

"First of all, Einstein, it was Sacco and Vanzetti—not Franco and Vanzetti. Franco and Vanzetti sounds like a fucking spaghetti sauce. Second, for your information, Sacco and Vanzetti didn't steal the Lindbergh baby."

"Well, that's what you say. But from what I've read there was proof."

"Sacco and Vanzetti were convicted of killing a guard in a shoe factory. It was a different case, moron. They had nothing to do with the Lindbergh baby."

"That's right. I meant the Rosenbergs."

"What?"

"Julius and Ethel Rosenberg."

"They didn't steal the Lindbergh baby, either."

"There was *proof,* Evan."

"The Rosenbergs were spies, nitwit. Wrong case."

"Yeah, well, whatever." I picked up the newspaper. "That's what I feel like."

He said I was going to feel like Jimmy Hoffa if I didn't get rid of that dog soon. I told him he was in a pretty foul mood for someone who'd spent the night tied to a bed and staring at a shaved vulva.

"Don't ever repeat that," he said. "I'm serious. I should never have told you that."

"That's right, you shouldn't have. Every time I see her now, that's all I can think about."

"Well, erase it from memory, okay? Besides, you've got your own girlfriend to think about."

"*Au contraire,* Pierre. Not anymore."

I told him what had happened with Maria. I had called her when I got back from the Frog Bar, but she wouldn't talk to me. Evan said he had a simple solution: We could get rid of the dog, and Maria would come back, and then we would all be happy. I would have a girl-friend, and Evan would be able to return to his apartment, where currently he was unable to reside.

"I went there yesterday to change my clothes, and I thought I was going to pass out," he said. "The place reeks, Reilly. The smell is never going to come out of the furniture. My album covers are going to stink forever. They might even rot."

Evan believed that Coco directed her abuse specifically at him. She had chewed up his Nike running shoes. She had torn apart a Spock doll that he kept on his bureau. She had shat in his room—again. I assured him that Coco had no way of knowing which room was his, or which things were his. He said he wouldn't be so sure. How could I explain the fact that none of my belongings had been ruined?

"Maybe if you tried being nicer to her," I said. "Maybe if you spent some time with her."

"Reilly," he said, "she shat in my room."

"She's a dog," I said. "She can't help it. And I can't believe you're getting so freaked out about a pair of shitty old sneakers and a *Star Trek* doll."

"For your information, those were hundred-dollar running shoes. And it was not a doll, it was a figurine."

"Figurine? Wait a minute. Do you hear that siren? I think my gaydar is going off."

"Your gaydar," he said, "is on perpetual red alert." He slumped back in his chair. He stared at the ceiling. "Reilly," he said, "do you know how odor works? It's tiny particles suspended in the air. The little particles lodge in our sinuses, and that's how we smell things. In the case of our apartment, the air right now is filled with tiny particles of dog shit. You walk into that apartment, and you are ingesting microscopic particles of dog shit. Are you listening? Do you hear me?"

"Yes, I'm listening," I said. But actually I wasn't.

I spent the morning cruising Internet Relay Chat channels. Evan was working on his business plan. He had decided not to quit Ionic right away; he would stay and collect a salary and make plans to make what he called the Big Leap. Evan was too broke to quit. In fact, he was more than broke; he was in trouble. His parents refused to bail him out; they'd bailed him out twice already. American Express had turned his account over to a collection agency. They called every day, making threats. Evan hung up on them.

"The irony," he said, "is that in about five minutes I could hack into the American Express system and erase my account and be done with them forever. Hell, I could make them owe *me* money. But instead, no, here I am, I'm trying to be a good citizen, I'm trying to do the right thing. And this is what I get for it."

"It's a shame," I said. "A crying shame."

I was logged into a sadomasochism channel, talking to a woman named Gloria whose interests included bondage, discipline, hot wax, golden showers, and shaving. Evan said Gloria might not be a buxom blond twenty-seven-year-old investment banker in Manhattan, as she claimed, but rather a fifty-year-old fat guy sitting in the Bronx wearing nothing but a pair of pee-stained underpants.

"Have you considered that?" he said.

"As a matter of fact," I said, "no. But thank you."

A line appeared on the screen: I NEED TO BE SHAVED. WOULD YOU DO THAT FOR ME?

"Tell him you'll shave his back," Evan said.

I started to type. But then I couldn't. "You ruined it," I said, and logged off.

"Why don't you try the amputee channels? See if there are any wannabe amputees looking for hot role-play action."

"Enough," I said.

It was almost noon. I had to go home to check on Coco. That morning when I woke up I had found her stretched out on the floor in front of the fan, wheezing. The heat was unbearable. I filled the bathtub with cold water and put her in it to help her cool off. I left the water in the tub so she could splash around during the day, and I left the fan going too, on high speed. Still I was worried about her. Greyhounds have a really hard time in hot weather. For some reason they are especially susceptible to heat stroke. For a week now the temperature in Boston had been at or above one hundred degrees, and the humidity had been close to one hundred percent. Stepping outside was like opening the door to a blast furnace. In five minutes you were soaked with sweat. I had arrived at work looking as if I had ridden my bike through a car wash.

I went home, and found her lying on the couch, in front of the fan, doing fine. She had eaten the food that I'd left out for her in the morning, and she had lapped up a bowl of water. So her appetite was okay. Still, just to be safe, I led her to the bathroom. She leaped into the tub and lay down so that the water came up over her back. She closed her eyes and sat still while I scooped handfuls of water over her ears and face, running my fingers down along her nose and up under her chin. When we were done, I got her out and patted her dry with a towel and put her back down in front of the fan. I put a bowl of ice cubes behind the fan. When I left, she was wagging her tail. And for a moment I felt happy, too. But then on my way out of the North End I rode my bike past the goons, and panic set in again.

I returned to work with a pizza and was listening to Evan threaten again to plant a virus on the American Express mainframe when suddenly the solution came to me.

"Buddy," I said, "you worked in a bank once, right?"

"Just for a summer."

"And you know about mainframes."

"I know about the IBM 3090."

"So you could hack into a bank?"

He leaned back in his chair. For once I was out ahead of him on something.

"That depends," he said. "Why?"

"But you could."

He shrugged. "If they were using a 3090, yes. No problem."

"You could get in and get out and nobody would know?"

"Reilly," he said, "on a 3090 I'm Jesus Christ, okay? I can walk on water."

"The question is who uses 3090s."

He took another slice of pizza. "MassBank does," he says.

"Are you sure?"

"No," he said, "I'm making this up."

"Here." I switched on my modem. "Start dialing."

Ninety minutes later Evan looked up from his screen and said, "We're in."

"In, as in, *in?*"

"No, in as in *out.* Now are you going to tell me what this is all about?"

I told him to create a new account, using the name Gloria D'Amico, and to give her a balance of two hundred dollars. He did, and then we were on to Phase Two, in which we would test to see if Phase One had worked.

We went to a MassBank branch office in Central Square. Evan said he wanted to make a deposit into his wife's account. He said he didn't have her passbook with him, but he knew her account number.

That was fine, the teller said. She was about twenty years old, with big hair and too much green eye shadow. It was Thursday afternoon, four o'clock. She wasn't sitting there worrying about being scammed; she was counting the minutes until she could leave. Plus, as Evan had explained to me, the thing to remember about banks is that as long as you're putting money into them, they don't care if you're Saddam Hussein. It's only when you want to take money out that they start getting antsy.

He gave the teller the name Gloria D'Amico and the account number we had made up. The teller called the account up on her screen. Apparently everything was in order. She took a hundred dollars from Evan, entered the deposit, and handed him a receipt that showed a three hundred–dollar balance.

"It worked," I said, when we got outside.

"Of course it worked," he said.

We moved on to Phase Three, which involved a visit to a Mass-Bank branch office in Harvard Square, where I opened an account in my name and was given a passbook. The assistant manager who waited on me was a middle-aged guy with greasy hair and eyeglasses that turned dark in sunlight. His lenses were dark gray, edging toward black: it was sunny outside, and we were sitting near a window. He produced a sheaf of forms for me to fill out. When I was done he disappeared out back, leaving me to admire the quaint Honeywell mainframe terminal on his desk with its little orange characters. It's always shocking to see these machines. They're like something out of the Stone Age—the kind of machines that you expect to see the Flintstones using. I've had the same experience at airport ticket counters, leaning over and wondering how on earth they manage to keep planes in the air using computers that are older than I am. Finally Mr. Dark Eyes returned with a passbook and a little laminated card with my account number written on it. I walked outside where Evan was waiting, standing beside his bike wearing his mountain-climber glasses, scanning the street and trying not to look suspicious.

We moved on to Phase Four. Back home we took a Polaroid photo of Coco standing beside a copy of that morning's *Herald*. We put the photo in a manila envelope with a note instructing Giaccalone to expect our call at ten o'clock. On the outside of the envelope I wrote: "Regarding Coco—Urgent" in Magic Marker. Then I snuck into Caffe Vesuvio through the side entrance on Maynard Street and left the envelope in the men's room downstairs.

31

AT TEN O'CLOCK we set up our voice changer and made the call. Coco sat beside me, watching. We had come home to discover that she had taken a massive dump, and not on the paper—a signal, I suppose, that she was growing restless to leave. Which was just as well, because Evan was feeling the same way. No amount of air freshener could dispel the stink this time. "The place smells like a Cuban whorehouse," he said. He was wearing a bandanna tied around his face. He said he wished he had an oxygen tank.

The phone rang three times, and then a man answered; one of the goons, probably. "I take it you're expecting my call," I said.

"Yessir," he said.

"Is this the dog's owner?"

"This is Lou. You can speak to me."

There was a click on the line, and then a hissing sound. I asked him if they were taping the call. He said they weren't. But they were, of course. Evan said they might even have the police involved, tracing the call. It was a risk we had to take. But probably there wasn't too much of a risk, since I couldn't really imagine that Giaccalone would allow the police to set up shop in his café. Nor could I imagine that the police would be too anxious to help him.

"We need to make arrangements," I said. "But I want to speak to the owner."

"All right, there, Willie Mays," Lou said. "But let me ask you something. You've got the dog, right?"

"Did you see the photo?"

"Yes."

"And what did you think, we used a stunt double? Of course we have the dog."

"She's there with you?"

"She's sitting right here."

There were numbers tattooed in the dog's left ear, he said. He wanted me to read him the numbers. I glanced at Evan. He was listening on an extension. He looked in Coco's ear, wrote the numbers on a piece of paper, and held it up so that I could see it.

"Two, seven, five, five, three, one," I said.

"Shit." Lou rustled through some papers. There were voices in the background. "Okay," he said. "Now the other ear. What's in the other ear?"

Evan checked, then held up the paper again.

"Seven, nine, A," I said.

"Seven, nine, A," Lou called out. There was commotion on their end—chairs being pushed back, voices. I heard Tony say, "They got her? Who is it?"

Lou said, "Okay, we can give you directions to the café, or we can come to see you, whichever is easier for you, whichever you prefer. I know Mr. Giaccalone will be very happy to meet you. Have you been to the North End before? We'll have quite a dinner, and you'll be in all the papers, I'm sure. We'll call the papers now. But whatever you'd like to do, however you'd like to do this, maybe you'd like your privacy—we'll accommodate your needs, okay?"

"I have instructions for you," I said. "I want you to write this down."

"What's this?"

"I'm going to give you a bank account number where you can deposit the money. When the money shows up in the account, you'll get the dog."

"A bank account? My friend, please. Come down here to the café and you'll get your reward, okay? But we can't go putting money in a bank account without you bring us the dog. We can't do that."

"Then we don't have a deal," I said.

"My friend, you're being ridiculous."

I looked at Evan. He gave me his little-kid-lost-in-the-mall look.

"Thank you for your time," I said. "We'll go kill the dog now. Sorry to bother you."

"What's that?"

"We'll go kill the dog. And we'll be sure to send photographs to Mr. Giaccalone, with a note about your role in this. Thank you again."

"Wait a minute," he said. "Hold on."

A moment later Giaccalone came on. "This is the owner," he said. "What's this about a bank account?"

I explained it to him.

"That's stupid," he said. "We're not going to do that."

"Fine. Do you want to say good-bye to your dog? She's right here."

"Wait, okay, hold on," he said. "Let me hear the dog bark."

"What?"

"Make her bark, dick-breath."

"Who are you calling dick-breath?"

"You, you dog-stealing fuck."

"The price," I said, "just went to twenty thousand."

"You know what? I'm going to trace this call, and I'm going to come get you, and I'm going to kill you."

Evan waved his hands. He drew a finger across his throat. He started making a "hang up" motion in the air.

"Mr. Giaccalone," I said, "we've tried to be polite about this. We've tried to handle this in a professional manner. But we're tired of fooling around. The price is now twenty thousand."

"Fuck you," Giaccalone said.

"The price," I said, "is now thirty."

"Jesus." He muttered something. Then he said, "Look, how do I know the dog is still alive?"

"We sent you a photograph."

"From this morning. I want to be sure she's okay now."

"She's not okay," I said. "She hasn't eaten in three days. And if you make us wait another day we're going to put her into a woodchipper and turn her into hamburger. Maybe we'll cut her throat and let her bleed to death first. We'll make a videotape. You can play the tape over and over, and tell yourself, 'Hey, if I weren't such a cheap piece of shit, this might not have happened.'"

"Enough," he said. "We'll take care of the money. But I want to hear her bark."

I snapped my fingers. Coco ran over, wagging her tail. I hated to do this, but I had to. I put the phone next to her mouth, then wrapped my arm around her neck and pinched her, hard, just below her ear. She yelped.

"Coco?" Giaccalone gasped. "Coco, baby, are you all right? Daddy's here, baby."

She recognized his voice, and barked at the phone.

"Enough," I said, and pushed her away. Evan grabbed Coco and held her mouth shut so she wouldn't bark again.

"You sick fuck," Giaccalone said. "If I ever find you, I swear to God."

"Deposit the money by noon tomorrow," I said. "Thirty thousand. No funny business. I'm sick of you bastards."

"I can't do thirty," he said. "I can do ten."

"The price is thirty. Otherwise we'll stick a piece of dynamite up her ass and blow her to pieces."

"What did you say?"

"You heard me."

"You sick, dog-stealing fuck." He paused. I could imagine him turning red, clenching his teeth. "Okay, look, we'll get the thirty. But if we don't see that dog by tomorrow at five o'clock, we're gonna come looking for you, okay? And we'll put a stick of dynamite up *your* ass, punk."

I gave him the number for Gloria D'Amico's account at Mass-Bank. I made him read it back to me.

"See you tomorrow, *punk*," I said. Then I hung up.

I whistled to Coco. She looked at me, but wouldn't come.

"Hamburger?" Evan said. "A woodchipper? Dynamite in her ass?"

"I had to talk his language," I said. "I had to get his attention."

"You're a deviant, Reilly. A complete and utter deviant."

He packed a bag. He was going to stay with Agnes. He glanced at Coco, who was lying on the floor by the fan, looking miserable. "See you in the morning," he said. "If you live that long."

I called Maria, and got her machine. I thought about going over there. But I knew that wouldn't do any good.

I went to bed. Coco stayed in the living room. I called to her, but she wouldn't come. Finally I got up and went out to see her. "Look, I'm sorry," I said. She was lying on the couch. "I didn't want to do it," I said.

She slumped down, and put her paws over her face.

"Come on to bed," I said.

But she wouldn't.

I N THE MORNING we used Evan's SPARCstation to tap into the MassBank system. It was dangerous to hack in and stay connected, but on the other hand it was Friday morning and probably the losers in the MassBank data center were still making coffee and yukking it up about their weekend plans. There wasn't much chance that some ever vigilant soul would be poking through the accounts database looking for intruders.

Evan scooted through the MassBank code as if he'd written it himself. Apparently the software was pretty much the same as the stuff he'd worked on during his summer job all those years before. I had never bothered to learn COBOL, but I knew that COBOL programs always had trapdoors—secret entrances that the developers left behind so they could get in if the system crashed. Evan knew exactly where to find them. The MassBank system had a Unix firewall too, but we didn't have much trouble getting past it.

The only trouble was that you could not go past the firewall without leaving traces. Whether or not the traces were discovered depended on how alert the people in the bank's data center were. If they were using a sniffer they could, in theory, have seen us the first time we came through the firewall. "They could be watching us right now," Evan said. "They could be tracing the connection. The police could be on their way here right now."

It was nine o'clock. The money had not been deposited yet. We logged off, then checked again at nine-thirty, ten, ten-thirty, and eleven. Still nothing. We began to give up hope. Then, at eleven-thirty, we checked and found that the thirty thousand dollars had been deposited. Evan transferred the money from Gloria's account into mine.

Naturally it occurred to us that if we could siphon the balance from Gloria D'Amico's account, we could do the same from other accounts as well. "Here, look," Evan said, and showed me rows of account numbers and balances. "Look at this," he said, and produced a list of just the accounts whose balances exceeded one million dollars. "Never knew there were so many millionaires, did you?" I shook my head. It was staggering. It was like knocking a hole in a wall and finding a secret compartment piled high with gold.

It was entirely possible, Evan said, to draw money out in such a trickle that nobody would notice. "Anybody who's ever worked in a bank has figured that one out," he said. You could find all the accounts with balances of more than one million dollars, and withdraw from each account a tiny increment—say, one-tenth of one percent. For someone with a million dollars that would be one thousand dollars—an amount so tiny that it would be masked by the exigencies of interest rate fluctuations, rounding errors, and assumable margins of error. Nobody would notice that, not even the bank's own auditors.

But then of course there are the moral arguments. Only those aren't very compelling, either. Why on earth should anyone with a million dollars mind giving up a thousand dollars? It's a speck of dust. Scoop up five hundred of those specks, however, and you've got half a million dollars. Not bad for clicking a few keys.

The trouble was that you couldn't get the money out of the bank. You could move it around all you liked and probably never get caught. But how did you get your hands on it? You couldn't put the skim into

a single account and then go make a half-million-dollar cash withdrawal. But maybe you could set up fifty fake accounts and distribute
ten thousand dollars to each one and then close them gradually, over
time. Or you could move the money into business accounts and then
write checks against them. Or you could transfer the money in
smaller amounts to other banks and then draw it out from them. But
no matter what you did, you would leave a trail. And sooner or later,
chances were, you would get caught.

"That's the odds, anyway," Evan said. "You can imagine what
happens if you get caught stealing half a million dollars. You don't get
probation and community service. You get put in a cell with some
Mike Tyson look-alike. No, believe me, it's not worth it. You'd be insane to try."

By the time he was telling me this we were standing across the
street from a MassBank branch in Brookline Village, and I was
preparing to go in and withdraw the money. I was feeling dizzy.

"One last thing," Evan said. "Did I ever tell you about the guy I
knew at MIT who got arrested for breaking into DARPA computers?
All he was doing was looking around. Hadn't stolen anything. But
they gave him eighteen months. Last I knew he had his legs shaved
and was wearing a skirt."

"I don't think I need to hear that story right now," I said. I got off my
bike and stood there shaking my arms and taking deep breaths. I felt the
way I had in high school before a wrestling match: the butterflies, the
sweat between the shoulder blades, the glances at my opponent who I
knew was going to destroy me. I wrestled for one season, at one hundred and ten pounds, and lost every match.

Evan explained to me again all of the ways in which things can go
wrong when a person walks into a bank and asks to withdraw thirty
thousand dollars in cash. First of all, banks have to report large cash
withdrawals to the FDIC. It's government policy. So sooner or later
there would be a report that a man named Glen Timothy Reilly with-
drew thirty thousand dollars from his account. Which may or may not
be a problem. But other issues presented themselves. For example, the

bank might not have the cash on hand, so they might tell me to come back on Monday. Or Giaccalone might have gone to the police, and the police might have told the people at MassBank branches to be looking out for anyone making large withdrawals. And even if that hadn't happened, the bank might have a policy of reporting all large cash withdrawals to the police, figuring that the people making them were involved in drugs. And once the police were called, forget it. Even if I could get past the guard, the surveillance cameras would have my picture. They would find me, for sure.

"If the police do show up," I told Evan, "you run, okay? Just drop my bike, and take off."

"As opposed to what?" he said. "Walking over and telling them that I'm your accomplice?" He held out his hands. "Here, cuff me, too. If he goes, I go."

"You're a real pal," I said.

Before I went into the bank, he reminded me again of the list of crimes that we were committing. First, we had hacked into a bank, which from a legal standpoint was the same as breaking in through the wall with a bulldozer. We had created false accounts. We had transferred funds illegally.

"We can walk away right now," he said. "We can forget this ever happened."

I thought for a minute. I knew he was right. This was stupid and crazy. But I was not going to stop now. I felt like a bungee jumper, standing on the edge, praying that the cord would hold. *"Adios,"* I said, and walked across the street into the bank.

33

THE TELLER WAS A BLACK WOMAN with hair that had been scooped and styled like chocolate ice cream. She checked her screen, then slid me a piece of paper. The balance was $30,301.20.

"I'd like to withdraw thirty thousand," I said. "In cash."

She tried not to scowl. But it wasn't easy. "Cash?" she said.

"That's right." I smiled. You are an upstanding citizen, I told myself, making an honest transaction. There is nothing unusual about what you are doing. People do this all the time. I forced myself to keep my face down, so that the security cameras could not get a good picture.

"For that kind of thing you have to talk to the manager," she said. She pointed to an office in back. The woman there was about fifty, pale, gray-haired, thin. Her name was Lorraine Ellison—there was a sign on her desk—and she was talking on the phone. She smiled in a way that let me know she was annoyed. She cupped her hand over the receiver and said, "I'm going to be a minute."

I sat down. She went back to her call. The office was small and cramped, with crappy brown carpet and fake-wood paneling that had come loose in places. There was one window. Outside, treetops swayed in a breeze; the effect was like watching a silent movie. I began to be aware of a pulse in the side of my neck.

The manager finished her call and asked what she could do for me. She made a face when I told her.

"That's a lot of money to carry around in cash," she said.

I shrugged. She waited for me to say something else. I didn't. I told myself to stay cool. Before leaving the office I had put on a pair of Gap chinos and a white button-down shirt. You are a wealthy trust-fund kid, I told myself, drawing out cash to go buy yourself a sports car. You do this all the time. Your dad would laugh if you told him about this bank manager getting uptight about thirty thousand dollars.

"Wouldn't you be happier with a check?" she said. "If you're buying a car, or making a down payment on a house, we would be happy to have the money transferred, or to give you a cashier's check. That's just like cash. It's just as good."

In an accent that I had learned from Jeanie, and which I imagined to be vaguely mid-Atlantic, I said that I didn't know that bank managers were in the habit of asking depositors how they intended to use their money, but that I was not in the habit of discussing with bank managers my plans for my money. I said that since I had given her bank the privilege of using my money, I wondered if she might now show me the courtesy of doing what I asked her.

She gave me a smile so hard that I could almost hear the click as the corners of her mouth turned up. "Of course," she said. "Your business is very important to us." She turned to her computer, clicked at her keyboard. A few seconds later her printer spat out a withdrawal form. She showed me where to sign.

"I'll be right back," she said, "sir."

Three minutes passed. Then five. An image came to me: a man in a bad suit appearing in the doorway and informing me that he was with the FBI and that he wondered if we might have a little talk. The room began to feel hot. I wondered if they had turned off the air con-

ditioning. I was sweating under my shirt. When ten minutes had
gone by, I started to consider making a dash. There was a window
that overlooked a parking lot. But it was the kind that didn't open.
The only way out would be the way I had come in, through the front
door and past the guard. I'd noticed him on the way in: an old man in
a uniform, overweight, bored. Probably I could get past him before he
got to his gun.

Lorraine Ellis returned with a man in his early thirties whom she
introduced as Mr. Something-or-Other, the assistant manager. He
was blond, thin, wearing a blue seersucker suit that didn't fit him
well; the sleeves were too short. He took a long look at me. I glanced
at him, then went back to staring at the floor. My heart was pounding.
Sweat was pouring off me. I could feel my shirt sticking to the back of
the chair. I started trying to figure out how I could get out of the
country while I was awaiting trial. There was a guy from Connecticut
who'd done that; he was arrested for rape and then fled to Europe.
Maybe Mom could help me do that. She could get me a ticket to
Switzerland, send me money once in a while.

When I looked up, the man in the seersucker suit was stacking
bricks of money on the desk. I stared at his hands. They were small
and pale, with fingernails so square and perfect that they might have
been manicured; he had hands like an undertaker.

"There you are," he said. "Thirty thousand."

I put the money into my backpack. I still worried about a trap.
Maybe they needed to catch me with the money in hand. Maybe the
police were waiting outside. I walked ahead of them out to the lobby.
I felt stiff and awkward, as if I'd forgotten how to walk and was having
to learn all over again. One foot, then the next, then the next.

And then I was outside, and there were no police, and Evan was
across the street, holding the bikes and calling me Raskolnikov, and
we were free, and pedaling hard down Commonwealth Avenue, racing with the Green Line train which rumbled along beside us,
whooping to the passengers. We crossed the bridge back into Cambridge, feeling safe, somehow, as if the river were some kind of bar-

rier, as if we had entered a zone from which we could not be extra-dited. The sun was bright. There were rowers on the river, and sail-boats. On the lawns girls in bikinis were lying on blankets, working on their tans.

At the Ionic building we suddenly became somber: we nodded to the guard and rolled our bikes across the lobby, trying to act normal, which is not easy to do when you're carrying thirty thousand dollars in cash in your backpack.

"I can hear you in there," Nabeel said, when we got to our office and were inside counting the money. "Giggling like a pair of fucking schoolgirls."

He tried the door. It was locked. He knocked again. We told him we weren't there.

"Come on," he said. "Stop fucking around."

We stashed the money in a file cabinet, and let him in.

"What are you up to?" he said.

I shrugged.

He looked at Evan. "Did you get your venture money or some-thing? Did you actually convince some poor bastard to invest in your company?"

Evan shook his head.

"So what, then?"

"Nothing," Evan said.

"Okay, don't tell me. Whatever. Have you had lunch yet?"

"No," I said. "Have you?" Then we burst out laughing again.

"Are you high or something? Did you take fucking mushrooms or something? What is it?"

We just kept laughing. He walked away, shaking his head. "You two," he said, "are mad as fuck."

There was one last thing to do. We tapped into the MassBank system and vaporized both accounts.

"No fingerprints," I said. "No paper trail. Right?"

"Well," Evan said, "not exactly."

We might have left tracks, he said. You couldn't ever be a hundred percent sure. Besides, even if we were clear on the computers, and even if the FDIC didn't care about our withdrawal, and even if Giaccalone hadn't gone to the police, we still had one problem."

"Which is?"

"The dog," Evan said. "We've got to get rid of her."

"Right. Everything's under control."

"You said you had a plan."

"I do. It's in the gestation phase."

He groaned, and slumped in his chair. He put his face in his hands. "We just stole thirty thousand dollars from the mob," he said. "And you don't have a plan." He began to rock back and forth in his chair. He was making a little wheezing sound.

"So where should we go for lunch?" I said. "My treat. How about takeout? Subs from Tony Lena's. I'll bring you one back. What do you want? Meatball? Steak bomb? Tell you what. I'll get us one of each. Why not? We're loaded." I took a hundred-dollar bill from one of the bricks. "One steak bomb, one meatball," I said.

He shook his head, and kept rocking. "Go away," he said.

34

THIRTY MINUTES LATER I returned with the subs and found Evan sitting with his legs drawn up against his chest, rocking back and forth, looking catatonic. "They found Karl Wilson," he said. "His body, anyway. What's left of him. Some kids found the body. In a quarry. In New Hampshire." His face was twitching. "No head, no hands. Maria called. She was looking for you. The state cops were in the North End this morning. They interrogated Giaccalone."

I sat down. I didn't know what to say. If this was true—but it couldn't be true.

"There must be a mistake."

"I don't think so." His face was red. He had been crying. "Reilly," he said, "this isn't funny, okay? We got a guy killed."

I felt sick. I didn't know what to do. I called Maria. She was not happy. She said the police had not been able to arrest Giaccalone; apparently, they couldn't prove anything. And as soon as the cops left, more wiseguys had arrived. They were everywhere now, she said. They were staking out the neighborhood, waiting to see who dropped off the dog. Giaccalone had posted them at both ends of Hanover

Street, and on all of the cross streets. He was in his café, sitting by the phone, waiting for a call.

"You made him pay you thirty thousand?" She was half-whispering. "What were you thinking?"

"It just happened," I said.

"Where's the dog?"

"Same place."

"Jesus, Reilly. Have you got a death wish or something?"

She told me she had delivered groceries to the café. Cold cuts, bread. A man at the back door gave Maria a hundred dollars and told her to keep the change. Behind him she saw men in T-shirts smoking cigarettes and playing cards. There were at least twenty guys, she said. "And guns," she said. "Lots of guns. It's a war room."

"Have they been in our building?" I said. "Is it safe for us to come home?"

"Hold on." She put the phone down. I could hear her talking to Gus. She came back on. "Okay, Anthony, so ten cases of oranges, ten Red Delicious, ten Mackintosh, and that's it, all right? Okay. *Grazie*. See you later."

I N THE NORTH END the streets were empty and the vendors sat in the shade on the sidewalks, fanning themselves with newspapers. It looked as if the whole place ran on batteries and the batteries were running low. The sun was blinding, and the asphalt felt as if it were melting beneath our feet. The temperature was one hundred and five degrees, with a heat index that made it feel like one hundred and twenty.

Once, in one of Evan's MIT alumni magazines, I'd seen a map of Boston shot from outer space, showing variations in temperature. The coolest spots, shown in green on the map, were places with lots of trees and water: the Common, the Public Garden, the Esplanade. The hot places, shown in red, were places with lots of brick and concrete, and lots of flat, dark-colored rooftops. The North End was the worst part of the city; it glowed like the tip of a cigarette.

We stopped outside the store. Maria wasn't there. Gus sat in a folding chair. He moved his big hooded eyes like a lizard but otherwise did not acknowledge us. Beside him, on the sidewalk, two old men sat in lawn chairs with their feet stuck in buckets of water. They had rolled their pants up above their knees. Huge blue veins stood out on their legs.

"Maybe we should take off," Evan said. "We can come back later, in the middle of the night."

For all we knew, he said, the goons could be sitting upstairs in the apartment, waiting for us.

"We're fine," I told him.

We had talked this over already, back in Cambridge. My theory was that staying away would only make us seem more suspicious; we had to keep to our normal routine. Evan asked me how I had suddenly developed the instincts of a criminal.

We went upstairs. The hallway on the second floor felt like an oven: it was hot, stale, impossible to breathe. An overpowering smell seeped out from our doorway. The smell was of shit and urine and other things that could not be described, a stink so awful it made me gag when we opened the door. "Mother of God," Evan said, and put his hand over his mouth.

There was dog shit sprayed everywhere, over everything, and urine, too; it looked as if Coco had lost control of herself and just gone crazy. The windows were shut, the fan knocked over. The air in the apartment must have been one hundred and thirty degrees. The living room looked as if it had been hit by a cyclone. The trash had been tipped over and spread everywhere. Video game cartridges were scattered on the floor. The pillows on the couch had been torn open; their stuffing lay on the floor like snow.

And Coco was gone.

"Okay, we've got to think," Evan said. He was standing in the center of the room, turning in circles. "Think, right? What do we do?"

"First of all, stay calm," I said.

He stopped. He stared at me. "Excuse me," he said. "Did you say, 'Stay calm?' Is that what you said? 'Stay calm'?"

"If they've got the dog, maybe that's enough. Maybe they don't care about us. Maybe that's why they're not here."

"Sure, they're downstairs getting the parade ready for us. They're blowing up the balloons. They're . . . they're . . ."

He stopped talking. He began to shiver. That's when we heard the whimpering. We ran to my bedroom and found Coco splayed out on the floor, half-dead and struggling to breathe. Her eyes were clouded over. Foam had formed in the corners of her mouth. Her tongue was swollen and hanging out: it looked like a piece of strip steak. I knelt down beside her. She tried to lift her head, but she couldn't.

"Heat stroke," I said. I ran to the bathroom. The tub was empty. Somehow the plug had come loose. I started running water. I carried Coco to the tub and set her in the water and put a fan on the toilet to blow air over her. Evan ran around opening the windows hoping to vent out some of the hot air. She lay in the tub looking ready to die. In fact, she looked as if she would be happy to die if only to stop suffering. She was looking at me not so much with hatred as with sorrow, and distrust; it was the look a prisoner might give to the person who's been torturing her, a look that said, *Please stop.* "I'm sorry, baby," I said, and splashed water up over her back, and on her face. Slowly, she began to recover. Her breathing got better.

I got out a phone book and called the first veterinarian I could find. She told me to fill a bathtub with cold water and put the dog in the tub. I told her I'd done that. Next step, she said, was a cold water enema. We had to get the dog's body temperature down, and fast. Go to a drugstore, she said, and buy an enema bag. The closest drugstore was the one on Prince Street. The clerk who rang me up was the woman who had asked Evan and me which one of us did the cooking. She took a look at what I was buying and said, "Big night tonight, huh?" I gave her a twenty and told her to keep the change. "Look, he can't wait to get home with it," I heard her saying as I ran out the door.

There are worse things, I suppose, than having to give a dog an ice water enema. But right at the moment I couldn't think of any. We had put Coco in the tub, to make it easier to clean up afterward. She shivered but held still as I pumped the water into her. She seemed to be getting better. Her eyes were clearer. Now it was Evan I was worried about. He was holding Coco and rubbing her ears while I handled the business end of things. "You know," he said, "for future reference, you might want to make a mental note not to kidnap dogs during heat waves. And just for the record, I'm not going to clean this place up, okay? That's your job."

We filled Coco up three times. I could feel her skin getting cooler as her body temperature came down. When we were done, I washed out the tub and filled it up with clean cold water and let her lie down in it. She lay with her face in the water, looking unhappy—which is, I suppose, how anyone would look after taking three cold water enemas right in a row. I found Evan's sneaker and brought it to her. She ignored it.

"By the way, you're going to owe me for those shoes," Evan said. "A hundred dollars."

"You paid twenty-five. I was with you, remember? You got them at Filene's Basement."

"But they're hundred-dollar shoes. That's what it'll cost to replace them."

I took a brick of money from the backpack and peeled off a hundred-dollar bill. "Here," I said. "Happy now?"

"Ecstatic." He stuffed the bill into his pocket. "Fucking overjoyed. Jesus. Look at this place."

I sat down on the floor next to Coco. I put my hand on her head. She growled.

Evan said he had a plan: We could leave Coco in the apartment with food and water and a bathtub full of ice, fly to Canada, and then fly to Cuba. In Cuba we'd be safe. There was no extradition. We'd get a hotel room in Havana and call Giaccalone and tell him where to find his dog.

It was not a bad idea. The only problem, I said, was that we would never be able to come back.

"Who cares?" Evan said. "Honestly. I could use some time off. We'll go down there, finish Nectar, and in six months, or a year, when everything is cooled off, we'll come back."

We were in the living room. I was using our bath towels to mop up dog shit. Apparently one of the symptoms of heat stroke is diarrhea. Coco hadn't missed a spot.

"I don't know," I said. I thought again about that guy who fled to Europe to avoid the rape charges. He stayed away for about ten years, but then he couldn't take it anymore. And he was living it up in the Alps, not sweating his ass off in Cuba.

Evan took off his glasses and wiped them clean. He looked out the window.

"We've got to do something," he said.

That's when Lucia started pounding on our door.

She wore bicycle shorts and a sports bra. Her midriff was awash in rolls of fat, her legs dimpled with cellulite: she looked as if she'd gone for liposuction and they had accidentally set the machine on reverse.

"This is it," she said. "I've had it."

She tried to come into the apartment, but I blocked her. Evan had gone into the bathroom to keep Coco quiet.

"What's with this smell?" she said. I told her that in the future we would definitely start using more lime on the corpses.

"I wouldn't doubt it," she said. "You two are like Jeffrey Dahmer. You're probably picking up teenage boys and eating them for dinner. You're probably out digging up graves. God! Can you not smell it? How can you live in there?"

"I don't know what you're talking about," I said.

"The smell! *This.*" She waved her hands in the air, as if I could see the smell if I pointed to it. "The odor!"

"I don't think it's coming from here."

"Of course it is. It's coming straight from your apartment! And I know what you're doing. You're trying to get yourself evicted, right? You're boiling fishheads or something in there, trying to get yourselves kicked out, because Gus won't let you out of your lease. And you know what? You win. I'm going to complain to Gus. I'm sick of this. This is my home, okay? For you, I know, this is someplace you live for a year, and then you move on. But I've been here for twenty years, okay? This is my home. And I can't live like this. I can't breathe."

"Maybe you should wear some kind of gas mask," I said. "From the army surplus store."

"Maybe you should leap to your death from the roof of the building."

The man at the end of the hall opened his door. This was Mr. Tomasino, a.k.a. the Phantom. In all the months we'd lived here we'd never actually seen him. We'd heard him inside his apartment when we walked by in the hallway. We would hear him moving around, we would hear his television. Sometimes too we would hear him opening the locks on his door—it sounded as if there were about a dozen—and we would rush out to the hallway hoping to catch a glimpse of him. But the most we had ever seen was a flash of his hair as he vanished down the back stairs. So now, for the first time ever, I was seeing the Phantom in the flesh. He was pale, and gaunt, and ghoulish, somewhere in middle age: more than forty-five, less than ninety. He wore plaid shorts, and black socks with sandals.

"What's going on? Is there a problem?" His voice was high, almost feminine. He stood with most of his body still inside his doorway.

"The problem, Charles," Lucia said, without looking at him, "is that this building smells so bad that you can't breathe."

"I can't smell anything," he said.

"You see?" I said.

"He lives in his own filth," Lucia said. "Of course he can't smell anything. He's as bad as you are. Worse, probably." She spun toward the Phantom. He leaped back inside and started clicking his locks.

I said maybe Lucia should go harass Gus and leave us law-abiding citizens alone. She told me to start packing my bags. "You won't get your security deposit back," she said. "I hope you thought of that. No way."

"Well," I said, closing the door, "thanks for stopping by. And thanks for the coffee cake. We'll have to have you over again soon, okay? Great. 'Bye now."

THERE WERE TWO STAIRWAYS in the building, one in front and one in back. To get to either one we had to go down the hallway past Lucia and the Phantom, both of whom were sure to be glued to their peepholes. To make matters worse, at dusk the goons began fanning out through the streets. "They've got every corner covered," Evan said. "Whoever pulls up with the dog—*wham.*" We were sitting by the front window. He let the curtain fall back across the window. Coco was still in the bathroom, stretched out in the tub.

I had cleaned up the apartment as best I could, but the place still stank. Evan said that once this was over, he was moving out. Gus could take him to court if he wanted, but no way would he ever bathe in that tub after what he had seen take place there. I said I didn't care if he wanted to move out; right now we had more pressing concerns.

"We need a diversion," Evan said. "A bomb scare. Or a fire alarm. We can call something in. We'll say there's a bomb in Giaccalone's café. Just anything that will get attention away from here."

It wasn't the greatest idea. And it didn't matter, anyway, because before we could mull it over we heard somebody open the downstairs door and start climbing up the back stairs. Then the footsteps were in our hallway, coming toward our door. We went to the door. I looked out the peephole. It was Gus. He was right outside. He was sweating, trying to catch his breath, and frowning at the smell. He stared right at me. His chest was heaving from the effort of climbing the stairs. I stood there, looking at him, not daring to move or take a breath.

Lucia opened her door and dragged Gus inside. I fell away from the door, my heart pounding.

And then it came to me: the plan. I explained it to Evan. It was risky, he said. But it was the best we had. We waited five minutes, long enough for Gus and Lucia to get out of their clothes. Then Evan ran to his room to get his trench coat, and I ran down the hall to get the Phantom. It took a few minutes to get him to open his door, and even when he did, he only opened it a crack. "It's Lucia," I told him. "It's an emergency. We heard this crash, and then there was this moaning sound. I can still hear her in there. I don't know what to do."

"Did you knock on her door?"

"I tried. There's no answer. There's just this moaning sound, like I said. Come here, I'll show you."

He stepped out, taking little steps, like a cat. I led him to her door.

"Listen," I said. We leaned close. "Can you hear it?"

"I better go get Gus," he said. He ran down the stairs. As soon as he was gone, I went inside and got Evan. He had Coco ready. She stood under the trench coat, looking confused. I took her by the collar and led her into the hallway. She trotted along, with her head peeking out from under the coat. At the stairs she hesitated. Greyhounds have this thing about going down stairs. There was no time to waste trying to coax her. I picked her up and carried her down to the alley. Evan slid the trench coat off of her. She stood there, her black coat shining under the streetlights.

"Go on," I said. "Get."

She just stood there.

"*Get,*" I said.

She ran off a few yards, then stopped and turned back, wagging her tail.

"Go on," I said, and picked up a rock. She sprinted away.

That's when the shrieking began. Lucia was screaming in Italian. Gus was braying and bellowing and howling, as if he'd been stuck in the side with a hot knife. The Phantom was stuttering and stammering and saying he didn't understand, there had been some kind of mistake. And Maria, who had gone upstairs with the Phantom, was yelling at Gus to calm down. We heard him pounding down the stairs. Then he stepped out onto the back landing in his boxer shorts and T-shirt. His face was bright red, his hair messed up. Maria ran out after him. "Uncle, wait," she said.

"Get away," he growled. That's when he noticed me and Evan. His face grew even darker. "You!" he said. He made a gesture whose meaning I did not understand but which I was fairly certain did not mean *Have a nice day.*

Lucia threw open her window. "You're sick!" she said. "All of you. You hear me? Sick! And you two are going to be evicted! That's it!"

Gus told her to shut up.

"Don't you tell me to shut up!" Lucia said.

"That's right, honey, you tell him," an old lady yelled from another building. All around us people were turning on their lights and leaning out their windows.

"You shut up, too!" Gus said. "You old whore!"

"Who are you calling an old whore?"

"You," Lucia said.

A man stuck his head out the next window. "Did you just call my wife a whore?" he said.

"Shut up, all of you, or I'll call the cops," somebody said. "And Gus, I already called your wife."

Gus put on his pants, and stomped away, barefoot. Maria stood there looking at me; if she'd had a gun, I am sure she would have shot me dead. Instead, she walked up and slapped me, hard, across the face. From the distance, on Hanover Street, there came the sound of people shouting, and then cheering. Coco had arrived at the café.

"So you pulled it off," she said. "Good for you. I'm happy for you. I hope you're proud of yourselves."

"It was a joke," I said. "That's all. A prank."

She stood, hands on her hips, eyeing me up and down; it was as if she wanted to say this just once and she wanted to say it exactly right.

"You know," she said, "these are real people who live here, okay? They have feelings. They're not little cartoon figures. This isn't a video game. We're not all here to entertain you. But you two run around here like a pair of assholes, and we're all supposed to be so impressed with you, right? We're supposed to be so *grateful* to be able to rent an apartment to a couple of guys who are as cool as you. But let me tell you something, Reilly. I am so sick of hearing you go on about your problems, and your job, and your little breakup with your little Jeanie. I mean, look around. Look at these rotten buildings, and these trash cans, and these weeds. This is where I grew up, okay? This is my life. These people that you go around making fun of, those are my family, and my friends, okay?"

I kept my hands up, in case she tried to slap me again.

"You know what you are?" she said. "You're a sociopath. You don't care about anyone else. You don't even know that you're hurting people. You don't know when you hurt my feelings. I'm just another part of the joke."

"Maria, please," I said. I tried to hug her. She pushed me away. I tried again. She struggled, but I got my arms around her.

"I hate you," she said.

"That's not true," I said.

"It is," she said. "I do."

In a moment she stopped fighting and pressed herself against me. Her shoulders began to shake. The front of my shirt became hot, then wet. "Come on upstairs," I said.

OUTSIDE, THE COMMOTION was spreading: People were leaning out windows, calling to their friends who were gathering in the street. Kids were running in packs toward Hanover Street. Somebody started blowing off firecrackers. "They'll be up all night," Maria said.

We were sitting in the living room, watching out the front windows. Evan said it was sick for people to be out celebrating, considering what Giaccalone had done to Karl Wilson. Maria said the Karl Wilson thing had all been a mistake. "They found him," she said.

"Right," Evan said. "No arms, no legs, no head. You told us."

"No, I mean they found him alive. He's in California. The body in New Hampshire, that wasn't him. The cops called Davio and apologized."

Wilson was in San Diego, hiding from Giaccalone. When the police called his sister and asked her to come identify his body, she didn't know what to do. So she told them yes, that was him. For a while Wilson had gone along with it. But then he had a change of heart and called the state police.

"So wait a minute," Evan said. "He's alive, the dog is returned, and we got the money. We got away with it."

"Right," Maria said, "you swindled an old man out of thirty thousand dollars. Congratulations. You must feel really good."

"As a matter of fact," Evan said, "I do."

He said we should go dancing. He went to his room to call Agnes.

Maria said she was going to go home. "I don't feel right about this," she said. "I wish I could come celebrate with you. But I wouldn't feel right."

I said I could appreciate that. I knew she didn't approve of what we had done. But I told her to look at it from our perspective. Giaccalone had screwed us, and now we had screwed him back. And besides, whatever money we had swindled out of Giaccalone was only money that he had swindled out of someone else. And she had to remember that we were talking about a man who cut off people's thumbs. Did she really have sympathy for somebody like that?

"Maria, what's done is done," I said. "We're sitting here, it's Friday night, and we've got thirty thousand dollars in cash, for God's sake. Thirty thousand dollars. In cash. Right here. In this bag."

I was holding the backpack on my lap, stroking it like a pet.

"That's what I mean," she said. "It's all the same, right? You swindle Davio, or you swindle some investors, or you swindle some customers. But it's all a swindle. Guys like you and Evan, you're not so different from Davio, I don't think. It just makes me . . . I don't know. Sad, I guess."

"And because of that, you feel like you can't go out dancing with us?"

"Not just that." She stood up. "I got an assignment letter." She looked at me. I didn't know what she was talking about. "From the Peace Corps," she said. "I got my letter."

They were sending her to Russia. St. Petersburg first, for language training. Then somewhere else, somewhere unpronounceable, up in the mountains. She was leaving in three weeks.

"I'm really lucky to get this," she said. "It's a really good assignment."

"Sure," I said. I was trying to look happy.

"What's the matter?"

"Nothing." I felt as if I had walked into a door. "I guess I just didn't expect . . . I don't know."

Down in the streets people were cheering, whooping it up, blowing car horns. I slumped in my chair. The bag of money slid down my legs to the floor. I felt a headache coming on.

"You knew I was leaving," Maria said.

I nodded. I got up and gave her a hug. "I'm happy for you," I said. "It's just that I'll miss you, that's all. In case you hadn't noticed, I kind of like you."

We were standing with our arms around each other, kissing, when Evan barged into the room. "Break it up," he said. He handed the phone to Maria. "Agnes says she'll go, but only if you go, too. So talk to her, okay?"

Maria took the phone to the other room.

Evan took a look at me and said, "What is it now? Are you all right?"

I told him.

"Jesus," he said. "I never thought she'd actually do it. Tough luck for you, eh?"

"You might say that."

"Talk about bad karma. You're setting records, buddy. What'd you do in your past life? Rape kids or something?"

I gazed across the street at Lonely Man's apartment. The place was empty, the lights off. Maybe he and his girlfriend had gone away for the weekend. Or maybe he had moved out for good. For a moment I imagined myself living over there in his rooms, standing at his windows, staring back across the street at myself.

Maria came back into the living room. "Okay, I agreed," she said. "God forgive me." She looked up at the ceiling, as if God might really be up there. "I'm going to go home and change. Agnes is on her way."

IKEPT WISHING THAT MARIA had some flaw, something that I could think about after she was gone that would keep me from missing her. If she had a crooked tooth, or a funny nose, or a mole on her chin; if she had an annoying laugh, or bad table manners; if she were boring, or stupid, or wore too much makeup. But she was smart, and beautiful, and effortlessly so. She could at least have tried to make herself ugly tonight, if only to spare my feelings. Instead, she looked more amazing than ever. We ate dinner in Chinatown, and Maria told us about her assignment. There would be some teaching, and some agricultural work. She wouldn't get the details until she arrived in St. Petersburg. I proposed a toast, and we all wished her the best. Out on the sidewalk, carrying a bottle of Dom Pérignon, I laughed and joked and pretended I was having the time of my life; but when my eyes met Maria's, I'm sure that she saw the truth.

We walked to the edge of the Combat Zone and tried to hail a cab. Evan started chatting with the hookers. A huge transvestite quoted us a price for four. Evan said thanks but we weren't in the mood for catching AIDS tonight. The hooker started spitting. Luckily a cab arrived. The fare to Faneuil was five dollars. Evan gave the driver a fifty and told him to keep the change. "I've always wanted to do that," he said. We sat on a bench beside a statue of Red Auerbach and finished the champagne before braving the crowd at the Black Rose, an Irish pub, where we hoisted pints of Guinness and sang "A Nation Once Again" and "What Shall We Do with the Drunken Sailor?" with some thick-necked idiots from South Boston who kept hitting on Agnes and Maria. They both were wearing short black dresses, and looking outstanding, which is basically the point that the Irish guys were trying to get across, albeit in a somewhat less than eloquent manner. "If there is anything worse than the Boston Irish," Evan said, "would someone please tell me?"

This prompted some angry comments, and threats of violence, and soon we were in another cab, rocketing across town, and I was making Evan promise not to give this guy fifty bucks, too. On Lansdowne Street there was the usual Friday night scene: kids from the suburbs in white stretch limos, wiseguys driving Mercedes 600SL coupes, Asian kids from BU driving M3s and Corrados. We bribed our way past the line at Xeno and paid another bribe to get a booth up on a raised platform at the side of the room. It was midnight, and the deejay was doing a nineties retrospective: Madonna, Prince, Us3. Evan said this summed up our generation; even our nostalgia was for ourselves.

"Everything's accelerating," he said. "Nostalgia used to have a twenty-year lag. In the seventies everyone was into the fifties. But then in the eighties everyone was into the seventies. Now, in the nineties, we're into the nineties. What's left? Nothing. Time folds in on itself, like a black hole. It's the millennium, the collapse of culture. *Götterdämmerung.*"

"Right," I said. "Let's dance."

The deejay was playing Deee-Lite's "Groove Is in the Heart," a song I remembered dancing to at a frat party during my freshman year at Michigan. That was seven years ago, but it seemed like more. I wondered if this was how it felt to get old. Lull told us once how the seventies craze had upset him, because he knew all of those disco songs from the first time around, and he realized now that he had officially become old. Thinking about Lull made me feel sad. Or maybe it was the drinking. Alcohol does that to me. I'm Irish, after all. I drink, and then I cry.

Back in the booth, Maria and Agnes were sitting pressed up against each other and talking about bisexuality. Agnes said everyone was bisexual but that most people had been conditioned to believe that heterosexuality was the norm. I said we should test her theory: we could get four hits of Ecstasy, go home, take off our clothes, and see what happened. Maria said it was fine by her, as long as we could have a few more martinis first. She said she had never tried the girl-girl thing, but what the hell, she was leaving town anyway, so why not?

The only holdout was Evan. He said he would watch, and perhaps join in—"selectively," he said and glanced at Maria. Agnes said fair was fair, and that if she and Maria were going to get it on for us, then we would have to get it on for them. There was nothing more erotic than watching two guys get it on, she said. Evan said he could think of, oh, say, about a zillion things more erotic than that.

I told him that Agnes was right, that fair was fair, and that once we got going it wouldn't be so bad. "I'll be gentle with you," I said. I put my arm around his neck and pulled his head down toward my lap. He pushed me away. I slapped him. He slapped me back.

"You bitch," I said. "You know you love it."

"You're the bitch," he said.

"You see?" Agnes said, turning to Maria. "You see how they are?"

"I know," Maria said. "It's incredible."

"What's incredible," Evan said, "is that I'm sitting here listening to this."

"Why do you fight it?" Agnes asked him. "You know you've got a thing for Reilly. You spend half your time at work sending each other porn magazines and ads for phone sex. You're always making jokes about each other being gay." She turned to Maria. "You should see them. They're always wrestling, and fighting, and grabbing each other. Basically, they're in love with each other."

"Right," Evan said. "Dream on."

"You love Reilly," Agnes said, "because he's got the whole Motor City boy-boy thing going, and you always wished you could be like that; and Reilly loves you because you're a genius, which is, well, something he's not. You're like a married couple. You live together, you work together, you bicker all the time. The only thing you don't do is have sex, and the only reason you don't do that is that you're afraid, because society tells you it's wrong."

Maria said she had long suspected the same thing. Evan said it was bad enough that Agnes was crazy without Maria becoming a wacko, too.

"But what about the time," Maria said, "when you guys brought home that love doll and kept putting it back and forth in each other's beds? That went on for weeks. You don't think there was something symbolic about that? You don't think there was a homoerotic component to that?"

"No," Evan said, "I don't. It was a *joke*. And for the record, the doll was female." He waved to a waitress, who ignored him. He drained the last drops out of his martini glass and said he wanted to go home.

"Oh, relax," Maria said. "We're kidding." She took his hand and led him to the dance floor. Agnes did the same with me. Then suddenly somehow it was one-thirty and the music had stopped and the lights had come up and three bouncers who looked like life-size Transformer dolls were marching around telling everyone to put down their drinks and get out. It's awful when the lights come up and everyone mills around looking not nearly as good as they looked in the dark and then you're massing along in that herd of uglies toward the street.

Outside it had rained: the pavement glistened, the air was cool. A bunch of club kids stood on a corner daring cabbies to veer through an enormous puddle and splash them. The cabbies were happy to oblige. The kids were soaked, laughing their heads off.

We piled into a cab. Agnes gave the driver her address in Allston. By the time we left Kenmore Square, she and Evan were asleep.

Maria leaned against me. I ran my fingers through her hair. The cab driver scowled at me in his mirror. He was Middle Eastern, and clearly disgusted, although by what, exactly, I wasn't sure.

In Allston, Agnes tried to shake Evan awake, but he was out cold. She kissed him on the cheek and told us to take care of him. Back in the North End, we paid the driver some ridiculous amount of money and found our way upstairs. We had left the windows open, with the fans on; the apartment was cool, and the smell had mostly gone away. Evan stumbled off to his room. Maria and I toppled onto my bed and fell asleep.

ARLY THE NEXT MORNING I was awakened by the sound of a garbage truck in the street below our window; it was groaning like some awful prehistoric creature, while barrels clanged and clattered and two men shouted at each other over the din of the hopper. The truck rolled ahead, then ground to a halt again, its air brakes hissing; there was more shouting, more barrels banging. My head was killing me.

"What time is it?" Maria said.

"I don't know. Early." Without my glasses I couldn't read the alarm clock.

Somehow during the night we had managed to get partially undressed. We were both in our underwear. I had no idea how this had happened. Maria got up and put on my POLITICALLY ERECT T-shirt and led me to Evan's room. He lay on his side, snoring like a lumberjack. Maria slipped into the bed in front of him, and placed his arm around her waist. I climbed in behind him, and put my hand on his shoulder. I tickled his nose with a lock of Maria's hair. He woke up, brushing the hair away. "Maria?" he said.

"Quiet," I whispered. "You'll wake her up."

"Huh?" He turned. "What the—"

"Shhh. How's your ass? Does it hurt?"

"What the fuck are you talking about?"

"You don't remember? You were kind of getting into it. It wasn't as weird as I thought it would be. It was pretty cool."

"Right."

"Tonight," I said, "it's your turn."

Maria began to giggle. Evan said we were both sick. He lifted himself up, then got dizzy and lay back down. He asked me what time it was. I told him I didn't know. He got up and went to the bathroom.

The garbage truck heaved away down the street, out of range. There was no sound but the fan humming in the window. Maria and I lay on our backs with our eyes closed. She was running her fingers through my hair. Somewhere in the neighborhood, girls were playing jump rope, clapping hands, and singing: *"Oh Mary Mack, Mack, Mack, all dressed in black, black, black, with silver buttons, buttons, buttons, all down her back, back, back . . ."*

Then we heard the barking. It was far away at first, just one sound amid all the others in the neighborhood; but it kept getting closer, and then it was very close—it was right outside our building— and I realized what was happening. I couldn't believe it. It was like waking up from a bad dream and finding out that you hadn't actually been dreaming. I ran to the window.

There, on our front steps, stood Coco. She saw me, and started barking louder, and wagging her tail.

"Say it ain't so," Evan said.

He ran to the window. So did Maria. The three of us sat there staring down at Coco and the crowd that had begun to gather on the sidewalk behind her. They were looking up at us. Gus came out of the store. "Maria!" he shouted. "What the hell are you doing up there? I've been looking for you."

Then it began to dawn on him: the prank we had pulled on him, Lucia's complaints about the odor. I could see the realization spreading across his face.

Tony ran around the corner, followed by two goons.

"What is it?" he said. "What's going on?"

"Up there." Gus pointed at us. "They're the ones."

They ran into the building. We could hear them pounding up the stairs. Then they were banging on our door. "Open up!" Lucia shouted. "Open the door! There's people here to see you. They know all about you."

Evan picked up the phone. He was going to call the police.

"Forget the police," Maria said. "We'll be dead before they get here. Come on."

Tony and the others were trying to smash the deadbolt through the wall. The molding had started to crack. Any second now it would give way.

I stood there in a panic.

"Up to the roof," Maria said. "Get your car keys and the backpack."

Maria went first, then Evan, then me. I put a stick through the skylight latch to keep it from opening. We had climbed over the roof and were moving down the fire escape when the goons broke through the door of the apartment: there was a snap like a tree branch breaking and then a boom as the door smashed to the floor. By the time they got to roof, we were already down in the alley and running toward Commercial Street, where I'd left my car. I fired up the engine and tore around the corner and then screeched to a halt because Coco was standing in the middle of street, smiling at us, wagging her tail.

In the distance, Tony and the others were running through the alleys. We could hear their footsteps, and their voices, shouting.

I opened my door and whistled to Coco. Sure enough, she ran over and jumped into the car. She climbed across my lap and got into the backseat with Evan. We sped off, tires squealing, just as Tony and the goons came around the corner.

One of the goons pulled out a gun. But Tony pulled his arm away—there were people all around. The last thing I saw in the rearview mirror was Tony punching the air and gesturing at the goons to get going.

THERE WAS NO SENSE DRIVING like a maniac, Maria said, since obviously Tony and the others didn't know which highway we had taken, or otherwise they would have caught up with us already. We were on Route 95 in southern Massachusetts, near the Rhode Island border. Clearly they had lost our trail, Maria said, and the best thing to do now was to drive the speed limit and try to avoid the police. Imagine what a trooper would think, she said, if he pulled over a car and found three people dressed in underwear, with a stolen racing dog and a bag full of money.

"I'm sure stranger things have happened," I said.

"Not to me."

I took her advice and slowed down to seventy-five, braking to sixty-five when the radar detector beeped. We drove south through Rhode Island, passing signs for Nooseneck, Moscow, Wyoming, and Hope Valley.

The sun was high, and brutally hot. The Bimmer did not have air conditioning; all we could do was keep the windows open and let the air rush through. At one time I had thought about having an air-conditioning system retrofitted into the car, but had decided it would be too expensive. Now it seemed like it would have been worth every penny.

Coco rode in back with Evan holding her face in the jet stream, her ears flapping. Every so often she would shift over and lean against Evan, and he would push her away. Evan was in no mood for snuggling. He sat there sulking, with his face turned toward the window, gazing at the mess of buildings and tattered billboards that passed for a landscape.

We crossed into Connecticut and now, feeling safe, we stopped in a Wal-Mart plaza for clothes. It was noon, the pavement merciless on my bare feet. In the trunk I found a pair of flip-flops and an old Ocean Pacific bathing suit that had been there since one day in June when we had gone to the beach. The bathing suit was rolled up into a ball, and had hardened from the salt water: it looked like some kind of fossil. Evan managed to unroll the suit and get himself into it. He went into a Wal-Mart and came out with a bag of clothes: shorts, T-shirts, underwear, flip-flops.

We dressed in the car. Evan had bought himself a pair of khaki shorts, a plain green pocket T-shirt, and a Yankees baseball cap. My outfit, on the other hand, consisted of a New Kids on the Block baseball cap, a purple Barney T-shirt, and madras shorts with a thirty-six-inch waist that kept sliding down off my hips. For Maria, Evan had selected a pair of Daisy Duke jean shorts with red patches on them, as well as a white T-shirt with gold appliqués in the shape of butterflies. He said he had just grabbed whatever he saw first. I said fine, then why didn't he and I switch outfits?

Maria told me to drop it; we had bigger things to worry about than dorky clothes. I put on my stupid cap and drove to a gas station, where I filled the tank and checked the oil. Then I got back up on the highway and drove in the center lane, at exactly sixty-five miles an hour. Coco stuck her head out the window. People in other cars were pointing at her and waving. We were near the coast now, heading through Old Lyme and Old Saybrook. It was low tide. The air stank.

Maria explained to Evan the plan that we had worked out while he was in the Wal-Mart.

"Miami?" He leaned into the front. "Are you serious? We're going to drive to Miami? What the hell is in Miami, other than my grandparents?"

"Maria has a cousin there," I said. "His name is Santo. She says he'll let us stay with him."

She had called her cousin from a pay phone. He told her to get to Miami and he would take care of everything. When I asked her who this cousin was and what he did for a living, she told me I was better off not asking so many questions.

"What if I don't want to go to Florida?" Evan said.

"It's only for a little while," I told him. "Until this blows over."

"How long is that?"

"I don't know. We'll see. If it's any consolation, we don't like this any better than you do."

"Sure," he said. "That's a big consolation."

I said we had to make a pact—either we stayed together or we split up. "Right here, right now, we have to decide," I said. "If anyone wants to go their own way, they can go now. Otherwise, we stick to the plan."

I looked at Maria.

"I'm in," she said.

I turned to Evan. He was sitting with his legs pulled up against his chest.

"Well?" I said.

He scowled. "Just drive."

41

WE DROVE THROUGH NEW JERSEY and skirted Philadelphia, then nibbed through the top of Delaware before crossing into Maryland. Night was falling. But still the air was unbearably hot. I was worried about the Bimmer overheating, and kept my eyes on the temperature gauge, whose needle kept moving dangerously close to the red zone. When we stopped for gas, I added some antifreeze and prayed that it would hold us. Meanwhile, Evan and Maria had been bickering since Hartford. First it was over the radio station: Evan wanted jazz, Maria wanted anything else. Then it was the windows: Maria wanted them open all the way, Evan said that was too much. Then Evan wanted to change places with Maria, so he could get away from Coco, who he claimed was drooling on him. Coco, for her part, just lay there on the backseat looking miserable.

Near Baltimore, we pulled off and found a Burger King. The kid working behind the counter had a giant white zit in the center of his forehead. Evan said imagine what would happen if that monster exploded when he was leaning over the grill. "Thanks," Maria said. "Now I can't eat." She threw out her cheeseburger and fries and took her diet Coke out to the car.

Back on the road, Evan started complaining again about Coco. He claimed she was taking up more than half of the backseat. I told him that if he didn't sit still and be quiet I was going to turn this car around right now and go home. Maria was less tolerant: she told him to shut up and go to sleep. He said he couldn't sleep in an upright position, especially not when it was a hundred degrees and there were bugs flying through the window and smacking him in the face and a giant dog slobbering on him. Maria turned on the radio.

Near midnight, just south of Richmond, Virginia, the radar detector chirped and I hit the brakes but it was too late—a siren erupted behind us and a set of red-and-blue lights appeared in the rearview mirror. We had been cruising at about a hundred, which was reasonable considering the car we were in and the condition of the road, which was smooth and wide and almost completely empty. But good luck explaining that to a cop.

I pulled into the breakdown lane, turned on the dome light, put my hands on the wheel where the cop could see them, and waited. Evan kept jumping around, turning to look out the rear window and then turning to stare straight ahead, tugging at his hair and his shirt. This was it, he said. No doubt Giaccalone had gone to the police, and now every highway patrol on the East Coast was looking for us. Maria told him to be quiet.

"Just sit there and try to look innocent," she said.

"Are you kidding?" Evan said. "Look at me." His hair was matted to his head, his beard was frazzled: in the glare of the dome light he looked like a terrorist and a drug trafficker and a child molester all rolled into one. "Do you have any idea what they do to Jews down here?" he said. "Do the words *Ku Klux Klan* ring a bell? And what about the dog? What's this guy going to think when he sees this dog? And what if he finds the money? What's he going to think when he sees thirty thousand bucks in a backpack?"

Before we could answer, the trooper had arrived at the window. He was holding his flashlight up on his shoulder and aiming it at my face. I squinted. He was black, and a giant. The top of my window came about level with his waist. Looking up at his face was like trying to see up into the top branches of a tree. He asked me if I had any idea how fast I'd been going. "Sixty?" I said. He sighed, and asked for my license and registration.

When dealing with cops you have to remember that the people who become police usually do so because it gives them something they wouldn't have in most other jobs—namely, the opportunity to deal almost exclusively with people who are even less intelligent than they are. When that is not the case—when they encounter someone with an IQ above one hundred—they tend to get defensive. The best thing to do is play dumb, look scared, and be polite.

He asked me what we were doing in Virginia. He shined the flashlight in my eyes again. In a shaking, timid voice (which was not fake) I explained that we were on vacation, driving to Florida. He aimed the flashlight into the backseat. Coco stood up and tried to stick her head out my window. Evan pulled her back. In the rearview mirror I caught a glimpse of Evan's face: he was terrified. If I were a cop and I saw someone looking like that, I would radio for help and start tearing open the fenders looking for drugs.

"That animal should be restrained," the cop said.

Evan grabbed Coco by the collar and pulled her back into the seat beside him. She barked, and tried to get free. I told the trooper that I was sorry, that my dog got excited when she saw police officers. "My dad's a policeman, up in Michigan," I said. "She just probably thinks you're one of his friends or something."

He smirked, and walked back to his cruiser.

"We're dead," Evan said. "He'll run your plates. He'll find out who we are."

"Buddy," I said, "I'm getting a speeding ticket, okay? I've gotten them before."

But not like this one. The fine was two hundred and twenty-five dollars, payable on the spot. The trooper had a little credit card reader. I gave him my Visa card. He ran it through, gave me a receipt, and told me to have a nice day and to keep the speed down. I assured him I would.

When we got under way again Evan said that if we came to a rest area he'd like to stop because he needed to throw out his underpants. I laughed. Maria did not. I asked her what was wrong. She pretended not to hear me.

I switched on the radio, and found nothing but country-and-western. On the AM band I found a call-in show: mental cases calling in for help, a woman psychologist hurling abuse. Maria turned the radio off. I said nothing. We drove on silence, listening to the hum of the Bridgestones on the pavement. I held the speed at sixty-five. When we crossed into North Carolina, I thought about speeding up again but was too tired. Evan was asleep in back. Maria had her eyes closed but I knew she was still awake.

The road was empty and dark. There were few exits, no billboards, nothing outside the swath of our headlights. The road was flat and smooth and straight: it seemed as if we were sitting still while the highway rolled toward us. At about two o'clock Coco began whimpering and scratching at the seat. I knew what that meant. I pulled into a rest area. The huge eighteen-wheelers were laid up in rows beside each other like sleeping dinosaurs. They sat with their diesel engines rumbling, their running lights on. Mosquitoes snapped into a blue bug-zapper. The sign on the building said: TOURIST INFORMATION. There were brochures and maps in the window. Why on earth anyone in their right mind would come here for a vacation was beyond me. But I could imagine the little blue-haired ladies working behind the counter during the day, serving coffee and touting the wonders of the local caves or the slave cabins or whatever else they had in North Carolina.

Out back, behind the building, Coco trotted away to the edge of a clearing and took a crap in the dark near the woods. I could just see her figure in the shadows. When she was finished, she straightened up and stretched her legs; and then she started to run. She jogged to the far side of the field, and for a moment I feared she was running away. But then she made a broad, sweeping turn, and ran back toward me, gaining speed. She zoomed past, so close that at the last moment

I feared she would hit me and knock me over. She looped around the perimeter of the field, moving so fast now that she seemed not to be touching the ground.

Most dogs run like horses: there is only one point in their stride when all four feet are off the ground. But greyhounds run like cats, in a double-suspension gallop, meaning there are two points when their feet are off the ground—first, when their feet are underneath their body, and then when their feet are stretched out in front and behind them. This is what gives them their speed. In the dim light Coco was barely a shadow, a dark shape whooshing past. I stood still, and closed my eyes, and listened to the drumming of her feet. I thought about the consequences of being hit by a seventy-pound animal moving at forty miles per hour. Coco passed within inches of my legs. I felt the wind on my knees. When I opened my eyes, she was streaking across the far side of the field. One corner of the field was lit by a sulphur lamp in the parking lot. She burst through the splash of light, and the effect was remarkable: it was as if she took form for a second and then vanished again.

Finally she slowed down and ran over to me, swishing her tail, breathing hard, smiling. I suppose it felt good to be out of the city and breathing fresh air again. Probably this was the first decent run she'd had since Giaccalone took her. I crouched down, and rubbed her neck and shoulders. She looked at me like a child who has just done something to impress a parent. I swear it was as if she were speaking to me. My legs were still trembling from her last pass in front of me.

She jogged away a few feet; then she stopped and looked back over her shoulder. She wanted me to follow her. She ran back, and nudged me with her head. She grabbed my shirt in her teeth, and pulled. She ran off again, lifting her head, cantering like a horse. Then she looked back over her shoulder. *Come on,* she seemed to say, as if she wanted me to come run with her. I stayed where I was. She began running loops again, showing off. I had the idea that she was trying to tell me who she was, in case maybe I didn't know already.

MARIA WAS SITTING on the hood of the car when I got back. "I don't feel like sleeping," she said.

"Me either."

"But I guess we should. Maybe I'll close my eyes for a little while."

Evan was still in the car, out cold. Coco drank some water—I'd filled up a cup for her—then jumped in back and curled up beside him.

Out on the highway, a lone truck rumbled past. Maria watched it roll away, and kept watching even after it was out of sight. The trucks in the parking lot grunted and huffed smoke. Above us the sky was empty and dark.

"I guess this wasn't exactly how you expected to spend your last few weeks in the States," I said.

"Actually, I'm supposed to be doing inventory this week," she said. "In a way this is a blessing."

I told her what I'd been thinking: In the morning we could take her to a bus station and give her some money to get home. She could give us her cousin's phone number and we could look him up ourselves when we got to Miami. Or she could call him and tell him that we were coming. She didn't have to actually be there with us.

"It's better if I go with you," she said. "Besides, it's only a few more hours. So we'll get you to Miami, and then if you want me to leave, I'll leave."

"It's not that I want you to leave," I said.

"Then maybe I'll stay," she said. She slid down off the hood and put her arms around my neck.

"I don't understand why you're helping us," I said. "You said we were being stupid."

"You were," she said. "You still are, I guess. So why am I helping you? I don't know. That's a good question. Maybe you noticed that I kind of have this thing for you. Have you noticed that? And I guess I feel this need to save you from yourself. My aunt always used to say that I didn't have boyfriends, I had projects. I guess I like the idea of people who need to be fixed in some way. And if anyone ever needed fixing, it's you, my friend."

We kissed. Her hand slid down over my belly. I pressed myself against her.

"Let's go for a walk," she said.

Out back, behind the building, there was a picnic table under a tree. The ground was strewn with fallen apples. Their smell hung in the air. All I could think about, as we made love, was that in three weeks Maria would be gone and I would never see her again.

"I wish you weren't leaving," I said.

I was whispering; our faces were only inches apart.

"Please don't do this." A tear formed in her left eye and ran down across her cheek. Then her eyes flashed and she said, "Come on," and pulled me against her.

But I couldn't continue. "I'm sorry," I said. "I can't. I don't know. I just—"

"It's okay," she said, and pulled my face against her neck. We lay there, breathing, not talking. Then finally we got up and walked back to the car and closed our eyes and lay in our seats, pretending to sleep.

A T SIX, the air was humid and hot. A gray mist hung like steam over the fields, and the trees at the edge of the woods were wreathed in fog. The parking lot was empty; the trucks had rumbled away. In the daylight the buildings looked drab. The parking lot was strewn with litter. Maria was still sleeping. So was Coco. Evan was gone. I saw him over at the far side of the parking lot, using a pay phone. I got out and went over to him. He was leaving voice mail for Lull, saying that we had both come down sick with a stomach virus and wouldn't be in for a few days.

I reached over and hung up the phone.

"Evan," I said, "think. Where are we? What are we doing? We don't have to call in sick. We don't work at Ionic anymore. We don't live in Boston anymore. Everything in the apartment is gone. It's trashed. It's out on the street. Giaccalone is setting it on fire."

His face fell. "Most of those records can't be replaced," he said. "They're first editions. They're worth . . . God only knows. They're priceless. Do you know how much that stereo cost? I've got to go back."

I grabbed him by the shoulders. I told him to forget about it, to let it go. "As of today," I said, "as of right now, all you own is what's in your pockets."

He pulled himself free. "You're psychotic."

"Come on," I said, and took him by the arm, the way you would with your senile grandfather when you've discovered him escaping from the nursing home. "Let's go back to the car."

We rolled down into the South, past pig farms and fields of cotton, past wooden shacks and junk cars, past Cracker Barrel restaurants and billboards advertising subdivisions with names like Forest Acres and Runnymeade, places which, when we saw them, seemed bleaker than anything on the planet: little identical boxes crowded onto bare spits of land. It was Sunday morning. I could imagine the scene being played out in every small town we passed: church bells ringing, Christians clapping their hands and rolling on the floor and praying for God to kill Jews and homosexuals.

The air grew hotter, the sun brighter, and you could feel the IQs falling. At each truck stop the attendants seemed to have thicker accents and fewer teeth, both of which made them more difficult to understand. By the time we got to Georgia, I could only point at the high octane pump and use hand signals to indicate the need for water for the dog.

This was *Dukes of Hazzard* land, and on the highway we were surrounded by redneck dream-mobiles—old Z-28s and Trans Ams and Roadrunners, Oldsmobile 442s and Corvettes and Barracudas. Every time one of them pulled up beside me, I downshifted and got ready to give some hillbilly the surprise of his life, but then as the turbocharger began to surge I would catch Maria frowning and I would shift back into fifth and try to think about something else: baseball scores, the periodic table. I thought about Ionic, and Nectar, and my nonfuture in the software industry; and soon I was going sixty-five again.

Evan sat in back imitating a line from a Ku Klux Klan phone recording that he had downloaded from the Internet and used to play on his computer at work. "Wake up, white people," he drawled, cupping his hands around his mouth, shouting out the window at the people in other cars. "Wake up, white people. Wake up, white people." He did this for about half an hour, until Maria turned around and said that if he said that one more time, she was going to climb into the backseat and kill him with her bare hands.

He got quiet for a while. But then he started talking about Microsoft and the Illuminati. This was paranoid stuff he picked up on the Internet. We let him ramble. It made the time pass. The Illuminati, he said, were an occult society that secretly controlled governments and banks. In 1975, the leaders of the Illuminati convened in Turkey and decided to move their organization to the United States. That year, oddly enough, was the year that Microsoft was founded. Also, on the Microsoft campus there was a pentagon-shaped building accessible only through secret passageways from other buildings and known only to five people, one of whom was Bill Gates. Oddly enough, "Gates" was the name of a magician in an Aleister Crowley novel. And if you converted the letters B-I-L-L-G-A-T-E-S to their ASCII number values you got a total of 663, and if you remembered that Bill Gates was actually William Gates III, and you added three to your previous total, you got 666, the number of the beast.

"Coincidence?" Evan said. "I don't think so."

Maria yawned, and turned on the radio.

We pulled into a truck stop in Georgia for breakfast. Maria and I ordered biscuits and gravy. Evan sat sulking over a cup of black coffee, staring out the window. He hadn't spoken for almost an hour.

In the next booth a hooker was showing photographs of her daughter to a trucker. They laughed together; it was almost tender. The hooker was overweight, with enormous breasts and bad skin and a huge gap between her front teeth. In a *Hee-Haw* drawl she was telling the trucker how intelligent her daughter was. "That's my baby," she said, putting the photo back into her purse.

Maria went to a pay phone and called her cousin. She came back looking sick. I asked her what was wrong. She glanced at the door. Her hands were shaking.

"He said—" She stopped.

"What?"

"There's a reward," she said. "Giaccalone put out a reward for us. Fifty thousand dollars, no questions asked. He says to get down there as fast as possible."

We ran out to the car. When we were under way I asked her how her cousin had come to know these things about Giaccalone. "Is he"—I searched for a polite way to say this—"is he one of these guys, too?"

"He knows people," Maria said.

"I see."

"He's making arrangements about the dog," she said. "He says he thinks we can sell her. Then he'll get us out of the country for a while."

In back, Evan began to moan.

Maria got out the map and tried to figure out how far we were from Miami. We were just south of Savannah; so maybe four hundred miles.

"Reilly," she said, "how fast will this car go?"

We flew down into Florida, past Jacksonville, Daytona Beach, Edgewater, Titusville, Merritt Island, Cocoa Beach, Melbourne, Vero Beach. Now when I downshifted and the engine lurched, Maria didn't complain—she just gripped the dashboard and braced her feet against the firewall. I drove in the outside lane, flashing my lights at the cars ahead of us, cutting over and passing on the right when some bozo in a minivan or four-by-four wouldn't yield.

From the highway we saw palm trees and sand, and at the gas stations people seemed to be speaking English again. Twice I asked Maria what day it was. Sunday, she told me. I tried to remember the last time I'd had a shower: it was Friday morning. Since then I'd tried to wash up in various men's rooms, but nevertheless I stank.

The smell was archeological, built in layers: champagne, Guinness, pot smoke, a chicken-fried steak that I had eaten in some truck stop.

In Fort Lauderdale we stopped for gas, and when we tried to get back on the highway, I missed a turn and we ended up in a parking lot near the beach. We got out and spread the map on the hood of the car and tried to figure out how to get back to the highway. Gulls wheeled in the sky, squawking. Girls in bikinis rode around on dune buggies. Evan said maybe we should just stay here. We could rent a little cottage and smoke pot and ask girls if they needed help putting suntan lotion on their backs. "Wake up, white people," he said, cupping his hands around his mouth and addressing the parking lot.

Maria told him to shut up. Evan said he was sick of Maria telling him to shut up. "Who died and made you God?" he said. Maria said Evan might try to remember that right now, even as we spoke, there were people who were trying to find us in order to kill us. As she said this, an old man with oily hair and a thin mustache approached from the corner of the parking lot, pushing an ice cream cart. The cart had a radio strapped to the lid and a red umbrella mounted to its side. On the radio Seals and Crofts were singing "Summer Breeze," and all I could think was that this was not the way I wanted to die, in a parking lot in Fort Lauderdale, listening to a soft rock station.

"Ices!" the man called. "Raspberry, orange, lemon, and lime. Hey, kids. You want the ice, kids?" He opened the lid and reached inside. My heart stopped. The whole thing seemed to be happening in slow motion. I looked at Maria and saw that she was thinking the same thing I was. She glanced at the man's hand, then back at me, and it dawned on both of us that it was too late to run—we were dead.

But instead of a gun the man took out a paper cup and a scoop and said, "What is this, a funeral? Who wants the ice, huh? The ice! Who's got the ice? I've got the ice! Who wants the ice?"

"Maybe you could come back," Maria said.

"Oh . . . I . . . don't . . . think . . . so." The old man closed the lid. "You get one chance with the ice man. Ice doesn't last, day like today." He rolled away, tilting his head back and calling out, "Who's got the ice? I've got the ice! Raspberry, orange, lemon, and lime!"

Maria leaned against the car and began to cry. I went to her. She pushed me away. "Just drive," she said.

The highway was jammed with traffic. The sun was so bright it hurt. Near the Hollywood exit we got another scare when two Cubans in a black 740i caught sight of us in their rearview mirror and slowed down and fell in beside us. The window on the passenger side rolled down. I was getting ready to duck when the guy called out, "Hey, dude, is that a factory turbo?" I told him it was. "Sweet ride," he said, and gave me a thumbs-up. They pulled ahead.

"I can't take much more of this," I said.

"We're almost there," Maria said. A few minutes later she said, "That's it, right there, up ahead. Get in the right lane, and take the next exit."

44

SANTO'S HOUSE was a brown ranch with white trim—the word *nondescript* sprang to mind. The shrubs were overgrown, the lawn needed mowing. Santo was going through a divorce, Maria said. A rough one, from the look of things. The shades were drawn. The shutters were flaking and in need of paint. The brick wall surrounding the yard was cracked in places and crumbling at the corners. The house itself seemed to sag, as if Santo's depression were weighing it down. Or maybe it was the heat, which was worse here than in New England. At the driveway two pillars stood holding a wrought-iron gate that groaned as it opened.

"I'm sorry for the hassle with the gate and everything," Santo said, when we pulled up in front of the house and piled out of the car. "But you can't be too careful down here."

He told me to put the car in the garage. "Just a precaution," he said. "But you never know. Better to be safe, right?"

He was thin, dark, with a face that looked older than I knew he was and the kind of perfectly black hair that you only see in magazines. His eyes were black too, and his gaze was disconcerting; you did not want to look directly at him for any length of time. He wore sandals, khaki shorts, and a green T-shirt. Maria gave him a hug and a kiss. When she turned to introduce us, still with her arm around his waist, I saw the family resemblance.

Coco was romping on the lawn with Dex, Santo's little terrier, who had come running up to the car when we arrived. Dex yapped and chased Coco around the lawn. Coco would leap away, then stand still and wait for Dex to catch up, and then leap away again.

"She's a beautiful animal," Santo said. He called to her, and she ran over. He crouched down and ran his hands over her shoulders and down along her sides. Dex stood there yapping, wanting attention. "I've never actually seen a greyhound up close like this," Santo said. "I've only seen them at the track."

I told him about the night before, at the rest area, when I had seen Coco running circles. "She's been clocked at forty-seven miles an hour," I said.

"That's pretty fast," he said, without looking at me.

I suppose he despised us. And why shouldn't he? We had put Maria's life in danger and now we were putting his in danger, too. He looked like someone who didn't need another thing to worry about. He was smiling at Maria and trying to seem happy. But he had forgotten to shave, and his clothes had food stains on them. His wife had been gone for two months, Maria said. She had taken the kids and would probably get custody. Santo had the look of a broken man: stooped shoulders, dark eyes. Probably he had been wearing these clothes for days now.

I knew what he was going through. I wished I could tell him that. I know all about it, I wanted to tell him. I know how you lose track of time, how the weeks go by, how one day you look up and realize that it's a different month than the last time you checked. I know how you keep losing things—your keys, your wallet—and thinking that somehow this is a metaphor for your life. I know how your own life suddenly becomes strange and unfamiliar, as if you are wandering, lost, in a huge building that you ought to recognize, but don't.

"You guys must be tired," Santo said. "Put the car away, and then come on inside. We'd better bring the dog inside, too."

The inside of the house was as drab as the outside. I kept thinking that it was no wonder Santo's wife had left him. The furniture looked as if it came from Sears. Photographs of Santo's kids, a boy and a girl, hung on the walls. In one photograph there was also a woman: blond, pretty, but tough-looking. Something about the corners of her mouth, the shape of her eyes. You would not mess with her. This, I presumed, was his wife.

A housekeeper showed us to our rooms. Her name was Susanna. She was middle-aged, gray-haired, thick-waisted. She had been the nanny for Santo's kids and had stayed on to cook his meals and take care of the house.

We were wiped out. We had driven the last four hundred miles in five hours, and now the adrenaline was draining away, like a drug wearing off.

"Take a shower, and get some sleep," Santo said. "I'll wake you up for dinner, and we can talk about what to do."

45

SANTO HAD TRIED TO ARRANGE a deal with Giaccalone. Through an intermediary he had offered to return the dog and the money, if Giaccalone would agree to leave us alone. Giaccalone told the intermediary that he was not going to make any deals with anybody, and that when he found out who the intermediary was representing, there was going to be hell to pay.

"He's being unreasonable," Santo said. "He's letting his anger get in the way of getting his dog back. That tells us two things. First, that he's weak. Second, that he's dangerous."

We were having dinner on the screened porch at the back of the house. Susanna had served gazpacho, then shrimp salad, then steaks. Halfway through the meal the sky had darkened and then suddenly exploded with rain. Now the rain had ended and the air smelled like laundry just out of the wash. We were drinking Cuban coffee: strong and black, in little cups. Coco and Dex were stretched out at the edge of the porch, snoozing.

Santo had a new plan. He had found Karl Wilson in California and arranged for us to sell Coco to him. "It's not ideal," Santo said, "but it's the best thing you can do. Get rid of the dog, get out of the country, and let things cool off."

I asked him how he had managed to find Wilson. He said he had talked to people who had talked to people. He had friends who had friends. Maria gave me a look. I started to wonder about Santo. But at the same time I got the sense that I would be better off if I did not ask too many questions. Wilson was taking a red-eye from San Diego and would meet us in Fort Myers in the morning.

"He's got friends there," Santo said. "He figures it's safer there than in Miami. He can get in and get out. Here in Miami he might be spotted."

Wilson would pay us twenty-five thousand for the dog, the same amount he had been willing to pay Giaccalone. We would take the twenty-five thousand, plus the thirty we already had, and go to Belize. Santo had a house there. In three weeks Maria would leave for Russia; then Evan and I would be on our own.

"I'm sorry," he said. "But it's the best I can do."

Evan said he didn't want to sound ungrateful but this was all happening kind of fast, and what were we supposed to do when our time ran out in Belize? Where were we going to go then? Santo made a face; he looked as if he had just tasted something unpleasant.

"I'll be honest with you," he said. "The only thing I care about here is Maria. As for you two guys, nothing personal, but it really doesn't matter to me what happens to you. You can leave right now. Take the dog with you. Drive away, and no hard feelings. Be my guest. Or don't be my guest, as the case may be."

He said this all in a quiet voice, between sips of coffee. Evan stared down at his plate. I had never seen anyone shut him up like that. I decided that I liked Santo, even if he did not like me.

Maria said we weren't in any position to be complaining. "Santo doesn't even know you," she said, "and he's going out of his way to help you. He's taking a big risk here. He doesn't need to get mixed up in this."

I said we appreciated everything that Santo was doing for us, and

that certainly we would figure out where to go after Belize. Santo
sighed and pushed his chair back from the table. "Let's go look at the
sky," he said. "It's beautiful after a storm." He whistled to Dex, who
jumped up and followed him out to the yard, with Coco close behind.

We stood outside on the wet grass admiring the long shafts of
light, which rose upward like pillars into the massive white clouds.
The sun had just dipped below the horizon, and the top of the sky
was growing dark, with bands of purple and pink stretched above a
line of bright red: it looked as if someone had pulled a shade over a
light but had left a crack open at the bottom. Even now, in the
evening, the heat was stunning. It made the heat wave in Boston
seem like nothing. The air was thick and sultry. Cicadas chirred in
the hedges.

Santo tossed a Frisbee for the dogs. Coco streaked around the
yard, with Dex yapping at her heels. I asked Santo if he knew how
much Giaccalone was offering as a reward for our capture. He said
that first of all the reward was not for our capture but for something
else altogether; and second, he didn't think it would do us any good
to talk about it. "It's bad luck," he said, taking the Frisbee from Coco,
who had just made a spectacular catch at the far end of the yard.

Santo had arranged for us to use a van for the drive to Fort Myers.
The van would help keep us from being recognized, he said. We
would leave at dawn, and if all went according to plan we would be
back by the early afternoon and out of the country by dinnertime.

"The only dangerous part of this thing is the drive to Fort Myers
and back," he said. "But you'll be okay. Just go there, drop off the dog,
get the money, and come straight back. Don't hang around. Don't talk
to strangers."

Despite the heat, I felt a chill running through me. Now that we
had stopped running I was starting to realize how much trouble we
were in. Until now this had all seemed a bit like a game; but suddenly
it seemed all too real.

I tried to explain this to Santo. He nodded. There was a story, he
said, about shearing sheep instead of wolves. He didn't know exactly

how the story went, but the point was that there was a reason for shearing sheep instead of wolves. "You guys," he said, "sheared a wolf. Not a big wolf, luckily. But a wolf nonetheless. And who knows? Maybe a little wolf is worse than a big wolf, because the little wolf gets his pride hurt more easily."

He smiled, and led us back into the house. Evan shuffled along behind me like a prisoner, walking as if his feet were shackled together, gazing down at the ground, not speaking. Coco and Dex ran to the kitchen for their water bowls.

Santo said he had errands to do. Maria agreed to go with him. They would be gone for a few hours, Santo said. He would wake us up at five for the trip to Fort Myers.

"I don't think I'll be able to sleep," I said.

"Try," Santo said. "You're going to need it."

46

"S ANTO GIVES ME THE CREEPS," Evan said. "And what's up with Wilson? And how did Santo find him? And Belize? Are you kidding? Where the hell is Belize?"

We were in the room that must have belonged to Santo's son. The wallpaper had little baseball players. Toys and games were stacked in the corner, and there was a pile of Sega Genesis cartridges next to a little TV set. Next to the bureau there was a fish tank that had been shut off but not emptied. The water was green, stagnant. I could imagine Santo coming in here to look at his son's stuff and just sitting on the bed, crying.

Evan turned on the TV. On the screen a woman in a Mexican soap opera was sobbing and saying, "Ay, Dios! Ay, Dios!" It was midnight. Coco and Dex were curled up on the floor asleep. Santo and Maria had been gone for hours. Evan said we should reconsider his original plan, which was to call the FBI and turn ourselves in. The FBI could arrange to return the money to Giaccalone, and they could protect us, too. With a good lawyer we'd probably stay out of jail.

It seemed to me, however, that while the FBI might not care about us ripping off Giaccalone, they certainly might have problems with what we had done to MassBank. And they might want to make an example of us. That's what they had done to Kevin Mitnick. All he did was hack into some Internet sites and harass people a little bit. He never stole anything. Still, the FBI had prosecuted him and he was sent to federal prison. There were magazine articles, books, TV shows. They made Mitnick into a kind of comic book arch villain, a twisted freak driven by self-loathing to commit heinous hacker crimes. Actually he was just another fat guy with a laptop and too much time on his hands and too few friends.

I could imagine how the newspapers would report our story. We wouldn't be two guys who had played a prank—we would be two geeks who had used our computer expertise to break into a bank. "They'd make us into Bonnie and Clyde," I said.

"That's okay," Evan said, "as long as I get to be Clyde."

"Think again, monkey man, because in prison, you and I would both be Bonnie."

I told him the one about the little nerdy white guy who goes to prison and gets put into a cell with a huge black guy. Black guy tells white guy there's nothing to be afraid of in prison. "All you gots to do," the black guy says, "is decide whether you want to be the husband or the wife. Whichever you want, that's fine by me. And then everything's cool." White guy says okay, well, he'd like to be the husband. Black guy smiles. "That's fine," he says. He pats his lap. "Now come on over here and suck your new wife's dick."

Evan lay on his back, staring at the ceiling. "That's not funny," he said.

I told him that everything was going to be all right. We would go to Belize and then after that we could go somewhere else. Bolivia, maybe. "Do you have any idea how long you can live on fifty thousand dollars in a place like Bolivia? And nobody can find you. That's why all the Nazis went there after the war."

"Great," he said. "We're going to live with the Nazis."

"We'll live like kings. We'll get a house, we'll go to the beach, we'll drink coconut drinks, whatever. Don't look so upset. You were going to quit Ionic anyway. You're going to start your own company."

"I don't think I'm going to be starting my own company in fucking Bolivia. Look at this." He pointed to the TV, where two Mexicans were having some kind of conversation. "Can you understand a word of this? Because I sure can't."

He shut off the TV. I got up and went to my room. Coco and Dex came with me.

Maria got back at two in the morning. I was lying in bed, awake, with Coco and Dex on either side of me, when I heard the motor in the garage door groaning. A moment later I heard Santo and Maria come in through the kitchen, and then Maria slipped into the room, trying to be quiet. The dogs jumped up and ran to her.

"Hey," I said. "It's okay. I'm awake."

"I figured you were asleep."

"No such luck. Turn the lights on if you want."

She switched on a lamp on the desk. The shade was in the form of a clown's head. All my life I have hated clowns. This one had a malicious smile—more of a leer than a smile. I tried not to look at it.

She leaned over the dresser, looking at herself in the mirror, taking off her earrings. I had the feeling that she didn't want to look at me. I wondered what she and Santo had been talking about. She said they had gone to a club in South Beach and Santo had talked about his divorce. "The poor guy," she said. "My heart breaks for him." She turned off the lamp and got into bed and told me the story: Santo's wife, Judy, had cheated on him. Santo found out, and Judy moved out, and now Judy had hired a lawyer who was going to take Santo for half of everything. "I've known Judy all my life," Maria said. "She was like a sister to me. I swear she was the nicest person I ever knew. They've been going out since high school, and now they're at each other's throats. I just can't believe it. It's scary."

She was lying beside me, her body warm beneath the cool sheets. The house was silent. The dogs had curled up on the floor at the foot of the bed.

"He asked me about you," she said. "About us."

"What did you tell him?"

"I don't know. What's there to say? I'm going away, right?"

"He probably thinks I'm an idiot."

"Not exactly."

"Tell me," I said.

"He thinks I'm an idiot, for getting involved with you."

"Nice."

"He wants me to stay here tomorrow. Just in case something goes wrong."

"I guess that's a good idea."

My heart began to flutter. A lump formed in my throat. That pre-wrestling-match feeling again, imagining all of the terrible things that were going to happen to me on the mat the next day. I knew that this was self-destructive—that thinking these thoughts would only contribute to my failure. But still I couldn't stop myself.

Now all sorts of paranoia flashed through my mind. What if we drove to Fort Myers and came back and Maria was gone? What if Santo were just trying to get rid of us for the day so that he could get Maria safely out of the country? What if we were ambushed? What if Santo was in league with Giaccalone? Maybe this whole thing was a setup. Maybe Maria was in on it, too. Maybe that's what she and Santo had been talking about. Maybe she had called Giaccalone and told him where we were . . .

I told myself not to think like that. Maria wouldn't betray me. There she was, falling asleep beside me, her hand resting on my shoulder. The smell of her perfume made me think of that first night we kissed, in the church garden. I traced my hand down over her belly, past her navel, letting my fingers drift into the tangle of hair. But she pulled my hand away. "I can't," she said. "I'm all worked up. I can't relax."

We lay in the dark. The air conditioner hummed. Maria's eyes were closed; but I could tell from her breathing that she wasn't asleep.

"Maria," I whispered.

She opened her eyes. In the moonlight her face looked pale, almost blue.

"What?" she said.

But then I didn't know what I wanted to say. Or I knew, but I didn't dare say it.

"I'm sorry," I said. "For all of this."

She sighed, and rolled over. "Go to sleep," she said.

WE TOOK ROUTE 41 through the Everglades, stopping only once, on the outskirts of Miami, for a Burger King breakfast that neither of us could eat. We ended up throwing the coffee out the window and giving our potato patties and sausage sandwiches to Coco, who seemed to enjoy them.

The van was a white Ford Econoline that belonged to Santo's company. I drove. Evan rode shotgun, glancing at the map and giving voice to his paranoia. What if Santo and Giaccalone were in this together? What if Santo had set us up? I told him that I had considered all of these things too, but had concluded finally that Maria wouldn't do that to us. I remembered the way she had kissed me that morning; the kiss had convinced me. It was five o'clock, the sun just breaking into the sky, and she had come outside to see us off. The air was cool, the sky gray. The lawn glistened; a little rain had fallen during the night. She kissed me for real—not some peck on the cheek—and I told myself that no way could you kiss someone like that and then send them off to get killed.

"She wouldn't do that to us," I said. "That's all you have to think about. She wouldn't do that."

"Maybe she doesn't know." Evan had the map spread out on the dashboard and was tapping it with his fingers. "Maybe Santo is getting us out of the way, and he'll tell her about it later. Or maybe he won't ever tell her at all. Like in *The Godfather,* when Al Pacino has Talia Shire's husband killed, and he pretends he had nothing to do with it. Maybe he'll just lie to her about it."

"Right, except this isn't *The Godfather,* and Maria's cousin isn't Michael Corleone, he's Santo Bava, king of the cuckolds. Think about it. His wife cheated on him, and then left him for the other guy, and now she's suing Santo for divorce. You think she'd be doing that to Michael Corleone? Buddy, he's an accountant."

"Maybe he made a deal," Evan said. "That's all I'm saying. For example, why do we have to deliver the dog? Why didn't Santo just get us out of the country and then take care of the dog himself? And why do we have to go to Fort Myers? Why didn't he have Wilson come pick up the dog in Miami?"

"Asked and answered," I said. "We've already talked about this stuff."

We were halfway across the Everglades, the landscape scrubby and severe, the sun merciless; the trip had begun to seem surreal, almost hallucinogenic. "All I know," Evan said, "is that this is not what my parents had in mind when they sent me to college."

"Me neither," I said, although really I had no idea what either of my parents had ever had in mind for me. Maybe the expectations were not so much my parents' as my own. If you're a nice middle-class American kid like me or Evan, you go through life knowing pretty much what to expect: college, job, house, kids, retirement. Maybe a summer cottage somewhere, a few rounds of golf, then with any luck a painless death, a nice funeral, and *adios,* roll the credits. But a life of crime? Exile in South America? These were not on the program. Still, here we were.

Wilson met us in a Wendy's parking lot in Fort Myers at exactly twelve o'clock, or "high noon," as Evan kept saying. He pulled up beside us in a maroon Honda Accord and got out. He wore khaki shorts, a blue polo shirt, and huarache sandals. He looked nothing like Carl Wilson of the Beach Boys. He was about fifty years old, about five feet six inches tall, with a round face and a little potbelly and oily black hair combed across a bald spot from a low part just above his left ear. He spoke with a thick New England accent.

"You're the guys from Boston," he said. He shook our hands. "I don't know whether to shoot you or kiss you. You guys almost got me killed. Then again, you did get my dog back. Where is she?"

We opened the back door of the van. Coco ran over and nuzzled up against him. "How's my girl?" he said. "Eh? How's my girl?"

I said that I didn't mean to be rude but that we were in a bit of a hurry and we wondered if we might do the swap and be on our way.

"I was thinking we might have lunch," Wilson said. "There's a nice place downtown."

I said that we appreciated the offer but that we really had to get going. Wilson said he really thought we should join him for lunch. "I've got a proposal for you," he said.

Evan said that we really would like to sit and have a nice lunch and listen to proposals, but that maybe Wilson had heard that a certain mobster and his friends were right now, at this very minute, trying to find us so that they could drill us both new assholes. "So the thing is," Evan said, "we'd really just like to take the money and get going, if that's okay with you."

"That's what the proposal is about," Wilson said. "The money. That's what I want to talk to you about."

He was holding Coco, rubbing behind her ears.

"Are you saying," Evan said, "that you don't have the money?"

"Not exactly."

"Not exactly?"

"Have lunch with me, and we'll talk."

Evan pushed Coco back into the truck and shut the door and said that we both thanked Wilson very much for wasting our time and that now if he didn't mind we were going to take the dog back to Miami and find someone else to buy her.

Wilson started laughing. "Look," he said, "I know you're worried about getting ripped off. But that's not what I'm doing here. You're going to get your money, just like we agreed. In fact, I'm going to get you even more money than we agreed on. Maybe a lot more. I just need your help with something, that's all. Now just follow me downtown and we'll have lunch like civilized people and we'll have a talk, okay?" He looked at me, then back at Evan. "Okay? Guys? Can we have a talk?"

He laughed, and patted me on the back. There seemed to be nothing to do but laugh along with him. It was noon, and we were in a Wendy's parking lot, engaged in criminal activity.

We followed him into Fort Myers and ate lunch at an outdoor restaurant where the waitresses wore Lycra shorts and every table had a blue-and-white beach umbrella. The umbrellas snapped and shuddered in the wind.

"So here's the proposal," Wilson said. "There's a dog track north of here, a new place. Bayshore Park. It's run by Indians. Apaches or something. They made a lot of money with casinos, so now they've got a dog track. And they don't know what they're doing. They're clueless."

This was the proposal: Wilson had a friend, a trainer named Peter Hakanson, who had a kennel at Bayshore. Hakanson had a black dog registered for the evening card. The dog was a four-year-old Class D racer named Sweet Sue who had a lousy record and ran at odds as high as forty to one. We would take Coco to the track and swap her for Sweet Sue. The track judge was supposed to do a last-minute check to make sure the dogs' serial numbers matched the numbers on the registration sheets—but Hakanson could take care of the track judge. Coco would get onto the track, running as Sweet Sue. We would bet on Sweet Sue, and clean up.

The betting was where we came in. Wilson couldn't simply place a huge bet at the track—as soon as you did that, the odds came down. We would have to bet off-track, with bookies. Three of us would put down one thousand dollars at three separate shops. We would do this at precisely the same time, just before the race went off. The bookies would take the action, and before they could figure out what was going on the race would be over. Wilson had already chosen the bookies. He had addresses and directions written on three-by-five cards, and pagers for us to carry.

Sweet Sue was expected to run at thirty to one. At those odds we would make ninety thousand dollars, which we would split three ways: thirty for Hakanson, thirty for Wilson, and thirty for us.

Evan pointed out that this wasn't much better than the twenty-five thousand we had already agreed upon for doing nothing. So what was the point?

"The point," Wilson said, "is that if you don't help me out, you get nothing. Because that's exactly what I've got for you—nothing. So, if you want your money, you'll help me out, and instead of twenty-five, like we agreed, you'll get thirty, or maybe even more. If the dog runs at forty, which could happen, we'll get a hundred and twenty, which means forty for each of us, and that's not bad. You make forty thousand bucks for a day's work, and where I come from that's a decent paycheck. If you're not interested, well, fine, fuck you and the horse you rode in on, take the dog back to Miami and see if anyone in the world wants to buy her once word gets around about who she belongs to. And consider this: How long do you think it will take for that shit-ass Giaccalone to track you down once my friends call him up and tell him where you are?"

He smiled. He was a greasy little bastard and I hated him more than I have ever hated anyone in my life. But what could we do? There were a million ways to run a con, but they all relied on the same thing, which was the promise of getting more than you deserved. My grandfather had taught me that when I was a kid. Now I was hearing my grandfather's voice inside my head and he was telling me that no matter what we did, we were going to end up with no dog and no money. Another of his sayings came to me: When rape is inevitable, lie back and try to enjoy it. I looked across the table at Wilson, at his fat smiling face and his happy little pig's eyes, and felt my sphincter tighten.

Once when I was in high school my friend Herb got a bunch of guys to go in together on a pound of pot. The going rate for a pound was two thousand dollars, but Herb had found a guy in Detroit who sold pounds for fifteen hundred, which meant a clear five hundred for Herb, on top of what he would make for breaking up the pound. I drove Herb to a bus station in the Cass Corridor and waited outside in the car. He went in with the money and came out empty-handed. The guy had told him to wait and said he would be right back with the pot. For fifteen minutes, then twenty, then thirty, Herb sat there growing pale. Finally he went into the bus station. A few minutes later he came out, crying. He was a big fat guy, a tackle on the football team, and it wasn't pretty to see him cry. It took him a year to pay everyone back.

"We need to talk," I said. "In privacy."

"Fair enough," Wilson said. "I'll go for a walk around the block."

We waited until he was around the corner and then both agreed that basically we were screwed. My opinion was that we should take the dog back to Miami and take our chances there. Evan said we should call Santo and see what he thought about that. We went to a pay phone and called his cell phone number. "I think you should do what he wants you to do," Santo said. "I don't see that you have much choice. And who knows? Maybe he really will pay you. If not, maybe we can catch up with him. At least you get rid of the dog. That's the important thing right now."

I hung up feeling sick. I knew this was all going to end badly. We went back to the table and found Wilson waiting. He smiled when we gave him our answer. "That's great," he said. "So we're partners. That's great."

He asked the waitress for the bill, and paid her in cash. Then he said there was one thing we had to do before we made things official. "We need to see Coco run," he said. "We don't want to take any crazy chances, right?"

In a racing blanket, Coco seemed like a different dog. Her eyes were bright. She strained at the leash. Her legs were twitching, and when I tried to pet her, she growled. "Don't get too close to her," Wilson said. "And don't put your hands near her mouth." It was the blanket, he said. Racing dogs know what the blanket means. A well-trained dog, like Coco, doesn't even need the rabbit. "You put the blanket on her, and she's off in another zone. She's not Coco the pet. She's a hunting dog. You see? Look at her neck. You see the muscles flexing?"

We were at a high school football stadium. Wilson was holding Coco at the starting line. The track was made out of some kind of rubber, which Wilson said would be faster than the dirt on a dog track; but still we could get an idea what kind of shape she was in. "She's gained some weight," he said, "and she hasn't been practicing. So we'll see. In sixty seconds we'll know if we're going to make money tonight."

On a count of three he let go of Coco's collar and shouted, "Ha!" and clicked a stopwatch that he was holding in his right hand. Coco sped off down the track as if she'd been shot out of a cannon. She tore into the first corner, then gained speed as she came into the second straightaway, then gained even more speed again as she came into the back corner. I was thinking about the first time I'd seen her run, at Wonderland, and also about the other night, when I had seen her run in the field at the rest area. I wanted to tell Wilson about those things, but I hated him too much to give him the satisfaction.

He stood there glancing down at the watch and then back at Coco; a wide grin was spreading across his face. Evan, meanwhile, just stood there with his jaw hanging open. There are few animals on the planet that can run like a greyhound; and seeing one at such close range sends shivers up your back. Even the people who work with them all the time probably never lose this feeling. Coco rounded the back corner, and blew past us in a blur. Wilson stared down at his stopwatch.

"So?" Evan said. "Was that good?"

Wilson looked up. Then he burst out laughing. He put his arm around Evan's shoulders and said, "Evan, you're a pretty funny guy, you know that?"

WILSON HAD A ROOM IN A MOTEL near the track. The plan was to go there and hang out until evening. We followed him there, waving to Coco, who stood in the backseat of Wilson's car, barking at us. At the stadium Wilson had put Coco into his car, and I'd almost said something; but then I didn't want to make a big deal out of it. The problem with growing up middle class is that you're trained to be polite. The very rich and the very poor don't mind being rude. But middle-class people are polite. That's how car salesmen make their living—they know that the average middle-class person would rather get ripped off than be thought to have bad manners. People like me and Evan can't come right out and accuse someone of ripping us off, even when it's true.

The pinch was smooth: Wilson whistled and Coco jumped into the car, and then Wilson looked over and smiled at me as if we were just a bunch of good old boys out having fun. Wasn't it cool to be making new friends? In his eyes there was something flinty—a challenge; a dare—and I had the feeling that he was testing us, seeing if we'd be hard-assed about things and tell them that until we got our money we would hold the dog, thank you very much. Instead, we had wimped out, and it seemed to me that in that moment a large weight had tipped in his favor.

Somehow Evan had started believing that things were going to work out for us. He said we might as well believe. Later on, if we got ripped off, we would have plenty of time to feel bitter and anxious. For now, he said, he was sticking to the notion that Wilson was a man who kept his word and that in twelve hours we were going to have our money and that by tomorrow afternoon we would be in Belize, sipping rum drinks from coconuts.

Evan had invented a scenario in which we spent a year in Belize and the islands and then returned to the United States. It was as if he imagined that the mob had some kind of statute of limitations, or that Giaccalone would just forget about us. "Time heals all wounds," he said, and he was only half-kidding.

In Evan's imagination we would take a year to enjoy a *Gilligan's Island* lifestyle: surfing, making langorous love to sloe-eyed tropical beauties, waking early each morning to work on our code. When the program was ready, we would move to Silicon Valley with the now-perfected Nectar software. We would pick up where we'd left off—get venture capital, go public, become millionaires.

"And then what?" I said. "Let me guess. You beat Deep Blue at chess, and then you and Winona Ryder live happily ever after."

"Exactly," he said.

We rolled past a miserable scattered landscape of billboards and motels and condos, a faded wasteland of sand and scrub brush and scrawny palm trees, and my heart grew ever sicker. We passed a sign for the highway to Miami. I suggested to Evan that we just turn onto the highway now and forget about the whole thing. "We could just drive back right now," I said. "To hell with the money. We're not going to get it anyway. Leave Coco with Wilson, and let's get out of here. We can be back in Miami for dinner, and out of the country tonight. We've still got the thirty thousand. Or most of it, anyway."

"Fuck that," Evan said. "In for a penny, in for a pound."

"What the fuck does that mean?"

"It means you got us into this fucking mess, so shut the fuck up."

Now that we were full-fledged criminals we felt obliged to use the word *fuck* as often as possible.

I told him again that I had a bad fucking feeling about this.

"Me fucking too," he said. "So just fucking drive."

The motel was called the Seaview. It was a miserable little one-story place with no view of the sea at all. We kept the shades drawn. There was pea-green carpeting, orange curtains, two ratty chairs and a ratty lamp, an old television that got three stations, and an air conditioner that rattled and knocked and only managed to produce a trickle of cool air. Outside, in the parking lot, seagulls squawked noisily around a row of trash cans. Even with the TV on we could hear them.

Coco curled up in an armchair and fell asleep. Wilson and Evan spent the afternoon playing chess on a portable set that Wilson carried with him. Naturally Evan was making short work of Wilson, and now, fired up by his chess victories, he started bragging about our hacker exploits in Boston—the break-in at MassBank, the phone pranks on Janet Scuto—and I was feeling once again the same nausea that I had felt years before on that day when Herb and I sat in the car outside the bus station in the Cass Corridor waiting for the dope dealer who wasn't coming back.

I was stretched out on the bed watching Ricki Lake's audience chastise a woman for having an affair with her husband's nephew. Watching them shout and sputter, I felt the dread in my heart being moved aside and replaced with an inexorable sadness. I thought about something Whit had once told me—"Desire is the cause of all suffering"—and now that rang more true than ever. Here were these cretins on TV whose lives were ruined because they lacked the ability to control their impulses. And here was I, trapped in a motel in Florida because I didn't have the good sense to control my greed.

If only we hadn't come to Fort Myers. If only we hadn't come to Florida. If only we hadn't stolen Coco. If only I hadn't moved to the North End. If only I hadn't gone out with Jeanie or moved to Boston or worked at Ionic Software. If only I had gone to graduate school and done a Ph.D. Why hadn't I done that? Why had I done what I'd done? I felt like an atom bouncing around in one of Heisenberg's experiments. I wondered if all of my life would be this random.

At six o'clock, Wilson got up and went out to his car. He came back with pagers and three-by-five cards. One address was a produce store. That would be my target. The other was a biker bar. That would be Evan's. Wilson went over the plan with us again. We would wait near our targets. When things were set up, Hakanson would signal Wilson, and Wilson would signal us. A string of zeroes—00000—meant that something had gone wrong at the track, and the plan was off. We should go stand outside and wait to be picked up. A string of sevens—77777—meant we should go ahead and place our bets. We would say that we had been sent by Mr. Scranton. This was a name that Hakanson used when he bet on the dogs. Apparently it was pretty common for trainers to bet through fake identities.

Hakanson did a lot of nickel-and-dime betting, and then every once in a while he bet large. He lost nearly as often as he won. You had to, if you wanted them to keep taking your bets. The trick was to keep your losses smaller than your wins. You had to think in terms of margins. You won a hundred, and then lost eighty, and you kept the difference. Over the long run you could make a decent living doing this. But it was a slow process. You couldn't just go in and make a killing. You picked up a hundred here, five hundred there. Pocket money. Usually you could stay a little ahead of the bookies. Sometimes you could let yourself get a little behind. When you were behind it was the best, because then they would definitely take your money.

All three of our bookies had gotten ahead of Hakanson. They would be happy to see us. We would place two bets—we would put five hundred dollars on the sixth race, which we would lose, and then one thousand on the seventh. Hakanson had been to all three bookies yesterday and had lost a few hundred dollars at each one, betting a hundred dollars at a time, always in the name of Mr. Scranton.

"They'll be ready for you," he said. "They'll be glad to see you. They won't be so glad to see you when you win, though. So you don't want to be there. You want to be gone by then. Just bet the seventh race, get a ticket, and walk out." He glanced at his watch. "And now, my friends, it's time to go."

SWEET SUE WAS SMALLER THAN COCO, and not as dark, and she had a small patch of white fur underneath her chin; but from the grandstand nobody would notice, Wilson said. We were in the paddock at the back of the track, and Sweet Sue was licking the back of my hand through the mesh of her cage. There were dozens of greyhounds around us, all of them in cages. Half of them were asleep; the others lay stretched out, looking bored. The room stank of dog crap and urine.

A few trainers were hanging around, chatting with each other. Most of them were older guys, greasy-haired and in need of a shave. They talked with good-old-boy southern accents and punctuated their conversations with squirts of tobacco juice, which they would deliver to the cement floor with a delicate sideways motion of the head. Several gave off an odor of alcohol. They paid no attention to us.

Hakanson had been waiting outside when we pulled up. He and Wilson shook hands without smiling and Wilson introduced us. Hakanson nodded and shook our hands but said nothing. He was about fifty years old, with rheumy eyes and blotchy skin. He wore Bay Rum Aftershave, a smell that reminded me of my grandfather, and a pair of dirty jeans and an old white tennis shirt. He had a handsome, almost patrician face, with faint gin blossoms in his cheeks and a nose that was in the early stages of being ruined by drink; he gave the impression of someone who had once been well-to-do but had fallen on hard times.

He led us through the paddock, treating us like tourists, explaining how the dogs were divided into different classes and how the trainers took them out to practice on the days when they weren't racing.

He took Sweet Sue out of her cage and put on her blanket and muzzle. She stood like a statue while he fixed the straps behind her ears. We crouched down and rubbed her head. She was a four-year-old with a mixed record: She had won a few Class C races during her second season, but this year she'd moved down to Class D and had only lost. Soon she would be retired, which meant she would either get adopted or be put to sleep. Like Coco, she had big dark eyes that seemed eerily human. I wondered if she knew what lay in store for her. Did the dogs go out onto the track knowing that they were running for their lives?

A door opened, and the lead-outs came into the paddock to take the first eight dogs out to the track. The dogs began to howl and bark and spin in their cages. The first race was Class A, and the eight dogs strode out of the paddock like royalty. Compared to the other dogs, the Class A dogs seemed like gods; it was like seeing Michael Jordan and Magic Johnson and the rest of the Olympic dream team walking past a bunch of schoolyard players. But even the Class A dogs were nothing compared to Coco. Now I realized how much I had taken for granted with Coco. These Class A dogs were the cream of the crop, and even so they all seemed smaller, slower—just less, in every way, than Coco.

I asked Wilson whether we were making a mistake putting Coco in a Class D race. The idea, after all, was for her to win without attracting too much attention. The illusion that we needed to create was that old Sweet Sue had reached deep down inside her soul and pulled up enough courage to squeak past the competition. Even in

Class A, Coco would blow the others off the track. In Class D, it would look as if one of the dogs had been running with rockets attached to her legs.

"It'll be fine," Hakanson said. "That kind of blow-out actually happens, believe it or not. Not often, but it happens. You get one dog who gets out of the gate real good, and the others lose heart. You'll get a twenty-length win sometimes. As long as we make the swap on the way in and the swap on the way out, we're okay. There's just those two times when everything has to go right." He finished buckling up Sweet Sue's muzzle. He groaned, and stood up. He rubbed the space between his nose and his upper lip—a habit of his, I'd noticed. "I guess we should go see our friend in the van, eh?"

He led us through the back of the paddock and into a cinder-block room that led to another hallway and then to a door to the parking lot. The door was supposed to be kept locked. But Hakanson had put tape over the latch. This was how he would get Coco in and out. We had parked the van near the door, beside a Dumpster.

"I've never actually seen this dog," Hakanson said. "Heard a lot about her, of course. I couldn't believe that guy in Boston retired her. What's that guy's name?"

"Giaccalone," Wilson said, and made a face, as if the name tasted bad in his mouth. The name had an effect on me, too. I felt a shiver run down my neck. I tried not to think about where Giaccalone might be right now.

"Right," Hakanson said. "Giaccalone. He's not a trainer, is he?"

"He's an asshole," Wilson said.

Wilson opened the van. Evan and I played lookout. Hakanson said it didn't matter, because nobody would pay any attention to us. There were owners and dogs going back and forth all the time. "Mother of God," I heard him say. He had climbed into the van with a blanket and muzzle. The blanket was blue, with the number 5 on it, just like the one Sweet Sue was wearing. I glanced inside. Coco had never seemed as magnificent as she did now, dressed in her racing blanket. Maybe she could smell the other dogs, or had heard them barking;

but she knew she was at a racetrack, and once again she seemed to have been transformed into a different animal than the one we had known in our apartment in Boston.

I suppose it was like seeing a fighter in the locker room before he goes into the ring. In those moments when he is fighting, he is not the man who lives with his wife, or plays with his children. For a few minutes he becomes something else—something more, in a way, and at the same time something less. So it was with Coco. The dog who had played fetch in our living room and slept on my bed at night was gone. Her eyes now were wide and clear and fierce, her tail stood out stiff and straight, the muscles in her legs were twitching and flexing. From somewhere deep in her throat there came a high sound—it seemed as if she were trying to bark but was too keyed up.

I called her name. She looked, but seemed not to recognize me. Hakanson attached her muzzle. The muzzle was a grille of thin metal bars, which slipped over her snout and attached by straps around the back of her head. Coco's eyes darted from side to side, and her toes clicked on the metal floor of the van; but otherwise she stood frozen like a statue, just as Sweet Sue had done, and let Hakanson tighten the straps.

Of course Coco was a lot more dog than Sweet Sue, and it was hard to believe that anybody was going to be fooled. An idiot would be able to tell they were not the same dog. And it seemed to me that there might be a problem with the videotape. The track tapes every race. Hakanson insisted that there was nothing to worry about. "We've got the whole thing worked out," he said, and looked at Wilson, who nodded and said, "He's right, there's nothing to worry about."

Hakanson rubbed Coco's shoulders and down over her flanks. "You're going show us something tonight," he said, his voice soft and low. "Isn't that right? You're a good dog, aren't you? Sure you are." He ran his hand down over her back legs, feeling the muscles. "You see how strong her legs are, right here?" he said, glancing at me. "And her chest—here, you see? You see how deep she is through here? And how tall she is? That's the key, I think, is her size. Amazing."

Wilson said we had better get going if we were going to all get into position on time. Coco would run in the seventh race, which gave us some time to get ready. The races went off every fifteen minutes. The first race would go off at 7:00 P.M. The seventh race would go off at about 8:30. There would be a crucial moment just before the sixth race when the dogs for the sixth race would be taken to the track and the dogs for the seventh race would be brought from the main kennel to a holding kennel. Somehow during that move Hakanson would swap Coco for Sweet Sue. Apparently he had a deal with one of the lead-outs.

"So we're all set?" Wilson said. "You're going to be okay?"

Hakanson nodded. He was holding Coco by the collar.

"Okay," Wilson said. "See you later."

We left the van parked where it was, and gave Hakanson the keys. Then the three of us got into Wilson's car and drove downtown.

We dropped Evan off first, at a bar called The King of Clubs. There was an air conditioner humming above the front door and a row of Harleys parked outside. Wilson handed Evan two stacks of money. One stack contained five hundred-dollar bills. The other contained ten of them. Evan was trying not to look scared.

"Nobody's going to bother you in there," Wilson said. "Just go in, sit at the bar, order a beer, and you'll be fine. Anybody at the bar talks to you, just be polite, and leave it at that. Just mind your own business. When you get the signal on your beeper, tell the bartender that you want to talk to Tommy. He's your guy. You tell Tommy that you represent Mr. Scranton. You put five hundred on the sixth race. He'll take the money. Then you wait, you get your second signal, and you put a thousand on the seventh, and then you walk out. Don't wait for the race. You don't want to be there when your winner comes in. You just go outside and walk down the block to that pay phone." He pointed across the street, to a pay phone on the corner. "Right over there is where I'm going to pick you up. All right?"

"Sure," Evan said. He got out, walked to the door, glanced back at us, then opened the door, peered inside, hesitated, then glanced back at us. Wilson beeped the horn. Evan disappeared into the bar.

We drove off to my location, which was about a mile away on the same strip. Here instead of Harleys there were sagging Chevrolets and pimped-out Toyotas, and all of the signs were in Spanish. The produce store was called Mendoza's.

"They're Cubans," Wilson said. "Nothing to worry about. Cubans are practically white people. You go in, hang around, look at the plantains, whatever. When you get the beeper, go to the counter and ask for Eddie. Same deal. Tell him you represent Mr. Scranton. Here's your money. Bet the sixth, wait, then bet the seventh and walk out. Daddy's Little Girl in the sixth, and Sweet Sue in the seventh. Same as Evan—you've got to make sure you get out of there before the seventh race goes off. You do not want to be in that store when the winner comes in, trust me. So you just walk out, calmly, and I'll meet you around the corner, over there."

The idea, Wilson had explained earlier, was to lose in the sixth and then to appear desperate in the seventh. The only problem would be if the bookies started talking to each other after the sixth race. Chances are they wouldn't, since Evan was betting with bikers, I was betting with Cubans, and Wilson was betting at an Irish pub that fronted for the IRA, and none of these groups had much to do with any of the others. If they didn't talk we had nothing to worry about.

If they did talk, there might be problems. The worst that could happen would be that they would smell a scam and so would refuse to take our money on the seventh race. If that happened, we had simple instructions: Be polite, and get out fast.

But probably they would take our money for the seventh. We would bet just before the race began, so the bookies would not have time to check with one another and discover that they were all taking large money on the same dog. In the best-case scenario, the bookies never talked to one another and so each one just figured he had been hit on a fluke and he paid off, no questions asked. In the worst case, they got suspicious and started calling around to see if anyone else had been hit, too.

"And what if that happens?" I said.

"By then the race is over," Wilson said. "They owe us the money."

"But won't they be a bit reluctant to pay off?"

"Maybe, maybe not," Wilson said. "They all get hit this hard once in a while. There was a Super Bowl a few years ago when all of these guys got hit for a hundred thousand, some of them more."

"They keep that kind of money on hand?"

"That little Cuban," he said, nodding toward the store, from which two old ladies were emerging with bags of groceries, "probably has a quarter of a million in cash sitting out back in a safe right now. Our thing is going to piss him off, but it's not going to break him. So he'll pay. And he won't deal with Mr. Scranton ever again. Which is fine, since Mr. Scranton is moving to Maryland next week anyway."

"But what if they balk? What if they just tell us to fuck off? What happens then?"

He opened his glove box and removed an automatic pistol, which he slid into the space beside his seat. I wasn't sure if he meant to reassure me or to threaten me. He took a cigarette from a pack of Old Golds on the dashboard, lit it, and let the smoke trail out against the windshield.

"Me and Hack have done this before," he said.

He nodded to my door handle. I got out and walked across the street to the produce store. Wilson drove away, headed for his Irish bar. It was two minutes past eight. I thought about that pay phone where I was supposed to meet him afterward. For a moment I considered going there and calling Maria and telling her to come get us. A vision came to me, like something out of a bad dream: Evan and I were trapped against a brick wall, with a gang of bikers, a bunch of Cubans, and some IRA hoodlums all marching toward us, with Hakanson and Wilson nowhere to be found.

But there was no backing out now. I took a deep breath and walked into Mendoza's. The store was crowded. I lingered in back, near the yucca. At ten minutes past eight I felt a buzzing on my leg;

the beeper was going off in my pocket. I took it out and saw a string of sevens. Which meant: The dogs for the sixth race were on the track, and Coco had made it to the holding kennel for the seventh. I went to the counter and asked for Eddie. The guy behind the counter was heavyset, dark-skinned, wearing a blue flannel shirt. I had my hands in my pockets. They were sweating through the fabric onto my legs. The guy in the flannel asked me why I wanted to see Eddie. I told him I was a friend of Mr. Scranton.

He looked me over, as if he didn't believe me. "Mr. Scranton," he said.

"That's right."

"Okay, hold on."

He disappeared through a curtain. A moment later he stuck his head out and said, "Hey." He gestured for me to come with him. I went around behind the counter and followed him out to the back.

WE LOST THE SIXTH RACE, and bet on the seventh. Wilson picked us up—me first, then Evan—and we listened to the race in the car. We heard the dogs being led into the gates, and then the bell. The announcer had a calm voice, a southern accent made gravelly by smoking. I remembered when I was young and my grandfather and I would take the radio out to the porch and listen to Tigers games. We could have watched them on TV but my grandfather liked the radio better. TV controlled what you saw, he said, while with radio you could see the whole thing.

It was the same way now with the dogs. I could see the track, and hear the crowd, and smell the food in the stands. Out of the gates a dog named Windy City took the lead, followed by Blazing Silver and two others whose names I didn't catch. Sweet Sue was running in the back of the pack.

Here was a contingency we hadn't expected: what if Coco didn't win? It seemed inconceivable; and yet maybe it made sense. Coco hadn't run in months. She was overweight, out of shape. Maybe she was confused by the other dogs, the unfamiliar track; maybe she was dazzled by the lights and the audience, all of the smells and memories rushing at her.

Wilson was trying to seem calm. But he was gripping the steering wheel so tightly that his knuckles had turned white. He pulled over into a taqueria parking lot and turned up the radio. He put his hands to his face. Outside, the sky grew pale, as if the color were being drained away. At the far edge of the parking lot there was an irrigation ditch with a stand of scrubby willow trees and then beyond that the highway.

In the back stretch the pack tightened. Windy City gave up the lead to Blazing Silver, but then recovered and moved back into first. The two dogs ran neck and neck. Then in the third turn Coco came alive. She cut to the outside and exploded past the pack and the two front-runners and was still accelerating when she crossed the finish in first place, ahead by two lengths. Sweet Sue, the announcer said, would pay off at thirty-two to one.

"You can almost hear those bookies groaning," Wilson said, and chuckled and lit a cigarette. He was trying very hard not to let on how frightened he had been.

Evan made no such effort. He had been scared to death in the biker bar and was still shaking. The biker bookie, Tommy, had kept a gun on the table in his office out back, and he had said at first that no way would he take a thousand dollars on a dog race. Evan said, Okay, thank you, I guess I'll leave. Hold on, Tommy said. Sit down. He asked Evan why he was so anxious to leave. Evan said he had instructions to deliver a bet and if the bet could not be placed, then he was to leave. Tommy nodded. He scratched his chin. He asked Evan if he was running a scam. He said he better not be running a scam because if he was, then Tommy and his friends would track Evan down and tear him limb from limb.

Evan insisted that he was simply a messenger, that he was paid to come here and deliver money and return with a ticket, and that was all he knew, and that if Tommy didn't want to take the bet that was fine by him. He was ready to make a break for the door when Tommy said,

"Okay, give me the money." Evan handed over the thousand dollars, got a ticket, then walked out as fast as he could. He jumped into the backseat and told us the whole story in a single breath and then said that if we didn't mind he would like to stop someplace and get sick.

My experience had been substantially better. Eddie, my bookie, was a man in his sixties who wore leather sandals and a long white linen shirt, neatly pressed, with creases in the sleeves and across the front. He took the five hundred for the sixth race and asked me how Mr. Scranton was doing. Fine, I told him. When I returned to bet on the seventh race, he consoled me about the sixth and said, "Yes, of course, please come in, a thousand is fine, it's no problem." Probably by now he was sitting there tearing out his hair; or maybe he was loading a gun.

"They'll find us," Evan said. "That's what Tommy said. He'll come looking for us. He'll track us down."

"Relax," Wilson said. "He's a bookie, okay? He takes bets, he pays out. It's what he does. And there's nothing for you to worry about. Your work is done. All you have to do now is hang around in the motel room and wait to get your money. Drink a beer, watch some TV, and get paid. Okay? It's over. Hack and I are going to take care of the collections."

He pulled back out into traffic, headed for the motel. On the radio they had gone to a commercial between races. There was an ad from a local computer store offering discounts on memory modules. The price of DRAM chips had been dropping all summer. The Japanese were flooding the market. Soon, it seemed, memory would cost nothing at all. Everybody could have as much as they wanted. What a world that would be.

"Hey," Wilson said, as we approached a McDonald's. "Who's hungry?"

We went to the motel and ate our Big Macs and waited for Hakanson. In about half an hour he pulled up in the van and flashed his lights in our window. "Time to make the donuts," Wilson said. We went outside with him. Hakanson gave us a thumbs-up and a ridiculous grin. Wilson opened the passenger door and said, "Soon we'll all be rich," and Hakanson laughed a little too hard, and his eyes met mine and then darted away toward Wilson, and suddenly a panicky image came to me: I saw myself and Evan sitting in the motel room, waiting for our money; then the sun coming up, and still no word from Wilson and Hakanson; and then the two of us dragging ourselves back to Miami.

"Wait," I said. "Hold on."

The engine was running. Wilson had his door half shut already. I put my body in the way so he couldn't close it.

"What's the problem?" He was smiling, but he didn't hide the fact that he was irritated.

"I want to keep the dog here with us," I said.

He smiled. I smiled back.

"You mean you don't trust us," he said.

"Well," I said, "as a matter of fact . . ."

He took the pistol from his waistband and put it into the glovebox. He said he was trying very hard not to feel insulted. I told him that I didn't mean to insult him but that I did want to remind him that the van he was sitting in was mine, and for that matter so was the dog, and that unless we got to keep the dog as collateral, then we were going to assume we were being ripped off, in which case I would have no choice but to go call Giaccalone and tell him that we were no longer the ones he should be looking for.

Wilson suggested another possibility: He could take us into our room and shoot us both in the back of the head, and then we would not be making any phone calls to anyone. He said this casually, hypothetically; and I couldn't tell whether he meant it or not, but Hakanson said, "Hey, everybody, now come on, let's not be like this, okay?" He forced a chuckle and said everybody was feeling keyed up right now but we had to remember that we were all in this together. "Nobody's going to get ripped off," he said. "You boys, I can understand you being worried. But it isn't like that. It just isn't."

"The dog shouldn't be riding around in the truck anyway," I said.

"She should lie down, get some rest, have something to eat, whatever. She shouldn't be out where someone might hurt her, or steal her. I don't see why you have a problem with leaving her here."

"We don't have a problem," Hakanson said. "There's no problem with that at all. Right, Karl?"

"Sure," Wilson said.

"Great," I said. I opened the panel door and helped Coco down out of the truck. Evan led her to the room.

"We'll see you soon," I said.

Wilson slammed his door shut and grunted something in response.

Coco ate a Quarter Pounder with Cheese and then jumped onto the bed and fell asleep, snoring. Evan sprawled out on the other bed, with his head propped up. He was drinking beer and watching *Sanford and Son* on TV. There was no cable, just an old antenna that got two stations, both of them miserable. I sat on the couch wondering how people lived before there was cable. The seagulls were still making a racket in the parking lot. I tried to figure out how Wilson and Hakanson were planning to scam us. Maybe they wouldn't even bother to trick us. Maybe they would simply walk in with guns and tell us they were taking the dog and that would be that. In the room next to ours a man was talking on the phone, and laughing; I could hear his voice but couldn't make out what he was saying.

An hour passed, then two hours. By eleven-thirty, I began to get worried. "Maybe they're not coming back," I said. "Maybe they don't care about the dog. After all, whoever's got the dog, Giaccalone is going to come after them, right? Maybe the whole thing was a setup, and all they wanted was the money."

"They'll be back," Evan said. "They probably just went out drinking or something. Here, hand me another beer."

I picked up the phone and called Santo's cell phone number. Maria answered. I told her what was going on. She put Santo on the line. He said we should just take the dog and drive back now and forget about the money. "You can get the money later," he said. "For now you should just get back here."

I told him we couldn't get back, because Wilson had our van. I was explaining how that had come to be the case when a pair of headlights appeared in the parking lot outside our room. Evan went to the window. I told Santo I would call him back.

E VAN WENT TO THE PEEPHOLE. "Jesus," he said, and then the door burst open and he fell back against the wall clutching his face. For a moment he held himself up, then he slid to the floor.

Standing in the doorway were the two guys Giaccalone had hired in Boston—the one with pockmarks, and the young one with the brush cut. Pockmarks was wearing white shoes and a white vinyl belt. In a different situation he would have seemed comical, but in this situation he had a gun and was telling us to lie on the floor face-down and put our hands behind our fucking heads.

We didn't struggle. We did what they said. Evan was moaning. His face was covered with blood. Pockmarks shut the door and told Evan to be quiet. They rifled through the dresser and the side tables and the closet. They looked between the mattresses and under the beds. The guy with the brush cut held Coco and tried to calm her down. "It's all right," he said, in a soft voice. "It's all right."

"Billy," Pockmarks said, "let go of the dog and let's finish what we're doing here, okay?"

Evan's blood was fanning out into the carpet beneath my elbow.

"He's hurt," I said. Pockmarks told me to shut up. Billy turned Evan over onto his back and propped up his head with a pillow.

Pockmarks asked me what we'd done with Giaccalone's money. I told him we didn't have the money with us but we would get it for them, no problem. My throat was dry; I could barely speak. "It's in Miami," I said. "We still have most of it."

"All right," Billy said. "Thank you."

Pockmarks told Evan to stop moaning. "It's making me sick," he said. "I'm serious. The kid's making me sick."

"My nose is broken," Evan mumbled.

"I'll get you some ice," Billy said. "Then we're all going to sit here, and we're going to be quiet, all right? We're going to relax and be quiet." He opened a cell phone and dialed a number. "Okay, we're here," he said. "Right. We're not going anywhere."

Billy went out and came back with a bucket of ice. He put the ice in a plastic bag and wrapped the plastic bag in a towel. He gave the icepack to Evan and told him to hold it against his face. "You okay there, buddy?" he said. "Here, let me take a look." I recognized his accent: pure Detroit, from the East Side, or maybe downriver. I wondered how he'd ended up working for Davio in Boston.

Evan's nose was enormous. Both of his eyes had gone purple. Billy told him to lie back down and rest the icepack on his face. He gave Evan a little pat on the shoulder. "You're going to be okay," he said. "You've got a broken nose is all. It bleeds like hell, and it hurts a lot, but it's really not so bad. It hurts a lot worse than it is."

Pockmarks said, "Hey, that's a good one. *It hurts a lot worse than it is.* You oughta tell that to your wife on your wedding night."

Billy ignored him. I looked at him out of the corner of my eye. He wasn't much older than I was. He sat down on the couch and started complaining about the bachelor party that he'd had to cancel because of this trip. Pockmarks said nobody ever died from not having a bachelor party. He said the guy who married his daughter didn't even bother trying to have one. I could not imagine what Pockmark's daughter must look like, or who on earth would marry her.

I could, however, imagine Billy in his tuxedo, drinking champagne and dancing with his new bride. He was just like all of the guys I grew up with.

"I better move the car away from the door," Pockmarks said. "Leave the space for Davio. You know how the fucker is about his parking space."

Evan groaned—as if the name itself caused him pain. I closed my eyes and tried to remember the words to the rosary.

Pockmarks said there was a restaurant in Miami where the two of them could go afterward, a place that made snails cooked in garlic and butter. Billy said you would have to be crazy to eat shellfish. They were scavengers, he said. They spent their whole lives eating the shit of other fish. "A lobster," he said, "will eat its *own* shit. I'm not shitting you. I've seen this. My brother has a fish market."

"Enough," Pockmarks said. "Put on the TV."

They found Montel Williams. The subject seemed to be infidelity: two angry black women, and one poor black guy caught in the middle.

"Look at this," Pockmarks said. "Planet of the Fucking Apes. They got their own TV shows now. Hello."

"Your tax dollars at work," Billy said. "Living on welfare, every one of them. I'd bet you a hundred bucks right now."

Pockmarks had a theory on this. They should make it a law, he said, that if you were going to collect welfare then you had to come up with some embarrassing information about yourself and go on TV with it. "We're paying to support them, so they entertain us. They're like, you know, those guys they used to have in the Renaissance. The guys with the hats."

"Jesters," Billy said.

"That's it. Jesters. You get it?"

"Try it, but the lazy bastards would complain," Billy said. "Jesse Jackson would be out there picketing. Louis fucking Farrakhan would do another million *muli* march."

"No shit."

"But you're right. Least they could do is entertain us. Tell jokes, tap dance, whatever." He patted the couch. "Hey, Coco, come up here, baby. Come on. That's it. Look at this dog, huh? Come here, baby. Who's the baby? Huh? Who's the baby?"

Coco wagged her tail and climbed up onto the couch beside him. People say dogs are loyal. But the truth is, a dog will be friends with anyone.

A car pulled up outside. Billy pulled back the curtain and looked out.

"Is it Davio?" Pockmarks said.

Billy shook his head. He motioned for Pockmarks to turn off the TV. The headlights shut off. There were footsteps on the pavement outside our room.

I must admit that I took some pleasure in seeing Wilson's face when he stepped inside and saw the guns pointed at him. Pockmarks cracked him across the face and pulled him inside. Hakanson ran, but Billy caught him and dragged him back. Pockmarks knelt on Wilson and tied his hands behind his back. For good measure they tied us up, too. The four of us lay side by side like sardines in a can.

"Place is crowded," Pockmarks said.

"Six guys in one room," Billy said. "We get a couple strippers, and a case of beer, this could be a decent bachelor party. Except for Nose Boy there." He nudged Evan with his foot. "How you doing, Nose Boy? You hanging in?"

"The ice is melted," Evan said, in a voice I almost didn't recognize.

"Yeah, well," Billy said. "You just hang in there."

Pockmarks said Billy should go move the van. "And take a look around in there," he said. "See what you see."

"There's nothing in the van," Wilson said.

"What's that?" Billy said. He tapped his foot against Wilson's head. "You say something?"

"No," Wilson said.

Billy came back in a few minutes carrying a brown paper grocery bag. "Check it out," he said. He put the bag down on the coffee table. "It's a lot."

Pockmarks stacked the bricks of money on the table. "You want to save me the trouble and tell me how much this is?" he said.

"Ninety-six thousand," Wilson said.

Pockmarks whistled, softly. He put the money back into the bag. Billy turned the TV back on. The people in Montel's audience were shouting at the black guy. Billy switched to CNN. Halfway through the financial news a car pulled up outside. Billy looked out the window and said, "Okay, here we go."

Outside the room a car door slammed. Someone belched, and Giaccalone said, "Tony, for Christ's sake." Billy opened the door for them. Giaccalone was wearing a shell suit and a Panama hat. He was smoking a cigar and no doubt feeling like a big shot. Tony walked in behind him, carrying a hockey bag. Giaccalone looked us over and said, "How many guys we got in here? It's like a fucking convention. And who's this? Karl Wilson? You miserable fuck. What'd you do? Pay these faggots to steal my dog?"

Wilson lifted himself from the floor and said, "Look, it's not like that." Before he could continue Tony swung out his foot, like a dancer, and caught him on the side of his face. Wilson fell over like a toy. The floor was concrete with thin carpeting over it and if the kick hadn't knocked Wilson out the force of his head hitting the floor would have done the trick.

I glanced at the clock radio on the table by the bed. It was 4:11 in the morning.

Giaccalone sat down in the armchair. Coco ran over and sat at his feet. Giaccalone set his cigar down in an ashtray and rubbed Coco's head and said, "Okay, so let's have a talk."

BILLY SHOWED GIACCALONE the bag of money. Giaccalone said, "What are you doing carrying around that kind of money, Karl?"

Wilson didn't answer. Hakanson, who was lying face-down beside him, said that before this went any further, he wondered if he might be allowed to say something. Giaccalone said fine, go ahead.

"I didn't have anything to do with stealing your dog," Hakanson said. "All I was involved in was the thing at the track, and the bookies. That money in the bag, you can have it. It's yours. All I want is to walk away from this thing, okay? I'm an innocent bystander."

"There's no such thing as an innocent bystander," Giaccalone said. "But thank you very much for letting me keep the money."

Tony leaned over and asked me how I was doing. I didn't answer him. He pressed his toe into the crack of my ass and said, "Can't you hear me, bitch?"

Billy said, "The money's in Miami. That's what they told us."

"Where in Miami?" Giaccalone said.

I didn't answer. I wasn't going to drag Maria and Santo into this.

"Hello? Did you hear me? I said where in Miami?"

"If you kill us," I said, "you'll never find it."

"Thank you," Giaccalone said. "I never would have thought of that on my own." He got up and kicked me, hard, in the ribs. I rolled to my side, reaching for breath. "How about if I do that? Will I find my money if I do that?"

Hakanson said that he was sorry to interrupt again but he wanted to point out once more that this really did not appear to be a matter that involved him and that since he really had nothing to do with any of this he thought it would be best if he just got up and left—but as he was speaking Tony wound up and delivered two kicks, the first one across Hakanson's ribs, and the second a punch with his heel down into Hakanson's kidneys.

Coco whimpered and leaned up beside Giaccalone. He rubbed her neck and said, "Shhhh, it's all right, baby, it's all right. What a dog, huh? Look at this." He cleared his throat. He picked up his cigar, which had gone out, and lit the end. The thick smoke rose and curled above his head. An awful stink filled the room. I thought about the ten-cent stogies that my grandfather used to fire up after dinner.

"We'll get your money for you," I said.

"Oh," Giaccalone said, "now we're getting someplace."

"We're sorry about this. We didn't mean for this to happen."

He leaned forward. "I don't think I heard you correctly," he said. "You say you didn't *mean* it? Because I don't understand what you mean when you say you didn't mean it. Maybe you can explain that to me. Are you saying that all of this happened by accident?"

"Well," I said, "not an accident, exactly."

"No. I didn't think so." He sat back. He puffed on his cigar. He exhaled a long plume of blue smoke. "You probably think I'm going to kill you, right?"

"I don't know. " My voice came out sounding high, ridiculous.

"Well, I'm not. All we're going to do is have a little talk. You're going to tell me where my money is, and how I can get it back. Is that okay with you?"

I nodded.

"Good." He grinned. "And then, once you tell me how to get my money, I'm going to cut off your hands."

The room tilted like a ride in an amusement park. I felt as if I'd been drugged. They were laughing, their voices strange, their faces grotesque and distorted. I told myself that they were kidding, that this was some sick joke; because nobody went around cutting off people's hands.

Giaccalone was going on about Arab countries and how if you get caught stealing, they cut off your hands, and if you get caught committing adultery, they cut off your dick. He said that maybe Wilson and Hakanson would be able to drive me to the hospital and I could have my hands reattached like that guy who had gotten his dick chopped off by his wife or the other guy who had got his arms torn off in a thresher and had them sewn back on. Then he nodded to Billy, who was looking a little bit sick about this, and said, "Okay, come on."

Billy lifted me up. A sharp pain hooked me in the ribs. Everything went white, then black, and then came back to normal again. Billy leaned me against the coffee table, kneeling with my arms stretched across the top. I was shaking, and suddenly cold. I remembered when I was a kid and went swimming in Lake Michigan and came out with my skin turning blue. Tony tied a rope around each of my wrists and ran the ropes down under the table and tied them off. Then he opened his hockey bag and removed a hatchet. Giaccalone picked up the hatchet and took a couple of practice swings. Then he placed the hatchet on the table and said, "Okay, now tell me, are you a leftie or a rightie?"

My lips were trembling; I couldn't speak. I shook my head. Tears were forming in my eyes. I managed to say, "Please." Giaccalone laughed. Coco, beside him, was staring at me, her eyes wide. I knelt there wondering how much this was going to hurt and wondering if the doctors would be able to make me a set of plastic hands, and if so, whether I'd be able to do anything with them.

"No preference?" Giaccalone said.

I shrugged. I tried again to speak, but could only babble, which made them laugh. Giaccalone held up the hatchet. He looked like a shop teacher giving a lecture on the proper use of wood-chopping tools. He took the cigar from the corner of his mouth and placed it into the ashtray.

"What I like about this," he said, glancing at Pockmarks, "is that really it's worse than killing somebody. Because if you kill somebody, that's it, right? They're dead. But with this, they've got to go on with their life, only now there are certain things that are kind of hard to do." He turned to look at me. "For example, every day, when you take a dump, you're going to need someone to come in and wipe your ass for you, right? You see what I mean? That's more pleasurable for me than if you were dead."

"You're goddamn sick," I said, and was surprised to hear my voice, which came out low and loud and full of its original downriver Detroit accent. The accent caught Billy's attention. He glanced at me, and in his eyes there was something like pity; for a moment I hoped that he might tell Giaccalone to stop. But no. Billy was a good soldier.

Tony asked me if I had any last requests. "You got anything you want to do with that hand? You want to go beat off one last time?"

At this point it seemed important simply to endure this with as much dignity as possible. Behind me Evan was saying, "Oh man, oh man, oh man." Giaccalone raised the hatchet and took a few more practice swings, in slow motion, each one coming closer and closer to my right wrist. As the swings got closer, my stomach tightened and I felt as if I might be sick; I closed my eyes. The nervous laughter trickled off and the room became quiet and then suddenly Giaccalone let out a scream and brought the hatchet crashing down into the table. I felt nothing. I opened my eyes. The hatchet was sunk into the table, an inch away from my arm.

Tony and Giaccalone burst out laughing. Pockmarks and Billy sat there looking more relieved than anything else. I suppose they couldn't have been looking forward to the sight of a severed hand. Evan was still muttering on the floor. Beside him, Wilson was awake again. Maybe the scream had brought him around.

"Check it out," Tony said, pointing to my shorts, where a wet spot had formed.

Pockmarks said, "Davio, you're fucking unbalanced, you know that? You made the kid piss his pants."

"I know." Giaccalone stopped laughing and wiped a tear from his eye. "I know. Okay, I'll get serious." He pried the hatchet out of the table. He took a deep breath, and tried to calm down. "Okay," he said. "Here we go. You guys ready to see this? Billy, you better go get a fucking towel or something, okay?"

"Sure," Billy said. He glanced out the window—then glanced again. "Hey," he said. "There's a car. Someone pulling up." He watched for a moment. "They're getting out. A man and a woman."

"So what?" Giaccalone said. "This is a motel, right?"

"They're walking toward this room," Billy said.

"Cops?"

Billy shook his head. I was praying that he was wrong. God only knew how the police would have found us, but maybe they had.

There was a knock at the door, and a voice I recognized said, "It's Santo Bava. Open the door."

BILLY SEEMED NOT TO BELIEVE THIS. He looked at Giaccalone. "He says it's Santo Bava."

Giaccalone slumped in his chair, as if someone had let the air out of him. "I heard," he said.

The word *Bava* zipped through the room like an electric current; Billy and Pockmarks exchanged a glance.

"You think it's really him?" Billy said.

Giaccalone sighed, and put the hatchet behind the couch. "Open the door," he said.

Santo walked in with Maria. The room was crowded already; we had to squeeze to let them fit inside. Maria was carrying my backpack. She wouldn't look at me.

Santo nodded at Giaccalone. "You know who I am," he said.

"Of course." Giaccalone smiled, nervously. He was stroking Coco's head, tying to stay calm.

Santo seemed irritated; he looked like a CEO who's been called down to the mailroom to settle an argument between two clerks. He nodded toward the table where I was tied up.

"What's this?" he said.

"Mr. Bava—" Giaccalone said.

"Untie him," Santo said.

Giaccalone nodded to Tony. Tony started to protest, but Giaccalone said, "Do what he says."

There was an awkward moment as Tony struggled to untie the knots. Pockmarks and Billy stood there staring at Santo. Finally Tony got the knots undone. I shook my hands to get the blood flowing again. My fingers tingled. The ropes had left grooves in my wrists.

Giaccalone cleared his throat and said that he hoped Mr. Bava would understand that he'd been wronged. "I'm the grieved party here," he said.

Maria handed over the backpack. "It's all there," she said. "The whole thirty thousand."

Giaccalone started mumbling about expenses: the cost of flying down here, the car rentals, the investigators he'd had to hire. Maria asked Giaccalone if he wanted her to call her uncle and tell him that Giaccalone had kidnapped her fiancé and tried to kill him.

Tony said, "Wait a minute. You're going to marry this dickhead?"

"That's right," she said.

"I don't believe it."

"I don't care what you believe." Maria stood there with her hands on her hips.

Giaccalone said, "Just so you know, Mr. Bava, we weren't going to kill them. We just wanted our money back. I have nothing but respect for your father, for your whole family. When Maria came to live in Boston, we took her in like she was part of our family."

Santo looked at Giaccalone the way you might look at a beggar who comes up and corners you on the subway. "Let's go," he said.

Maria helped Evan get to his feet. His face was swollen and caked with blood. The words *Elephant Man* came to mind.

"He needs a hospital," I said.

Santo nodded. Wilson and Hakanson got up, too. We all started for the door. Coco, seeing us leaving, began to whimper and slap her tail.

"Wait," Wilson said. He turned to Giaccalone. "You said I could buy

Coco back for fifty thousand dollars. There's ninety-six in that bag."

Giaccalone's face darkened. "Karl," he said, "I wouldn't sell you this dog for all the money in the world. You could kneel down right here and blow me and I wouldn't sell you this dog."

"She should be running," Wilson said. "It's where she belongs."

The side of Wilson's face was blue where Tony had kicked him, and his voice came out sounding like he had pebbles in his mouth. I wondered if he had a broken jaw. A thin line of blood trailed down from a gash on his temple.

Wilson said he would make Giaccalone the same deal he had offered before: Giaccalone could have a share of Coco's winnings, and when she retired he could have her back.

"Right, and then you walk out of here, and I never see you again," Giaccalone said. "You see an *S* on my head for *Stupid*?"

"All I want is the dog gets a chance to run," Wilson said.

"And all *I* want," Giaccalone said, "is my dog. You don't understand. I love this dog."

"If you really loved this dog, you'd let her race," Wilson said. "That's what she was bred to do. She's a champion. And she's still got two good years, maybe more. And you're going to rob her of that."

Giaccalone sat there, his jaw clenched. He was staring at the wall, shaking his head.

"I'm not leaving without the dog," Wilson said.

"Fine," Giaccalone said. "So don't leave. Stay here the rest of your fucking life. Live here in this room. All I know is, I'm leaving. And I'm leaving with the dog, and you're not going to get in my way."

Santo cleared his throat. Everybody looked at him. "Davio," he said, "this isn't personal, it's business. It's business, but you're making it personal."

"It *is* personal," Giaccalone said.

"The guy is going to give you a hundred thousand dollars for a dog," Santo said. "Plus a share of the dog's winnings, and you can keep the dog after she retires, which means you can breed her. You let her race a couple years, and win some races, set some records, and your breeding fees are going to be higher. See? And you can still visit her whenever you want." He turned to Wilson. "Right? He can visit her?"

"Sure," Wilson said.

"I should get *all* of her winnings," Giaccalone said. "Not just a share."

"Davio," Santo said, "be reasonable."

"Reasonable? You think it's reasonable what these fucks put me through? Who's to say they're not going to screw me over?"

"I am," Santo said. "I'm the one to say. And I'm telling you, right here, right now, you let Wilson have the dog and he'll stick to the bargain. And if he doesn't, you come to me, okay? *Capito?* He turned to Wilson. "You understand this, right? You break the deal, you answer to me."

"That's fine," Wilson said.

Santo turned back to Giaccalone. "Well?" he said.

Giaccalone sat there wringing his hands. "Do I have any choice?"

Santo shook his head. "Not really."

"Great. Thank you very much. Story of my life. Every time I turn around I get fucked in the ass. Okay, here." He handed Coco's leash to Wilson. "Take her."

Wilson led Coco toward the door. Giaccalone closed his eyes. He couldn't bear to see this. And then something awful happened: Coco broke free and ran back to Giaccalone and jumped up and tried to lick his face. This was more than the poor bastard could take. He pushed her away. "Come on, get her out of here," he said.

They led the dog out to the parking lot. Giaccalone sat in the chair staring at the wall and clutching the backpack and the paper bag like some crazy old man you might see on a bus. I wanted to say something—tell him I was sorry, at least. But Maria grabbed my arm and pulled me out of the room.

In the parking lot we all stood looking up at the sky like people who have been in a car crash and still can't believe they've survived. The sun was coming up, but there were still a few stars in the sky. The seagulls squawked. Coco barked as Wilson put her into the backseat of his car. Through the window of the motel room we heard Giaccalone shouting, and then there was something that sounded like crying.

Wilson and Hakanson drove away without saying good-bye. Santo helped Evan get into the backseat of his car.

I took Maria's hand. "What's this about your uncle?" I said.

She turned away. "I don't want to talk about it."

Of course I had heard the name Bava before, usually in sentences that also included names like Gotti, Gambino, and Genovese. But for all the times I had heard Maria introduce herself it had never occurred to me that she was from that family. Maybe because I had never heard her say her name the way Billy had said it: in a hushed, solemn voice, the two syllables, *Bah-vah*, falling off his tongue with a mixture of fear and disbelief—the inflection a priest uses when he raises the host and tells you it's the body of Christ, or that the doctor uses when he tilts his head and says, "Cancer."

"You could have stopped this up in Boston," I said. "You could have stepped in right at the beginning."

"That's not true." She gazed off in the direction of the highway. Both sides were jammed with traffic. Twin torrents of light: white in one direction, red in the other. Somehow it did not seem possible that all of those people were headed off to work, just like any other day. Maria stood there, unable to look at me.

"And what about us being engaged?" I said.

"I had to say something."

"So we're not engaged?"

"Stop it." She turned. Color rose in her face. She pointed to the van and said, "Go."

54

THERE ARE MOMENTS when life seems to open up and present itself to you, when you are amazed by the sheer size and wonder of the world and startled by its secrets and surprises, as you would be if somehow one night the canopy of the sky were to fold back like a curtain and reveal another world, or set of worlds, that you had not known existed. Even if that were to happen I would not have been more amazed than I was that night, as I piloted my car down Ocean Drive in Miami with a warm breeze spilling across my face and Maria Bava, the *principessa* of La Famiglia Bava, riding beside me. All around us lay the circus of South Beach: the buzzing neon, the shimmering palm trees, the fashion models who called to each other and leaned down to kiss their boyfriends, like swans bending for crumbs of bread. The air throbbed with salsa and techno and hip-hop.

Evan had stayed home with Santo. When we left, they were sitting at the kitchen table eating Chinese takeout and talking about Nectar. That afternoon Santo had taken Evan to a doctor who set his nose and taped it in place with a metal splint. Evan looked nasty. I suppose Santo felt bad for him. By the time they got back from the doctor's office, they were joking around like old friends.

Maria and I, on the other hand, still had not managed to have a decent conversation. She spent the afternoon out by herself doing errands, while I stayed home and washed Sigrid and played Doom on the Macintosh that Santo's son had left behind in his room. Maria got back late and said she wanted to take me out to dinner. "We need to talk," she said. From the look on her face I figured I would be getting the official declaration that our relationship was over, and I resolved to take this like a man. But then when we got in the car and drove into South Beach, Maria cheered up, and I began to think that maybe things were going to work out.

We ate dinner in a Cuban restaurant, a place that Santo had recommended. We sat outdoors, on a patio. There was music playing, and candlelight. Every so often people would get up from their tables and go to a little clearing to dance. Off to one side a large Cuban family, perhaps twenty people, were eating together, with an elderly couple—the grandparents, I suppose—sitting at the head of the table. The grandparents were handsome and well-dressed and you could imagine how beautiful they both had been when they were young; they sat holding hands, whispering like lovers, and when they got up and danced, the old man spun his wife and then dipped her and all of the family cheered and I thought how good it would be to grow old with a woman you loved and children and grandchildren who took you to dinner and applauded you on the dance floor.

After dinner we walked down to the waterfront, where sailboats tugged at their moorings and little waves lapped at the piers, a sound like a cat drinking milk from a bowl. Most of the boats were empty, their lights off; but in a few there were lights on, and voices floating out from the cabins. We walked to the end of a pier and stood beneath a sky crowded with stars. Maybe it was the wine we'd had with dinner, or the air, or the fact that we were holding hands and we knew that something big was about to happen, but we found ourselves shivering. I was wearing clothes that Santo had loaned me: linen pants, a white cotton shirt, sandals. Maria wore a thin summer dress she had bought that afternoon.

"I'm going to tell you about my family," she said. "I'll tell you the whole thing, just once, and then I don't want to talk about it ever again."

Her father was in federal prison in Kentucky. He had been there since she was eleven years old. Which was why Maria had been shipped off after her mother died. She was twelve years old and she was given a choice: she could live with her cousins in Miami—her father's side of the family—or she could go to Boston and live with Gus, a relative on her mother's side. And so a rich girl became a poor girl; a princess became an orphan.

"I didn't want anything to do with my father's family," she said. "I still don't."

I said that I could understand her being angry at her father, but that at the same time it seemed to me that if she had been holding this trump card all along, she might have helped us out when we were still back in Boston.

She said that first of all she wasn't sure if Giaccalone would have listened to her if she were making the case by herself rather than with Santo. "You might have noticed," she said, "that people like Davio tend not to take women too seriously."

But another reason and perhaps the more important reason was that she had simply been embarrassed. "I'm not proud of my family. You understand? That's what I liked about you; you didn't know who I was. You just liked me for *me*. I mean, can you imagine what it was like for me growing up in the North End? With guys like Tony asking me out, figuring they could get to meet my father? Either that or guys avoiding me because of who I was? Why do you think I'm going to the Peace Corps? All of my life, all I've wanted to do is to get as far away from them as possible."

"I'm sorry," I said.

"So am I."

We stood looking over the water. In the distance a yacht moved across the bay, its running lights leaving a trail in the dark water.

"I was thinking," I said. "About what you said to those guys this afternoon. About us being engaged."

She sighed. "Reilly," she said, "don't do this." The sailboats rose and fell in their slips; the pier groaned at the effort of holding them. In the distance, a fat moon hung above the buildings. Searchlights spun and wheeled in the sky. Another wave washed in against the pier, lifting the boats, and I thought about the huge tilt and spin of the earth. This, I thought, is how it feels when your life is about to change.

"I have to do this," I said. I took her by the shoulders and held her. "Maria," I said, "I'm in love with you. I don't care about your family, or anything else. Just you."

A breeze blew her hair across her face. She pulled it back behind her ear. She said that if I really loved her, there was one way I could prove it.

"Name it," I said.

"Come to Russia," she said.

I looked at her. I didn't know what to say. And right then, right there—in that moment, which I would never forget—I blew it. I should have said, yes, I'll go, I'll walk to Russia if I have to; instead, I stood there shifting my weight from side to side and thinking about my job and my future and trying to think of something clever to say.

"Right." She nodded. She pressed her lips together, and gave me a tight smile. "That's what I thought."

I felt dizzy, and stupid, and ridiculous. I was afraid to speak, for fear that whatever I said would only make things worse. Besides, what could I say? I wasn't going to quit my job and move to Russia, for God's sake.

"I'm sorry," I told her. It was the best I could do.

"It's all right. You're just not ready, that's all."

She wiped a tear from her face. In a sailboat near us, people burst out laughing.

"I'll get myself together," I said. "I promise."

"I know." She smiled. "I wish I could be here when it happens." She kissed me, and then we stood holding each other.

The people in the sailboat came up on deck. In the dark we could not see their faces, just their shapes. A man said, "Hey, young lovers!" and they all laughed.

Maria took my hand. "Come on," she said. "Let's go home."

Evan and Santo had a bottle of Dewar's and a bowl of ice on the kitchen table, along with a yellow legal pad and a pile of notes. They shouted when we came through the door. "We're celebrating," Evan said, grinning from behind his splints. He was drunk. "We're going into business together. You and me and Santo. He's got some friends. They're going to invest. He made a few phone calls, and boom, we've got a million and a half. Can you believe it? We'll do another round in six months."

Maria looked at Santo. He shrugged. He was drunk, too.

"Come on, have a drink," Evan said. "Meet the new board of directors of Nectar Software Corporation. Or most of it, anyway. We're going to have to give Santo's friend Italico a seat on the board, too." He turned to Santo. "Right?"

Santo shrugged. He held out a chair for me. Maria stood there, looking at us. Her eyes welled with tears, and she said, "I'm going to bed," and then walked away.

"What's wrong with her?" Santo said.

I told him about us breaking up. He tried to seem surprised. But I'm sure Maria had told him beforehand. He showed me a photograph of his wife, which he had brought out earlier to show to Evan. "Maybe it's for the best," he said. I didn't know if he was talking about my situation or his. "Everything works out in the end," he said. He poured me a glass of Dewar's and told me to drink up. "Trust me," he said. "It'll make you feel better."

WE DROVE BACK TO BOSTON, and I spent a few days helping Maria pack her things and put them into storage; then a few days later Evan and I drove her to Logan and saw her off at the gate. Right at the last minute she started having second thoughts. The plane had boarded, and she was standing beside me holding her ticket and staring out the window at the darkening sky and the rows of lights on the runway. She kept saying in a voice that was a little too high and a little too fast that she couldn't believe that in ten hours she was going to be standing in St. Petersburg and she didn't speak a word of Russian and she didn't know a soul in the whole country; she didn't even know what kind of food they ate. I was about to tell her that she could change her mind, that she didn't have to go; but then they made the final boarding call and she grabbed me and said, "All right, see you later."

She gave me a quick squeeze and a kiss and then hurried away, stopping once at the bend in the chute to turn and look back and wave. Her hair was pulled into a ponytail, and she had a fleece pullover wrapped around her waist and a backpack on her shoulder; she looked like a kid going off to the first day of school. She was leaving everything behind, and she was terrified—I could see it in her eyes—but she was determined not to back down. It occurred to me that Maria had a lot more guts than I did, that she was doing something that I would never dare to do; and for the first time ever, I envied her.

It occurred to me too that I might never see her again. We had talked about plane fares and e-mail and letters and phone calls. But when she started down the chute I panicked, because suddenly it seemed that all of that talk had been nothing but talk, just things we had said to keep ourselves from freaking out. I knew what would happen: For a few months we would write, but then the letters would trail off, and the phone calls would become too expensive, and we would meet other people, and for the rest of my life I would carry with me the image of Maria summoning up her courage—the courage that I did not have—and walking away. I would remember the Levi's she was wearing, brand-new and bought for the trip; I would remember her black Italian shoes with the chunky heels, her green MEI backpack, her red Columbia pullover, her marvelous thick black hair, her lovely quick frightened smile when she turned and waved good-bye. I would remember her Boston accent and the way she took a breath and said, "All right, see you later," and the way I stood there after she was gone, gazing down the chute, feeling like a coward and a fool.

I wanted to wait and watch the plane take off; but Evan said only morons did that, it was a pointless gesture, and besides, we were parked at a thirty-minute meter. Sure enough, when we got to the car there was a ticket on the windshield.

A week later Evan and I were packed and gone too—off to San Francisco, where Evan had found office space in a converted warehouse on Ninth Street and an apartment in the Upper Haight. We hired the cutest receptionist we could find—a blue-eyed blond former aerobics instructor named Blair—and bought some desks at a used furniture store. Evan convinced his friend Saul to leave McKinsey and become our president, with a five percent share. Saul didn't like the fact that we had taken funding from Santo and "those people," and he also thought we had given "those people" too much control. Santo and his partners owned thirty percent of the company, while Evan and I owned ten percent each. Down the road, Saul said, we were going to have to rewrite that agreement.

A few weeks later we hired Nabeel and Upendra, and gave them both five percent shares. Saul objected; he wanted to give them two and a half each. He said that if we went public with a valuation of fifty million dollars, a five percent share was going to be worth two and a half million, and that was a lot of money to give people for joining a project at the last minute. The real problem, I think, was that he didn't like the idea of Nabeel and Upendra having the same share that he did.

Evan overruled Saul, saying that Nabeel and Upendra were the best programmers he knew and besides they were friends and he wanted to do something good for them—a statement he regretted when Nabeel arrived and revealed that during his last few weeks in Boston he had been sleeping with Agnes. This was a pretty serious violation of the Code of Men—Rule Number One: You don't sleep with your friend's ex-girlfriend—but then again we were living in San Francisco, a city where there were three single women for every single heterosexual man, and you couldn't stay angry for long. Besides, Evan was already dating Blair, the receptionist, and had, on more than one occasion, actually bounced quarters off various parts of her body, just to see if it could be done. "My shiksa goddess," he called her. Most nights she stayed with Evan, at our apartment, and there was no way not to hear them.

Evan said it was like living in a Budweiser commercial. And the fact that even I had done some dating was proof enough for me. There was the girl I met in a dance club, and another I met one day when I was walking around in Golden Gate Park. In San Francisco women just came right up to you and started talking. The problem was that going out with other women only made me feel worse about Maria. She and I were trading e-mail every day—there were computers at her language center—and she told me about St. Petersburg: the canals, the cathedrals, the street musicians on Nevsky Prospekt.

She mailed me photos of herself standing in front the Winter Palace. She had cut her hair—long hair was too much hassle, she said—and she looked like a different person. Even her smile was different. I kept wondering who she was smiling at. Who was taking the photos? But I didn't ask; I just told her how much I missed her. She said she missed me, too. She told me about her new friends, the closest of whom was a guy she called Bryan from Ohio—to distinguish him from the other Bryan in her program, who was from New Jersey. Bryan from Ohio had gone to Haverford and had spent time in Central America before joining the Peace Corps.

Maria insisted that she and Bryan were only friends; but I could see where they were headed. One day I would go to work and find no e-mail from her, and then a few days would go by like that, and then I would get a note saying that she was sorry that she had not been writing but she had been struggling with how to tell me this, because she and Bryan had become involved. Worse still, she would not tell me anything until she sent me an apology and a wedding announcement.

"Dude," Evan said, "how can you be so messed up? I mean, look where we are, dude."

It was a Sunday afternoon in October and we were standing on our mountain bikes at the top of Mount Tamalpais, looking out over the city. And these were the eleventh and twelfth times, respectively, that Evan had called me "dude" since we had left home that morning. Evan loved California. He had bought a Jeep, and dropped his New York accent in favor of a surfer drawl. He wore contact lenses now, and worked out in a gym, and spent his evenings with Blair, boogie-boarding in wet suits at Stinson Beach. Nectar was close to being finished, thanks in large part to Nabeel, who turned out to be every bit as brilliant as he had always claimed to be. Lately we had started generating a buzz in the industry—calls from journalists and venture capitalists, invitations to speak at conferences. Saul was lining up prospective customers and talking to investment bankers about our stock offering.

"I just don't understand how you can be unhappy," Evan said. "Everybody out here is happy. They put Prozac in the drinking water, for Christ's sake."

I tried to explain that this was precisely the problem. Any day now, the Happy Police are going to extradite me back to the East Coast," I said.

It didn't help that when Maria wrote to me about the despair of people living in communal apartments with not enough food, I could only reply with stories about the despair of people who have too much of everything. I was living with grown people who told you with complete seriousness that their top goal in life was to be able to run a marathon, or to climb Mount McKinley. This was either going to kill me or make me crazy and I didn't know which was worse.

"Come visit me," Maria said. We were talking on the phone, the connection fading in and out, like short-wave radio. "I've got a semester break in November. Just come here and see what it's like. You can meet my friends. You'd like them. I can show you the city. We can take the overnight train to Moscow. We'll get a sleeper car."

I told her I would think about it. The next afternoon, after a meeting in which Evan used the word *dude* twenty-seven times, I decided that I had done enough thinking. I went to my office and called a travel agent. Two weeks from now, Maria would meet me at the airport and big things would happen; I could feel it. I told Evan that I just needed a little break, a chance to relax; but secretly I fantasized about never coming back.

Maybe somehow Evan knew this, because the day before I was supposed to leave, he and Saul burst into my office and told me I had to cancel my trip. "Saul just got a call from Microsoft," he said. "They want us there tomorrow."

"So go," I said. "You don't need me."

"They want the whole team. The three of us."

"Take Nabeel. He can pretend to be me."

"Dude," Evan said, "I'm sorry. But you can't go, okay? Not if you want to be part of this company."

I had been expecting them to pull something like this, but not this early. I'd figured they would wait until my bags were packed, and then out of the blue I would get a call from the Russian embassy telling me that my visa had been revoked, or a call from United Airlines telling me that their computers had crashed and all their reservations had been scrambled but they would be happy to refund my ticket.

But this wasn't a prank. Saul closed the door and said we needed to have a talk. He was a fat guy with a goatee, little round glasses, and a Harvard MBA. He'd done time as a McKinsey consultant working for a toy company. Now he was our president and I had never been able to warm up to him. Saul was a bully and a braggart. He had a tendency to exaggerate and sometimes to just plain lie—things that may serve you well in business but had never been what I looked for in a friend. At first I thought he was brilliant. But lately I had noticed that there was an inverse relationship between Saul's knowledge of a subject and the pace at which he discussed it: the less he knew, the faster he went. I suppose that was something they taught you at business school.

Our company was too small for any real back-stabbing or office politics. But I suppose Saul saw me as a chance to practice. He resented the fact that I owned a bigger share of the company than he did, and he had talked to Evan about wanting an equal share. I wondered if he was making this stink about my trip not so much because he begrudged me a vacation but because he recognized a chance to drive me out of the company. Our contracts said that if you quit before the product shipped, you lost your share. I'm sure Saul would have been glad to get back my ten percent; and maybe he could convince Evan to shift five of that to him, so that he and Evan could be equal partners.

"There are certain people," Saul said, "who are not exactly psyched about the fact that while they're working around the clock, one of the founders is going off on a vacation. And you can't blame them. Think about how it looks."

"What people?" I said. "There's only ten of us, and five of us are owners, and one is Blair, and the other four are testers, and they've only been here for a month. So who's complaining?"

Saul looked at Evan, as if to say, *You see what I mean?* They both stood there staring at me, like doctors in a mental hospital examining a new patient.

"What are you saying?" I said. "If I go on this trip, then what? You're going to fire me? I'll come back and my office will be cleaned out?"

"Dude," Evan said, "you just have to decide what's important to you, that's all."

I looked at him. I couldn't believe it. "Dude," I said, "get out of my office."

They left, whispering to each other like murderers in some Shakespeare play. I called Maria. She said she wasn't angry so much as disappointed; but I could tell she was angry, too. She had turned down a chance to go to Yalta over the semester break with the people in her program. Now she would be stuck in St. Petersburg, alone.

I told her I could come over in January. By January she would be in Tashkent, she said. It was another of those crazy satellite connections, the signal going in and out.

"Are you there?" I said.

"I'm here."

"I'll visit you in Tashkent," I said. "In January."

She sighed. "We'd better wrap this up," she said.

That night I flew with Evan and Saul to Seattle. The two of them had seats together, toward the front. My seat was in back.

We got to the hotel and checked in. As soon as I got to my room, I called Maria. It was eleven o'clock my time, six in the morning for her. There was no answer. I tried not to think about where she might be.

In the morning we drove to Microsoft and met with a team of engineers. Saul explained our business model, and Evan gave them a demonstration of Nectar. The Microsoft engineers were not impressed. "We could do this in a week," one of them said.

Later we were taken to a different building, where we met with Gates himself. I felt like James Bond being led into Dr. Evil's secret headquarters; I half-expected to find a glass floor above a tank of piranha. But Gates disappointed me. He had the build of a skinny guy who has gone to seed: narrow shoulders and a pigeon chest, then a gut that was too big for the rest of his body. He sat sprawled out across his captain's chair, looking like a python trying to digest a meal. We talked for five minutes. Then he thanked us for our time and told us they would stay in touch. Saul got up and held out his hand and then bowed slightly; for a fleeting moment I thought he might genuflect.

By the time we got back to San Francisco, it became clear to us what had just happened: all Microsoft had wanted was to get a look at what we were doing so that down the road they could copy it and put us out of business. "That's why we were meeting with engineers," Saul said. "Those guys were taking notes." I resisted the temptation to point out that it had been Saul, the Harvard wunderkind, who had arranged the meeting in the first place.

But really, it didn't matter. We had to get to market, as soon as possible. Saul nailed down a beta customer, a catalog business that would use Nectar to sell clothing over the Web. It was a big break for us. But it meant we had to work even harder. The customer was in Chicago. We had to go there, install the software, show them how to use it, fix problems as they occurred.

At least one of us had to stay in Chicago. Naturally, Saul recommended me. I suppose this was my punishment for having wanted to take a vacation. Or maybe it was another way to convince me to quit. No matter. I saluted the flag, pledged allegiance, and went to Chicago like a good soldier. I spent my days in a cubicle, fixing bugs, and spent my nights in a hotel room, eating miserable room-service meals and reminding myself of how much my ten percent was going to be worth when we went public.

There were no days off, no weekends or holidays. On Thanksgiving I packed a turkey sandwich and went to the office, and even forced a laugh when Saul called and said that everybody was there at his apartment having a turkey dinner and they wanted me to know how much they appreciated me being a team player. They put me on speakerphone. Evan said if it was any consolation, the weather in San Francisco was lousy. Nabeel said he had saved me a drumstick and would FedEx it to me in the morning. I pretended to have a call coming in on my second line, and told them I had to go.

I N DECEMBER, my mother came to Chicago and took me out to dinner at a place called Too Chez. Outside, snow fell dizzily against the windows. Mom was frazzled, as always. She drank two martinis before dinner, and smoked all through the meal, and she waited until dessert to tell me that she had not come to Chicago for a trial but rather to tell me that my grandmother had had a stroke and was in the hospital. The doctors did not think she would recover.

At first I didn't realize what she was saying. Then I did. "God," I said.

Mom blinked. Her eyes were wet. She lit another cigarette and gazed off toward the bar and seemed not to notice the waiter who had arrived with our bill and was standing beside her.

"And how is everything here?" the waiter said in a nursery school voice. "Can I get you anything else, or are we all set?"

Mom nodded. She stared off into the distance. The waiter placed the bill on the table and told us to have a nice evening.

Ten days later, Nana died. Mom called and woke me up in my hotel room. I called Evan and woke him up and told him.

"Your grandmother?" he said. "Can't you just send a card or something?"

There were things I wanted to say—"I quit" came to mind. But instead I said, "No, Evan, I can't just send a card."

He grumbled, but said okay, they would put Upendra on a flight; he could cover for me until I got back.

Nana was eighty-seven years old, which meant there weren't many people coming to the calling hours. The few friends she had left were all living in nursing homes. A few of them straggled into the funeral home, limping along on walkers and canes. The next day a priest said a funeral mass in the funeral home. It was easier than taking the body to a church, he said, and if you weren't expecting a big crowd . . .

We weren't. Mom and I were the only ones there. At the cemetery we stood with our arms around each other looking at the tiny casket set on planks above the grave. The sky hung low and gray, as it always did in Detroit in winter. I was thinking about my grandfather, who had died on a day like this. He was buried right here, too. The snow lay on the ground like a dirty blanket, soot-gray and uneven. It was bitter cold, below zero with the wind chill. The gravediggers had needed jackhammers to break open the earth. The hard dirt lay in mounds around the opening. The priest wore ski gloves and fumbled with the pages in his prayer book. He ran through a few prayers, trying to keep his teeth from chattering; and then two gravediggers— beefy Polish guys from Hamtramck, bundled up in ski parkas— lowered Nana into the ground.

We went to Nana's house, the house where Mom had grown up and where she and I had moved after her divorce, and I don't know whether her whole life was flashing before her eyes but I would guess the memories were rushing at her, because they certainly were at me. There was the same stale smell, the same dank curtains, the same drab kitchen with its cracked linoleum and crooked cabinets. We went through every room making sure the storm windows were shut and that the doors and windows were locked. We unplugged the appliances, threw out the food in the refrigerator. Mom said she would have to sell the place quickly. You couldn't leave a house empty for very long in Detroit or something bad would happen: graffiti, or a fire.

She sat down on the couch. She asked me if I remembered when Grandpa bought this couch. We had just moved in, and Grandpa was embarrassed because the old couch was ratty, so he went out to Sears and bought this one, which was gold with white brocade on the cushions. At the time it had seemed extravagant. Now the couch was old and frayed and dappled with tea stains.

"Look at me—I've got old, too." She laughed. "I don't know how it happened, but there it is."

"You're not old," I said.

But she was. Her hair had gone gray, and her face had changed; it was as if there was some threshold that separated the old from the young, and now, with both her parents dead, she had stepped across that threshold and inhabited the world of the old. She was only in her fifties, but already I could see how she was going to look in her coffin.

After we checked the lights and the locks one more time, we went back to Mom's house in Birmingham. It was a big brick monster of a house, with pillars out front and a circular driveway. I had never been able to imagine her living here all by herself. And the house agreed. Most of the rooms looked as if nobody ever went into them. Mom heated up some chicken soup—storebought, from a deli in Bloomfield Hills. As we ate I told her about Jeanie, and then about Coco, and Maria. I told her about Evan, and Saul, and how they had kept me from going to Russia and made me work through Thanksgiving and probably would make me work through Christmas, and how I felt bad about things with Maria because for a while I had really thought she was the one, but on the other hand my share of the company was going to be worth five million dollars, which was a pretty good consolation prize. If I could just hang in for another year, I said, then everything would be okay.

Mom put down her spoon and started telling me about a guy who had wanted to marry her when she was in law school. "You were little then," she said. "You didn't know about him."

His name was Tom. He sent her flowers, and cards, and chocolate; he took her to dinner at the Whitney, and wanted to take her to Bermuda on vacation, and he had no problem with the fact that she had been married and had a kid.

"Like a fool," she said, "I broke it off. I was waiting for your father. I kept thinking he was going to get his act together. Plus, I figured, Hey, I just got out of one relationship, I don't want to dive right back into another one, right? It was the seventies. I wanted to play the field." She laughed. "Now here I am, it's twenty years later, and you know what? There wasn't any field to play. Your father never came back. Tom married someone else. Twenty years, and they went by like this." She snapped her fingers. "And what have I got? I've got a nice house, and nice furniture, and a nice car—and I'm all by myself. Go figure."

She got up and cleared the table. She stood rinsing the bowls at the sink, silhouetted against the window, and suddenly I understood her life: I imagined her standing there, gazing into the backyard, wondering what might have been.

"I guess what I'm trying to tell you," she said, "is that I thought there were all sorts of people in the world ready to love me. Everybody thinks that way when they're young. But if there's one thing I've learned, it's that there aren't that many people who will ever really love you, and really stick by you. If you find even one, I think you're pretty lucky."

She made coffee, and we sat at the kitchen table looking through old photos. There was one of me and my grandfather, both wearing Red Wings shirts, heading off to a game. There was one of my mother and father with me on the day they brought me home from the hospital. Of course I had seen this one a million times before: Mom and Dad are standing in front of their new house, holding their new baby, beaming. They look ridiculously young, ridiculously sure of themselves, like people who know that nothing bad will ever happen to them.

"Well," she said, closing the photo album, "we'd better go."

*　　　*　　　*

The airport was crazy—huge lines, crying babies, families waiting. A blizzard was shutting down airports in places like Kansas City and Omaha. Flights were being canceled. Bored students, stranded in Detroit, lay sprawled on the floor beside their backpacks. My flight to Chicago had been delayed, but they were still hoping to take off tonight. The storm was edging into Chicago, but O'Hare was still open. I sat down on the floor with the students. Some were sleeping, others were were playing cards, and others were reading books that only students read: *Moby-Dick,* the *Odyssey.*

I unzipped my bag, looking for a copy of *Rolling Stone* that I had bought in Chicago. Instead, I found my Russian phrase book, my passport, and the Russian visa the travel agent had sent me back in November. I looked at the visa with its funny writing. I glanced through the phrase book: *Privyet, sdravstvuitye, gde tualet?* It was hard to believe, but for a while I had practiced, sitting in my living room at night, my tongue tripping on too many consonants. I had imagined myself with Maria: fur hats, a little apartment, shopping for vegetables on Nevsky Prospekt, the two of us miraculously fluent. Where was she right now? Probably up in a dorm room with a bunch of Peace Corps hippies, drinking vodka and talking about Marx.

Nearby, there was a commotion around a gate. A plane had landed. A crowd quickly formed—families there to greet the passengers. The plane was hours late. One of the first people off was a man who spotted his wife and daughter and ran to them and leaned over and took his little girl up into his arms. An Indian family standing off to the side spotted an old couple—grandparents, presumably—and called to them, and there were hugs all around. At the back of the crowd a girl stood nervous, alone, stretching up to see over the others. Her boyfriend was one of the last ones off the plane. He was a tall kid, a serviceman in uniform. She saw him, and shouted, "Jackie!" and then began to cry. He pulled her up against his chest and held her and they didn't care who saw them; and I thought again about what my mother had said about loving someone and being loved.

Here all around me were these hundreds of people, all of us coming and going and gazing at each other like strangers passing in a dream, and what would any of us ever know about the others except that once briefly we had chanced to be in the same place at the same time? Outside, the snow had given way to rain, which fell softly against the windows and washed away the little piles of snow at the edges of the runways. A silvery light descended. The gloaming, my grandfather used to call this. Night was falling, and as the light dwindled there was a moment when it was possible both to see through the windows and also to see reflections in them. I gazed at the image of myself floating ghostlike among the images from the world outside: the planes and trucks and blinking lights, the men in yellow slickers, the long paved runways and the thick stand of trees. Then slowly the sky darkened and the outside world disappeared from the glass and there was only myself and I realized that I was vanishing too—we all were vanishing, faster than we could imagine.

I went to a pay phone and dialed St. Petersburg. The circuits were down. I tried again. Same thing. I stood there staring at the phone. I thought about calling my mother, asking her what I should do. But I didn't need to call her. I hurried to the Northwest international counter. There was a flight to St. Petersburg at 5:50 P.M., with seats available. It was 5:40 now. "You'll have to hurry," the agent said.

I explained my situation. I showed her my passport and my visa. I told her I was supposed to be going back to Chicago to work, but I hated my job, and I loved my girlfriend, and just now, right over there at Gate E-21, I had done some thinking. All I had to do, I told her, was call Maria and see what she said. If she said okay, I would go.

"Our phones don't dial outside the airport," the agent told me. "Besides, there's no time for making calls. As it is, you'll barely make it."

I stood there, perplexed. I thought about Chicago. I thought about Evan, and Saul, and my five million dollars. It was a lot of money to throw away. Maybe this was a stupid gesture, arriving in St. Petersburg with nothing but an overnight bag and a Visa card. And God only knew what I would find when I got there. Maybe the late